PRAISE FOR VAUGHN C. HARDACKER

"In this hard-hitting crime novel . . . Hardacker keeps the action flowing all the way to the violent climax."

—*Publishers Weekly* on *Black Orchid*

"Fast paced and action packed, *Black Orchid* takes the Hollywood private eye novel in a bold and exciting new direction. You won't want to put it down."

—Paul Doiron, author of *The Precipice* on *Black Orchid*

"Hardacker is a writer as comfortably at home on the dark streets of Boston as he is in the north woods of Maine. In both places, his story of a twisted serial killer will make you feel like you're there even as he keeps you right on the edge of your chair. This ensemble of strong men, strong women, good bad guys, and bad bad guys will take you on a trip you won't want to miss."

—Kate Flora, winner of the 2013 Maine Literary Award
for Crime Fiction on *The Fisherman*

"Born in Southie and forged by the Marine Corps, there's no way Boston police detective Mike Houston is going to sit still for a sniper shooting up his city, never mind going after the people he loves. A tense and exciting duel that turns the pages for you."

—Stephen D. Rogers, author of *Shot to Death* on *Sniper*

WENDIGO

Also by Vaughn C. Hardacker

Sniper
The Fisherman
Black Orchid

WENDIGO

A THRILLER

VAUGHN C. HARDACKER

Skyhorse Publishing

Excerpts from pages xi–xii from *Manitous: The Spiritual World of The Ojibway* by Basil Johnston, Copyright 1995 by Basil H. Johnston. Reprinted by permission of HarperCollins Publishers and Beverly Slopen Literary Agency, 131 Bloor Street West, Toronto, Canada M5S1S3.

Skyhorse Publishing books may be purchased in bulk at special discounts for sales promotion, corporate gifts, fund-raising, or educational purposes. Special editions can also be created to specifications. For details, contact the Special Sales Department, Skyhorse Publishing, 307 West 36th Street, 11th Floor, New York, NY 10018 or info@skyhorsepublishing.com.

Skyhorse® and Skyhorse Publishing® are registered trademarks of Skyhorse Publishing, Inc.®, a Delaware corporation.

Visit our website at www.skyhorsepublishing.com.

10 9 8 7 6 5 4 3 2

Library of Congress Cataloging-in-Publication Data is available on file.

Cover design by Erin Seaward-Hiatt

Print ISBN: 978-1-5107-1591-2
Ebook ISBN: 978-1-5107-1593-6

Printed in the United States of America

DEDICATION

To Connie, who was my first fan and supporter, and to Leslie Jane, my current number-one fan and supporter, who said this one scared the crap out of her!

ACKNOWLEDGMENTS

As with any work, there are many people who were invaluable to me in completing *Wendigo*. I would like to take a moment to thank a few of them.

The North Maine Woods covers more than 3.5 million acres (14,000 square kilometers) of forestland. While global economic changes and other factors have hurt Maine's forest-resources industry, forest products are still a key part of the state's economy. Maine has two hundred forest-products businesses employing some twenty-four thousand people. The forest-products industry directly contributes some $1.8 billion to the state's economy each year. Maine is the second largest paper producing state. The North Maine Woods is managed by North Maine Woods, Inc., in Ashland, Maine. Executive Director Al Cowperthwaite was a great resource quickly answering my questions about the woods industry, and about geographical features of the woods.

Thanks are also owed to Warden Ryan Fitzpatrick of the Maine Department of Inland Fisheries and Wildlife Warden Service, who gave me assistance on warden procedures and organization.

Ojibway teacher and scholar from Ontario Basil Johnston's book on Native American gods, *The Manitous*, was instrumental, particularly in its well-written chapter on the Wendigo, spelled Weendigo in the book. Johnston brings out the point that the myth does have its real-world counterparts. He states that the Wendigo is never satisfied: the more it eats, the more it grows, and the more it grows, the more it needs to eat; it is constantly hungry. He argues that the modern-day Wendigo is the logging industry, in that the more timber they cut, the more they need to cut, leaving our natural woodlands looking like the result of a humongous bomb detonation or the impact of an interstellar body similar to the meteor (or asteroid) that exterminated the dinosaurs.

To Maxim Brown, my editor at Skyhorse Publishing, for his insight and patience while I made major revisions based on his recommendations. To Jay Cassell of Skyhorse Publishing, who took a chance on me, and now we are up to book number four with number five under contract (hang in there, you who are awaiting more of Ed Traynor).

You, the reader, give me the fortitude to keep writing, to fight off the deadly impact of procrastination on those days when I'd rather goof off than place myself in front of a word processor—thank you.

Stockholm, Maine
2016

Of the evil beings who dwelt on the periphery of the world of the Anishinaubae peoples, none was more terrifying than the Weendigo. It was a creature loathsome to behold and as loathsome in its habits, conduct, and manners.

The Weendigo was a giant manitou in the form of a man or a woman, who towered five to eight times above the height of a tall man. But the Weendigo was a giant in height only; in girth and strength, it was not. Because it was afflicted with never-ending hunger and could never get enough to eat, it was always on the verge of starvation. The Weendigo was gaunt to the point of emaciation, its desiccated skin pulled tautly over its bones. With its bones pushing out against its skin, its complexion the ash gray of death, and its eyes pushed back deep into their sockets, the Weendigo looked like a gaunt skeleton recently disinterred from the grave. What lips it had were tattered and bloody from its constant chewing with jagged teeth.

Unclean and suffering from suppurations of the flesh, the Weendigo gave off a strange and eerie odor of decay and decomposition, of death and corruption.

When the Weendigo set to attack a human being, a dark snow cloud would shroud its upper body from the waist up. The air would turn cold, so the trees crackled. Then a wind would rise, no more than a breath at first, but in moments whining and driving, transformed into a blizzard.

Behind the odor and chill of death and the killing blizzard came the Weendigo.

Even before the Weendigo laid hands on them, many people died in their tracks from fright; just to see the Weendigo's sepulchral face was enough to induce heart failure and death. For others, the monster's shriek was more than they could bear.

Those who died of fright were lucky; their death was merciful and painless. But for those who had the misfortune to live through their terror, death was slow and agonizing.

The Weendigo seized its victim and tore him, or her, limb from limb with its hands and teeth, eating the flesh and bones and drinking the blood while its victim screamed and struggled. The pain of others meant nothing to the Weendigo; all that mattered was its survival.

The Weendigo gorged itself and glutted its belly as if it would never eat again. But a remarkable thing always occurred. As the Weendigo ate, it grew, and as it grew so did its hunger, so that no matter how much it ate, its hunger always remained in proportion to its size. The Weendigo could never requite either its unnatural lust for human flesh or its unnatural appetite. It could never stop as animals do when bloated, unable to ingest another morsel, or sense as humans sense that enough is enough for the present. For the unfortunate Weendigo, the more it ate, the bigger it grew; and the bigger it grew, the more it wanted and needed.

The Anishinaubae people had every reason to fear and abhor the Weendigo. It was a giant cannibal that fed only on human flesh, bones, blood. But the Weendigo represented not only the worst that a human can do to another human being and ultimately to himself or herself, but exemplified other despicable traits. Even the term "Weendigo" evokes images of offensive traits. It may be derived from *ween dagoh*, which means "solely for self," or from *weenin n'd'igooh*, which means "fat" or excess.

The Weendigo inspired fear. There was no human sanction or punishment to compare to death at the hands of the Weendigo . . .

THE LEGEND

The Saint John River, near what is now the Madawaska Maliseet First Nation, New Brunswick, Canada, 1683

A gust of frigid wind caught and snapped the deerskin flap. The small fire at the center of the lodge struggled to ward off the cold while its light made the occupants' shadows dance on the thin walls like an eerie shadow-puppet play. An old Maliseet man faced the five wide-eyed children who were huddled together as close as they could to the fire, several of them wrapped together in blankets, trying to absorb as much warmth as possible. The old man's low, raspy voice filled the room above the periodic popping of the wood fire and the howling of the wind. His breath was visible in the air as his tale held his young audience captive.

"It happened years ago, after Kji-kinap created the six worlds and the people. Many years before the French came to our lands and destroyed the balance of life, the people had shared with the Earth World from the time of creation. The people knew that for three seasons the Earth

World worked hard providing crops so the people could survive the fourth season, when the Earth World rested. The balance was always uncertain, some seasons were dry and crops suffered, others were wet and again crops suffered. Then the whites came and killed the Earth World's animals for the pleasure of it. They left the carcasses, taking only the prize meats, leaving the rest of the valuable gift to rot on the forest floor. Soon game was not so plentiful and Kji-kinap was displeased with the way both the French and the Algonquins had treated the Earth World. To teach the people a lesson and to get them to return to the old ways, Kji-kinap sent Wendigo to the land.

"Wendigo has always been a cruel teacher. He visits during the Hunger Moon, when food is scarce and the people are weak with starvation. His lessons always bring death and suffering.

"Over the land came a winter worse than anything the people had ever known. They knew Kji-kinap was angry and punished them for abusing the blessings that the Earth World provided. Snow fell for days at a time and soon was so deep even the deer and moose moved to the south. Many of the people died from the cold and lack of food.

"There was among the people a great warrior named Plawej. He stood head and shoulders above the next tallest man in the village. He saw that the people's need was great and declared he would take a band of hunters far away, toward the setting sun to seek food for the tribe. There was great celebration in the village, for Plawej was renowned throughout the land as a great hunter. "Surely," the people said," if there is anyone who can find game it is he." The villagers were so sure that the hunt would be successful that they gave most of their food to the hunters for their journey.

"The party was gone two moons with no word of them. One day, when it was so cold the air froze into fine crystals of ice, Wijik, one of the hunters, crawled into the village. The villagers took him before the council and placed him before a fire to warm. The warrior had been in the frigid cold for so long he was reluctant to sit close to the fire; its heat too painful for his cold flesh. He gathered the council around and this is the tale he told:

'We traveled many days to the south and west, past the great lake shaped like the antlers of the moose. The cold and snow made travel hard and we saw no game. Plawej led us into a great cedar swamp where the snow was not so deep, but hoarfrost was everywhere. Never have I seen such a frozen and foreboding place. Ice coated the trees and their branches hung to the ground as if they were the arms of a great frozen monster, waiting to grab us up. It was there that Plawej decided to set our hunting camp. Many of the hunters were not happy with the place. The swamp air was so frigid that it seemed to freeze on our faces and every breath brought the glacial chill deep into our chests. On the ground, the hoarfrost was so thick and hard it was all we could do to chop through it for water. Plawej challenged anyone who doubted his decision. We all knew his prowess as a warrior, so no one challenged him.

'We hunted around the great lake for seven suns and found no game. We told Plawej we should return home because we were running out of food. It is far better to starve with your people than to die alone in the deep woods. He refused us. Again he issued his challenge. No one took it.

'The next morning when we arose, Skun and Njiknam were gone. We saw their tracks going toward the rising sun and believed they had given up and returned home. The following morning Tia'm and Mi'kmwesu were gone, the day after, Miskwekepu'j and Antawesk. The desertions continued until only Plawej and I remained.

'Hunger and cold were the only truths we knew. I had lost much weight and was weakening. I knew I too had to leave while I still had enough strength to get home. Plawej, as was his habit, had left camp early, climbing one of the high ridges that surrounded the swamp. I was suspicious of his going off alone and I set out to find him. I walked on the ice, seeking the place where his tracks left the frozen bog and entered the deep snow. I followed his footprints out of the swamp and up the great ridge. I was almost atop the incline when I first smelled something foul. It smelled as if a great battle had taken place and the smell of spilled blood and death rode the gusting wind. The ledge was too steep for me to climb while carrying a notched arrow, so I took my war axe in hand, hung my bow across my shoulder and slowly climbed to the top.

'Once atop the ridge, I heard cracking sounds and sought cover in some evergreen trees. Curious about what the sounds were, I crept toward their *source. In a short time the cracking ended and a great beast, I hoped it was a moose, could be heard walking down the ridge. I notched an arrow in my bow and stepped out of the tangled evergreens.*

'What I found there will remain with me always. I was in an area of pine, beech, and great maple trees. Suspended from the trees were the remains of men. They had been devoured . . . the ground beneath the hanging carcasses covered with broken bones, the very marrow gone as if it had been sucked out. To one side I found a pile of clothing and weapons: Tia'm's bow was there, as was Mi'kmwesu's moccasins and Miskwekepu'j's blanket. I looked up into the maple tree and saw what remained of Antawesk hanging by the neck in a forked branch. The fiend had lifted him up and left him there, no doubt to keep its food safe from other animals. At first I wanted to find Plawej, but was afraid the monster might return, smell my scent and follow me. I decided to return to my hiding place in the evergreens and wait.

'The sun was halfway across the sky when I heard it. I waited for him to get settled for his midday meal. I soon heard the cracking noises again and pushed aside the evergreen boughs.

'I could not believe what I saw. There sat the creature—only it was not an animal!

'It was Plawej. He squatted with his back to me, chewing and sucking the marrow out of one of Antawesk's broken leg bones—he had become Wendigo.

'I knew that even at full strength, I was no match for him, so I crept away. Once I reached the bottom of the ridge I ran and ran until I thought I could run no more—then I ran more. I ran until I dropped from exhaustion. Several times I heard Plawej call to me, asking me to wait for him so that we could travel together. I was too afraid to do anything but run. . . .'"

The children sat entranced. Only the smallest, her eyes wide with horror, was brave enough to speak. "What happened then, Grandfather?"

"The next morning when Plawej arrived at the village, unaware Wijik had beaten him there, the people fell upon him and killed him. Because a Wendigo will resurrect unless his icy heart is melted in a great fire, they cut his body into pieces and burned the pieces.

"But, that was not the end . . ."

"It wasn't?" the youngest said, her eyes wide and she leaned forward.

"No, the villagers were too hasty. They did not remember all there is to know about the Wendigo. Although they are gaunt in appearance, no mortal man can move faster. It is said that it would be easier to outrun the wind than a Wendigo. It was impossible for Wijik to have outrun one.

"As the fire in which Plawej burned died down, Wijik suddenly grew to over twenty feet tall. He snatched up two of the village children and disappeared into the woods, leaving only his laughter behind."

The children gasped as one. "You mean—" said the eldest.

"Yes, Wijik was the Wendigo. That is why you must always be good children. When the winter wind blows hardest and coldest the Wendigo comes for bad children. It always has and it always will. . . ."

1

Township 19, Range 11 West of the Easterly Line of the State (T19, R11), North Maine Woods

Ryan Kelly sped along the remote tote road with a wary eye on the rapidly darkening sky. Even on a sunny day, night came early in January in northern Maine. But that day was overcast and clouds hung ominously low. Night would come earlier than normal. Getting lost in the dark would be the final blow to what had been a foolhardy endeavor in the first place. Running to Frontière Lake in advance of the annual fishing derby to check out the ice and a site for his portable ice fishing shack was a dumb idea. This time of year, the conditions could change in a heartbeat. What was clear ice today could be covered with deep snow by next Saturday.

Ryan looked at the trees bordering the road and saw the first snowflakes appear against the gray-black backdrop. Suddenly the wind escalated into what the locals called the Montreal Express and blasted his face with stinging sleet. He hunched forward and bent into the wind, wishing he had stayed back in Lyndon Station with his sister and her boyfriend.

The headlamps of his Bearcat illuminated the shape of something in the road ahead. At first he thought it was a moose. But as he neared, he realized it was much too tall. A large moose stood five feet at its shoulders; this shape was at least three feet taller than that. Kelly slowed his sled—if it was a bear he didn't want to get too close. It couldn't be a bear, he decided. They'd all been in hibernation for the better part of a month.

The figure noticed his lights and turned. When it turned and faced him, Kelly realized that it was humanoid. His heart skipped. All his life he'd been told that there had been Bigfoot sightings here in the crown of Maine. Was he looking at a Sasquatch? He shook his head as if to clear away a drunken mirage.

The shape began walking toward him and he slowed his sled even more. As he watched it approach, he debated whether to spin around and leave this thing behind. *But*, he asked himself, *what if it's just a big person in need of help?* He made a decision and crept forward.

As he neared the form, Kelly saw that it was indeed a human being. He raised his hand in greeting.

Suddenly a dark cloud covered the man from the waist up, the temperature dropped so dramatically that several trees cracked, the wind escalated from a gentle breeze to a raging blizzard, and an overwhelming odor of death and decay and corruption permeated the air. Icy hands gripped Kelly and began tearing him apart while jagged teeth ripped into his body and he felt his blood being drunk. Kelly fought for his life and screamed and died.

2

Lyndon Station, Maine

Warden Larry Murphy drove slowly. The road was slick with snow and ice that had been packed by passing cars and trucks until it was as hard as the pavement it covered. When he stepped on the brake, the pickup's rear end fishtailed and he steered in the direction of the skid to bring the vehicle back under control. The tires suddenly came into contact with the road's paved surface and straightened, snapping the four-by-four to the left. Murphy pulled into the parking lot of McBrietty's Outpost.

Wendell "Del" McBrietty was the wealthiest man in Lyndon Station and his gas station, general store, restaurant, and rental cabins formed a gauntlet along the only major thoroughfare in the minuscule town. He provided just about everything a resident of—or a visitor to—the remote town could need.

Like the majority of small Maine towns, Lyndon had no police force of its own. Law enforcement was handled by a consortium consisting of the Maine State Police, Aroostook County Sheriff's Office, and Murphy, a member of the warden service of the Department of Inland Fisheries and Wildlife. While Murphy's primary responsibility was enforcement of the state's many hunting and fishing laws, members of the warden service are also police officers. They are required to successfully complete the Maine Criminal Justice Academy as well as a number of physical tests specific to the job. The warden service has the responsibility of conducting search and rescue operations throughout Maine's extensive woodlands—which was why Murphy was at McBrietty's.

Murphy parked his truck in front of the store and walked inside. The difference between the minus-twenty degrees outside and the store's eighty-plus temperature hit Murphy like a wall. He felt as if he had entered a blast furnace.

McBrietty, who was in his midseventies, harbored fond memories of a bygone era and anyone entering one of his buildings for the first time would think they'd entered a time capsule from the 1930s. In the middle of the room was a pot-bellied wood-burning stove—the source of the super-heated, arid air—surrounded by a number of wooden chairs. A large metal coffee pot sat on top of the woodstove and the aroma of percolated coffee filled the air. Del McBrietty stood beside the stove and seemed to be in serious conversation with several men of his own age. Del was a large man, both in stature and in girth. He wore hunter-green wool trousers that were secured by both a wide leather belt and a pair of red suspenders over a red-and-black plaid flannel shirt. He sported a full beard and mustache, and his long hair fanned out from beneath a ball cap that had DEL's embroidered on the front.

In similar fashion, the men seated around the stove wore the unofficial uniform of northern Maine's long, long winter season: heavy flannel shirts, wool trousers, and L.L. Bean boots. When he spied the warden, Del stopped talking midsentence and said, "Hey, Murph. I take it you're here about that idiot snowmobiler from away."

"Yeah. How you doin', Del?"

"If business was any slower, I'd have to shut the place down."

Murphy grinned. For as long as he'd known Del, the man had complained that business was so slow he was going broke—a fact belied by the fancy Cadillac Escalade Del drove. Del's Place was a gold mine and everyone in Lyndon Station and the surrounding towns knew it. Everyone agreed that if the store were to go out of business it could very well be the end of the town and locals would have to drive to Fort Kent, almost thirty miles away, to buy their cigarettes, booze, and lottery tickets. Regardless, there was no way Del was ever going to close his doors—at least not while he was still looking at the grass from the green-side-down. Murphy expressed his opinion of Del's complaint. "I seriously doubt that. What's the story on this lost sledder?"

"Friggin' idjut from away decided he wasn't gonna let cold weather keep him from takin' a ride in the North Maine Woods. He left out of here yesterday mornin' headed up towards Lake Frontière."

"That's a long ride in this weather."

"It's a long ride in any weather. But like I said, the guy's an idjut. He's a young fella with more guts than brains, if you ask me. He told me that he wanted to check things out before the ice fishing derby this coming weekend."

"It's unusual for out-of-state fishermen to go up to Frontière. They usually stay around the more accessible lakes along the Fish River."

"The kid's from Massachusetts—that tells me all I need to know."

Murphy sighed. There was a lot of country between Lyndon Station and Frontière Lake . . . a trip of about thirty miles along isolated woods, roads, and trails. It was, he believed, going to be an exercise in futility. For all anyone knew the guy had crossed over into Quebec and was holed up someplace—not that there were any places to hole up in—unless he had found an unoccupied camp and broke in. He believed however, that the missing rider was most likely dead from prolonged exposure to subzero temperatures. Either way, Murphy was going to have to head up that way. "Was he here alone?"

"Nope, he was staying with a couple of others. . . . At least they had enough sense to stay inside until this weather breaks. Gonna have a heat wave, supposed to be up to twenty degrees by Tuesday."

"I'll make it a point to keep my bathing suit handy. What cabin were these guys in?"

"Hell, there's only four back there. . . . Look for the one with a bright-yellow Hummer parked in front."

Murphy left the warmth of the store and immediately felt the moisture inside his nose freeze as he circled the building and crossed the parking lot. He spotted the yellow Hummer parked in front of one of McBrietty's rental cabins. Wood smoke furled from the stone chimney and the windows were covered with a layer of heavy frost. He stepped onto the wooden porch and rapped on the door. A muffled voice called out, "Who's there?"

"Maine Warden Service."

Murphy heard footsteps stomping across the cabin's wood floor and envisioned their source as a large person. He was surprised when a slender woman, who he assumed to be in her early thirties, opened the door. She stepped aside and said, "Come on in, no sense trying to heat the outdoors."

Murphy stepped inside and removed his bombardier hat. "I'm Warden Larry Murphy. Did you report a missing sledder?"

"No, my boyfriend did." She raised her voice and called, "Steven, there's a warden here about Ryan."

A small man, barely taller than the woman, walked out of the bedroom. "Have they found him?" he asked.

"That's hardly likely," Murphy said, "seeing as how we haven't started looking yet."

A reddish hue covered the young man's face. "I was hoping that maybe he'd gotten back or something."

"There're a lot of woods out there and before I head out I need to know anything you might know that will help me narrow down the search area," Murphy said.

"Of, course, I'll do anything I can to help." The young man held his hand out and said, "I'm Steve Millhouse. . . ." He turned to the woman. "This is my fiancée, Lisa Kelly."

"And the name of the missing man?" Murphy asked.

"Ryan . . . Ryan Kelly," Lisa said. "He's my younger brother."

"Del . . . Mr. McBrietty told me that he was headed up to Frontière Lake. Is he familiar with the area?"

"Our father grew up around here, over by Saint Francis. We've been coming up here since we were little kids."

Murphy nodded. Her answer made the selection of Frontière Lake as a potential ice fishing location a bit more understandable. "Did your brother say which trail he was going to take?"

"He said he was going to take Lake Road to Cross Lake Road and then cut across Block Road until he came to the lake. He marked it on a map for us." She walked to the room's small couch and picked up a copy of DeLorme's *Maine Atlas and Gazetteer*. She opened the book to the appropriate map and traced her brother's alleged route. Murphy scanned the page and saw that Ryan Kelly did know something about the area. The only remaining questions were about the youngster's readiness for a trip in subzero weather. "What type of condition is his sled in?"

"Tip-top," Millhouse replied. "It's a new Arctic Cat Bearcat 570. He was dressed for the cold, too."

"What about food and water?"

"I don't think he took any," Kelly said. "He was planning on riding up and back in one day, said all he was going to do was check out the ice conditions before next week's derby."

Murphy grunted. It wasn't the first time he'd come across people whose one-day ride turned into an exercise in survival. He could only hope that Ryan Kelly was still alive. "Okay, I'll head up there." He took a notebook from his coat pocket and wrote a number down. "Do either of you have a phone?"

"We both do," the young woman replied.

Murphy jotted a number down. "This is the number of the Department of Inland Fisheries and Wildlife Regional Headquarters in Ashland. If you hear anything from your brother, call them and they'll get in touch with me. Does he have a cell phone too?"

"Yes," Lisa answered.

"And I'm assuming that he hasn't called."

"We figured that there aren't any towers up here."

"Oh, you can usually get one, either in the U.S. or from across the border in Quebec."

"Unless," Millhouse interjected, "his battery is dead."

Murphy opened the door and stepped out into the freezing temperatures. As he walked to his truck, he hoped that the only thing dead was Ryan Kelly's cell phone.

3

Little Black Checkpoint, North Maine Woods

Murphy walked inside the checkpoint and nodded to Sean O'Gill. As he walked to the pot behind the desk and helped himself to a cup of coffee, Murphy asked, "Did a sledder named Kelly come through here yesterday?"

"Don't know, I was off."

"Suppose you could check the log?"

"Suppose I could." O'Gill smiled at the warden. "Carole was on yesterday, so I know that nobody slipped through without her seeing them. What'd this guy do?"

"It's what he didn't do—he didn't come back. Told everyone that he was riding up to Frontière Lake to check it out before the derby next weekend. He hasn't been heard from since."

"He may have gone through Dickey checkpoint."

"Could have, but he was staying at Del's in Lyndon Station and Dickey is the wrong direction."

O'Gill accessed the computer on his desk. "I got him. It looks like he came through at ten forty-five yesterday morning. Don't see where he came back though. Of course if he came through after nine last night there was no one here."

"What are the roads like between here and Frontière?"

"If I were goin' up there, I think I'd take a sled. Not much cutting goin' on in that area so I doubt that plowin' those roads is a priority. They'll make sure some of the roads are open for next weekend, but that's a few days away."

"You're probably right. Will it be a problem if I leave my truck here?"

"Nope, you need a hand getting your sled out of the bed?"

"Nah, I got a set of ramps."

Murphy drank the last of his coffee, crumpled the disposable cup, and tossed it in a waste can.

"Well, if you decide you need me, holler."

"I will. Okay if I suit up in the restroom?"

"Be my guest."

It took Murphy ten minutes to don his snowmobile suit, heavy insulated boots, and helmet. He thanked O'Gill for the coffee, went outside, and unloaded his sled from the back of his truck. He let the motor warm for a few minutes while he checked that all of his equipment was in working order.

Lake Road was maintained by logging companies and Murphy was able to race along its plowed surface at forty-five miles per hour. After thirty minutes he left Lake Road, turned onto the unplowed Cross Lake Road, which would take him to Frontière Lake, and followed a trail of snowmobile tracks. Two miles down the road he saw where a single set of tracks turned onto an unnamed tote road and followed it. After a mile and a half, he broke out of the trees and spied a well-worked Ski-Doo with attached trapper sled parked beside a blue and white painted Arctic Cat Bearcat. He stopped behind it and raised the visor on his helmet. As he got off his sled and approached the Ski-Doo, a familiar figure stepped out of the woods that lined the trail. "That you, Louie?" Murphy asked.

Louis Cote raised his visor. "Yup, you been lookin' for this feller, Murph?"

"I am looking for a sledder who was reported missing this morning. He was reported to be riding one of those."

"Well, it looks like he ain't missing anymore."

"That's a load off my mind," Murphy said, he looked at the Arctic Cat and saw what appeared to be blood on the seat. "Is he hurt?"

"Not anymore."

Murphy turned toward the woods and saw a blood trail. "Maybe you better explain. . . ."

"He's dead," Cote said.

Murphy gave Cote a stern look and said, "I don't think finding a dead body is something you ought to get cute about. Maybe you better tell me what you're doing out here and what you found."

"I left home before first light this morning, checking out my trapline. I came across this sled, saw the blood, and got curious. As you can see, anyone—even a city dweller—can follow that trail. I stuck my nose in there. You got any idea who he was?"

"If he's my guy, his name was Ryan Kelly. He was staying at Del's. I went over there and met with his sister, who told me he was headed up to Frontière Lake."

"What's in Frontière Lake?"

"Next weekend is the ice fishing derby."

Cote nodded as if Murphy's answer was all the explanation required. He looked at the registration sticker on the Arctic Cat. "That's a Massachusetts registration."

"Yeah, but the family is originally from Saint Francis. They come up here several times a year. . . . Apparently the kid knew his way around. In fact he was smart enough to leave an itinerary with his sister."

During winter, darkness comes early in the north. Murphy glanced at his watch, the luminous dial said 5:25 p.m. and the sun was already below the trees cloaking the ground beneath them in deep shadows. Murphy walked to his sled and got a flashlight. He shined the beam on the Arctic Cat's seat.

"I thought that looked like blood," Cote said. "That's when I decided to look around for him. There's a trail leading into the alders over here." He pointed toward the copse of brush. "The body is in there."

"Have you looked at it?"

"Not up close. Once I got to the point where I knew it was a body I backed off. I didn't want to fuck up the area."

Murphy nodded. "I appreciate the effort, but out here, during the winter there won't be much to fuck up. C'mon, let's have a look at it." He retrieved his Maglite and followed Cote.

They pushed their way through the knee-deep snow following the trail Cote had blazed earlier. In the concentrated beams of their flashlights the world seemed confined, almost claustrophobic. The red left by Kelly's blood stood out in stark contrast to the white background of the snow.

When they reached the copse of alder bushes, Cote forged ahead and peered into the small stand of leafless bushes. He hesitated before entering the thicket.

"You okay?" Murphy asked.

"Yeah."

"You say you didn't go in there?"

"Just far enough to see that he was there. From all the blood, I knew he was dead and backed out. . . . That's when I met you."

Murphy lightly grabbed Cote's shoulder, restraining him, and moved ahead, spreading the alders and pushed his way inside. The carnage that greeted him was horrific and his stomach lurched, trying to evacuate its contents. Whoever had killed Kelly—if this was Ryan Kelly—had ripped the body apart. For some strange reason Murphy visualized a medieval pagan feast where everyone around the table grabbed meat with their hands and ripped it apart with their teeth. Murphy forced his revulsion aside and squatted beside the body to inspect it. He expected to see damage from where predator animals had been at the corpse— this was over and above any damage he'd ever seen done by scavenger animals. Starting at the head, he slowly trolled the light's beam over the body and stopped when he reached the chest cavity. The body had lain in the cold long enough to have frozen and everything looked crystalline in the light of his Maglite. "Christ . . . ," Murphy whispered—then he realized that the boy's legs and buttocks were gone.

"What you say?" Cote asked.

"Nothing." Murphy spread the snowsuit open. As he spread the fabric, the frozen blood that covered it cracked and snapped. He peered inside and saw the chest cavity had been ripped open rather than cut and appeared to have been ravaged by teeth. He rocked back on his heels, took a deep breath, and rose. As he stepped out of the brush, he said, "Did you contact anyone else?"

"Like I said, I got here just ahead of you. Was gonna see if I had any bars on my phone when you came along. It don't take no doctor to see there ain't no rush to get no ambulance out here—he's beyond their help," Cote said. "Even if they was of a mind to come, the closest they'll be able to get an ambulance will be Cross Lake Road."

"I could call for a helicopter to get him out of here. Nearest hospital is Fort Kent and that's, what . . . thirty, forty miles away?"

"By helicopter, yeah, maybe as close as twenty if they cut across Canadian airspace."

"Well, I better call. Where's the nearest place a chopper can get in?"

Cote thought for a minute and then said, "About a mile south there's a clearing that might be big enough, but it'd take an idiot to try and land there at night."

Murphy glanced upward at the black sky, "I left my truck back at the Little Black checkpoint. Looks like I'm in for a long night."

"I could swing by Little Black and have them send someone up here."

Murphy checked his watch. "The checkpoint will be closed before you get there. I'll see what I can do with my cell phone."

"We could pull him out of here, put him in my trapper sled, and head back there. Somebody will have to collect his sled tomorrow though—I got no way to haul it." Cote scrutinized the warden. "Murph, I can't help but notice that you seem a bit shaken. What did you find in there?"

"Whoever killed that boy tore him apart. There are parts of him missing. You head on, I don't want to disturb things any more than I have to."

"You gonna spend the night out here?"

"Might have to." Murphy shined the beam around the ominous trees. In the monochromatic world of the winter night, snow falling from the pine and evergreen boughs resembled white cirrus clouds. "If you don't mind, in the event I can't reach anyone, when you get back to Lyndon, would you call 9-1-1 and report this?"

"Sure."

When Cote was out of sight and the whine of his motor faded, Murphy began a quick search of the area. Returning to the thicket, he scanned the area with the flashlight's beam. If there was one single positive thing about a winter crime scene it was the difficulty a perpetrator had in obscuring his or her tracks. After a short time he found one. He took care not to disturb the area any more than he had to and estimated the distance from the track to the thicket to be approximately six feet. He perused the area around the footprint and discovered another, also about six feet away. *If he ain't running, he's one tall son of a bitch*, Murphy thought. He reached inside his winter snowmobile suit and took out a folding knife. He cut several long, full boughs from a pine and carefully laid them over the two tracks to protect them from drifting snow.

He straightened and inhaled deeply. There was an odor hanging in the air. Murphy couldn't describe it except to say it smelled like rot and decay. It was as if he was standing beside a corpse that had been lying in the summer sun for a week. Suddenly Murphy was overcome with the feeling that he was not alone. He slid his nine-millimeter pistol from its holster and held it in his right hand while he swept the area with the flashlight in his left.

The wind increased, causing the trees to rustle and creak. Snow drifted through the light beam and settled on Murphy. *Time to build some sort of shelter for the night*, he thought, and he stepped wide of the crime scene and trudged back to his sled.

It took him the better part of an hour to scoop out an impromptu shelter in the snow, pausing several times when the wind escalated and the trees groaned as they swayed, stressing their frozen trunks. *It is going to be one long night*, he mused as he settled into the crude shelter.

4

Viverette Settlement

It walked across the clearing toward the abandoned village. No one had lived in the settlement for almost fifty years. Still, it kept a wary eye out for any sign that someone had been in the area. But the snow along what in summer was a dirt street showed no sign of anyone having walked on it.

The lane ran between a number of depressions that were the foundation remnants of buildings that had succumbed to the ravages of time and the weight of the snow of many winters. There was a time when the settlement was a small but thriving village, but then the lumber companies determined they'd harvested all of the trees of any value and moved on to more lucrative wood lots, effectively killing any chance Viverette had of ever again being anything but a ghost town. The only proof of its existence was a small dot and notation on topographic maps. The deep snow, which would be hip-deep on a person of normal height, barely came midway up its shins. It proceeded effortlessly across the open dell and approached one of the two remaining structures, a collapsing shanty. It pulled the door open, stooped down to avoid banging its head on the top of the entrance's threshold, letting the portal swing closed. In spite of the cold, its breath was not visible when he exhaled. Now that the hunger had lessened, the monster was at peace.

It walked back outside, carried the rest of his provisions inside, and placed them on the counter next to the sink. When placed beside the legs and the pieces of rump, the liver looked tiny. Too small to sate hunger, still it would make a passable snack. The gigantic being stared through the small, grime-coated window that was centered over the sink, opened the window, placing the meat in a wooden box fastened to the sill, and closed it, secure in the belief that the food would be there when wanted.

It walked over to the elongated cot that lay along the wall of the one-room hovel and flopped down on it. Like any sated animal, now that it'd fed, it would sleep—until the hunger came again.

Unnamed Logging Road, T19, R11, North Maine Woods

Murphy heard the sleds several minutes before he saw them. Awake since dawn, he had left the snow shelter he'd made, and had been crouching on the leeward side of his snowmobile, using it as a windbreak. He would be the last to admit it, but when he saw the two sleds he felt an immense wave of relief flow over him and he stood up for the first time since leaving the body.

The two machines stopped beside Murphy's. Not sure who the riders were, Murphy removed his helmet and remained silent. The rider on the sled closest to him stepped off and removed his helmet. Murphy immediately recognized the man. "Hey, John," he greeted John Bear, the DIF&W Crimes Investigation Division investigator.

"Murph, long time no see." John Bear looked around the area. "Could you have found a worse day to discover a body?"

Murphy grinned. "Believe me, it ain't something I planned."

The second man rounded the sleds, carrying his helmet in his left hand. "Looks like you found a way to screw up my week, Murph," Bob Pelky said.

Murphy nodded to Bob Pelky, the Maine State Police officer assigned to Lyndon Station. "Wish I hadn't, that's for sure. It's the goddamnedest thing I ever come across," Murphy answered. He pointed to the mound. "You guys should probably take a look for yourselves."

John Bear took the lead. When he reached the corpse he stood beside it for several seconds, looking around the area. "Things pretty much the way you found them?"

"I tried to keep the scene undisturbed as much as I could. But, with the snow and everything there ain't gonna be a hell of a lot of forensics takin' place," Murphy answered.

John Bear said nothing as he surveyed the corpse and their surroundings. After several seconds, he turned to Pelky who squatted beside him and said, "seen enough?"

Pelky nodded. "For the time being."

The two men stood. Pelky turned to Murphy and asked, "You find any sign of who did this?"

"A couple tracks."

"Show us," John said.

Murphy led them to the first track and raised the pine bough he had used to cover it. Pelky saw the bough and looked at him. Murphy said, "Hey, the way it's blowin' I wanted to preserve it as much as I could. I was careful to disturb the snow as little as possible."

Pelky shrugged and looked at the track. He asked John, "What you think—a snowshoe maybe?"

"It sure as hell ain't a human boot," John answered. He turned to Murphy. "This all you found . . . a single track?" He reached inside his cold-weather suit and took out a small digital camera and took several photos of the depressions.

"There's another about six feet over there." Murphy pointed to a dark spot in the snow. He shrugged with embarrassment. "Yeah, I know . . . another pine bough."

Pelky looked skeptical. "That's it? Two tracks about, what, five or six feet apart?"

"Believe me, Bob, I looked everywhere to see if there were any others that may have drifted in—didn't find a single one. Like I said, it's the goddamnedest thing I ever saw. It's like the killer escaped like Tarzan, swinging from one tree to another."

John squatted beside the huge humanoid footprint and studied it. The killer, if these were his tracks, was gigantic. He bent cautiously over the packed depression, eyeing it with trepidation, as if he were afraid it would attack him. The print was sharp and clearly defined; wind blew snow across the area and some was caught by the depression, but had not yet filled it with drifting snow. John studied the footprint. Other than its size there was something peculiar about it. He bent over the track, intently studying its shape, and then he caught a whiff of a repugnant odor, similar to that of a rotten carcass.

John's eyes returned to the track. He knew when fully expanded each of his hands measured nine inches from the tip of his little finger to his thumb's end, a technique he had used for years to measure fish he caught. He touched his thumbs together and spread his fingers as wide as he could. He placed his hands into the track. He touched his left pinky to the heel and made a mark where his right pinkie ended. There was still an inch of space between his pinkie and the toe of the track! Allowing for distortion in the snow, John guessed the track to be near twenty-four inches long and its width about ten inches! Cold sweat soaked through John's heavy wool shirt. He slowly stood up and moved deeper into the woods, his eyes searching, expecting who-knew-what to jump out of every clump of brush he saw. He cast a last look around and began back-tracking. A gust of wind blew through the trees and made a sound not unlike a howl. He spun around, trying to identify the source of the eerie sound, but all he saw were gray trees and snow drifting through the air. Another gust of wind sent the trees creaking and swaying. The hair on the back of his neck stood up; he thought he could detect a foul smell in the wind, similar to the odor of decaying flesh. Just as he was about to give in to fight or flight, he heard Murphy shout, "Where are you, John?"

Without removing his eyes from the woods in front of him, John answered, "Over here!"

John returned to the body and said, "The body was like this when you found him?"

"Yeah, you notice anything unusual about the vic?"

John spread the remnants of the dead man's snowmobile suit and saw the ravaged chest cavity. "It looks like scavengers got to him before you found him." He took several photos of the body.

"If they did, I sure as hell didn't see them—besides, the only tracks I saw were the two I showed you. When I found him there was no heat in the cavity. The wounds are not sharp and precise." Murphy said. "His legs and ass are gone. If I didn't know better I'd think he was slaughtered and butchered like a cow."

"So, what now?" Pelky asked.

"Let's take him down to the Little Black checkpoint. The rangers there can babysit him until the medical examiner can get someone out here to check him over." John looked at the sky and noted the lowering clouds. "Gonna be snowing soon. There's no way we'll find anything in this weather. . . ."

"I suppose you're right," Pelky said. "Any evidence is buried deep in the snow and ain't goin' nowhere. I'll bring a crime scene tech out here first thing in the morning and look things over." He turned to Murphy. "That okay with you?"

"Guys," Murphy said, "I been out here since yesterday afternoon, I'm more than ready for some heat and a few hours' sleep."

5

Viverette Settlement

I t sat in the darkness, listening to the blowing wind, and staring at the snow flying past the filthy window of the cabin. Its mind drifted back to a time when it had been someone different. His name had been Paul Condor. . . .

Oslo, Maine, 1996

It was the January thaw, a brief period of unseasonable warmth which usually preceded the really cold weather of February and March. Paul Condor stood silently staring out the filthy window of the ramshackle hut where he lived with his father. His eyes followed his father, a solitary, drunken figure who held his collar closed around his neck as he staggered through the pouring rain. Paul watched with dismay as his father pulled a pint of gin from his pocket, took a deep swallow from it, and succeeded in returning it to its resting place in his pocket on the second try. His father's feet slid in the mud that covered the road's shoulder and the drunken man took several quick steps to try to right himself, but Wally Condor was unable to maintain his balance and he tumbled face-first into the mud. Paul watched his father lying in the mud and knew that the cold rain was soaking through his coat and shirt, plastering it to his back. He heard Wally curse and saw him spitting mud out of his mouth as he scooped a handful of snow from the snowbank that bordered the road and washed the mud from his face. He must have thought about the pint of whiskey he had put in his coat pocket and began patting his pockets, searching for it. He extracted the unbroken bottle of Seagram's, unscrewed the cap, and took a drink. He wiped his mouth with the back of his muddy hand, spit out the debris that wiping his face had left in his mouth, staggered to his feet, and plodded toward the shack.

Paul knew his father's brain was swimming in an Olympic-size pool of alcohol and he muttered in fear and frustration. He knew his father bemoaned his lot in life—cursing because everything was shit, as usual. It would only be a matter of seconds before the old man began to vent his anger on Paul. He would start by blaming Paul for the death of his mother and from there Paul would become the object of all that was wrong in Wally's life. By the time Wally stepped through the door, the alcohol would have fueled his anger into a raging conflagration—one that would consume him until he doused it by beating his son unconscious.

Paul dropped the burlap bag they used as a curtain for the filthy window and crawled into his bed. He pulled the blanket over his head, hoping that by feigning sleep maybe the old man would leave him be. He listened, in stoic silence, to the sounds of his father staggering into the cabin's main room. The old man was swearing at no one in particular and Paul heard the wet plop of a coat hitting the floor. That, Paul knew, was not a good sign. Wally's level of sobriety could be measured by the length of the clothing trail he left on his way to the greasy mattress where he slept. Whenever he dropped his coat immediately upon opening the door, that meant he was really loaded. The door to the small room where

Paul and Wally slept swung open so violently that it slammed into the wall and a loud bang echoed through the shanty. A jar fell to the floor in the section of the main room that served as kitchen and dining room and shattered. "Get out here you mother-killer," Wally shouted.

Paul tightly shut his eyes and feigned sleep while bracing for the inevitable beating that always followed when Wally was drunk.

Wally Condor appeared in the door, teetering back and forth as he stared at the figure of the boy. The volume of Wally's voice increased as he began to rant, "You ain't foolin' me you overgrown bastard! You ain't asleep. Now git on your feet and take it like a man, not an oversized pussy!"

Paul lay still.

"Have it your way then. . . ." Wally took two stumbling steps forward and with all the strength his anger could muster, he punched Paul in the face.

The boy's head bounced from the recoil of the blow his father had delivered and white spots danced before his eyes, rendering him temporarily blind. He curled into a fetal ball, a futile attempt at self-preservation, but his maneuvering only served to further enrage his attacker. Wally continued to pummel and curse at the boy until Paul was a bloody, crying mess.

Wally landed one final punch and then, exhausted from his efforts, flopped onto the bed across the room. In moments, he began to snore in a deep, drunken sleep.

Paul slowly regained consciousness. He rolled over and began to sob, fighting to keep the sounds of his despair muffled. He did not want to risk awakening his father to resume his assault. He silently lamented his lot and began to beg for help from any quarter. He began to chant, a chant his maternal grandfather had taught him, one the old man had said would summon the gods in a time of great need.

The temperature in the room suddenly plummeted and Paul felt the presence of something, or someone, in the room. He ceased chanting and slowly opened his swollen, bruised eyelids. A heavy mist hovered in the far corner of the room. Paul stared into it, mesmerized. The mist began to swirl around with increasing speed. Paul's eyes widened. There was something in the twisting fog but it was barely discernable. Of one thing he was certain: whatever it was appeared to be gigantic. The haze now filled the room to the rafters, and Paul felt that the inhabitant was looking down on him with a scowl of disgust.

Suddenly Paul was struck by the realization that he might be looking at a god! Possibly Kitchi-Manitou, the greatest of the gods! Paul slid from the filthy mattress and fell to his knees. He became aware of someone or something speaking to him and he opened his mind, allowing the unexpected message to enter. In his beaten and battered condition, Paul found the voice soothing. *I am Wendigo, god of the Algonquin people. I have seen your plight and have sensed your pain. It need not be so, if you but accept me all can be made well again. . . .*

Paul slowly rocked back and forth as the words seemed to heal him, both physically and mentally. He slowly raised his head and wiped the blood that still trickled from his nose, flinching when his hand touched his battered and split lips. "H-how do I do that?" His smashed mouth made his words slurred.

Open your mind and soul to me! Let me enter your body and all will be over!

The Wendigo stared down at Paul. *Open to me, Paul—Now!!!*

Paul raised his face. He stared out the dirt-encrusted window of the shack and saw the clouds suddenly part. The moon illuminated the room like a celestial laser beam. He turned his head back to face the mist, which had morphed into a dark cloud. Before Paul was able to stop it, the revolving storm descended around him. At the last minute, Paul felt the evil of the Wendigo and began to fight back. It was too late; the spirit permeated his body, soul, and mind. Paul Condor, with a cry of utter despair, ceased to be.

The body convulsed as the Wendigo assaulted and killed what was left of Paul Condor. The boy collapsed in a heap and clouds obscured the moon. The night was split by the drumming crescendo of another unseasonable storm.

Thunder boomed as a monstrous storm settled over Oslo with a display of power and force that rattled windows throughout the tiny village, shattering several. The Condor shack vibrated with the force of the thunder and the windows blew out of their frames. Wally was shocked awake and, although still drunk, leapt to his feet. He stood still in a state of vertigo for a moment and then saw Paul curled in a ball on the floor. "Git up you chicken-shit coward. It's only a fuckin' storm. . . ." He launched a kick at the boy's side.

A powerful hand reached out, grabbed Condor's foot, and flipped him across the room. Wally bounced off the wall and looked at his son. Instead of a cowering boy, he found himself looking at a malevolent face. Its eyes were as large as an owl's and seemed to be swimming in pools of blood. He inadvertently turned his eyes away from the hate-filled orbs.

Paul reached down and grabbed his leg and lifted him. Wally shouted, "Leggo my leg, you simple bastard—or you'll live to regret it!"

Rather than cower, as he usually did, Paul lifted him with a single hand and Wally found himself suspended by one leg and staring at the floor like a deer that had been hung out to bleed before butchering. Without saying a word, Paul spun him around and smashed him into the wall. He dropped his stunned and bleeding father to the floor and left the room. Standing in the kitchen, Paul watched Wally stagger to his knees and before he could regain his feet, Paul returned to further punish him.

On hands and knees, Wally scrambled across the floor. He reached under his cot, found what he sought, and turned to defend himself. Lightning lit up the room and sparkled on the blade of Wally's most prized possession, a bowie knife he'd bought at the pawnshop in Caribou. Paul reached down, grabbed Wally by the throat, and held him there.

Wally drove the knife into his son's midsection and was astonished when the boy did not even flinch as the large blade penetrated him. Wally drove the knife home two more times, yet no matter how viciously he attacked, Paul's unbelievable strength imprisoned him. He opened his mouth to scream but his shout was quickly stifled. Paul grabbed his lower jaw and with a horrendous twist, ripped it from its socket. Wally howled in pain, his jaw hanging loose and flapping like a storefront sign in a strong wind.

Wally's eyes bulged with horror when his captor pulled him from the wall and carried him into the kitchen. Paul slammed him onto the table. Oxygen depletion sapped Wally's strength and he dropped the knife and grabbed Paul's hand with both of his in a vain attempt to stop the strangulation. Suddenly the huge hand released his throat and Wally gasped as he sought the air he needed to survive. Before Wally was able to fill his lungs, Paul forced Wally's head to the left exposing his neck. With his teeth he ripped through the flesh and severed the artery. He sounded like a nursing infant as he sucked blood from his father's carotid.

Wally screamed as his son tore his chest open and grasped his heart and with a final mighty pull, yanked it out of his chest. Before death finally ended the brutal attack, Wally saw Paul raise the heart, blood pulsing out of it, and smile at his victim as he bit into it.

The Wendigo, now in control of Paul, went into a feeding frenzy. He tore, ripped, and gorged himself on the body, cramming chunks of raw meat into his mouth until he was stuffed. In a final act of depravity, he ripped the head off the body and paused in the quiet, staring at the waves of steam rising from the body as it gave up its heat in the cabin's cooling interior air. Wendigo heard the rhythmic sound of the blood slowly draining from the head suspended in his right hand by the hair. The soft impacts of the blood hitting the floor sounded like cymbals to the sated beast.

Plop.

The Wendigo felt his new stomach heave under the weight of all the meat it contained.

Plop. Plop.

His stomach lurched.

Plop. Plop. Plop.

The Wendigo threw Wally's carcass across the room and bent forward, vomiting a gushing torrent of raw meat and tepid blood. When the heaving ceased, the Wendigo wiped the excess vomit from his face with the back of his hand. He admonished himself. It had been so long since he had eaten that he had overlooked entirely the fact that his new body would have to be trained. It would require a period of time before it would be ready for its new diet.

The Wendigo grabbed the legs he had butchered from Wally's body and carried them with him as he stepped out of the dark cabin and into the sudden light of the lightning storm.

Viverette Settlement

The room seemed as hot as a furnace. He opened the window over the sink and retrieved the meat he'd stored there. It was frozen but his hunger was so great that he ripped into it and gulped it down. He realized that he was still hungry. It was time for another hunt. This time he'd go further south, there was usually heavy snowmobile traffic around Rocky Mountain.

6

***

Fort Kent, Maine

It was just past eight when John drove into Serge Shapiro's yard. He walked to the door and knocked. After a few seconds, a small woman with streaks of gray in her hair opened the door. "Can I help you?"

John took out his badge and offered it to her. "I'm John Bear, Wildlife Crimes Investigation Division, is Serge at home?"

She took the badge, scrutinized it for a second and handed it back. "He's downstairs," she said and stepped aside to let him in.

Without a word, she led him down a short flight of stairs and into a finished basement. "Serge," she announced, "you have a visitor."

A short, gray-haired man, at least thirty pounds overweight and with a gray mustache and full beard, appeared in the doorway. He looked at John for a second and then his face lit up in recognition. "John, how've you been?"

John held out his hand and Shapiro gave it a hearty shake. "I been fine, Serge, busy but fine."

"C'mon in. Julia would you bring us some coffee?"

Shapiro's wife nodded and climbed back up to the main house while Serge led John into his inner sanctum. John paused and looked at the room. On a rectangular table lay an impressive array of handguns. There were revolvers and pistols lying in a row. One of the revolvers was disassembled and a rag and a bottle of Hoppe's No. 9 solvent lay beside it. Shapiro saw John glance from the weapons to the walls, which were covered with posters. The posters were assorted, everything from NRA advertisements to intricate how-to placards on the care of firearms and firearms safety. "I teach NRA handgun safety courses," Shapiro commented. "Completion of one is a requirement for a concealed carry permit."

John looked past Shapiro into a small room that held several rows of shelving, each filled with assorted parts for weapons, even parts for machine guns. "I'm one of the few dealers licensed to sell machine guns and machine gun parts by the ATF."

John looked at his host, obviously intrigued. "There a lot of demand for machine guns?"

"More than you might imagine. Someone has to service the legal collectors . . . even sold some to one of the major movie production companies."

"I had no idea. How many classes you give?"

"Before the governor made it legal for anyone in Maine to carry concealed, I'd do two a month . . . mostly on Sundays." He handed John a small business card that listed him as a legal dealer and manufacturer of machine guns and silencers.

Julia Shapiro reappeared carrying a tray on which sat a complete coffee service. She placed it on the table and departed without saying anything. Shapiro poured two cups of steaming coffee and asked, "Cream and sugar?"

"Black is fine."

Shapiro sat in the chair in front of the disassembled revolver and motioned for John to sit across from him. "What brings you here?"

"Two days ago we found a body, up near Lake Frontière."

"That would be the young fellow from Massachusetts. I did a preliminary autopsy on him yesterday. I took one look at him and knew that it was going to require a hell of a lot more testing than I could do here. The body is being transported to Augusta for a more complete one."

"What can you tell me?"

"Cause of death was massive blood loss and trauma to most of his internal organs. I have no idea what the killer used as a weapon."

"So it's a homicide?"

"By legal definition: anytime someone dies of other than natural causes it's a homicide. . . . However, this was a murder and a particularly brutal one at that."

"Can you tell me anything else?"

"Nothing, other than the fact that he was brutalized before dying and something had been eating him?"

"Animals get to him?"

"Right now I can't say, they'll have a better idea once the people down in Augusta go over the cadaver. I will give you my personal opinion though, whatever was rooting around inside that young man had a flat snout—more like that of a human than that of any four-legged predator I ever saw."

John was silent as he processed the information. After several moments, John said, "I wonder if there may be a Native American link."

"Are you alluding to the fact that in some tribes it was believed that if a warrior ate the liver of a worthy enemy he would gain that warrior's courage and strength?" Shapiro asked. "I will admit that the thought crossed my mind. There's anthropological proof that some tribes ate the bodies of dead captives to induce fear in their enemies. There's also Wendigo psychosis."

"Wendigo psychosis?"

"Wendigo psychosis is what shrinks call a mental state where the sufferer has an intense craving for human flesh; some believe that they see people as edible animals. It appears to be culture bound."

"What do you mean by *culture bound*?"

"Very few, if any, cases have involved ethnicities other than Native Americans."

"Are you saying that this only happened to Indians?"

"I'd even go further than that. It seems to be prevalent in people from tribes in the Algonquin nation, which runs from the Canadian Maritime provinces west to Minnesota and south to the Ohio River, the greatest numbers being in Quebec and Ontario."

Something in John's mind snapped. Like a lightning strike, awareness burst through the barriers his mind had formed to hold back the primordial fear that had been nagging him. He thought that he knew what had made the track and his heart leapt! It took him several long seconds to squelch his superstitions and childish fears. Still, a chill raced through him. A horrific word echoed through his head, one that adults had used to scare him into behaving when he was a child. The most evil of all the Algonquin spirits—*the Wendigo*!

John recalled the tales his grandfather had told him. The old man, in his eighties when John was eight, had mesmerized him with tales of the old days and of the Wendigo. John remembered the old man's response when asked if he really believed that such a creature existed: "No," his grandfather replied, "but I saw his tracks once. . . ." John wondered if he, like his grandfather before him, had looked at the track of a Wendigo. While John listened to Serge, his mind was busy, recalling everything he had ever heard about the Wendigo.

"So there are people who suffer from this psychosis?"

"Prior to 1900 it occurred frequently among Algonquin cultures, one of which is your Maliseet tribe, but since Native American urbanization the incidence has fallen dramatically."

"But not completely . . ."

"Nothing ever stops completely. By the way, the success rate in curing a patient with this particular psychosis is lower than the success rate treatment centers have in getting addicts off their drug of choice . . . only about 14 percent versus 20. The only thing I know of with a higher rate of recidivism is nicotine addiction."

"Just what I need," John said, "a psychopath who thinks people are on the menu."

"Are you trying to say we're dealing with someone suffering from the Wendigo psychosis?" Serge said.

John said, "I hope that's all. . . ."

7

Maliseet First Nation, Edmundston, New Brunswick, Canada

John Bear coasted to a stop in front of the small house. He sat in the stillness and stared at the light glowing from the kitchen window. He slid from the seat, walked onto the porch, and knocked on the door. He heard the shuffling footsteps of his father's ancient tread from within. He swallowed nervously, not knowing what type of reception he would get. It had been over four years since he had last visited the old man and the parting had not been good.

The door opened a crack and Charley Bear's rheumy eyes peered out into the darkness. The old man's craggy face curled as he squinted to focus his eyes. He gazed out trying to see who was disturbing him at this late hour. "John?" The gravel in his voice made John aware of how much the old man had aged.

"Yes, Father. May I come in?"

Charley Bear stepped back and his face cracked into a toothless smile. "Of course! Of course! My god, boy, I ain't heard from you since you called me on my birthday, two or three months ago. Where you been?" He closed the door as soon as his son stepped through the threshold.

"I'm still living across the line, in Ashland," John answered.

"Pretty country over there, used to hunt it a lot myself. You still a warden?"

"Yeah, another five years and I can retire."

"How's your brother?"

"Tom and Clarisse are fine, still living in Lyndon Station. We see each other a couple of times a month."

"Maybe you ought to get together and come and see your old man once in a while."

Rather than point out how Charley had been a nonentity in the lives of his sons during the years that their drunken mother had dominated them, John ignored the old man, allowing him to continue believing the fantasy that he was a good father. Instead he said, "We should do that."

The old man led John into the small kitchen and pulled a chair out for him. "Set yourself down, boy." He stood by the table, stooped with age, and assessed John for several long moments. John began to feel like a lab specimen. "You're looking good, if I must say so myself. You want some coffee?" the old man asked.

John became aware of the heady aromatic mixture of cigarette smoke and coffee that filled the small overly hot room and nodded. "I'll get it, you sit," he said. He took the old man by the arm to help him into a chair.

Charley Bear immediately yanked his arm free. "I may be old, but I ain't feeble. Now set down and I'll get it!"

John held his hands up in supplication, "Okay, okay. You get it." He could not help but smile at the old man's desire to appear self-sufficient. His father shuffled over to the stove, used the toe of his Red Wing work boot to hook open the firebox of the antiquated woodstove. He picked up two pieces of firewood from the stand to the immediate right of the stove, tossed them into the blaze, and pushed the door shut with his foot. He grabbed the coffeepot from the stovetop, hooked two mugs with the index finger of his left hand and returned to the table, taking a seat across from his son. He placed the mugs on the table and poured coffee into them, splattering the table as his hands shook from Parkinson's.

John ignored the spillage and accepted one of the mugs.

"Cream and sugar?" the old man asked.

"No, black is fine."

The arthritic knuckles of Charley Bear's hands seemed elevated as he fought to twist the cover off a jar of non-dairy creamer. He scooped five teaspoons of creamer into his mug, scattering most of it as his hands shook, and then repeated the chore to add an equal amount of sugar. Once his coffee was prepared to his liking, he fumbled to remove a cigarette from the pack that sat on the table beside an overflowing ashtray. He struggled for several seconds trying to align the Marlboro with his mouth. Once he'd achieved his objective, he broke three wooden matches attempting to light it. John removed a match, struck it on the side of the box, and held it before the old man, waiting patiently as his father sucked through loose lips. "You really ought to cut down on the sugar," John said.

"Hell, I'm sixty-eight years old and been using sugar all my life. Besides, once a man reaches my age he's living on borrowed time anyways. I can't chase women no more so I might as well enjoy what little I can." The old man waited for several seconds and then chuckled. "Ain't you gonna give me the *smoking will kill you* lecture?"

"Won't do any good. . . . You'll just give me the *borrowed time* answer again," John said. "Besides, I still have one from time to time."

Charley laughed again and slurped more coffee. He smoked the Marlboro and stared at his son through the spiraling smoke. "Boy, you're as tetchy as a cornered bobcat. What's eatin' at you?"

"Larry Murphy . . ."

"How is Murph?" the old man interrupted, "I ain't seen him in years either."

"Murph's fine, day before yesterday he went looking for a missing sledder . . . a young fellow from away, Massachusetts. Murph found his body up north of the Little Black River."

The old man sucked on his cigarette and took a long slurping drink from his coffee mug. "His death accidental?"

"We're still investigating."

John took a swallow of coffee and tried to decide how best to approach the heart of the matter. He decided that knowing his father, getting to the point was usually the best course of action. "Dad, tell me about the Wendigo."

Charley Bear froze for several seconds, his cigarette suspended before his lips. "What you want to know about *that* for?"

"I'm just interested."

"You didn't drive no hundred miles in the middle of a snow storm because you're interested in hearing about the Wendigo. Now level with me."

"The body Murph found . . ."

"What's that got to do with the Wendigo?"

"Whoever or whatever killed him tore him all to pieces and parts of the body are missing. I scouted the woods and came across a track. It was a giant track—human, yet not human." John held his hands up touching the thumbs together and spreading all his fingers as far as they'd go, approximating the size of the track. "It was about this big."

"I knowed it. Damn it! I told the RCMP years ago all them hunters they said was getting lost over across, and round here too, wasn't lost. I told them there was a Wendigo hereabouts. Stupid sons-a-whores wouldn't listen though. No siree. They wouldn't listen at all."

"Tell me about it. Not the myths, the truth."

"Wendigos is mean, boy. They eat human flesh and grow to great size. They don't like towns and such, stay in the woods, they do. They got enough strength to rip a man apart with their hands. They got no lips because they's always starvin' and over time they chew them off with their jagged teeth. The track you saw, did it have toes?"

"I couldn't tell in the snow. Why?"

"Wendigo only have one toe, the great one, kind of acts like a natural snowshoe. They have eyes like an owl, huge, only sunk into their head like a man who ain't had nothin' to eat for weeks. The eyes roll around in their head, crazy-like, truth is they floatin' in blood." As Charley Bear spoke of the creature, his hand wavered in front of his face in spasmodic loops. "Like I said, they grow tall, taller than any normal man, might even top twenty feet, and they're skinny as a rail . . . even their skin starts to turn yellow. Of course, they don't always look like that. Often they look as normal as you and me, only taller and skinnier. They's pathetic sons-a-bitches. The more they eat, the more they grow. . . . They can never get enough to eat. They smell like a cadaver, it's a heady, sweet smell of decay, hard to describe it, but once you smellit you'll always remember it. You might say they's a real-life version of one of them zombies they show on the TV." The old man once again froze, cigarette smoke trailing out of his nostrils. "Did it see you, son? If it did you're in great danger."

"I don't think so. How can you be sure if one sees you?"

"Hard to say, but they'll usually talk. The Wendigo speaks in many ways. It can mimic human voices to lure its prey, but mostly it speaks in high-pitched whistles and thunderous booms and it only does that when it sees or senses prey. It trails their victims, like a bloodhound, they never give up. Then after dark they seize and eat them. If you are dealing with a Wendigo, you better hope it's a young one."

"How can you tell if it's young or old?"

"Young ones still look human. Big, but could still pass as an unusually tall person. Old ones are another story. They are skinny and, like I said, what lips they have will be tattered and bloody from its constant chewing with jagged teeth. Chances are better than not that its bones will be pushing out against its skin, its skin is the ash gray of death, and its eyes pushed back deep into their sockets, and it looks like a giant skeleton recently dug up from the grave.

"How do they come to be?"

"There's three ways to become Wendigo. First, a shaman can place a curse upon you. Second, you can allow yourself to be possessed by the evil spirit, and third, you eat human flesh—and like it."

John Bear drank his coffee, took one of his father's cigarettes, and lit it. "How do you kill one?"

"There are few possibilities to defeat a Wendigo. Your best chance is during the day as they usually hunt at night, it's almost impossible to defeat them at night, since it is their favorite period to hunt. Also despite being animal-like, Wendigos are smart, as intelligent as humans, thus making them even more dangerous. Once it gets on your trail, Wendigos engage in a torturous game. They bait their prey, release shrieks or growls, and sometimes mimic human voices calling for help. When it begins hunting in earnest, a Wendigo becomes all business. It will race after you, upending trees, create animal stampedes, and stir up ice storms and tornadoes."

"Almost makes you want to lock your doors and hide. . . ."

"You ain't safe indoors either. The Wendigo can unlock doors and enter homes, where it will kill and eat the inhabitants before converting the cabins into Wendigo dens for hibernation."

"Hibernation?"

"More than anything, a Wendigo knows how to last long winters without food. It hibernates for years at a time. When it's awake, sometimes it keeps its victims alive. It stores them in dark isolated places so it can feed whenever it wants. Wendigos can stealthily stalk victims for long periods. What with fast speed, endurance, and heightened senses such as hearing so good they can hear the beat of panicked hearts from miles away, it ain't often that they don't get their prey."

"If you can't outrun a Wendigo, can you outgun it?"

"Conventional guns don't hurt it, they only piss it off. It's been said silver works. Silver bullets, knife blades, and ax heads work best—problem is I don't know who can afford them and sure as hell don't know where to get them. No matter what you use you got to get at its icy heart. I been told that you can shatter it, but the safest way is to burn it."

"So all I gotta do is buy silver bullets, find its lair, incapacitate it, then cut out its heart and burn it. . . ."

"You won't have to find it. If you fuck with this thing, it will find you."

8

Lyndon Station

B ob Pelky sat in front of the fireplace in his living room. He twirled ice around the glass of bourbon he was drinking while listening to country music on the radio. A loud knocking at the door brought his head around. He watched his wife open the door and then turned back to gazing at the fire.

"John, come in out of the cold," Elaine Pelky said. "Bob's in the front room."

Pelky bolted to his feet when John Bear walked into the room. "John, where in hell have you been?"

"Over home, I stopped by to see Serge Shapiro in Fort Kent, then went to the reservation to see my father."

"You visited your old man? Did you two settle your differences?"

"There're a lot of things still hangin' over us, but at least we can talk now."

"Well, I just thought it was strange you'd take off when we got a murder to solve."

"We're after a Wendigo, Bob."

"A what?"

John told Pelky about the legend, as well as the physical and supernatural powers of the beast. When John finished, Pelky looked at him, astonished. "Holy shit, John, that's the craziest fucking thing I've ever heard!"

"Such language," Elaine said as she entered the room. "Do you two eat with those filthy mouths?" Her smile contradicted the indignation of her words. "You two are a couple of real party-poopers. Bob hasn't said two words since he got home tonight. What's eating at you two? Does this have anything to do with the dead snowmobiler?"

John said, "Serge said he was murdered."

"Oh my God," Elaine whispered softly. She walked over to the bar and mixed a drink. "That's shocking. Bob told me that Murphy found a dead man, but murder—that scares me. It scares me. The last thing one expects in a small town like this is a murder." She took a drink. Satisfied with her efforts she walked back to the men.

The conversation lapsed into silence. The atmosphere in the normally cozy room became heavy with tension. "Please," Elaine implored them, let's don't make this the primary topic of conversation this evening, okay?" She directed herself to John. "I'm glad you came by. . . . You are staying for dinner, aren't you?"

"I don't want to impose. . . ."

"It's not an imposition. In fact, Laura Wells, an old friend of mine from college, called today and I've invited her over for dinner." Elaine gave John an impish look and added, "She'd be a good catch for you."

"Just what I need right now," John answered with a weak smile. "We've got a Wendigo running around and you're matchmaking."

"What did you say?" Elaine asked.

"John has lost his mind. He thinks the killer is a Wendigo," Pelky said. "It's mythical. . . ."

"I know what it is," she said. A look of abhorrence crossed her face. "You mean the body was . . ."

"Yes . . . ," John looked at Elaine before continuing. "The body was torn apart and . . . well, several parts were missing."

"Elaine," Pelky interjected, "are you saying there are reported cases of this?"

"Serge said there are cases of people goin' crazy and thinking they're a Wendigo," John added. "I don't think that our killer is a human being."

A knock on the door interrupted the conversation. Elaine turned to the men and warned them, "Remember you promised to let this lie for the night. Tomorrow I'll be more than happy to let you talk about it all day. Deal?"

"Deal," John and Pelky said in unison.

Elaine opened the door and Laura Wells stepped across the threshold, removing all thoughts of mutilated bodies and Wendigos from John's mind. He couldn't take his eyes off her. He admired her stature and figure. He guessed her height to be about five foot seven, just right when compared to his five feet, eleven inches. Her light-brown hair cascaded softly past her shoulders, accentuating her slender figure. John resisted the urge to reach out and touch it to test the softness for himself. She wore a bulky sweater, which did little to obscure the fullness of her breasts, tight blue jeans, and calf-high leather boots. She was one of the most desirable women he had seen in years.

After they had eaten Elaine pushed them into the living room while she cleaned up the dishes. John and Laura sat on the couch facing the fireplace. Pelky came out of the kitchen carrying a tray laden with steaming mugs of coffee, which he handed around. They sat in idle chatter for several minutes while they sipped on the hot beverage before Pelky stood up and announced that he was going to see if Elaine needed any help.

The door to the kitchen closed behind him and Laura smiled over her mug and said, "It looks as if we're all on our ownsies now."

John returned her smile, "This was probably planned out very carefully. Elaine has been trying to get me attached for quite a while."

"Welcome to the club," Laura said with an understanding look. "She's always been at me too."

"So tell me," John said, changing the subject. "What do you do for a living?"

"I'm a reporter for the *Bangor Post*. My editor sent me up here to look into the death of the snowmobiler they found. You know the one they found the night before last."

"One of my fellow wardens found him."

"You know about this," her demeanor suddenly turned professional.

"I'm with the Maine Department of Inland Fisheries and Wildlife Warden Service."

"A game warden?"

"Wildlife Criminal Investigation Division," John said. "It's my job to investigate any case involving a fatality in the woods."

Laura leaned toward him, her attention locked. "You're the investigator on this?"

"In a way, the investigating warden will probably be Warden Murphy, my job is more that of supervision and coordination. I don't know whether or not Bob will have any official presence—that's up to his superiors on the state police."

Her interest intensified. "I jumped when offered this assignment for two reasons. First, none of the more senior writers wanted to visit the far northwestern part of the state in midwinter. Secondly, it afforded me a chance to visit my best friend at the paper's expense. I had no idea I'd walk into a real story."

Laura sat back. Her posture and demeanor told John that she couldn't believe her luck. She opened her mouth to ask another question but was forestalled by the Pelkys entering the room.

John knew that the matchmaker in Elaine immediately picked up on the way Laura's body was inclined toward him and knew that it was obvious that they had been deeply engrossed in conversation when she asked: "Are we intruding?"

"Elaine Pelky, you'd been holding out on me," Laura accused with mock indignation.

"What do you mean?" Elaine responded, assuming that her friend was talking about John.

"You didn't tell me that John and your husband are investigating the murder."

"Well, my involvement could be temporary. Matter of fact, it wouldn't surprise me if an investigator from the Maine State Police Major Crimes Unit, North didn't show up soon."

They spent the remainder of the evening avoiding discussion of the killing. They talked until the chimes of Elaine's antique grandfather clock rang out eleven and John announced it was time for him to leave. "Tomorrow morning is going to be a long day."

"I should be leaving too," Laura said. "I've rented a small cabin at Del's Place. It has a woodstove and I need to put some wood in it or I'll freeze to death tonight."

"I'll follow you there," John said. "I live in Ashland, so I'm staying with my brother and his wife. You shouldn't be driving on these icy roads at night—especially now."

"I'll be all right," she protested.

"It's not a problem for me," John said. "It's on the way."

Elaine brought them their coats and stood in the door while they walked to their cars. Laura slid into her compact and turned the ignition. The motor turned over once and then stopped with a sickening *wruung-wruung*. "Damn," she cursed.

"Sounds like you got a dead battery. These cold days and nights will bring out any problem in a car," Pelky said. He turned to John and asked if he had jumper cables.

"No. I lent mine to one of the guys." John turned to Laura. "I can drop you off."

"Or," Elaine called, "you can crash here."

"Thanks," Laura said to Elaine, "but I'll go to the cabin. All my things are there."

"Okay, have it your way. I'll get someone over tomorrow to charge or, if needed, change your battery," Pelky said.

Laura slid into John's truck and John backed out of the drive, barely avoiding a collision with her car. He concentrated on his driving for several minutes and suddenly realized the silence was getting heavy.

"Are you going to look into this?" Laura asked.

"Yes. Even if it wasn't my job, I'd do it."

"Why?"

"If I don't do it, I'm afraid that after a while it will become a cold case and then no one will."

"Wouldn't the state police investigate?"

"I don't know. Bob might, if Augusta doesn't take the case from him. Bob's still a field officer, a uniform patrol officer, not a detective."

"Is there a difference between the two?"

"Bob has a territory to patrol and handles everything from traffic stops to domestic violence. However, murders, or homicides if you will, fall under the Major Crimes Unit, North. They have detectives assigned in Caribou and Houlton among other places."

"Will he be promoted to . . . what you said . . . Major Crimes?"

"I doubt it. He was offered the chance once, but turned it down. He likes being on patrol and not sitting around waiting for an assignment."

"But it seems to me that there would be plenty of cases."

"A lot less than you'd think—last year Maine had a total of twenty-five, most of them from Bangor south."

"But the missing hunters—"

"That's my primary responsibility. Some people refer to us wardens as dirt-road cops. I handle all deaths, accidental or otherwise, and missing persons in the woods. However, depending on the crime, the state police or even county sheriff can take it away."

"They do that often?"

"No, we're all overworked and underpaid."

The remainder of the trip to the motel was completed in silence, each of them content to spend the time alone with their thoughts. John pulled into Del's parking lot, circled the store, and slowed down to cruise along the front of the cabins. "It's the fourth from the office," Laura said.

As he drove past the cabin with the yellow Hummer in front, John said, "I probably shouldn't tell you this, but five minutes after you go over to Del's for coffee someone'll tell you that that cabin is where the victim's sister and her boyfriend are staying."

Wells looked with interest at the vehicle. "Thanks, maybe I'll try to get an interview tomorrow."

John pulled up in front of her door and said, "How about I buy you dinner before you go back?"

"That sounds fine," Laura said opening the door and stepping out into the freezing night air. "I'll wait to hear from you then."

John pointed to the smoke spiraling from the small cabin's chimney, "Looks like Del decided to warm the place up for you."

"Thank God for small favors," she said with a smile. "Thanks for the lift. I'm going to hold you to that dinner promise."

John smiled and said, "Don't get your hopes up. There ain't any fancy restaurants in Lyndon Station."

"I'm sure we'll make do," she replied. "Thanks again." She shut the door and walked into the cabin's.

John remained parked in front of the small cabin until he saw her enter and close the door behind her. As he drove out of the parking lot he realized he was looking forward to taking her out. He smiled to himself all the way home.

It had been years since John had been interested in a woman. It was not like he didn't have his share of chances—he was not a bad-looking man. Elaine told him that often enough. Women just didn't seem to fit into his lifestyle. He lived in a two-room cabin in Ashland, not because he had to, but because he held little if any regard for material things. He had more than enough money to keep him living in comfort. In fact, if he didn't want to work as a game warden ever again, he could sit in front of his fireplace and read. The job just seemed to fit his solitary ways, and gave him a reason to be in the outdoors most of the time. John Bear was not the type to be domesticated or housebroken. He liked being alone. In fact he *chose* to be alone. But of late he had found himself questioning his lifestyle more and more. Was he finally ready, at the age of forty-three, to get serious about a woman? Was he ready to start a family? The turmoil of his childhood came to mind and John shrugged the thoughts out of his mind. He was not sure if he was ready for that degree of responsibility or commitment. Let alone to trust a woman that much. There was, however, one thing he couldn't deny. He found Laura Wells very intriguing.

9

Lyndon Station

John swallowed the last of his coffee and rinsed the mug in the sink. He stared through the kitchen window at the predawn darkness. He turned his eyes to the left and looked at the thermometer on the outside window frame. The needle pointed to the twenty-below-zero mark.

On the table, his brother's radio was on and the disc jockey was reading the weather forecast. It was going to be cold. John already knew that. However the rest of the forecast was ominous. It called for the weather to warm up ahead of a frontal passage later in the day. That meant snow. They were calling for twelve to eighteen inches, and, when coupled with the forecasted thirty-five-mile-an-hour winds (with gusts to fifty miles an hour), it was more than enough to hinder John's search. He knew it was today or never. He shook his head and remarked about the weather forecast. "Now ain't that just goddamned great."

"Good morning."

John jumped with surprise; he had yet to get used to having anyone in the house with him. "You really get a charge out of sneaking up on people, don't you?" he snapped at his brother, Tom.

Tom smiled, undaunted by his older brother's gruff behavior. "It's not my fault you can't think and hear at the same time."

"I'm sorry. I'm just a little jumpy. I didn't want to disturb you."

"I'm usually an early riser," Tom lied. The last thing he wanted to do was to tell John that neither he nor his wife, Clarisse, had slept all night. The thought of what John was about to do had kept them awake and they were afraid to say anything that could upset him. So they had suffered in silence.

John rinsed his coffee mug with water and placed it in the sink. "I'd better get going. We're due for some weather today and tomorrow. I don't have much time."

"John, I heard that forecast—they're calling for another nor'easter. Can't this investigation of yours wait until after the storm?"

"No. If I wait I'll never find its trail—at least not before it comes back and kills someone else. This town is so damned small I guarantee the next victim will be someone I know."

Tom decided to make one last plea to dissuade him. "It's bad enough you're going into the wilderness after who knows what but with the weather forecasted, you'll be risking death from exposure."

"Give it a rest, okay? I'm going," The tone of his voice told Tom the issue was settled. John struggled into his heavy coat and added, "I've got a cell. Hell, it even has a built-in GPS! If it starts to get bad and you don't hear from me for two days, call the warden service. They'll come and get me with a plane."

"Planes don't fly in blizzards."

Damn, John thought, *he's as stubborn as I am*. Although he was not about to admit it, John knew Tom was right. But this was his job, what the state paid him to do. He picked up his rifle and pistol. "I'll be careful," he said. He gave Tom a weak smile, patted him on the shoulder, and walked through the door into the frozen darkness.

John was less than a mile from his brother's house when his cell phone rang. "John Bear," he said.

"It's Murph. We got another one."

"Where?"

"Same area . . . the victim is Raymond Labelle. He ran a trap line."

"Where are you now?"

"A couple of miles from where we found Kelly. This one looks like he's been here for a while."

"Give me an hour."

"Hurry up, John. I have to confess that I'm not enjoying being out here alone."

T19, R11

The body was in much the same condition as Kelly's. Who or whatever had killed Raymond Labelle had slaughtered him. Once again the chest cavity had been ripped open and the legs were gone. John was sure that Serge would find the heart and liver missing. This time the killer had had more time to do his work.

John studied the area. "Just like Kelly, finding anything is gonna be a problem."

Murphy said, "Like that crime scene, I found tracks over there under a tree." He pointed down the road. "They're old, but more legible than the ones near the Kelly kid."

"Who else you call?" John asked.

"The state police. They're sending a chopper in here to lift him out."

"Let's take a look at those tracks."

They walked down the road and once again found large tracks similar to those found at Kelly's murder scene. The killer had stayed on the road until it intersected an animal trail and had then turned off into the woods. The two wardens stood beside the road and looked where the tracks disappeared into the dense tree cover.

"What's in that direction," John asked.

Murphy, who was familiar with the area, answered, "Not much. Viverette Settlement is northwest about twenty-five miles . . . but beyond that we got no jurisdiction. It's Quebec."

Their musing was interrupted by the sound of an approaching helicopter and they turned back to meet it. As they neared the body, Murphy asked, "John, you think we have any chance of finding this guy?"

"I think that there will be one hell of a body count if we don't."

"What possible motive can the killer have?"

"If it's what I think it is, it's hunting."

"Hunting for what?"

"What men have hunted for thousands of years—food."

When the departing helicopter was a small dot against the low-hanging clouds, John turned to Murphy. "You got room on your trailer for my sled?"

"I should have. Where are you going?"

"I'm going to follow those tracks—" John lifted the cover to his sled's storage department and took out a pair of snowshoes, "—afoot. If we get the snow that's forecast, we may not get another chance to find out who or what we're dealing with."

"Are you sure about this? There's over three feet of snow in the woods." Murphy stared at John as if he was uncertain whether or not he should speak what was on his mind. After a pause he asked, "When were you on snowshoes last?"

John grinned as he dropped the shoes into the snow. "Been a while, that's for sure."

Murphy picked up one of the snowshoes. He turned it over and studied it. The bottom of the shoe was orange and was supported by a sturdy aluminum frame; the boot was similar to that of a ski in that it only allowed the wearer's heel to rise up to make walking easier. "These things have come a long way. How long is it?"

"L.L. Bean catalog lists it as thirty inches. It fits into the storage compartment perfectly."

"It's still gonna be hard, especially if you aren't used to shoeing in deep snow."

"Yeah, only problem is that I don't see any other way."

10

T19, R11

John adjusted the straps of his backpack and the sling on his rifle so they would not dig into his shoulder and walked in the direction the track led, keeping his eyes on the ground until he found the second track. The footprints had to be eight or ten feet apart. Even if the killer was running, he had to be one big bastard to cover that much ground in a single step. He was glad he had brought his snowshoes. Even though this was his first time on shoes this winter and his legs ached from the unaccustomed exertion, it beat trudging through calf-deep snow. He saw a line of tracks equidistant to each other and, for the next hour, he followed them.

The trail continued to go southwest, never faltering nor drifting away from their tack. The trail did not circumvent dense brush and tree limbs, the murderer merely busted through, apparently paying them little, if any, mind. *He definitely knows where he's going*, John surmised. *He's making a beeline to some place.*

John glanced upward. What he saw in the sky did not please him. The clouds appeared to be dropping lower and lower, a sure sign of snow. He knew from experience that before long the forecasted storm would be upon him. The wind began to add to his discomfort by whipping and gusting through the trees knocking snow from the heavily burdened branches onto his head and shoulders. "Of all times for the weatherman to be right," he groaned in frustration. "Why did he have to pick today?"

John looked at his watch. It was three in the afternoon and he had been snowshoeing for almost three hours with only a couple of short breaks. He was cold, and his legs were sore from walking on snowshoes. In an hour and a half it would be sunset, not enough time for him to make it back to Lyndon Station. He needed to find a place to settle in for the night and the last thing he wanted to do was set up camp in the dark. He decided to continue on until he found a suitable place to construct some sort of shelter for the night. He was determined to track this killer to the end, even if it meant weathering the storm in a makeshift lean-to. Blizzard or no blizzard, he was not going back until he had found the Wendigo.

Just prior to three, the snowflakes started to fall. At first they were large and heavy, what one usually encountered in a short, fast-moving squall. However in a half hour they turned into light, fine flakes—the type associated with prolonged and serious accumulation. The wind increased and each gust whipped the crystalline water against John's exposed face, stinging his flesh like a swarm of stinging insects. The airborne snow rolled across the landscape, giving the appearance of a tidal wave—a mammoth wave of frozen water rolling over, around, and (John was sure) through him. This was going to be a much stronger storm than the weatherman had predicted; John was not going to be able to stay out in this.

Suddenly, John found himself in a small meadow. He saw several large pines scattered through the clearing and spied one whose boughs were arched downward under the weight of snow, creating a natural shelter. He crawled inside and shrugged with approval when he found himself sheltered from the wind and snow. He removed the cell phone from his pocket and checked the display—it read: NO SERVICE. Before he could return it to his pocket, he froze in place. He stared out through the pine branches, which spread over his head and surveyed the clearing.

Something was there. Something big.

Slowly and without taking his eyes off the figure, John slipped the phone into his pocket, and crept forward. He stopped at the perimeter of his shelter, still partially hidden by the tree and studied the gigantic figure. It was almost impossible to determine whether it was animal or human with the blowing snow obscuring visibility. John's heart hammered in his chest. He worried that whatever stood before him would hear its clamorous thudding.

The wind suddenly died down and when the swirling snow settled, John saw the unmistakable outline of a moose. The large bull pushed snow around using its front hooves and snout. It seemed to sense John's presence and stopped its foraging. The huge head turned and stared at him. One of its antlers was missing. John was unsure whether it had lost one during a rutting fight or if it had dropped it (during December and January, Moose dropped their antlers, growing new ones in spring and summer) after the annual rut.

John remained still; sight is not the strongest of a moose's senses. Although usually docile, a startled moose will run, and not in any particular direction. It could charge as easily as it could flee. Passive or not, a half-ton animal could do a lot of damage if it ran over you. The animal studied him for a minute and then lumbered away, entering into the trees at the far end of the dell, and disappeared into the storm.

John settled back, sighed, and set about arranging the shelter for the night. He slid deeper into the protective confines of the pine and cleared away an area beneath the large lower boughs. Despite the calm in his impromptu camp, each time the wind gusted, snow drifted through the tree and settled on his head and shoulders. John opened his pack and extracted a tarpaulin, unfolded it, and then interwove it through the branches. Satisfied that he would be sheltered from falling snow, John staked the sides of the tarp in place with metal tent pegs. Using cord, he tied the back around the tree's trunk and, even though it was probably unnecessary, staked it into the frozen ground. The makeshift tent more than met his satisfaction. The tarp was big enough that a portion of it hung down in front and would serve as a door. It was not insulated, but it would keep snow from falling on him and he would be dry and out of the wind.

Finally, John banked snow around the bottom edges of the impromptu tent and crawled inside. He untied his goose-down sleeping bag from the pack and spread it out. He retrieved a flashlight and switched it on so he could see to unload the rest of his gear. Supper was a can of beans, eaten cold. His meal finished, he placed the empty can in his pack and sat on the sleeping bag. He debated whether or not he should remove his insulated boots when the effects of the day caught up with him. Suddenly, after a day of unaccustomed labor, his legs cramped and he massaged them until the spasms subsided. As he fell asleep his last thought was: *All the comforts of home.*

A loud thundering boom woke John up. He listened to the wind racing through the clearing and remembered what Charley Bear had told him about the Wendigo. He peered out of his rudimentary shelter. The front had passed on, leaving behind a cold wind, clear sky, and a brilliant landscape illuminated by a full moon. Then he saw a dark figure standing at the far end of the clearing. This time it was not a moose; it was humanoid. Jesus, he thought, the old man was right—the damned thing does exist! He reached behind his body and grasped his rifle.

The Wendigo charged, heading directly at John's hiding place beneath the pine. Its gigantic strides covered the distance between them at a speed John had heretofore thought impossible. There was no way anything so large could also be so fast! He pulled the high-powered rifle forward and into his shoulder, took aim, and squeezed the trigger.

The rifle's sharp *crack* was immediately followed by a dull *thud* as the bullet found its target.

The Wendigo was within fifty yards of his quarry when he saw the man raise his rifle. He feinted to the right and saw a flash of light burst from the weapon. A tremendous force hit him in the left shoulder, hammering him as if he'd been struck by a falling tree, and he stepped back, fell on his side, and for a few seconds lay in a heap.

John was unsure whether or not he had killed the Wendigo and stayed in place, still aiming his weapon at the form that lay on the snow. He thought: *Anything less than the .44 Magnum and I wouldn't have stopped him!*

The gargantuan suddenly leapt to its feet and John realized that it was only wounded. Once again, the beast's agility and speed shocked him. It charged again and John fired once more, hearing the unmistakable *crack*, *thud* of a high-velocity, large-caliber bullet finding its mark.

Once again, a tremendous force slammed the Wendigo backward. He realized he had only one choice and that was to flee so he might live. Although he knew the man's weapon would not kill him; it was capable of incapacitating him for a time—leaving him vulnerable to being cut open! He leapt to his feet and ran toward the side of the clearing away from the man with the deadly rifle. He quickly widened the gap between him and the man and then veered left. Without so much as a backward glance, the Wendigo fled into the safety of the woods.

John was amazed that the Wendigo was still able to run; the high-caliber bullets would have killed an elephant. The wind carried a sweet, almost sickening smell, like a slaughterhouse floor, and John thought he would vomit from its heady aroma. Before he was able to bring the rifle to bear and get off a third shot, the Wendigo had disappeared in the woods.

John shifted his shooting position and fired again. The rifle's report disappeared into frozen landscape. John knew that his last shot had been a futile attempt at best and doubted that he had scored another hit. He saw that the semiautomatic rifle's ejection port was locked open, the magazine was empty. John rolled over, fumbling inside the sleeping bag for his nine-millimeter service pistol. It seemed an eternity passed before he found it and felt as if he was moving in slow motion. He expected to see his assailant return to finish him off but forced his panic down. He struggled to his feet and stepped outside the shelter, aiming the handgun toward the direction the Wendigo had fled. He heard noises like those made by a large animal running through the forest and fired a couple of shots in the direction of the sound. The echoes of the gunshots were quickly swallowed by the wind.

John found himself standing alone defiantly looking after the Wendigo. He realized he was no match for the beast, especially at night. He quickly scanned all of the surrounding trees, trying to determine whether or not it was circling around, looking for a different angle of attack. All he saw were dark, threatening shadows that seemed to be on the move, and all he heard were the sounds of the wind and trees creaking as they swayed. He hoped he had hurt it and that all it cared about was flight.

John turned his attention to his own situation. He knew that if the .44 had not dropped the beast for good, his nine-millimeter would be as useful as a peashooter. He reached inside his shelter for the rifle. He wiped at the weapon, trying to clear it of any snow or debris it may have gathered when he discarded it. Without taking his eyes away from the surrounding forest, he patted his pockets until he located his backup magazine, which he quickly placed in the weapon.

After several tense minutes, John believed the beast had fled the area. He found his flashlight, turned it on, and scanned the area. Now that his adrenaline rush had abated, he suddenly felt the frigid temperature and crawled inside his shelter.

The windchill plummeted and John was forced to continually fight to remain conscious, his cold body needing and wanting rest. Under ordinary circumstances, in weather like this, he could curl up in his cold-weather, down-filled sleeping bag. But in this situation, going to sleep could turn into a fatal act; should the Wendigo return to finish him, the last thing he wanted to be was trapped inside the bag or unconscious.

John's head bobbed forward and he shook it violently trying to force himself awake. He washed his face with snow, trying to shock himself to full consciousness, but he was so cold he felt no difference between his skin temperature and that of the snow. He decided to throw caution to the wind, crawled outside, found a dead tree, and gathered some twigs and branches for a fire. Once he was back in the security of the pine, he started a small blaze and huddled near it as he awaited the dawn.

11

Viverette Settlement

Shortly before dawn, he entered the cabin and sat on his cot, back resting against the wall, and felt safe. He ignored the agonizing pain racking his shoulder and side while channeling his powers to heal the frightful damage his body had absorbed. He knew if he was to survive he had to go on the offensive once again.

The Wendigo was perplexed. For years he'd been successfully hunting these remote woods and no one had ever stood up to him or had even suspected his presence—until now. Rather than cower or try to escape, this man had fought him and it was obvious he was not about to give up.

T19, R11

The morning broke to reveal a cloudless sky, no discernable wind, and a temperature well below zero. John carried his rifle when he crawled out of his shelter and stretched, trying to force life into his tired and sore muscles. He looked for depressions in the snow, found traces of blood, and shuddered when he realized how close the Wendigo had gotten to him. He stared off in the direction the Wendigo had fled and wondered if he was doing the right thing by taking this thing on alone. "Well," he muttered, "sane or insane, I'm in it up to my ass now. . . ." He scanned the trees that bordered the clearing one last time and then returned to the shelter and broke camp.

Once he had finished packing his gear, John checked his weapons to ensure they were still in working order and not frozen. He looped the backpack over his shoulders and set off in pursuit of the Wendigo.

He trudged through the new snow until two in the afternoon, when he came to Camp 75 Road, a half mile south of the abandoned McClintock Mountain lookout tower. The road was a major thoroughfare for the large eighteen-wheel lumber trucks that hauled from the various cutting sites to mills in Maine and across the line in Canada, and had been recently plowed. John sat on the snow bank and sighed. He was cold, hungry, and tired to the point of exhaustion. That, coupled with the fact that he had no idea which way the Wendigo had gone, had him debating how much further he should go. He decided that he would give up for the day and head back. There was at most two hours of daylight remaining and the Little Black checkpoint, where he had left his truck, was about twenty miles away by the road.

John strapped his snowshoes to his pack and started walking south. He had walked a mile and a half when he heard the unmistakable rumble of an approaching truck. He turned and waved. When the driver downshifted and broke, the trailer, which was stacked twenty feet high with timber fishtailed slightly.

The side windows of the truck were coated with salt and grit and John could not see the driver's face. The window rolled down and the driver said, "Jeez crow, I almos' run you over—you nuts or sumptin'?"

John recognized the driver. He was a local named Rene Thibeau.

Thibeau stared out the open window with eyes that were squinted. "That you, John Bear?"

John knew Thibeau needed glasses, but refused to get them—not that it would make much difference, the windshield of the truck was so splattered with mud that it was doubtful much of anything was visible through it.

Any other time John would have cited him for driving with obstructed vision, but he was too fatigued and wanted a ride. "*Bon jour*, Rene, I need a ride to the Little Black checkpoint."

"Well, don' be standin' dere. Get yourself in."

John walked around the front of the big truck, reached up and opened the door. He placed his rifle and rucksack on the floor and climbed in. No sooner had he shut the door than Rene shifted gears and had the truck moving forward.

The lumberman had the stub of an extinguished cigar clenched in his teeth and the truck's cab smelled like an ashtray that should have been dumped days ago. When the truck was up to cruising speed (which was about ten miles an hour faster than what John would have considered safe for the road conditions), Rene glanced at John's gear and said, "You carryin' a lot of guns. How come? It's too late in the year to be huntin' bear, you after a wounded animal or somet'ing?"

John knew that to tell Rene what he was hunting would make him sound crazy, so rather than risk it, said, "Yeah. You see anything on the road?"

"Nope, I bin haulin' from up on Estcourt Road an' ain't even seen a fuckin' coyote. . . ."

John grunted in acknowledgement and settled back in the seat. The truck looked like it was on its last legs and the interior was coated in dust and cigar ash, but it had a damned good heater. In short time the heat penetrated John and he nodded off.

Little Black Checkpoint

John waved as Rene drove off and turned toward the gatehouse. A cloud of steam rolled out when he opened the door to the heated interior and he stepped inside, quickly pulling the door shut behind him.

Sean O'Connell was on duty and he looked up at John. "I thought that was your truck parked outside. You been out all night?"

John picked up a disposable coffee cup and filled it with hot black coffee. Yeah, I camped up near Lake Frontière."

O'Connell turned around in his swivel chair and studied John for a few seconds. "Right now ain't exactly ideal campin' weather."

All John could think of to say was, "That's no shit."

John settled into another chair and sipped the scalding beverage. He savored the beverage's heat as it flowed down his throat and into his body. "Are there any fools still in the woods?"

"Damned if I know. Once they pay the toll and enter, who knows where they go. They can head north and come out in Estcourt Station or go west to St. Pamphile. . . . Roads are all plowed between the major checkpoints. Hell, it's possible they made a big loop and came out at Dickey. Why you askin'?" O'Connell paused for a second. "This got anything to do with those two fellows that died?"

"Yeah. How'd you hear about them?" John was always amazed at how fast word traveled even in the sparsely populated woods.

"It's been all over the CB. Damn fools from away. Ain't got enough sense to check the goddamn weather report."

John swallowed another mouthful of coffee. "Weather had nothing to do with it—the last guy, Raymond Labelle, was a local. They were both murdered."

O'Connell's head snapped around. "No shit?"

"No shit."

John stood up and walked back to the coffee pot. He refilled his cup and returned to the chair. "Sean, you heard about anything . . . I guess unusual is as good a word as any?"

"Now that you mention it, some idiot from away stopped in a couple weeks back and swore he saw a grizzly bear up north—at Mud Pond I think he said. We almost laughed in his face."

John finished his coffee and looked at the clock on the wall. It was approaching four in the afternoon and through the window he saw that it was already dark. He still had a ten-mile drive, most of it on unpaved logging road, to get to Lyndon Station. He crumpled the cup and tossed it in a waste can. "Well, I better get the lead outta my ass and head back. If you get any more reports of a grizzly, call me."

O'Connell smiled and said, "Sure, you'll be the first person I call."

"I'm serious. One report we can laugh off, two might be something—most likely not a bear, but something."

O'Connell turned and stared at John. "Jesus Christ, I believe you're serious."

"I am." John turned to the door. He opened it and said, "Stay warm, Sean."

"You too."

John stepped from the warmth of the gatehouse into the cold early evening air. He started his truck and turned east, heading home. As he drove, it took all of his concentration to keep from falling asleep. He cranked the side window down, hoping the frigid night air would keep him awake. As he stared into the tunnel created by his headlights and the six-foot tall snowbanks that the snowplows had pushed up alongside of the road, he wondered what he should do next.

12

Lyndon Station

John drove into his brother's driveway and coasted to a stop. He saw the curtain in the kitchen window move and knew that his sister-in-law, Clarisse, had been watching for him. He could not help but smile when he thought about how she mothered him whenever he stayed in her home.

When John entered the kitchen, Clarisse sat at the table, two cups of steaming coffee sat in front of her. He sat across from her, pulled one of the mugs toward him and took a drink.

"Pardon my bluntness, but you look like shit. What have you been doing?" she asked.

"Last night I tracked the Lake Frontière killer into the woods—shot it too."

She stood and looked out the window. "I don't see anything in your truck."

"I said I shot it . . . not killed it."

Clarisse returned to the table. "John Bear, you been shooting since you were old enough to hold a rifle, there is no way that you shot at anyone and didn't kill him unless you meant not to."

John sipped at the coffee and nodded toward the pack of cigarettes that sat beside her mug. "Can I have one?"

"Of course."

John took a cigarette, lit it with a match, and shook the taper a few times before he threw it into the ashtray. He exhaled and waited for Clarisse to ask the next question. She did not disappoint him.

"You're sure you didn't kill him? He may have crawled away into the woods and died."

"All I'm going to say is that I shot it twice with a .44 Magnum and didn't kill it. I checked all around the clearing . . . there's no way it crawled. If anything, it ran."

"*It*? You make it sound as if this killer isn't human."

"It isn't, it's a Wendigo. . . ."

Clarisse stared at her brother-in-law. "Wendigo . . . have you been smoking wacky-tobaccy?"

"Do you ever wonder if all those crazy stories we were told as kids were true?"

"I always thought that the Wendigo was just a story to scare us into staying close to home—our own Indian version of the boogeyman."

John looked into Clarisse's eyes. "I don't think that's the case."

"John, I'm beginning to think that you're serious. . . ."

"Clarisse, I'm as serious as death—in fact I met it in the woods last night."

"You met which—death or the Wendigo?"

"Both."

Clarisse finished her coffee and walked to the counter. She picked up the pot and asked, "You need a refill?"

"No thanks, I'm fine." John walked over to the wall phone. He flipped through the phonebook and dialed a number. He listened for a few seconds and then said, "Laura Wells, please." Holding his hand over the mouthpiece he said, "I won't be home for supper."

"Oh?"

"I'm eating out tonight."

"With this Laura?"

"If I'm lucky—Hello, Laura?" he listened for a second. "It's John from the other night. You up for that dinner invitation?" He paused, glanced at the clock above the sink, and then said, "Great, I'll be over in about three hours." He hung up, finished his coffee and grinned at Clarisse. "Yes, with this Laura. But first, I need a couple hours' sleep, a shower, and change of clothes." He walked out of the kitchen.

Del's Place

John and Laura walked into McBrietty's dining room and took a table near the back. Lyndon Station was a small community, so small that the locals said it was the perfect example of a one-horse town after the horse had left. In truth, it was not too great an exaggeration. Lyndon Station did not even have a railroad station. The town was named for a long-defunct trading post, known as The Station, and owned by an early settler named Jonathon Lyndon. Downtown was Del McBrietty's. The nearest thing to a railroad station was in Fort Kent, forty miles to the east and it was truly just a spur of a railroad that crossed the border from Clair, New Brunswick.

John seated Laura and then circled the table and sat. He glanced around the room to see who was in attendance and then turned his attention to his date. "I know it ain't much," he said, "but it's the only place within an hour's drive."

Laura studied the rustic decor for several seconds, noting the moose head that hung over the bar. Dust covered the animal's head and face and cobwebs hung from its antlers. The walls were adorned with stuffed fish and throughout the room a number of stuffed animals were on display, many of which greeted diners with bared fangs or claws. The tables were covered with red-and-white checkerboard tablecloths and the chairs were heavy wooden replicas of something one would expect to find in a logging or hunting camp. Her eyes went back to the moose and, based upon the state of the mounted head, she wondered how clean the kitchen was. "This is fine," she told John. "Quaint. And it kind of emphasizes the local atmosphere."

She knew John saw that she was less than thrilled by the place. He looked like an awkward teenager on a first date when he grinned and said, "It ain't much as far as aesthetics goes, but the food is all right and portions big."

McBrietty walked to their table. "Evening, John, ain't seen you in a while. You looking into the killings?"

"Yeah."

"You learn anything?"

"Nothin' that ain't already common knowledge."

McBrietty waited for a few seconds to see if John was about to say more. When it became obvious that he was not going to, he said, "Get you guys somethin' to drink?"

John motioned to Laura defaulting to her. "I'll have a vodka Collins," she said.

"Okay," McBrietty turned to John. "You havin' your usual?"

"Sure."

When McBrietty had left, Laura said, "You don't give away a lot, do you?"

"In what way?"

"If someone asks you a question you give them a short answer, but don't go into a lot of detail."

"It's a habit I learned over the years. Answer the question. If they want to know more, let them ask another one. Besides, you can't listen to people when you're talkin'—at least I can't."

She sat back and studied him for a second and then said, "I'm beginning to think that you're a lot deeper than you want people to know."

John grinned. "Just don't tell anyone else, okay?"

"Your secret is safe with me."

McBrietty returned and set their drinks on the table. "What'll it be?" he asked. As soon as they ordered, he disappeared into the kitchen.

"Now he'll put his chef's hat on," John commented.

Laura swirled the swizzle stick in slow circles, mixing her drink. "So," she said, "who is this mysterious man named John Bear?"

John took a drink from his glass and replied, "Who's asking—Laura the woman or Laura the reporter?"

"Both . . . to be honest, I've gotten to that point where most of the time even I can't tell the difference."

"Well, where do you want me to start?"

When she asked him, "Why did you become a game warden? I did some research and it seems that the requirements are almost identical to those of being a state policeman," she knew it sounded more like a professional interview than a social conversation.

"For the most part they are, both wardens and state police have to complete the Maine Criminal Justice Academy, and after that each organization has some special training and requirements."

"Okay, all that aside, what attracted you to the warden service and not the state police?"

"I'm not too good with people. Being a warden, especially here in the north, allows me to work outside and alone most of the time."

"But, you're not just a district warden are you? Truthfully, I had no idea that the warden service had its own investigators. What is different about . . . what did you call it?"

John smiled; he had been asked this very question on many occasions. "WCID is the Wildlife Crimes Investigation Division. There are a number of investigators stationed throughout the state. I report to a lieutenant who in turn reports to the major in Augusta. As I said the other night, we investigate accidents involving serious personal injury and fatal hunting-related incidents as well as ATV, snowmobile, and boat crashes."

"What you didn't say was that you are basically the Inland Fisheries and Waterways version of the State Police Major Crimes Unit."

John became pensive. "Sometimes I think we're too much so."

"How's your investigation going?"

"Laura, I'd rather not discuss that. Besides, we haven't learned all that much."

"Okay, I understand about ongoing investigations and that stuff. What about John Bear, the man—who's he?"

"I grew up in Canada, at the Madawaska Maliseet First Nation."

He saw her brow furrow.

"It's between Edmundston and St. Basile. In fact, you pass through the Nation without knowing it when you drive between the two."

"What about your parents, are they still alive?"

"My father is."

"Any siblings?"

"I have a brother who lives here in Lyndon Station and a sister who we haven't heard from in years."

Laura glanced at him through the flickering dim light of the candle that was on the table. "I'm starting to get the impression that you don't like to talk about your family."

"Truthfully," John replied, "there ain't a lot to talk about. . . ."

For the first time since they had met, John Bear lied to her—they hadn't known each other long enough for him to feel comfortable answering her questions about his family. Before she could probe any deeper, McBrietty brought their meals and John sighed in relief.

13

Del's Place

John Bear pushed his plate away and sat back. He raised his coffee mug to his lips and, over the rim, saw Bob Pelky enter the diner. When Pelky slid into the booth across from his friend, John immediately recognized the conspiratorial smirk on his face. "You look like a raccoon caught raiding a garbage can," John commented.

"So," Pelky said, "how'd it go last night?"

John grinned, knowing how fast Lyndon Station's grapevine was. "How'd you know about last night, you a cop or something?"

"C'mon tell me what happened. Elaine will be grilling me as soon as I get home."

"Great, we had dinner and a couple of drinks and then I dropped her off at her cabin."

"That's it?"

"That's it—just two people out for dinner."

"Well," Pelky said, "that is gonna be a big letdown for Elaine."

John chuckled. "Besides, even if it did go further than that, I'm not about to say anything. This town is so small that when you smile your cheeks rub the borders. I'm certain that more than one set of eyes saw me leave her at her door."

"Makes you wonder doesn't it?"

"What makes me wonder?"

"In a town where everyone knows everyone else and nothing goes unobserved, no one has so much as a clue about who our murderer is."

John placed his mug on the table. "I know who—or what—our killer is. It's a Wendigo."

"Well, until we have it in custody, I'm going on the assumption that we're looking for a psychopath who believes he's a Wendigo."

John glanced over Pelky's shoulder and saw Del's only server, his daughter Nellie Corrigan, striding toward them carrying a carafe of coffee in one hand and a mug in the other. "Hold that thought," he said.

She poured Pelky a cup, refilled John's, and stepped back, waiting for Pelky to order. While Pelky perused the menu, even though everyone knew he would order the same thing he always did, Nellie said, "You boys didn't have to stop talking just because I'm here."

John laughed. "Sure, we didn't. This place is the central clearinghouse for all the gossip in Lyndon Station—not that you would say anything, but things have a way of getting out."

She leaned back, emphasizing her rotund figure and smiled. "Well, in a town with no newspaper or radio and TV stations, the news has to get out somehow."

Pelky returned the menu to its slot on the rack that held the salt, pepper, and sweeteners and said, "The usual, Nelly."

"Why does that not surprise me?" She retreated to the kitchen.

Once she was out of hearing, John said, "Bob, I need you to check something for me."

"Okay . . ."

"Can you find out if there are any unsolved killings or disappearances over the last, let's say twenty years? I don't think there's any sense going back over twenty years—go back to 1996. Check both Aroostook County and New Brunswick and Quebec."

"Jesus, John, twenty years? You're talking about a lot of paper-trailing. I hope you're on to something."

"I don't believe that this thing has just arrived in the area—it's been here for a while."

"Okay, I'll get on it. Oh, Elaine would like for you and Laura to come over for supper tonight."

"I could use some of her cooking. What time?"

Pelky Residence

Laura was already at the Pelky house when John arrived. He knocked on the door and she opened it. "Elaine's in the kitchen," she said and then stepped aside to allow him to enter.

They sat on the couch and John relaxed as his body absorbed the heat from the fireplace. John realized he was ravenously hungry.

"How about a cup of coffee," Laura offered.

"That would be great."

"I'll let Elaine know you're here." She opened the kitchen door, poked her head in and said, "John arrived, better bring a third coffee," and then returned to her perch on the couch.

He noticed that Laura sat mute, obviously taking time to organize what she wanted to say. Finally, in what she hoped was a soothing, encouraging tone of voice she asked, "Do you want to tell me about yesterday? At dinner last night you made a concerted effort to avoid the subject."

He suddenly became suspicious. "Again, I can't help but ask: do you want to know as a reporter, or as a concerned friend?"

"To cut through the bullshit and not play silly children's games, both. Does it make a difference to you?"

He mulled over her words for a few seconds and said, "I guess not. But I appreciate your honesty."

Elaine entered the room carrying a tray on which was their coffee. She placed it on the coffee table and noticed that her guests seemed to be in a very serious mood. "Am I interrupting anything?"

"No," Laura said. "John was about to tell me about his adventures while investigating the murder."

Elaine placed a cup of coffee in front of each of them and then settled into a loveseat that was perpendicular to the couch. "I'd like to hear this, too. Do you mind if I sit in?"

John shook his head. "Sooner or later Bob will tell you anyhow. To start off we're dealing with a Wendigo. It's a cannibal and may appear as a monster with some characteristics of a human, or as a spirit who has possessed a human being and made them become monstrous. . . ." John went on to relate his confrontation with the Wendigo.

When John finished his tale he felt strangely uplifted. He decided whoever had said confession is good for the soul knew what they were talking about.

Laura said, "It sounds like some type of Frankenstein's monster . . . a being that is, or was, human, but somehow isn't anymore—utterly alone and isolated from his kind for the rest of his life."

"Its existence is not what one would expect of a supernatural spirit. The Wendigo is in a constant state of need. The more he eats, the more he grows and the more he grows, the more he needs to eat. It's a vicious cycle."

Elaine interjected, "I can think of some corporate examples of that, for instance the lumber companies."

"So," Laura asked, "how do you stop it?"

"That's an entirely different story." John related what he'd learned from Charley Bear.

14

Pelky Residence

Bob Pelky walked in, stomping snow from his boots as he arrived home after a long, hard day of driving on icy, snow-covered roads. "There had better be something in those reports," he warned John. "I had to drive all the way to Houlton on these shitty roads to get them. It's so damned icy out there it's like driving on a rolling bottle."

John thanked him and immediately snatched up the handful of large manila envelopes that Pelky held in his hands. John looked as if he were holding on to a life-support system as he walked to the couch and took a seat. He perused the files for almost three hours, oblivious to the presence of the others, pausing only to join them for a meal of Yankee pot roast. His three companions began to think he had temporarily lost control of his faculties.

"Here it is!" John shouted. "I got the bastard!" His shout brought the others running into the room. "Laura," John said, as excited as a child on

Christmas, "how would you like to break a story about a series of killings going back thirteen years?"

"What are you talking about?" Laura asked.

"Here, look!" John said. His enthusiasm was beginning to infect the rest of them. "From 1996 to 2003 there's nothing that appears to be out of the ordinary. At least nothing other than what might be overlooked as being anything more than a normal level of activity. A couple of disappearances, one which turned out to be a suicide—hung himself in the woods—the other guy turned up in Chicago a year and a half later. He told his wife he was going hunting for a week and then took off.

"Then we come to the winter of 2003. A drunk, who was also half-Indian, I might add, gets murdered and mutilated in Oslo . . . and the body was in similar shape to ours."

"Shit," Pelky said, "Oslo is virtually a ghost town."

"Now it is. But back then there was a plywood mill there, as well as a fair-sized population. It became a ghost town after this guy was killed in a way that scared the bejesus out of everyone. The guy's name was Condor, Walter Condor.

"Now," John continued, "here's a missing-persons report for a fifteen-year-old kid; height between 6' 8" and 6' 10"; three-quarter-Indian. His name was Paul Condor, his mother was Nancy Condor, deceased 1988.

"The kid must have done in his old man and then took off for parts unknown. Then again those parts may not be so unknown. If we arrange the remaining missing persons reports in chronological order we have a definite trail that leads through New Brunswick from Grand Falls to Saint Leonard, then Edmundston, and over the line into Quebec. Notice the trail is leading away from populated areas and moving west along the border toward here. Taking into consideration the fact that every one of these missing persons was last seen entering the woods alone, and we can see a definite pattern.

"How can you be sure?" Pelky responded. "This is all conjecture. Besides, even if this thing was Condor, how does knowing this help us?"

"Maybe not a hell of a lot," John said. "But at least now we have someone we can tell the higher-ups about; I don't feel we have enough to call him our perp—yet. No way in hell are they gonna go along with giving us resources to chase a monster. We have a place to start looking."

"So what's our next step?"

"I think that we should take a trip to Oslo tomorrow."

State Route 129, near Oslo, Maine

John stared into the painfully bright glare of the midmorning sun reflecting off the new snow and blinked his eyes. "Should have brought my sunglasses," he commented to Pelky. "How much farther is it to Oslo anyhow?"

"About fifteen minutes."

"Are you sure the store there is still in business?"

"Yup, has been since 1939. Just relax, okay? I talked to Olaf Swenson on the phone this morning. He's expecting us, and yes, he does remember Paul Condor. So relax and enjoy the ride."

John took a careful sip of his coffee and muttered. "If anybody else tells me to relax I'm going to bust them one right in the mouth." He took another drink, then placed the lid back on the empty takeout container, and rubbed his temples. I'd give anything if this damned headache would just go away for a while. I've had it since I met that bastard in the clearing."

"Maybe its stress. You've been under quite a bit of it lately."

"I don't think its stress. I think it's the Wendigo and he's trying to mess with my mind. . . ."

Pelky cast John a skeptical look and said, "I think you're blowing things all out of proportion. You've become obsessed with this thing. Hell, you blame everything that's gone wrong in your life lately on it."

John looked away and stared at the snow-covered trees as they sped by the side window. He wiped his hand across his face and shuddered. He knew he was going to have to face the Wendigo again and it was going to be just the two of them, one on one. He had given it a lot of thought and decided there was no other way.

Oslo was exactly what John had been expecting. A town that was, when viewed from the hill overlooking it, nothing more than a crossroads in the middle of nowhere. As Pelky's cruiser drove down the icy, winding road John could make out the remnants of an old mill of some kind. He asked Pelky if he knew what it had been. "I believe that's the foundation of the old plywood mill. At one time, back in the seventies, it employed most of the town's inhabitants. When the mill moved down to Presque Isle—over on the old air base—the town just started to die." Bob ceased his soliloquy when they pulled up in front of a small store strategically located at the junction of the two roads that formed the crossroads. It was reminiscent of the town where he had grown up, and John was overwhelmed with childhood memories, most of them unpleasant.

The nostalgic feeling intensified when John followed Pelky into the old building. The store's interior was heated by a single woodstove which created a virtual wall from the blasting waves of dry heat radiating from the dull-black finish of its metal hull. John found himself enmeshed in a distinct feeling akin to that of déjà vu. He grappled with his childhood memories in a vain attempt to identify the memory the store had triggered and after several moments gave it up as a lost cause. John looked around the building and saw it was typical of many small stores throughout the area. A single counter occupied the eastern wall and behind it an elderly, balding man was earnestly retrieving a red-colored hot dog from the depths of a steamer. He deftly dropped the wiener into a resting place within the confines of a bun, layered a coating of mustard and chopped onions on it and then wrapped it in wax paper. He nodded to John and Pelky, and then started to write on the side of a paper sack with a pencil. He turned his attention to the two men standing before the counter and said, "That'll be . . . $6.55." He quickly grabbed the ten-dollar bill one of the men held and counted out the change before he filled the sack with the hot dogs, chips, and four beers the men had purchased. The men picked up their purchase and gave Pelky's state uniform a nervous look as they made for the door. "Now don't you boys go drinking that beer while you're driving," Pelky said, his face stern. The two men mumbled an answer and were close to running as they left the store.

Pelky watched the two woodsmen jump into a rusting and dented Ford pickup and drive out of the lot. They took extra care not to do anything that would give the officer cause to follow them.

Pelky turned to John and with a mischievous smile said, "Sometimes I just love this job."

John turned to the counter and the old man said, "Can I . . . help . . . you boys?" He spoke in a dry monotone and so slowly that John thought it had taken a full two minutes for the old Swede to speak the five words. John decided that when it came to talking, Olaf Swenson would most certainly lose a footrace to constipation.

"Yes," Pelky answered, "we're looking for Olaf."

"You found . . . him."

"I'm state trooper Bob Pelky. I phoned you this morning."

"Oh . . . yes . . . about the Condor boy." Swenson remarked.

"Yes." Pelky said. He turned to John and added, "This is John Bear. He's a game warden and good friend of mine, from up in Lyndon Station. He also has an interest in hearing about the Condor boy."

Swenson nodded to John and then retrieved a coffee pot from the burner near the hot dog steamer. "You boys . . . want coffee? It's free . . . ya know? The story of Paul Condor takes . . . a while. You can't talk about Paul . . . without talking about his . . . folks."

He poured coffee for his guests and led them to several straight-backed chairs that formed a ring around the woodstove. When John and Pelky had taken seats, Swenson walked to the door, placed a CLOSED sign in the glass, and locked the door. "Been . . . a mite slow . . . today," he said. "T'won't hurt a bit . . . to be closed . . . for an hour . . . or two."

Swenson took a chair opposite the two men and reached into his pocket for a cigarette. He slowly placed the cigarette in his mouth and then, with what appeared to be great effort, leaned forward and touched a wooden match to the hot surface of the woodstove, igniting it. He lit the cigarette and sat back in the chair. He took a sip of coffee and then inhaled the smoke with a slowness John found agonizing. Swenson looked at the two men and said, "There now. A man . . . needs to prepare . . . for a long . . . story."

John sighed in relief—Olaf was finally ready to talk. He removed a small portable cassette recorder from his pocket and showed it to the old man, "Do you mind if I record this?" he asked.

"Can't say . . . as I ever . . . been recorded . . . before. Suit . . . yourself. Let's see now. . . . Paul Condor . . . yuh, yuh . . . I remember that boy. Killed his father . . . must be . . . nigh onto twenty years or more by now."

Pelky found himself wanting to reach out and shake the words out of the old man. At his present rate of speech Swenson was going to be relating the story for the next six months. "2003," he added, trying to spur the old man into his tale.

"Yup. That'd be . . . about right . . .'03. That was a mighty poor year . . . around these parts. . . . What with the plywood mill . . . shuttin' down and all."

"Mr. Swenson," John said, "we've driven a long way to speak with you and we have a long drive home after we're done. Please just tell us about Paul Condor."

"Ain't a whole lot to it. He . . . just got tired of that . . . drunken father of his . . . beatin' the shit outta him and blamin' him . . . for his mother's death and . . . he . . . killed him."

The boy killed his mother?" John asked.

"Now . . . it ain't like it sounds." Swenson became defensive. "If the old man had been around and not off drunk . . . he could have gotten her down to Caribou . . . and into Cary Hospital. That boy . . . was so big . . . that when she dropped him . . . he all but tore her apart. . . . If'n she coulda had some medical help . . . maybe they coulda taken it. . . ." He struggled trying to find a word. "Oh . . . hell. You know . . . that operation they named after that . . . Roman feller."

"Caesarean," Pelky added.

"Yeah . . . that's it. He sure was one big heifer . . . that's for sure. Anyways . . . the old man beat that boy . . . like a redheaded stepchild. . . . Didn't seem to need any reason . . . either. . . . He'd just up and whale the shit out of that boy . . . for just any old thing. Sadie, that's my ol' woman.

She's been dead . . . nigh on ten year now. She always said that one day . . . that boy was going to get his fill . . . and then Wally would be wearing his asshole . . . for a necktie. Well . . . boys. She was right as rain. . . . By the ol' sweet Jesus was she ever right. That boy . . . finally had all he could stand . . . and he ripped ol' Wally apart . . . just like he was nothing but a sack of guts. . . . Which I guess is all he ever was anyhow. . . . Let me tell you boys about that night. . . . It was the January thaw . . . and raining like a cow pissin' on a flat rock, it was."

The old man sat back and smiled at his guests. "Yup . . . I'll sure as hell always . . . remember that night. Goddamnedest storm we ever had in these parts. . . . Thunder and lightnin'. . . . so hard it would scare your old woman right out of her monthly—"

"We get the point," John said, cutting the old man off.

"Well," the store owner went on, "they never did find out . . . who it was done it. I think it was the boy. . . . He ain't never been seen since."

It became evident to John they were not about to learn any more from the old man and he stood up. *If I have to listen to this guy's slow rambling any longer I'll go nuts*, he thought. "Well, Bob," he said, "I guess we've learned all there is to learn here, and it's a long drive back to Lyndon Station."

Bob stood up with a look of relief and nodded his grateful agreement. "Yup, I guess we'd better be going."

Neither man said anything until they were safely away from Swenson's store and Bob was expertly guiding the four-by-four through the snow-covered curves of the twisting secondary road leading out of Oslo. John broke the silence: "Well . . ." he said in a parody of Swenson, "what . . . do . . . you . . . think . . . of . . . that . . . story?"

Bob playfully punched him on the left arm and said, "Enough already! That old man makes clock-watching exciting!"

John chuckled and said, "Seriously. Do you think the kid did his old man in?"

"I've seen some pretty big fellahs get kicked around by their fathers, mothers too for that matter. I mean kids who outweigh the adults by fifty or sixty pounds and could hand them their heads in a wicker basket. But for some reason they let the parents beat the living shit out of them and don't lift a finger." Bob's face began to redden with a sudden searing anger. "Fuck, they even make excuses for the people who abuse them, say it's their fault for misbehaving.

"John you wouldn't believe some of the assholes that have kids! They beat the kids when they do something wrong; they beat them when they do something good; and they beat the kids when they do nothing at all!"

John listened to Pelky's harangue and found himself remembering his childhood and his mother's alcohol-fueled rages. He recalled her bending over and shoving her face into his, the alcohol on her breath reeking, shouting, and mocking him until he would cry. He remembered shaking in fear, knowing if he answered her questions she would beat him with the heavy wooden yard stick she always brandished when she was correcting him for some offense, real or imagined. He felt the hopelessness wash over him; to say something meant a beating, yet to say nothing also meant a severe walloping. To cry would leave him open to her favorite line, "Does the baby want a reason to cry?" John's mind filled with the vision of her face as she shook the menacing wooden stick, "Well I'll give you a reason to cry you goddamned sissy!" On the other hand, not to cry had always been interpreted as rebellion and it usually led to the most severe beatings of all.

John found his mind drifting to her funeral and the anger he felt as he stood dry eyed before her coffin. He was angry with his father for showing grief over the death of his son's tormentor. He was angry at the relatives who for years had downplayed her alcoholism. Their hushed denial robbing young John of anyone with whom he could talk out his anger and frustration, as well as his fear and hatred of his mother. And now, those very people were openly admitting she was a hard woman. He was most angry, however, because he felt grief for her death. In fact he was torn between a desire to cry and the desire to break out into a dance of joy singing *Ding-dong the bitch is dead, the wicked bitch is dead. . . .*

Two days after the funeral John had been sorting through a dresser in his old room and came across his baby book, and he began to leaf through it. He was astounded by what he read in the old book. The author, while he knew it to be his mother, was a stranger. She had written flowing passages about the firsts of her son's life with such obvious love and pride that John closed the book and hung his head in his hand. "Who was this woman?" he asked aloud. Suddenly sobs racked his body and tears rolled down his cheeks. He finally allowed himself to grieve. He grieved not for the woman who now lay cold in the ground but rather for the woman who had written in the baby book twenty-eight years before. John grieved for the loss of the mother he had once had, a woman he now had no memory of.

"John?"

"What?" Bob's voice brought John back from his journey into the past.

"You left me and went off inside yourself without answering my question. Do you think the kid killed his old man?"

"If the abuse was as bad as Swenson said I only wonder why it took him so long. John thought about his childhood: *Why did it take me so long to rebel against her? Why didn't I kill her?*

"Well," Pelky said, "when I get home I'm calling the Department of Child and Family Services and see if anything was ever reported about Paul Condor."

"Yeah, I'd like to know myself." John lit a cigarette, cracked his window, and leaned back in the seat, suddenly exhausted. "I hope the weather clears. The forecast is for a clear day but you couldn't tell it by this stuff." John inhaled on the cigarette and stared at the snowflakes diving through the car's headlights like white moths flying to a brilliant death. He slowly exhaled and forced his mind into nothingness.

It was close to six in the evening when Pelky and John drove into Lyndon Station. Neither had said much during the return trip from Oslo. Had they spoken the thoughts weighing heavy on their minds, they would have been amazed to discover how much they had in common, not only with each other but with the Wendigo as well. They were both struggling with empathetic feelings for the vile freak of nature.

When Pelky and John stepped out of the car in front of Pelky's house, Laura walked out to meet them. She looked at John and noticed he was still and haggard from the trip and the effects of the ordeal he had survived two days before. "Could you give me a ride to my room, John?"

John smiled weakly and said, "Sure. Just give me a minute okay?"

"Sure, I'll wait in your truck. I took the liberty of warming it up about a half hour ago."

John smiled and followed Pelky into the house.

He waited until Elaine released her husband from a long, welcoming embrace before he spoke. "I just wanted to thank you for the other night. It meant a lot to me."

Pelky shrugged off the thank you and said, "No problem. It was the least we could do."

"Well, it meant a lot. I don't know what I'd do without you guys. I'll see you in the morning, Bob. And, if you don't mind, I'll keep this." He held up the cassette tape containing Swenson's long soliloquy about Paul Condor.

"Sure. I doubt I could stand listening to that guy again. At least not for a few days anyhow."

John nodded and left to join Laura.

John parked in front of Laura's cabin and saw her compact parked alongside the building. "I see you got your car fixed," he said.

"John," Laura said, turning to face him. "Would you like to go to dinner with me? I really don't want to be alone right now."

"You too, huh?"

"Why don't you go over to the diner and get us some burgers and maybe pick up some beer? We can eat it here. That is, if you don't mind?"

"Sounds good to me. Do you want to come with me to the diner?"

"No, I'll get a fire going while you go."

"All right, give me a half hour." He watched her safely into the cabin and drove away.

———

Laura dumped the refuse from the inexpensive meal into a trash can and, carrying two fresh beers, rejoined John on the small couch. John had been mechanically watching the news on the small black-and-white television, and looked up when she sat next to him. "John, what did you guys find out today?"

"About Condor? I don't know if it's believable." He held out the tape. "This can tell you about it better than I can."

Laura took the tape and held it delicately in her hand. "Can I listen to it?"

"Sure. There's nothing there would stand up in court but, if you can stand that old man's slow tongue, I'll listen to it again. There ain't anything there proves Condor is the Wendigo. But, I do know there is one running loose out there in the woods."

She sipped on her beer and gave John a serious look. "Let's change the subject. Tell me about John Bear. You don't fit my picture of the type of person who runs around the woods for a living."

"Well," he said with an impish grin, "in the beginning I was born to a virgin. . . ."

She playfully punched him on the biceps, "Be serious, I'm interested in you—very interested."

"Okay, I was raised here in Aroostook County, got disillusioned with my life, joined the Marines, went to war, came home, and became a warden. That's me in a nutshell."

"Sounds pretty dull," she said in mock seriousness. "Something tells me there is more to you than that."

"I'm not sure what you mean by that," John replied, taking a drink. "There is always a lot more to people than they tell others. Now take Bob . . ."

"You really think a great deal of him don't you?"

"Bob and I have a lot in common. We both went to war full of delusions of grandeur, ideals, and enthusiasm. We came home filled with resentment, grief, and turmoil. I guess he's about the only person around here I feel understands me at all. We walked the same walk, so to speak."

"Tell me about how you saved his life."

John finished off the can of beer and she saw, for the first time, the pain he held imprisoned inside of himself. He slid down in the seat and rested his head on the back. "There isn't much to tell," he said. "Bob was captured by the enemy and I trailed them for two days before I found him. Wasn't all that exciting, just part of the job. . . ."

Laura found herself touched by the pain and grief in his voice and on his face. She saw he was trying to minimize it, without much success. *He doesn't realize it shows,* she thought, *but it's there like a boil that's about to burst. What he needs is someone to lance the boil and let the poisonous pain out. Then he and all the other veterans of that disgusting war can finally heal.*

"It sounds as if you have a good friend."

"My best, don't misunderstand me now, Murph's a good friend, too. But Bob, well with Bob there's an attachment most men can never hope to realize. It's sort of a brotherhood of pain. We went through a lot together." He stared off to a place only he could see and tears began to gather in the corner of his eyes. "I don't make a lot of friends," he said, his voice trailing off in a detached monotone, "but whether a man is my friend or not, no one deserves to die like Ryan Kelly did. He was butchered like an animal." His voice trailed off to a moving silence and he stared into his beer.

Laura sat still. She felt the weight of John's silence but was at a loss as to how she should break it. Again she was touched by his deep sense of loss over the violent, unnecessary death of a young man. She felt herself being pulled into his deep remorse, perhaps by some innate maternal instinct. When she looked at him she saw a lonesome man staring off into space. She slid across the couch and took him in her arms. She looked up into his downturned face and gently kissed him. They would later wonder if the passionate evening that followed was due to their attraction for each other or from the need of two bewildered people for intimate contact.

———————

It was early when John awoke. He lay quiet in the bed, staring at the ceiling, savoring the warmth of Laura's soft, nude body as she nestled against his side. He replayed the week's events in his mind, visualizing the sights of the dead bodies of both Ryan Kelly and Raymond Labelle as vividly as if they were in the room with him. The sound of his father's mournful monotone vibrated in his head. The thoughts haunted him. He recalled the confrontation in the woods and he decided upon a course of action. A course he was sure would put him in jeopardy of meeting a fate similar to that of Ryan and Raymond. John shuddered.

Laura sighed softly in her sleep and rolled over, pushing against him as she moved yet closer to the warmth of his body. Her feminine smell took his thoughts away from the Wendigo and its victims and pushed them in a softer, more pleasurable direction.

He suddenly felt the room's chilly temperature; the cabin's woodstove needed wood. Trying to keep from waking Laura, he placed one naked foot on the floor and hissed when the cold caused him to inhale sharply. *Damn it*, he thought, *why in hell doesn't Del put oil heat in these cabins?* Bracing his body against the chilly air, he slowly swiveled into a sitting position and placed his other foot onto the frigid hardwood floor. He eased himself out of the bed and felt his entire body erupt in a layer of goosebumps.

"John?" Laura mumbled from a state of half sleep.

"Yeah." He slid into his trousers.

"You leaving?"

"No, I'm just going to stoke the fire."

"Hurry back," she purred. She burrowed deeper into the blankets, preserving the warmth trapped there.

"Don't worry, I'll only be a few minutes."

John walked from the tiny bedroom and was in a quandary as to what he intended to do. The rational half of his brain was telling him to get dressed and to run like hell. Run until he was far from the horror and upheaval Lyndon Station had come to represent. However, the human brain is a complex computer, one that also has an emotional part, so logic and rational thinking did not always win out. The emotional half of his brain recalled one of his father's favorite sayings. Each and every time John had gone to the old man with a problem requiring actions contrary to those John wanted to take, he had heard the same thing. The nostalgic phrase came to the forefront of his mind: "Son," his father had said, "there are times when what we want to do and what we know deep in our hearts we must do are two entirely different things."

"But," the bewildered boy had answered, "how will I know which way to go?"

"Listen to your guts boy, the brain will lie to you—it is intelligent. Your guts now, they ain't got the sense God gave a housefly, but they react on instinct—on what they feel is right. Sometimes there just ain't any logical reason to do what your gut says has to be done, even though your brain will deny it, it just has to be done. I guarantee you, boy, if you ignore your gut instinct that brain of yours will turn on you later on and you'll wish you hadn't listened to it. When you don't know which way to go, just stop. Stop and listen to your gut. You'll never regret it."

There was no doubt in John's mind as to what he wanted to do. He wanted to run. Tuck his tail between his legs and run like a scalded dog. But he knew what his gut was saying and what he would do——tomorrow morning he was going to find the Wendigo. Even if it killed him.

John took out his cell phone and called the DIF&W district headquarters in Ashland. When the dispatcher answered he said, "This is John Bear. I need a plane in the morning."

When he'd made the necessary arrangements, he opened the stove door and tossed two good-sized pieces of firewood onto the glowing coals covering the bottom of the fire chamber. He saw the coals flare up into flames and then returned to the warmth of the bed, and Laura's willing body.

15

Northern Aroostook Airport, Frenchville, Maine

To the east the sky was lighting up enough to show that the day would be clear and cold. John Bear spotted the landing lights of the small airplane and watched in silence as its skis sent a cloud of snow trailing behind as it landed on the small landing field. He crushed out his cigarette and gulped down the last of his tepid coffee. John reached back into the four-wheel-drive Jeep and grabbed the rifle case lying on the back seat. He got out of the car and walked toward the plane. After he had taken several steps, he stopped and waited for the pilot to bring the aircraft around. The Cessna spun in a tight circle and stopped about twenty yards away. John trotted to it, hunched forward trying to avoid the icy blasts of wind and stinging snow the propeller sent swirling into the air.

John opened the door, leapt into the front seat and slammed the door shut against the frigid air. He nodded to the pilot, saw a set of headphones between the seats, and placed them on his head. He positioned the microphone in front of his mouth and said, "How you doing, Sébastien?"

The pilot's electronic voice came from the headphones. "Can't complain, John—no one wants to listen to me whine anyhow."

"You have much trouble flying up?"

"Other than fighting one bastard of a headwind all the way from Houlton?" Sébastien Lavallée, the warden service's pilot assigned to northern Aroostook County, grinned. "Made it interestin' though."

John was busy adjusting his headset and seatbelt and didn't notice Sébastien's harsh look when he saw the 30-06 rifle for the first time. "What in hell's that for?" Lavallée asked.

"I'm being cautious. I've heard reports of a rogue bear in the area," John answered.

"There's no way you think it was a bear that killed them fellahs. Hell, they're all in hibernation by now."

"Well, either way, bear or no bear, it ain't goin' to let us take it alive."

John buckled the seatbelt and waited for Lavallée to take off. John made sure the rifle was unloaded and then placed it between his legs, with the barrel pointing upward.

The pilot quickly checked to see that his passenger was buckled in and increased the motor's RPMs. He deftly swung the nose around 180 degrees until it faced into the wind and sped down the runway. When the airplane had gained enough speed, he pulled back on the wheel and the aircraft's nose lifted and they were airborne. I hope you brought sunglasses," Lavallée said. "The sun reflecting off this snow is going to be a real bitch."

John sat back and felt an unease creep through him. He refocused his mind to ward off what he was sure was an impending flashback to his tour in Afghanistan. He stared out the window and saw the ground falling away in the golden light of the early dawn. "I think we'll find it today . . . ," he said to no one in particular.

Lavallée looked at him. "It? I thought we were lookin' for a lost cross-country skier."

John leaned back and felt his stomach turn as the small plane was buffeted by the wind. "Just a figure of speech," he said. He looked out the side window and hoped that he would not lose his breakfast.

John had been intently watching the terrain passing by below the Cessna. They had been searching the woods for almost three hours and his attention had not waned. They were on the brink of turning back for lunch and to refuel when John asked, "How long would it take us to get over to Viverette Settlement?"

"Fifteen, twenty minutes. What's up there?"

"I don't know. That's why I thought we'd take a look."

"That place has been deserted for years. Thousand Islands built it when they were cutting out all the spruce on account of the spruce budworm infestation back in the sixties. Once they'd cut everything worth cutting they tore down most of what was theirs and hauled ass."

"So there's nothing there now?"

"A couple of shacks, if they ain't fallen in," Lavallée said.

"I'd still like to check it out. If we got enough fuel."

"We got enough."

Lavallée banked the plane and headed west.

True to his word, in less than twenty minutes they flew over Viverette Settlement. Lavallée dropped down so low that John was afraid that they'd hit the treetops as the settlement sped beneath them. The area where the settlement had existed was still clear of trees and John was surprised to see a snowmobile trail. He turned his eyes to the front and said, "I thought you said this place was deserted?"

"Always has been."

"Well there's a lot of sled tracks down there. Swing around one more time."

Lavallée made a turn and flew back toward the shack.

"There! I see someone," John shouted, pointing over the nose of the aircraft at a large form standing in front of one of the shacks.

Lavallée stared at the figure and said, "Christ, John, that's the biggest sonuvabitch I ever seen!"

"Can you land down there?"

"Don't know—who knows what's hidden under that layer of snow. All I'd have to do is hit something and we'd both be in a world of hurt."

They circled around and made another pass over the shack. A gigantic figure stood near the shack and looked up at the small aircraft.

"Are you certain that it's too dangerous to drop me off?"

"I don't know this area," Lavallée said. "Like I said, there could be anything under that snow—it ain't worth the risk."

"Then take me back. I need to get my gear and come back here."

"John, you got to be the craziest Indian I know," Lavallée said as he turned the Cessna and headed for Frenchville.

16

Northern Aroostook Airport

John Bear watched the warden service plane lift off from the small airport and waved to Lavallée as he circled the field before turning south toward his home airfield. The sound of the Cessna's motor faded while John walked to his truck. He started the motor and waited for it to smooth out as the oil warmed. As he sat in the cold cab watching his steamy breath drift upward, he planned his next action. At that point he was only certain of one thing; he had to go up to Viverette Settlement, if for no other reason than to question the man he'd seen. The trip was not going to be easy during this time of the year. Few, if any, of the roads would be plowed. Even Camp 75 Road, which connected the Little Black checkpoint and Estcourt Road, only came within ten miles of the road to Viverette Settlement. He recalled that the forest service maintained a fire watchtower up that way. He needed to contact them to get a list of people who worked the tower during the spring, summer, and fall—maybe they knew something about the man in the settlement. He opened the glove box and took out a notebook in which he made several notes.

The truck's motor was idling smoothly and John put the transmission in gear and drove toward Lyndon Station. When he went into the woods this time, he was going to be better prepared.

––––––––––

John arrived in Lyndon Station an hour and a half later and went immediately to his brother's house. He backed his truck up and attached the trailer carrying his snowmobile, to the hitch. Before he could get into his four-by-four, Clarisse walked onto the porch holding two steaming mugs of coffee. "You should eat," she said as she placed one of the mugs on the railing and returned to the warmth of the house.

The storm door closed with a loud bang and John stood in the yard watching the steam spiral up from the mug. *Shit,* John thought, *if I don't eat something she'll bust my ass for years.* In spite of his ire over the delay, he picked up the mug from the railing and was smiling as he entered the kitchen.

Clarisse was already seated at the table, a plate of donuts before her. John was overwhelmed by the pleasing aroma of freshly made donuts that filled the room, and grabbed one before he was completely seated.

"You're going back out there, aren't you?"

"I have to."

"Then take someone with you."

"Such as?"

"I don't know, another warden maybe."

"They're all busy. We still have two months of ice fishing season left, and the derby is in a couple of days. Keep in mind we only have five wardens to patrol an area larger than several states."

Clarisse took a drink of coffee and placed her mug on the table. It was evident to John that she was not about to be placated, at least not easily. "What about the state police? Bob Pelky would help, all you got to do is ask."

"This is something that I need to do on my own. . . . This case belongs to the warden service, not the state police."

Clarisse leaned back in her chair and glared at him. "You mean this case belongs to you. I think you've let this become something personal."

"Maybe I have," John admitted, "but only because the majority of people have no idea of what this thing is capable of. They still think it's human. . . . We know better."

"If by *we*, you mean us Mi'kmaq and Maliseet, you may be mistaken. Most of us know those old tales for what they are. They are myths used to scare little children into behaving, nothing more."

"Clarisse, you weren't with me out there. I saw it and it's no myth."

She stood, walked to the stove, and refilled her mug. She held the pot out, silently offering him a refill. He nodded and slid his mug toward her. As she poured, Clarisse said, "I don't know what it was you saw. But it was dark, snowing, and you were half-frozen to death. You may not know what it was you saw either."

John took a long drink of the hot coffee and felt it burn as it traveled through him. "All right, you win. If Murph has nothing going on, I'll take him with me and once I'm certain what I'm dealing with I promise to ask for appropriate assistance."

Clarisse sighed in an exaggerated show of relief. "I swear that talking to you and your brother is like praying. You believe there is someone there, but can never tell if they are truly listening." She walked toward the door leading to the living room. "Go on, do this thing you feel you must do. I only ask that you leave instructions."

"Instructions?"

"Yes, where you're going in case we have to search for you . . . and how you want your remains handled if we find you dead."

17

Viverette Settlement

The Wendigo saw the airplane before he heard it. He stood at the threshold and watched as the Cessna approached. He watched it pass overhead and then turn. He watched the plane as it turned again, made another flyover, and then headed southeast. In minutes the plane was a small dot in the sky and he cursed. It was obvious that the plane belonged to the warden service and he was certain that they'd be back. He entered the cabin and began gathering his meager belongings. At best he figured he'd have four or five hours before they would arrive. The warden service kept their planes at Eagle Lake, but it didn't have skis or pontoons and may have come from Frenchville; either way when they got here, he'd be long gone.

He tried to think of a place where he could go unobserved, no easy thing when you were seven feet eight inches tall. Anyplace he went he'd stand out like a cigar store Indian. He crammed his things into a worn backpack and left the ramshackle shack. He walked to a cache that he'd made from deadfall and bits and pieces of lumber that he'd found in the settlement. He crouched over and disappeared inside.

John Bear and Murphy arrived at Viverette Settlement as the sun was setting. They stopped their sleds about twenty yards from the shack and removed their helmets so they could hear one another. "Looks as if there's no one at home," John said, "The door is open and it ain't that warm."

"No smoke coming from the chimney either."

"What do you think? Maybe someone is inside and needs help?"

"Sounds like probable cause to me," Murphy said.

They slowly advanced to the front of the shack.

"You think the guy you saw was just curious and was looking at the place?" Murphy said.

"I suppose anything is possible, but for some reason I don't think so."

John dismounted and walked to the door. "Maine Warden Service," he called out. "Hello? Is anyone in there?" Without thinking about it, he drew his service pistol and stuck his head inside the shack. It took several seconds for his eyes to adjust to the dark, the sun had completely set and the interior was Stygian. "Murph, open the storage boot on my sled, grab my light, and bring it here, would you?"

Murphy turned to John's sled and retrieved a flashlight which he then handed to John who in turn shined it around the inside. "Looks as if someone's been living here."

Murphy visually scanned the room. "Recently, too," he added.

John Bear removed his right glove and placed it on the cast-iron woodstove. "Cold as ice. He probably lit out as soon as we flew away."

"That was what? Four, maybe five hours ago?"

"Yup, sum-bitch could be in Bangor by now."

"Well," Murphy said, "since we're here we may as well look around."

"I'll check this place out," John said.

"Okay, I'll look around outside."

Murphy stepped out of the shack and stared at the darkening woods. *Maybe twenty, twenty-five minutes of daylight left,* he thought. He took his flashlight out of the storage boot of his sled and followed the tracks to the back of the cabin. He noted that the tracks led to a pile of dead-wood, lumber, and sundry odds and ends, and then disappeared. He walked closer and inspected the pile of detritus and moved a couple of boards to see what lay beneath. In the light's harsh beam he found a door to what appeared to be an old root cellar. "Hey, John, I think I found something."

When John reached his side, Murphy shined the light on the door. "Looks like it may be an old root cellar," he said.

"So why would you bury it under all this debris?" John pondered.

"My thoughts exactly."

"Well," John said, "there's only one way to find out."

He grabbed the door handle and pulled the door—which surprised him when it opened with minimal effort. Murphy illuminated the opening with his flashlight beam. Stone steps, with the center worn from years of feet using them, led down into a black chasm. The strong odor of a dead animal, with a touch of a gross sweetness to it rose up from the dark abyss. It was so overpowering that both John and Murph put their hands over their noses and mouths.

"Jesus," Murphy said, his voice muffled by his hand.

John reached out his free hand and Murphy placed the flashlight in it. John descended into the crypt and stopped at the foot of the staircase. He panned the light around and dropped his hand from his mouth when he saw the carnage inside. The floor was littered with broken bones, both animal and human, that looked as if something had snapped them and sucked the marrow from them. Scattered around the sides of the floor were human skulls—too many for him to accurately count—each showing some form of trauma; one he saw had a jagged hole in its crown, another a similar wound in the back. He directed the light to the far corner and saw the source of the nauseating odor, a partially decom-posed—and devoured—body, with its mouth open as if it had died in mid-scream. John recalled what his father had told him: "... *sometimes it keeps its victims alive. It stores them in dark, isolated places so it can feed whenever it wants.*"

Having seen enough, John reentered the stairs and motioned for Murphy to climb out. Once they were in the fresh, cold night air John said, "We need a complete crime scene team out here."

"What did you see in there?"

"A vision of hell from the world of H. P. Lovecraft."

St. Francis, Maine

The Wendigo stood back in the trees, watching the log building. Country music blared from the beer joint and the yard was filled with snowmobiles of every make and model. He was so hungry that thought was impossible. He could leave and hunt someplace else, but this place, the only bar in town, showed the most promise. It was a matter of time before somebody would leave, then he'd hunt—and feed.

Steve Jackson staggered out of the Borderview Tavern and drove toward his home, his headlights were coated in dirt and road salt and he strained to see the road through the dark, moonless night. He had been drinking since that morning, after he'd arrived at work only to be told that the mill was closing down due to a decreasing market for wood pellets. *Goddamned foreigners*, Jackson mused, *make it impossible for a man to keep his job.*

He saw his home appear in his headlights and he shook his head trying to clear away the drunken haze. He pulled into the drive and got out, slipping on the icy surface. He slipped down onto one knee and cursed, goddamn!" He struggled to his feet, gripping the side of his vehicle for leverage and then scurried to the door, sliding along across the icy surface without lifting his feet. Jackson paused in front of the rusting mobile home gripping the railing of the ramp leading to a plywood mudroom attached to the entrance.

Jackson opened the woodstove, threw a log in, and lit some kindling before taking a bottle of whiskey from the cupboard. He sat at the kitchen table and poured whiskey into his glass and cast a drunken glance at the disarray of the small one-room home that was all that sheltered him from the cold wind blowing outside. His look was almost furtive, as if he was expecting the very structure itself to launch an attack on him. He raised the glass to his lips and felt the whiskey's heat spread through his chilled body; the liquor had long since ceased burning his throat and went down easy. Jackson stopped, holding the dirty tumbler against his lips. His eyes were fixed on the tiny window centered over the sink on the trailer home's back wall. *Something had been looking in through the window. He had seen the distinctive sparkle of lights reflecting off something—like eyes.* He slowly lowered the glass to the table and, convinced his mind was tricking him, forced himself to remain calm, to relax.

He nervously refilled the glass, wondering whether or not his alcohol-soaked brain was playing tricks on him. He drank in morose silence, fumbled for a cigarette and inhaled the smoke deep into his lungs. It took all his strength to remain calm and regain some serenity.

Jackson's mind raced from one paranoid thought to another and he drained the glass again. A noise came from the rear of the house, near the woodpile. Jackson jumped to his feet and raced over to the small window and peered out into the darkness. He saw nothing but the reflection of his own dilated pupils in the glass. The wind gusted and Jackson felt the house tremble as it resisted. Then the wind abated and he was struck by a silence so still that his ears rang in the quiet. He remained there for several moments concentrating on the silence, trying to detect any foreign noises that might come from the outside. He heard nothing but the sudden wail of the wind and the loud bang of the door hitting against the exterior wall. He suddenly realized there was another sound missing. The fire in his stove had stopped its comforting popping, warning Jackson that either the fire was dying or dead. The lack of the sound from the stove brought with it the awareness of chilling cold. The temperature of the room, although it was fully insulated, was dropping fast and he walked over to the stove. He raised a work boot–clad foot and hooked the latch on the front door of the stove. The door slowly swung open. Jackson squatted down and peered into the stove's interior; the fire was down to smoldering embers.

He reached into the wood box that sat near the stove and cursed when he found it empty. "Shit," he moaned. The last thing he wanted to do was to go out into the subzero cold and dark to replenish his wood supply. He scoffed at his hesitance and reached for his coat. "What are you, some dumb kid? Afraid of the dark? Goddamn it, man. Get a grip on yourself. . . ."

He knew words alone were insufficient to calm his nerves. He also knew he was not so much afraid of the dark as he was by what the darkness might hide. Inside the cabin he felt a sense of security, however small, but outside, with the woods a mere fifty feet away, he would feel no such security. He grabbed the worn parka from the nail upon which it hung and struggled to get his uncooperative arms into the sleeves. He returned to the table and picked up the half-filled glass of whiskey. He stared at the contents of the glass for several seconds and then drank it down. He cast a wary glance at the door and then sighed with resignation. *I might as well get this over with*, he decided. He zipped up his coat while walking to the door. He reached for the door latch and hesitated. Breathing deeply, he released the hook from its eyelet and cautiously pushed the door open. "Fuck it, man," he said as he stepped out the door and felt the cold quickly envelope him like a huge blanket, "you're forty friggin' years old and still afraid of the dark. . . ."

The effects of the whiskey he had drunk hit him and his legs felt wobbly. In an effort to steady himself, he placed a hand against the aluminum wall and fought back a wave of sudden nausea. He pulled his collar up against the cold as he turned to the left and began the journey around the building to the woodpile in the back.

Jackson detected movement out of the corner of his eye and stood immobile. He peered at the area from which the motion had come with such intensity he felt as if his eyes would leap from his head. He felt a deep cold enter his body and suddenly sweat covered his chest and back soaking through his inner clothing. A wave of nervous tension set his stomach to fluttering, a feeling much like a low-intensity itch—one he couldn't reach to scratch. A battle waged within him. His brain sent an urgent *SOS* to his feet and legs in an overt effort to get them to run back into the safety of the trailer's interior. He won the battle against his fears by talking to himself, "Shit, man, you either get wood or you freeze to death. Put your childhood fear behind you and grow up. . . ." The sound of his voice was strangely self-assuring and restored forward momentum to his feet, yet he still felt an uncontrollable urge to dive back through the trailer's open door. He struggled against the preservation instinct eating at him, and kept going toward the unlighted rear of the house, and his wood supply.

Jackson was a mere six feet from the chopping block when a loud bang startled him. He jumped back into a defensive posture, ready to fight for his life. Again he saw movement! By the chopping block! He stepped forward and almost laughed when a porcupine jumped to the ground. It gave him a look, which communicated its irritation at being disturbed, and then waddled across the snow and disappeared into the darkness. Jackson realized he had been holding his breath and slowly exhaled. He wiped sweat from his brow and walked forward.

He reached the woodpile without encountering any of his childhood monsters and he calmed down. He surveyed the chopping block used for splitting wood and saw his axe was in its usual resting place. He grabbed the axe and tugged on it. The handle was chewed beyond use and the blade hopelessly frozen into the block. Jackson cursed. The porcupine had chewed the handle, seeking the salt left by his sweat that permeated the wood. He knew the axe handle would have to be replaced. While the handle had not been chewed through, it would be too weak to use on anything as hard as firewood and decided against using it.

He rummaged through the woodpile until he found a piece of wood not frozen in place and pulled it from the pile. He used the wood as a battering ram and freed a number of pieces from their icy prison. He gathered up the pieces of wood—it was impossible for him to load more than four by himself—and started on the return trip to the cabin. The labor of freeing the wood completely dissipated his earlier fears and he whistled as he rounded the corner of the shack. Once he reached the front and spied the light-filled open door his thoughts returned to the day's events and fear came rampaging back into his inebriated brain. He began to run in a jerky trot. The light was one of the most welcome sights he had seen all day. Jackson happily vaulted through the door and into its safety. Once inside he slammed the door shut, locked it, and felt safe.

Jackson watched the fire until it caught and then returned to the table and his bottle. He poured half a glass of alcohol and sipped it. He was on his second sip when he heard a voice outside. "Help me!"

Jackson stood, walked into the chilly mudroom, and opened the door to the outside. "Who's there?"

"Help me!"

It sounded like Barry Boudreau, but he just left Barry at the Borderview. . . .

"Help me!"

It's Barry! Jackson turned the deadbolt and opened the door. He was immediately repulsed by a stench that reminded him of the putrid odor of a corpse he was hired to disinter several years before. He took an involuntary step back. He heard Barry call for help again and stepped through the threshold.

A powerful hand gripped Jackson's shirt and he was thrown out the door, landing on the frozen, ice-covered ground with such force his wind was driven from him. He blinked his eyes to stop the lights flashing before them and saw something rising and falling with his labored breathing. He stared into the bright exterior light unable to discern what he was looking at. The light from the trailer was suddenly blocked out and Jackson blinked his eyes in disbelief—a gigantic shadowy figure emerged. A large hand, horny with callouses, grasped him by the throat, completely enclosing it. It opened its twisted mouth, made a thunderous roar and yanked viciously upward.

The most intense pain Jackson had ever experienced tore through his ravaged neck, bringing an end to his disbelieving funk. He knew he had to act and act fast, but he had no strength. He attempted to free himself, hoping that if he got loose he might get to the handgun he kept inside. However he was consumed by a weariness that bore down on him as if he were Atlas holding up the earth.

Jackson watched, strangely mesmerized, as the giant raised him up, grabbed him in both hands and slammed him down across its bent knee, snapping his spine in half. Jackson felt a flash of pain and he screamed, then as quick as it had appeared the pain went away. He tried to raise his arm to hit the beast but neither his arms nor his legs would respond to his commands. The creature dropped him to the frozen dirt, placed a hand on each side of his head, placed a foot on his chest and yanked up, decapitating him.

Steve Jackson's last thought was: *I'm dead.*

The Wendigo bent over, grasped the severed head by the hair and held it up in front of his face. He watched, fascinated as the eyelids blinked in rapid succession for several seconds before the eyes within turned glassy. He tossed the head, blood still pouring from the severed neck, over his shoulder. The head spiraled through the air, turned three revolutions, and bounced through the open door, spraying the mudroom with a frightful red paint. It landed with a sickening thump and rolled over, coming to a stop in a corner resting on its right side. Steve Jackson's lifeless eyes remained open into a dimension only he could see while a mixture of sputum and blood trickled from his open mouth and puddled on the floor.

The Wendigo lifted the cadaver with his free hand, took a final glance up and down the road and carried it into the house. Upon entering, he threw the carcass on the table and recoiled at the heat emanating from the stove. He grabbed the cast-iron stove, ignoring the painful heat, walked into the mudroom, and threw it out the door.

18

P elky had just finished breakfast at Del's and was getting into his patrol car when his radio squawked. He picked it up. "Pelky, over."

"Bob, we need to check out a situation on Sunset Road in St. Francis, over."

"That's toward the Back Settlement, over."

"You got it. Actually it's in the Back Settlement. A passerby noticed the door open and what looked like a woodstove in the yard, over."

"Got an address, over?"

"Nope, caller said it was Steve Jackson's place though, over."

"I know it—on my way, out."

He had been trying to locate John Bear all morning to question him about the missing body. The search had thus far been anything but fruitful. The only thing Pelky could think of was that John was on another of his woods adventures.

Pelky knew something was wrong as soon as he turned into the driveway and saw the frozen blood on the ground. He snatched his radio and called for backup. The door to the crude addition built onto the ramshackle mobile home stood open and swung back and forth in the freezing wind, banging against the exterior wall each time it cycled. Pelky also noted there was a small woodstove lying across the hood of the pickup truck. One end was protruding through its smashed windshield, and was tipped at a forty-degree angle. Pelky exited his patrol car and loosened the strap on his holster. He removed his service pistol and held it alongside his leg as he looked inside the truck. He saw where coals from the stove had burned the hood, seat, and floor of the truck. It appeared that most of the coals had burst out of the burn chamber and had slid off to the side; only a couple landed in the interior or the truck would be a burned-out hulk. *Who would be capable of throwing a burning woodstove?* Pelky did not want to consider the possibilities.

The mercury that morning had plunged down to forty below zero—the wind chill was reported to be as cold as eighty below—not the type of weather that made a person want to throw open his door and air out the house. Pelky knew if Steve Jackson had passed out in this weather without a fire, he had surely frozen to death. Pelky stopped beside the police car and spied a large area of red ice in front of the single step leading into the cabin.

Pelky mechanically checked the handgun's load and slowly began the long walk to the open door. Each step closer to the entrance of the dwelling increased the nervous tension in his stomach. He felt the large breakfast he had eaten at Del's lay heavy in his gut. He felt as if he had swallowed a shot-put.

He came to the red spot in front of the door and squatted down to inspect the crimson-stained ice. The hair on the nape of his neck stood on edge when he recognized the color for what it was. It was frozen blood. A lot of blood.

Pelky looked up from the grisly discovery and strained his eyes to see through the fine blowing snow into the foreboding interior. "State police," he called. "Is anyone in there?"

No answer.

"Steve, Steve Jackson, are you in there?"

Still no answer.

Pelky concentrated all of his attention on the open door. He saw nothing but the dark opening he knew he must enter. He started with alarm when the door, once again caught by the winds, banged against the wall. He slowly rose from his squat and tentatively approached the ominous opening. He paused short of the threshold, a battle waging within him. His emotions told him: *Get back in that car and wait for backup to arrive. Just wait and let some other idiot walk in there with you— you don't have to do it alone.* On the other hand his logical side argued: *You have to go in. There may be someone who needs help in there.*

Pelky remained indecisive for several seconds before his sense of duty and honor won over his instinct for self-preservation. He pointed the handgun ahead and stepped inside.

The sudden transition from the bright, snow-reflected sunlight to the house's darkness rendered Pelky momentarily blind. He began to blink his eyes rapidly trying to adjust his vision to the diminished light; the room was as dark as the bowels of a cave.

A loud screech sent Pelky diving to the floor with a shout of surprise. He fired a shot in the direction of the sound as he dove. A shaft of light instantly appeared where the large-caliber bullet passed through the back, exterior wall. Pelky heard a loud flapping and, when he looked in that direction, he'd recovered his vision enough to see two large ravens launch from a table and pass over his head as they burst through the door. He noticed that the black predators carried what appeared to be entrails in their beaks as they fled from the unwelcome intruder who had interrupted their feast.

Pelky looked up at the table; it was covered with a mess. It reminded him of roadkill. He lowered his suddenly sweaty forehead onto his outstretched arms and listened to the echoes of birds cawing as they flew over the forest outside the shack. The wind and bird sounds died away to an eerie stillness. Pelky let out a long sigh and struggled to regain his control. It only took a few seconds for him to feel a semblance of control return and he raised his head.

Pelky's newfound self-control shattered like a beer bottle hitting a boulder. He stifled a scream of paranoid dread. He found himself looking into the terror-filled eyes of Steve Jackson's bodiless head!

Pelky bounded to his feet and staggered over to the table, trying to keep from blowing the contents of his stomach across the room. He blindly placed his hand on the tabletop and felt it slide through the slime covering it. He quickly pulled his hand back with revulsion. He stared at the exposed ribs and mutilated organs of some large animal.

Pelky's eyes roamed across the table. He stared at the grotesque mess with disgust. He forced his eyes away from the table and turned on the single bare lightbulb that hung over the table. He was appalled by the condition of the room. The walls were splattered with crimson paint—no not paint . . . blood. The place looked as if someone had opened gallon cans of the stuff and had thrown it helter-skelter around the room. He paused at the phrase *helter-skelter* (the phrase the Manson family painted on walls in the blood of their victims).

Pelky forced his attention back to the table and spied Jackson's Red Wing boots, which were dangling from the ends of a pair of flayed legs, the femurs exposed to the unforgiving light. Pelky's mind jumped. *Good Lord!* The table was not covered in animal guts. It was covered with the remnants of Jackson.

Pelky panicked. He dove through the open door, slid on his stomach across the scarlet ice, then scrambled to his knees until he was away from any evidence that he knew of and began to vomit. Pelky retched until there was nothing left. He felt his stomach lurch violently with each heave and thought it was going to push up into his throat. He believed the dry heaves would never stop.

Pelky began to suck in deep draughts of the cold air and felt relieved as the retching began to subside. He opened his eyes and stared into the sickening mixture of steaming vomit and frozen blood inches below his feverish face. The acidic odor of the mess filled his nostrils. With the look of a person who has just learned he has kissed a leper, he staggered to his feet and stumbled back to his cruiser.

Reeling like a drunken marine, he fumbled with the door handle, trying to pull the door open with fingers slippery with gore. It seemed an eternity passed before the door pulled open and he fell into the driver's seat. Pelky laid his pistol on the passenger seat, placed his hands on the steering wheel, and then rested his head on his hands. He felt his hands stick to his forehead and pulled back with abhorrence. He vaulted out of the car and scooped up handfuls of snow as he tried to wash his hands. When his hands were on the brink of frostbite, even then he was not sure his hands were as clean as possible, Pelky got back into the vehicle and closed the door. He fumbled around until he found some napkins stored in a panel on his door and wiped his hands, trying to dry them and increase blood flow to his numb fingers. Once again, he rested his head on the steering wheel and fought to get his thoughts in order. He remained motionless for several minutes feeling hot sweat drip off his brow. He tried to put the horror he had just experienced into perspective. He fell back in the seat, let his body have its way, and let it shake out its shock. When the shakes passed, he picked up the microphone to his radio and called Linda Bouchard, the dispatcher, asked when the backup would arrive, and placed an added request for a crime scene team. He locked all the doors, started the engine, turned up the heater for warmth, and sat, like a waxen-faced dummy until backup and the requested crime scene people arrived.

19

Lyndon Station

John Bear's cell phone rang, pulling him out of a deep sleep. It had been midnight when the forensics people had finished processing the Wendigo's larder and close to dawn before he and Murphy had finally arrived home. He glanced at the clock beside his bed and saw that he'd been asleep less than three hours. At first he tried to ignore the iPhone, but it was insistent and rang, went to voicemail, and then rang again. He gave up and answered it. "Bear."

"There's something you might want to see," Bob Pelky said.

"What?"

"It looks like your boy's been busy. I think it left us another body—at least parts of one."

John became alert. "Where?"

"St. Francis, Back Settlement."

"Give me an hour."

"Hurry up, the CSI team is here. I'll try and hold the body." He paused and then added, "What's left of it anyhow."

––––––––––

St. Francis

John Bear parked his DIF&W truck across from the trailer home. Like many homes in the area, what was once an aluminum mobile home was now half-metal, half-wood. He walked toward the group of men who stood before the door and nodded when he reached them. "Is Sergeant Pelky inside?"

"That you, John?" Pelky called from the interior.

"Yeah."

"The crime scene team has already worked the house, come on in."

John stepped out of the bright, sunny day into a world of carnage and horror. What remained of the victim was spread across the kitchen tabletop.

Pelky was standing to the left of the door. "Ain't nothing left of him but a pile of bones and guts."

John could not take his eyes off the table. The victim's thorax was ripped open from his neck to his crotch. Intestines, partially digested food, body waste, and fluid coated the floor immediately around it. Pelky handed him a jar of Vicks VapoRub and said, "Use this, it'll help . . . somewhat."

While John spread the Vicks across his upper lip, Pelky said, "I tried to reach you all day yesterday. Where were you?"

"Viverette Settlement. Murph and I found an old root cellar—full of this." He pointed to the evidence of the Wendigo's latest act of butchery.

Pelky shook his head and said, "Christ, this is like something from Jack the Ripper."

"Worse. The Ripper didn't eat his victims. Who found him?"

"A passerby noticed that something looked wrong and called 9-1-1."

"Someone must have heard something."

"If they did we haven't found him or her."

"You got any idea when he was murdered?"

"Nope. Sometime last night I'd guess, but I got no idea how they're gonna determine time of death. It was so frigging cold last night everything in here is frozen. The crime scene technicians had to take tissue samples by scraping them off the tabletop with putty knives."

John forced his eyes away from the table. "Damn Bob, you look like shit. How long you been here?"

"I got the call around seven this morning and arrived here around eight thirty."

"Anyone else live here?" John Bear asked.

"His wife passed away about five years ago. Don't know about kids. We'll know more once we check out a few places. He worked at the pellet factory. They'll know."

John Bear stared out the window for a second and then said, "So, once again we ain't got a damn thing to work on." John looked at the empty platform where the woodstove had stood. "Where's the stove?"

"The killer threw it, fire and all, out the door and through the windshield of Jackson's pickup."

John shook his head. "Bob, we got to figure out how we're goin' to get this piece of shit."

"We don't even know how it got here."

"I do," John said. "It ran here from Viverette Settlement."

"That's insane."

"Have we found one thing about this case that wasn't? All I know is that we saw it from the plane. It was there about ten yesterday morning."

20

Big Twenty Township, T20, R11

The Wendigo walked through knee-deep snow to the door of the abandoned trapper cabin. He used his left foot to sweep the piled snow away from the threshold and when the bottom step was free, pulled the door open. Once inside he surveyed the interior; everything appeared to be in order. He slammed the door and sat at the crude wood table in the middle of the shack's single room.

The Wendigo pondered the events of the past few days and tried to determine where he'd gone wrong. For over ten years this had been a fruitful hunting ground, but now that they had discovered a body, Viverette Settlement was unusable and all that was left were several backup locations. The wind gusted and the cedar shingles on the outside wall rattled. The Wendigo took a towel from the leather bag slug across its shoulder. He unwrapped the towel and laid a heart and a liver on the table. His hunger peaked and he reached for the uncooked meat.

As he ate, his thoughts turned to the mysterious man from the encountered of the other night. This was was the biggest threat he had ever faced. Suddenly, the Wendigo experienced an epiphany—the man was Anishinaubae; he knew of the existence of the Wendigos, and he'd also know how to stop one. The Wendigo began formulating a plan to deal with him.

Lyndon Station

John Bear walked into McBrietty's Outpost and flopped into his favorite booth, the one beneath the massive head of a bull moose whose antlers spanned over five feet. He glanced up and noted the cobwebs and dust bunnies that coated the trophy. His revelry was interrupted by Del's sudden appearance at his side. "Hey, John. You havin' the usual?"

"Yeah," John pointed at the moose. "You ever consider cleaning that?"

Del looked up at the huge head. "Once: I thought about it, laughed about it, and forgot about it."

"Really, what about now?"

"Still thinkin' on it. Be right back with your beer."

In minutes Del was back and placed a cold beer in front of John. He glanced around the room and seeing that besides John there were only two other customers, slid into the seat across the booth. He leaned forward as if he and the warden were co-conspirators and in a low voice inquired how the investigation was going.

"Del, I can't discuss an ongoing investigation, you know that. Let's say we're still looking into it and let it go at that."

"You got any idea who killed them guys?"

"Nope. All we know is the killer is very familiar with the area and must be as strong as a wounded bear."

"There's rumors that them bodies had parts missing. . . ."

John remained quiet.

Del went on: "I read this book where a guy was killing people so that they could use their organs. I think it was the heart because this cop was chasing him and had a heart attack. Turned out the killer was one of them serial killers and he enjoyed the game him and that cop was playing. He was killing people so they could give the cop a transplant and he could keep the game going. You don't suppose you're dealing with someone harvesting hearts?"

"Del, it's not likely. The window for transplants is real narrow . . . a matter of hours. No way the killer could get a heart from out here to a hospital in time."

Del sat back. "Then why in hell is this guy taking organs?" He paused for a minute and then said, "Hey, you don't suppose this is like that mountain man in the movie, do you? You know the one where the Indians killed his wife and kid and he kept fighting them one at a time? Didn't them Indians eat their victims' livers?" Del suddenly realized who he was talking to and his face reddened. He stood up. "Didn't mean no offense, John."

John smiled at McBrietty. "None taken Del. The answer is yes, some of the plains Indians did eat the heart and liver of a brave enemy they killed. They believed doing that would give them some of the vanquished warrior's bravery. But that's not what we have here. I'd appreciate it if you'd help put a stop to these rumors—only thing they'll do is scare the shit out of people."

Del nodded. "I suppose you're right, John."

"Who's been spreading these stories anyway?"

"Aww, it was just a bunch of the fellas sittin around havin' a few brews, you know how they get."

"Well, if any more of the *fellas* start spouting off again, tell them to get hold of Bob Pelky or me and we'll set them straight."

Del grinned. "No way in hell they'd ever approach you guys about this."

"I agree, but it'll give a couple of 'em a soft stool or two. Won't it?"

"That it will. You having a steak?"

"Yeah, medium—."

"Medium well, baked potato, and the vegetable of the day is Brussels sprouts."

"Hold the sprouts, things give me a soft stool."

Dell laughed, made a pistol with his index finger and thumb, and pointed it at John. "Gotcha."

John Bear walked out of the dining room and into the general store portion of McBrietty's. He walked to the cooler in the back of the room and took a twelve-pack of Pabst Blue Ribbon from the top shelf. Returning to the counter he overheard a local man say, "They ain't got a clue who's doin' them killins. Ain't safe to be out in the woods a'tall."

"What I hear," his companion said, "it's like the blind leadin' the blind. . . . I don't think they could catch a cold if they was skinny dippin' in a snowbank."

The two men noticed John standing in front of the counter and abruptly shut up and walked out of the store. Placing the twelve-pack on the counter, John commented, "Something like this happens and everyone becomes a law enforcement expert."

Del's day-man, George Harvey, rang up the sale and said, "These killings got everyone stirred up. Before you know it they'll be forming a posse and searching the woods for any one they don't know."

"That," John replied, "is the last thing I need—bunch of boozing, hyped-up vigilantes running around the woods. I'd spend more time dealing with them than I would finding this guy."

John paid for the beer and carried it out to his truck. He placed it on the passenger side floor and drove along State Route 161 toward his brother's house. A light snow began falling, and the flakes seemed huge in the brilliance of his high beams. He turned on the radio and tuned in to the Canadian Broadcast Corporation. He listened to the Québécois station until the weather came on. He listened intently, mentally adjusting temperatures and accumulation amounts from metric to English measurement. The resulting forecast was not encouraging—six to twelve inches of snow, followed by temperatures plummeting into the minus-forty range. It was going to be a good night to sit in front of a fire and drink a couple of beers.

He turned into his brother's drive and shut off the truck. He sat in the sudden stillness, listening to the motor tick as it cooled in the sub-freezing temperatures. After several moments, he grabbed the beer and got out of the truck. He entered the house and immediately felt the dry, super-warm heat of a wood fire. Tom and Clarisse sat at the kitchen table and smiled at him. "Hey, big brother, how you doin'?" Tom greeted him.

John held up the twelve-pack and said, "I come bearing gifts."

"I see." Tom kicked a chair away from the table. "Set your ass down and let's have a couple of them."

John placed the PBR on the table and opened the box. He took a cold beer out and offered it to his sister-in-law. "Clarisse?"

"No thanks, I'll stick with coffee." She gave her husband a stern look and said, "Don't you be gettin' drunk, Tom Bear."

Tom took the beer from John, popped the tab, and took a long drink. He put the now half-empty can on the table, wiped his mouth with the back of his hand and said, "Never crossed my mind." He grinned at his brother.

"Well," Clarisse said, "you two can sit here and drink. I'm going in the front room and watch some television."

"Watch a bunch of idiots buy a vowel is more like it," Tom said.

Clarisse gave him a disgusted *humph* and left them alone.

When she disappeared into the living room, John took a drink and said, "How you guys doing?"

"Been better . . . but then we been worse. Seems like this winter is never going to end."

"You fishin' the derby this year?"

"Don't know." Tom pointed over his shoulder with his right thumb. "The ol' woman don't think anyone should be out and about, what with all the goin's on of late. If I do I'll probably drive down to Eagle Lake or even Square—know some guys who got a shack out on Square. Too much goin' on around Frontière, if you know what I mean."

"Yeah, I do. What you been hearing around town?"

"Usual bullshit . . . everyone is scared shitless to go out in the woods. Hell, even the loggers ain't happy about cuttin' anywheres north o' Estcourt Road."

"Well—and this goes no further than here—we think this guy also killed a fella in St. Francis."

Tom finished off his beer and reached for another. "This guy gets around, huh?"

"Appears that way. Anyone capable of this come to your mind?"

"A bunch. You could start with that bunch of crazy-assed Dowds that live over around Kelly Brook Mountain."

"Oh?"

Tom drank another swallow of beer. "You go up there you better take a long gun and a squad of Marines—them folks don't take kindly to visitors."

21

Dowd Settlement, T1, R12

John Bear stopped before the metal gate that barred access to the narrow lane leading into the cluster of cabins and sheds known as Dowd Settlement. He notified the DIF&W dispatcher in Ashland of his location and chuckled when the reply crackled out of the two-way: "John, you be careful goin' in there. Those Dowds can be crazier than a surfeit of rabid skunks—over."

"So I hear—over." He hung the transmitter on its hook and checked his cell phone—zero bars.

He locked his truck and circumvented the barrier, following the road toward the buildings that he estimated to be two hundred yards further on. The road was more of a trail, both sides lined with snow-banks. During summer it consisted of two tracks separated by a median of tall grass which was now poking through the mounded snow. As he walked, John thought about what he'd learned from Del about the Dowd clan. The reigning patriarch, Linwood Dowd was in his late sixties. He was a Vietnam veteran, having served there with the U.S. Army. He returned, like many Viet vets, a disgruntled and disillusioned young man. He turned his back on the society that he believed tried to kill him, went off-grid, and settled into the woods west of Kelly Brook Mountain. Lin Dowd and his offspring lived by a simple code, *Don't be fuckin' with us and we won't be fuckin' with you.* The question that John needed to answer, and soon, was whether or not old man Dowd would consider a visit from a game warden as being *fucked with.* He got his answer in seconds.

"Stop right there."

John turned and saw a young woman on snowshoes in a stand of pine. She held what appeared to be a .30-30 lever-action rifle aimed in his general direction. "My name is John Bear. I'm with the warden service."

"I can see your uniform. What you want? Didn't you see the NO TRES-PASSING sign on the gate?"

"I'm here in my official capacity."

"We ain't been poachin' nothin'." She moved out of the pines and onto the road.

"I'm with Wildlife Crimes Investigation Division."

"So? Far as I know ain't no wildlife around here committed no crime. . . ."

John chuckled; at least this one seemed to have a good sense of humor. "I investigate accidents and crimes, such as killings, in the woods."

She stopped about ten feet in front of him, the rifle still held at the ready position. A sly smile came over her face. "We ain't had no accidents and as far as I know we ain't killed nobody. . . . not yet anyways."

She wore a heavy black parka and green wool trousers. Striking blond hair was visible around the border of the wool watch cap she wore. She stepped aside. "You armed?"

John unzipped his coat and showed her his service pistol.

"Nice," she said. "What is it, a nine-millimeter?"

"Yes and I'm not leaving it or handing it over."

"Just keep it under your coat."

John dropped the flap of the coat.

"Zip it up."

He complied with her wishes. "Might I ask who I'm talking with?"

"You might . . . won't do you no good though. Head on up to the house." She let him pass by and then followed him. "And keep your arms out away from your body."

"You people take turns being on guard duty?"

"Wasn't on no guard duty."

"Then why the rifle?"

"In case I meet a bear."

"In February?"

"You're a Bear, ain't you? Anyways, that's my story and it ain't gonna change."

When they broke out of the trees, John found himself facing a wide cleared expanse containing several ramshackle buildings, counted ten coyote hides stretched on the side of a shed that contained cords of firewood. "Head for the big house," his guide said.

John angled toward the largest building. It was constructed of logs and had been coated with tar or oil so often that it looked more black than brown. Smoke spiraled out of a chimney comprised of stone and concrete and the pleasant smell of wood smoke filled the area. A covered porch ran across the front and when they were within twenty feet of the steps leading up, a thin, wiry old man walked out of the door. He spit a wad of brown tobacco into the snow and said, "Who you got there, Amy?"

"Says he's some kinda special game warden."

He turned his attention to John. "We done something special?"

"You Linwood Dowd?" John asked.

The old man inclined his head toward John Bear and squinted, an obvious sign to the warden that the old man was in need of glasses. As he mounted the steps leading onto the porch, John saw a white area in the center of Dowd's eyes where cataracts had formed. The old man peered at the warden for several moments and then said, "Don't think I know you. . . ."

"My name is John Bear—"

"Bear . . . what in hell kind of name is that? You an Indian or some shit?"

"Maliseet, I grew up on the Madawaska Maliseet First Nation near Edmundston."

"How's a goddamned Indian . . . and a Canadian at that . . . get to be a game warden in Maine?"

"Just lucky, I guess."

"What you doin' on my land?"

"I'm investigating three murders—"

"Murders . . . you ain't tryin' to pin nothin' on us are you?"

"If you ain't done anything then you ain't got nothin' to worry about from me."

Linwood Dowd laughed and it turned into the phlegmy cough of a heavy smoker. "Ain't said that we ain't done nothin', we just ain't killed no one, not in a while anyhow." He turned toward the house. "Come on in an' we'll talk."

John Bear looked at Amy and saw that she had turned her rifle away from him and rested it in the crook of her arm. She climbed onto the porch, removed her snowshoes, and entered the house.

He followed the Dowd patriarch inside the house. He was immediately struck by two things: the intense dry heat from two fireplaces, one on each side of the room, which spanned the breadth of the cabin, and the overwhelming smell of cigarette smoke that seemed to radiate from every piece of furniture. He wondered what the cancer rate was among the Dowds.

The old man pointed toward a huge couch that faced the fireplace on the east wall and John took off his coat and placed it over the back. Dowd looked at John's service pistol. John ignored his stare and settled onto the couch. Mounted above the hearth was a moose head with the largest rack John had ever seen; to its right was a twelve-point buck and on the left a black bear. All three trophies appeared to have been prepared by a professional taxidermist. Dowd saw John's gaze and said, "All shot legal."

John smiled. "Nothin' else ever crossed my mind. Who did the preservation? It's really fine work."

"My oldest boy, Earl. It's a hobby of his."

On the mantle John saw two pictures, one of a much younger version of the old man who stood before him wearing an army fatigue uniform while holding an M-16 rifle; the other was of a beautiful young woman whose attire told him the picture was taken in the 1970s or at the latest, the 1980s. Again Dowd noted where he was looking. "That was me in '72, in Nam. The woman was my wife, Kera."

John nodded. "I heard you were a veteran, thanks for your service. . . ."

Dowd picked up an empty coffee can and spit into it. "Save me from the fuckin' platitudes. Where were all these people sayin' that when we came back? We didn't get any thanks, we got spit on, and cursed. Now people meet you and say that like everything is okay—well, fuck 'em. I went 'cause I was sent and I did what I had to do to get my ass home."

"Well, it's a different world now."

"These shitheads ain't got a clue. It'd be different if they meant it. It's like when people say *have a good day*. Do you think they really give a good goddamn whether or not you have a good day? Not a chance. You want something to drink?"

"No thanks."

The old man walked over to a chest of drawers and opened the top drawer. He took out a bottle of bourbon and twisted the cap off. "Suit yourself, but I'm having a snort or two." Dowd crossed the room and flopped into a Boston rocker. "Now what's this shit about murders?"

"There have been three murders in the last week."

"I heard. Now suppose you cut through the bullshit and tell me why you're sitting in my living room if you don't think me or mine done it."

John couldn't help but admire the old man's candor. "Mr. Dowd—"

"Lin or Linwood, Mr. Dowd was my father an' that contrary old bastard is long dead. We buried the bastard facedown in case he tried to dig his way out."

"Lin, you know this wilderness. In fact, I'd bet that between you and your family there ain't a road or game trail in fifty miles you don't know."

"You might be right. I been huntin', fishin', and trappin' these woods for over fifty years."

"I'm looking for someone of . . ." John paused for a second. "Well, he'd be almost a giant. I believe that he may have been living up around Viverette Settlement."

Dowd took another drink of whiskey. "*Askook.*"

"Excuse me, did you say *Askook*?"

"Yeah, I did. Only gigantic sonuvabitch I know of up that way is a guide and trapper named Askook. Only met him once or twice myself, but he was one goofy-acting sumbitch."

"What do you know of him?"

"Not much, just that he showed up here about ten, maybe twelve years ago. I believe he was from down around Houlton. He's taller than anyone I ever seen before or since. Looks like one o' them zombies you hear about. I hear he's as strong as any four men. Hauled a eight-hundred-pound cow moose out of the woods by himself." Dowd must have noticed the incredulous look on John Bear's face because he added, "Didn't see it myself mind you, but I heard about it many a time."

"Where might I find this man?"

"If he ain't in his shack out on Hafford Pond, I ain't got a clue. He's probably got lairs spread out all over the place." Dowd took another drink. "Now that I think of it, I believe that Askook was a Indian too—Mi'kmaq, if I ain't wrong."

"The name is Algonquin," John said. "Askook is our word for snake. You wouldn't by any chance know his first name, would you?"

"I heard it once didn't give a good goddamn about it or him so I don't remember it. Recollect it was some Indian thing—even if I did give a shit, it was too damned hard for me to say."

John heard a noise and turned his head to see Amy Dowd enter the room. She carried a glass of water in her right hand and an assortment of pills in her left. She looked at the whiskey bottle with disapproval. "Granddad you ain't supposed to be drinkin' that stuff. She gave him the water and pills, and then stood close by watching him toss the medication into his mouth and wash it down with a gulp of water. Dowd handed her the empty glass, then turned to John and said, "About all the goddamned army ever gave me was diabetes and them friggin' pills."

The old man seemed to be searching his memory for something. "You know I heard stories about another giant runnin' around. They say ain't nobody ever seen it and only a couple people ever heard it." A grin spread across Dowd's face. "I guess whoever he is, he ain't friendly like us—sounds like some friggin' ghoul to me."

John thought that the word *ghoul* was appropriate when talking about a Wendigo and then stood and said, "Thanks for your help, Lin. I'll look into Askook."

Amy Dowd walked to the door and picked up her parka. "I'll guide you out to your truck," she said.

"That ain't necessary," John said. "I can find my way out."

"Ain't no bother," Lin Dowd said. "Is it, Amy?"

"None at all."

John Bear donned his coat and as he left the warmth of the house and reentered the freezing outside world, he wondered what the Dowds were hiding that they didn't want him to see. However, he had bigger issues on his mind and filed the thought until sometime in the future.

22

Big Twenty Township, T20, R11

The February wind picked up and howled across the valley. Trees creaked and swayed, throwing off snow that drifted across the road like white clouds and obscured visibility. The Wendigo vaulted over the eight-foot-tall snowbank and stood in the road. His clothing was tattered and he was starved. He had not eaten in three days, and his last meal had consisted of a single bite of raw, frozen meat from his depleting cache.

He heard the approaching truck before he saw it. The eighteen-wheeler appeared out of the white-out like a plane emerging from a cloud. He waved his arms and the oversized load of timber swayed as the driver slowed. When the truck stopped, he reached up and opened the passenger-side door. "Thanks for stopping."

The driver studied his filthy clothes and disheveled appearance. "What in hell are you doing out here in the middle of nowhere?"

The Wendigo ignored his question. He opened the door, jumped onto the truck's running board, and yanked the driver out.

The Wendigo's fast was over.

McBrietty's Store

Del McBrietty was working behind the counter when the door opened and a blast of frigid air caused a cloud of steam in the threshold. "Close the friggin' door," Del shouted, "I ain't in the business of heating the outdoors."

A man ducked inside and when he straightened his head the ceiling was less than a foot over him. He shifted his head to the side to avoid bumping into the ceiling fan and approached the counter.

"Hey, Askook, ain't seen you in a while."

"I'm leavin' the area and got some loose ends to tie up."

McBrietty's internal alarm sounded. Megedagik Askook was carrying a $140 balance on his account.

"I'll be squarin' up my account with you, too."

Del hid his relief and said, "Give me a minute, I'll check on the balance of your account."

"You do that—but you and I both know you have it up here." Askook tapped the side of his head. "To the last penny."

Del disappeared into his office. In a few minutes he returned with a bill, and handed it to the huge trapper.

Askook glanced at the printout and then reached into his pocket and took out a roll of bills that Del estimated was over an inch in diameter. The trapper peeled off two one-hundred-dollar bills and gave them to McBrietty.

McBrietty opened the till, placed the cash under the money tray and then handed back sixty dollars. "Where you off to, if you don't mind my askin'?"

"Over home."

"Where might that be?"

"You're askin' a lot of questions, Del."

McBrietty shrugged. "Just interested, that's all. You must be having a good trapping season."

"No better than most." Askook turned and said no more as he left the store.

A few seconds later, McBrietty heard a snowmobile motor start and the sound of a sled racing away into the night. He stared at the cash register and wondered: *Askook must have had one hell of a season to get all that money.*

Del looked at the clock on the wall and started closing up.

John Bear met Laura Wells and Bob and Elaine for coffee at Del's. He settled into the booth and took a bite out of the donut he'd purchased. "Mornin'."

He believed that Laura looked as beautiful on an early-winter morning as most women did at midday on a mild, warm late-spring day. "Tell me, John," she asked, "why am I sitting here watching the sun rise over a friggin' snowbank?"

He laughed and said to Pelky. "Well, she may be pleasing to the eye early in the day, but a bit on the grumpy side."

"Hey," Pelky said, leaning back and holding his hands up in surrender, "don't involve me in your domestic disputes."

John turned serious. "Yesterday I went up to Dowd Settlement—"

"And got out in one piece?" Pelky commented, "Not a usual occurrence."

"I spoke with Linwood."

"How is that old geezer? He's got to be pushing seventy real hard."

"From what I've heard, I must have caught him in a good mood—he talked with me."

"What did you learn?" Laura asked.

John turned to her. "Laura, you got to promise me that you won't print a word of this until we get this guy."

"I understand."

"Okay. Linwood says there's only one man in the area that he believes is big enough and strong enough to be our perp."

John took a notebook out of his pocket. "Megedagik Askook."

"I've met Askook," Pelky said, "never knew his first name though. Sure is a mouthful."

"Roughly translated from the Algonquin his name means *Kills Many Snakes*."

"Nice," Laura said.

"According to his snowmobile registration, Askook lives near Hafford Pond. I'm heading up there today."

"Most likely, roads over that way won't be plowed."

"Got my sled on the back of my truck."

"You got room for a passenger?" Laura asked.

"Not this time. But I promise if anything develops I'll make sure you're in on it."

She didn't look happy with his answer but rather than push the issue said, "Okay, I'll let you off the hook this time. But the next time . . ."

Hafford Pond, T19, R12

The cabin was almost hidden by snow; in fact, if not for the thin stream of smoke arising from the chimney, John Bear may have missed it completely. As he slowly approached, John wondered about the old man's name: Kills Many Snakes. Knowing that his people named children according to some event or natural phenomenon, he wondered what Askook's family had done to earn that name. He stopped his sled in front and stepped off. There was a lean-to attached to the left side of the building and John saw a Polaris snowmobile and a four-wheeler ATV parked inside. He removed his helmet, placed it on the seat, and then put on his green uniform cap. The sudden quiet was broken by the unmistakable *chunk* of an axe splitting a piece of firewood. He heard a voice shout, "I'm out back."

There was a narrow path created by someone's repeated treading through the snow that led around the right side and John followed it. He heard the sound of the axe fall again, followed by the sound of two pieces of wood striking each other. When he turned the back corner, John stopped dead in his tracks. Hunched over a chopping block was the tallest human being he'd ever encountered. He said, "Megedagik Askook?"

The giant buried the blade of the axe into the tree stump that served as his chopping block and turned toward John. He was well over seven feet tall and John found the man's height to be somewhat intimidating, in fact he was tempted to open his coat, allowing access to his service pistol.

Askook squinted against the brilliance of the sun reflecting from the pristine white snow. "You pronounced my name like you speak the language." He stepped toward the warden and recognized the green uniform and the DIF&W crest on the front of John's cap. "What is an Anishinaubae doing wearing that uniform?"

"My name is John Bear, I'm a special investigator for the Maine Department of Inland Fisheries and Wildlife."

"You must be the Maliseet I heard about—the one who crossed over and turned his back on his people."

"Well, I wouldn't believe all you hear."

"You here about the Wendigo?"

John tried to cover up his surprise and knew that he had failed. "I don't know anything about a Wendigo but I am looking into a couple of murders in these parts."

"Don't bullshit me Warden." Askook took two long strides and passed John, headed for the front of the cabin. "C'mon, I got a fresh pot of coffee inside."

John Bear followed the towering figure inside the cabin. Askook was so tall he had to bend over to enter the door. "I wanted to make it taller," Askook said, "but couldn't find one big enough."

Everything inside the cabin was constructed with magnified dimensions. John found himself feeling like a small child in an adult's room. When he sat in the chair that Askook offered, his feet barely touched the floor. "You make all this furniture yourself?" he asked.

"I had to. They don't have too many big and tall men's furniture stores." Askook poured two mugs of coffee from a pot that sat on the top of a large wood cookstove. The pot reminded John Bear of the huge pots they used to show on chuck wagons in the old Western movies he loved as a kid. Askook slid a mug in front of John and said, "So, what sumbitch told you I was a Wendigo?"

John couldn't help but laugh. "Well, you gotta admit that you are tall enough."

"Contrary enough too. But, I ain't never et no human bein' and don't expect to either. I took steps." He motioned around the room. Dream catchers hung from nails driven into the rafters and frame of the house spaced no more than a foot apart.

Askook drank some coffee. "Bein' Maliseet, you know there's a few ways to become Wendigo, eatin' human flesh is most common, and, like I said, I ain't never done that and don't have any plans to either. The other way is to be possessed during a dream. As you can see I took steps to avoid that."

Askook's brow raised as if he'd just had an epiphany. "You been over to Dowd Settlement, ain't you?"

John Bear took another drink of coffee, refusing to either admit or deny Askook's assertion.

"Fuckin' Linwood Dowd tol' you I was some kind a nut, ain't that so? Well, I ain't no crazier than that fuckin' idjut."

"All I know is that there have been three mutilation murders in this area, that's three more than normal."

Askook looked at John. "What makes you so sure about that?"

"If there's more we haven't heard of them."

"There's lots o' shit goes on in these woods you wardens don't hear about. For instance how many people get lost and disappear and never git found? What about that woman down in the Hundred-Mile Wilderness?"

John Bear knew the case. The Hundred-Mile Wilderness is the section of the Appalachian Trail running between Abol Bridge just south of Baxter State Park and the town of Monson. It is generally considered the wildest section of the Appalachian Trail, and one of the most challenging to navigate and traverse. A female hiker had gone missing on the trail and in spite of an all-out search by the wardens, forest rangers, state police, and an army of volunteers—many of whom were trained professionals—her remains were not found for three years.

"Are you saying that her death is related?"

"Who the fuck knows? Dead is dead and gone is gone. You get taken by a Wendigo—or some sick bastard who thinks he's one—and you usually ain't never heard from again. . . ."

John sat quietly listening as the trapper rambled on. Nevertheless, he had to acknowledge that Askook was making some valid points. "Do you have firsthand knowledge of missing people?"

"A few."

"Locally?"

"And across the line in Quebec. This thing has been hunting for a long time."

John knew that the Wendigo was a very accomplished and skilled hunter, especially at night. Like a vampire its powers increased after the sunset and like a werewolf, it was capable of shape-shifting. He couldn't help but wonder how tall it would be if, as Askook said, it had been hunting for years.

"All in all," Askook said, "they're pretty miserable. The hunger drives them crazy. No sooner do they feed than they become hungry again. So they never stop hunting."

"In the thirty-something years you been working these woods, have you ever seen one?"

"If I had, I wouldn't be here talking to you."

John decided to test whether or not Askook was leading him on. "The Wendigo is a tale used to scare kids and warn against the evil of gluttony. Surely you don't believe it exists?"

"I do." Askook looked sincere when he said, "You do too, or you wouldn't be here."

The old trapper turned serious. "Whatever this killer is, it's one sick sumbitch and *has* been at this for quite a while." He glanced at the small window that faced west. "Gonna be dark in an hour. If you ain't planning on stayin' the night you better get your ass out of here. Wendigo or no Wendigo, it ain't smart to be running around alone after dark."

John looked at the sun and agreed that he was running out of daylight. "You know a guy named Paul Condor?"

"Never met him."

John stood up. "Well—"

"Don't be in such a damned rush," Askook said. "I never met Paul Condor . . . but I sure as hell heard about him. Killed his father about thirteen or fourteen years ago."

John Bear sat down again.

The Wendigo studied the cabin and hissed. Kills Many Snakes and the Indian warden had been in there for more than an hour. There was no doubt what the major discussion was. His existence was in jeopardy. They would both have to be dealt with if he wanted to remain alive. He turned away and trudged through the snow that would be waist high on most people, but was only knee deep on him. Askook wasn't as much of a threat as the game warden. Askook would be here whenever Wendigo wanted him.

The Wendigo disappeared into the darkening forest.

23

Del's Place

John Bear was in his usual seat below the dust-covered moose head when Laura Wells walked into the dining room at Del's. She slid into the seat across from him and looked up at the trophy. "You may regret doing that," he said.

Laura studied the cobwebs and dust bunnies for several seconds. "So long as he doesn't have a sinus infection or head cold, I should be all right."

John smiled at her. "The more I get to know you, the more I like you."

She grinned. "That's all part of the plan. . . . Besides—what's not to like?"

Del appeared and they placed their drink orders. As he walked across the room, Laura asked John, "So what've you been up to for the past couple of days? I've looked all over the place for you and no one has seen you."

"I been beating the hell out of the boonies."

"The boonies?"

"The woods. . . . It's short for the boondocks."

"Humph, and for years I called them the willy-wags."

"Willy-wags? I hope that if and when you write your article about this you don't use that phrase."

"Oh, I think I'll come up with something more professional than either boonies or willy-wags."

Del brought a couple of beers and placed them on the table. "You two eatin' or just drinkin' beer and bullshittin'?"

"My usual," John said.

"I figured as much," Del said.

"What is his usual?" Laura asked Del.

"Every time he comes in he orders a rib-eye steak, medium-well, mashed potato, and the vegetable of the day. It comes with bread and garden salad. He eats so many steaks his cholesterol must be through the roof—his arteries have got to be full of sludge." He smiled at her and said, "What about you?"

"Do you serve seafood?"

"I serve a great grilled salmon . . . it comes with all the fixings, choice of potato, veggie, and salad."

"That sounds terrific to me."

"Dressing on your salad?"

"Something low-calorie, if you have it."

"Got a great vinaigrette. Tonto here always wants French." Del chuckled and then was gone.

"Getting back to our conversation," Laura said. "Tell me what you've been up to."

"Well, I've been interviewing some of the local characters. I was up in Dowd Settlement—"

"Don't think I've ever heard of it."

"No reason you would have." He gave her the background information on Linwood Dowd and his family.

When he was finished, Laura said, "I think I saw them once . . . in the movie *Deliverance*."

"Between you and me, there isn't much difference."

He then told her about his visit to Megedagik Askook.

"You're serious when you say his name is Kills Many Snakes? The other day I thought you might be foolin' with the city girl."

"That's a rough translation, but close enough."

"I've got to meet this guy."

"Laura, these people make a hermit seem sociable. They live off the land—if I watched them for a week I could probably arrest them and put them away. The thing is, they only poach what they need and they waste nothing. Animal hides become either clothes or blankets and anything that isn't fit for human consumption becomes food for their dogs or bait when they hunt and fish."

"I have never encountered people like this in my entire life."

John laughed. "And these are the ones who at least border on normal. I can show you people who are far worse."

"So what is next?"

Del reappeared with their salads and a platter of freshly baked bread. "Entrees will be right up," he said.

When Del turned away, John said. "Both Dowd and Askook spoke of another giant in the area."

Del stopped and turned back. "Now there is a *real* piece of work."

"You know him?" John asked.

"I know who Askook is. Ain't nobody really knows him, if you get my drift. Matter of fact he was just in yesterday and paid his bill up to date."

"You act surprised," John replied.

"It ain't often that a trapper pulls a wad of money from his pocket, peels off two one-hundred-dollar bills, and hands it to you. I asked if he'd had a good season—he gave me a *nunya business* answer then got on his sled and left."

Del turned toward the kitchen. "I better see about your meals."

Laura stared at John across the table. "Where's this guy live?"

"Over by the Slash, on the western border. You can throw a stone and hit Quebec from there."

"The Slash? You people have more places that I've never heard of and each has its own name. What's the Slash?"

"Once you get below Estcourt Station, there's no natural line of demarcation between Maine and Quebec. So the United States and Canada cut a right-of-way, sort of like they do when they run a power line, only instead of puttin' up power poles, they placed concrete markers, called monuments, in the middle of it to mark the border."

"There's no fence or anything?"

"Nope, just a twenty-foot-wide slash through the woods, runs all the way from Maine to Washington state. It runs by Hafford Pond and right through the middle of Viverette Settlement."

"You going there in the morning?"

"Looks as if I got no choice." John sighed. "I was just up there a couple days ago. It's a long ride and I got to go by sled. There's no guarantee those roads have been plowed."

"Take me with you."

"What?"

"You promised that you'd give me an exclusive, but the story won't be any good unless I've experienced the land."

"Like I said, it's a long ride."

"I've been on snowmobiles since I was a kid. I can handle it."

"Are you willing to head out before sunrise?"

"I'm ready to do whatever it takes."

24

Dowd Settlement

Dwain Dowd walked into the kitchen and flopped into a vacant chair at the table. His aunt, Amy, glanced at him and he scowled at her.

"What's eatin' at you this morning?" she asked.

"The old man won't let me do nothin'."

Amy Dowd studied her angry nephew for several seconds. "Which *nothin'* won't he let you do?"

He crossed his arms across his chest and his face twisted into an adolescent pouting frown. "Don't matter which nothin', he won't let me do it."

"Maybe if you were a bit more specific I might be able to talk to him."

"Would you do that Aunt Amy?"

She sipped from the mug of coffee that sat in front of her. "Of course it would depend on what partic'lar nothin' I'm askin' him for."

The boy stood up, walked to the refrigerator, and opened it. He stared inside for several seconds, while he debated whether or not to tell his aunt what it was he wanted her to approach his father about. He came to a decision and closed the refrigerator door. I want to go over to the Cochrans and play with Murdock." He turned toward his aunt to plead his case. "Ain't nobody 'round here my age. They's all either older or just kids."

Amy suppressed a smile. Dwain fancied himself to be quite grown, but was still only thirteen years old. Granted he was mature, but still thirteen was thirteen and there were many potentially dangerous things living in the woods around them—and that didn't take into account the killer who was out there someplace.

"Dwain, it's over fifteen miles to the Cochran place over in Dickey an' it ain't safe to leave the settlement alone these days."

"Aw, c'mon, Aunt Amy, it ain't like I'm a little kid no more."

She sat back and pondered his request. The boy's father, her brother Buster, was not an unreasonable man, nowhere near as stubborn as their father, Earl, but still, once he made up his mind about something he seldom, if ever, reversed himself. However, as the youngest, and only female offspring of Earl Dowd, she knew the loneliness of not having someone to grow up with. She stood up and said, "I ain't makin' no promises now, but I'll talk to him. Maybe if he says it's okay, I can drive you over in one of the trucks.

Dwain's face lit up. "You'd do that?"

She smiled. "Boy, its fifteen degrees out there an' you'd freeze to death if you was to try walkin' it."

"I'd wear my snowmobile suit and boots. Tell Dad that I could ride over on the old Ski-Doo."

"Whoa, Dwain. Let's fight this war one battle at a time. Okay?"

He smiled a broad smile, which disappeared within minutes when he heard the argument that developed in the next room.

———————

"That goddamned kid put you up to this?" Buster Dowd scolded his sister.

"Well, he talked to me."

"Well the answer is still no. No one is leavin' this settlement until they catch whoever it is killing these people."

"Buster, be reasonable. There's no other kids his age here and he gets lonely for someone of his own age and gender—you remember how it was for me, don't you?"

"Yeah I do, Amy, but that don't change the fact that it ain't safe for him to be away from the settlement and that's the end of it. One more word and I'll grab hold of him and wear him out. He won't be able to sit for a week."

Hearing the abrupt end to the argument, Dwain ran to his room. He slid into his heavily insulated snowmobile suit and boots. He grabbed his helmet and gloves and crept out of the house. Once he was in the yard he ran to the large shed where the Dowds parked their ATVs, trucks, and snowmobiles.

———

Buster Dowd walked into the mudroom and beat snow and sawdust from his feet before entering the kitchen. He walked to the stove and poured a mug of coffee. He turned to Amy who was busy making bread for the family's supper. "Where's Dwain?"

"I haven't seen him since breakfast."

"You tell him about our talk?" Buster asked.

"Nope, haven't seen him since."

Buster's face reddened. "If that little shit overheard us and took off after I told him no. . . ." He gulped a mouthful of coffee and walked out of the kitchen.

"Buster, where you going?" Amy called, knowing her brother's temper and his predilection to act before he thought things through.

"I'm going to see if his sled is in the shed. If it ain't—"

Amy rushed to get her coat and followed Buster across the open yard. She caught up with him as he swung the door open and peered inside. "Sonuvabitch," his voice was fraught with anger.

"Buster, don't be gettin' all bent out of shape. He may be takin' a ride and hasn't left the settlement."

Buster turned and glared at her. "You an' me both know they's two chances of that . . . slim and none, and slim left town."

"What you goin' to do? Whip him for bein' just like his father? How many times did you act contrary to Dad's orders?"

The large man stopped in his tracks and a slow grin came across his face. "You sayin' the apple ain't fallin' far from the tree?"

"I'm saying the sins of the father will always fall on the son."

He slammed the shed door shut and turned away. "Well, him and me are due for a come-to-Jesus meeting." He paused halfway across the yard and spun around. He pointed an accusatory finger at his younger sister. "Don't you be defendin' him either. He disobeyed and he's gotta pay."

Amy stopped and stared at Buster. She struggled to keep from laughing at him. Buster had a quick temper, but he cooled down every bit as quick. By the time Dwain got home, he'd be in a much more reasonable frame of mind. Snowflakes began to drift down from the sky as Buster jumped inside of his massive logging truck and headed toward the wood lot where they were cutting timber. She knew everything would be okay, Buster would work off his anger and give his wayward son a sound tongue-lashing, but that was as far as it would go.

As she approached the house, her father opened the door for her. Steam rolled out of the warm kitchen as the moist, warm air met the cold, dry outside air. "Everything okay?" Earl Dowd asked.

"Just a minor father-son dispute," she said as she stepped inside.

"Dwain actin' like his father again?"

"Something along those lines."

Camp 106 Road, T16, R12

Dwain Dowd sat on the Ski-Doo staring at the brown sludge on the trail behind him. *The old man is really gonna kick my ass,* he thought. In spite of the heavily insulated snowmobile suit he wore, a chill set in and Dwain shivered. He wondered if anyone at home had discovered his absence. In one way he hoped they hadn't, but with the Ski-Doo all shot to hell there was no way he could hide his disobedience from his father. If he didn't get his ass kicked for taking off, he'd be getting it kicked for not checking the oil and gas in the sled.

It began to snow harder. Dwain had only a rough idea where he was, but knew that he was closer to the Dickey checkpoint than home. The checkpoint however, didn't offer him shelter. It was no longer a manned checkpoint, but there was an on-site radio call box that would connect him to the Little Black checkpoint. During this time of year, it got dark around five o'clock and he did not want to spend the night alone in the woods. If he didn't freeze to death, who knew what he might meet in the dark. He got off the sled and began walking.

After an hour of trudging toward the Dickey checkpoint, the snow had accumulated to three inches. Periodically, Dwain would turn and look at his back trail, which looked as if a huge snake had wound its way through the fresh snowpack. The snowfall had increased and the youngster knew it would be getting dark soon. He hoped that by now his father or someone at Dowd Settlement had noticed his absence and was looking for him. The sudden realization that that would make no difference caused him to pause. No one would be looking for him tonight. The Cochrans didn't know he was coming and his father would assume that he was spending the night with Murdock and his parents. He picked up his pace, fighting the cold and numbness in his feet.

Daylight was fleeing fast and visibility was down to mere yards. The wind had picked up and Dwain wondered if the storm was going to become what his father called a *real bejeezer*. Cold and walking in the heavy snowmobile boots had taken a toll on the boy, and it took a determined effort for him to place one foot in front of another. He wondered whether he should keep walking or look for some form of shelter where he could get out of the storm for the night. He estimated that so far six inches of snow had been dumped on the area and his tracks would have been filled in. He began looking for a place to hole up when he spied a downed tree. The massive pine's branches formed a natural windbreak and would be a perfect place for him to rest for a while. Dwain broke a trail through the snow that was so deep that he felt as if he was trying to run in water. Reaching his goal, the freezing boy used his hands to scoop out a depression in the space between two of the larger boughs.

The boy huddled in the inadequate shelter and wrapped his arms around himself, trying to preserve what warmth the winter suit provided. His eyelids began to close and he shook his head to ward off sleep. His father had told him that being sleepy was the first step in freezing to death. Dwain felt his throat constrict as he tried to stifle a sob. He scooped up a handful of snow and washed his face with it. His skin was so cold that he didn't feel the chill that he hoped would ward off sleep. He began to shiver violently and burrowed deeper into his hole. After a few minutes the shivering stopped and he felt sick to his stomach and a debilitating fatigue bore down on him. In seconds he was asleep.

The Wendigo had been following the solitary figure since it saw his machine break down. The boy was obviously lost and staggered as he walked—he'd be easy prey. When the target turned into the woods and sought refuge behind the downed tree, the Wendigo knew it was a matter of time before he'd be unconscious.

The falling snow blanketed the woods and muffled all sound except for the occasional rustle of tree branches when a burst of breeze passed. The Wendigo listened; his super-keen hearing enabled him to hear the accelerated heartbeat of frightened prey. However, the boy's heart had slowed so much that his heartbeat was barely discernable.

The Wendigo advanced and gathered the unconscious form. He looked at the young face and felt a minuscule bit of concern for the boy's well-being. The human moment was fleeting and quickly passed. The Wendigo carried his prize off into the darkness of the storm.

25

Tobique First Nation, Perth-Andover, New Brunswick, Canada

B enny Graywolf was the epitome of what everyone thought a
Royal Canadian Mounted Policeman should look like. He was
six feet, two inches tall, lean and mean. The only thing that took
away from his image was that he looked ten years older than he was.
Years of exposure to winter wind and summer sun had given him a ruddy,
weathered look. He gripped John Bear's hand with enough strength to
crush hazelnuts. "So you decided to come over and see how a *real* law
enforcement agency operates.

John returned Graywolf's crushing grip and said, "Actually, I wanted
to spend some time hanging out with some of your people."

Graywolf laughed. "You could have done that without driving seventy
miles. If I remember correct your old man still lives on the Madawaska
First Nation. So what is it you *really* want?"

John Bear gave the RCMP sergeant a serious look. "Is there someplace less public where we can talk?"

Graywolf led John Bear to a conference room and when they were seated said, "What's up?"

"You may know we've had several murders up my way."

"That I do, what about them brings you here?"

"Benny, I think I'm looking for a Wendigo."

Graywolf stared across the table. "What?"

"The bodies were torn so badly their own mothers wouldn't have been able to recognize them—and there's parts missing."

A female officer entered the room carrying two mugs of coffee, placed one in front of John Bear and the other before Graywolf, and then exited the conference room.

Graywolf took a drink of coffee, the heat from the beverage steamed his glasses. "Okay. Why *are* you here?"

"I've been told that this guy has been working both sides of the border."

"Here?"

"More likely the remote areas of eastern Quebec."

"And you want me to . . . ?"

"Have your people go back, maybe as much as twenty years and see how many hunters, fishermen, whatever have gone missing and never been found."

"These types of requests are usually handled through Ottawa and Washington, or even between Maine and the province in question."

"Benny," John leaned forward, "this perp has killed at least three times in the past month. Two days ago we discovered a root cellar filled with skeletons and bones—I believe it was one of his food caches. By the time the bureaucrats on both sides of the border get the paperwork done I could have who knows how many more bodies on my hands."

Graywolf sat back and thought for a second. "Okay."

"I know it'll take a day or two to get the information, so I'll come back in two or three days"

"You know Norman Levesque?"

"Not by name. May know him if I see him."

"His territory is up in Claire and the part of Quebec you're interested in. I'll get the info to him, that way all you got to do is drive to Fort Kent, save you a couple of hours of windshield time." Graywolf glanced at his watch. "It's twelve thirty—"

"Eleven thirty my time."

"Whatever, I'll call Norm and have him meet you in Claire. Who knows? He may already have something that you can use."

"When you get the information, call me and I'll meet him in Claire."

Big Twenty Township, T20, R11

Dwain awakened when early light filtered in through the dirt- and grime-coated old window. He was still in his snowmobile suit and he was covered with an old canvas. His face was numb with cold, but not as much as it had been when his sled broke down. *There'll be hell to pay when the old man finds that,* he thought. Dwain pulled the canvas up to his chin and smelled the mold and rot. As bad as it smelled, it was warm and at that moment he was reluctant to leave.

He scanned the shack with his eyes and saw spiderwebs stretched between the rafters, in some places so thick they looked like a white blanket. In the center of the room was a table with one leg broken so that it tipped to the side. Even at his young age he could tell it was devoid of any modern conveniences, such as electricity. The only source of heat was an old fireplace lined with a heavy coating of creosote. Beside the hearth was a pile of firewood and small bits of twigs and branches for kindling.

Dwain struggled out of his crude bed and used the kindling and a couple of pieces of the wood to create a miniature pyre in the firebox. As he searched around inside his one-piece snowsuit for his cigarettes, he was glad his old man hadn't yet learned that his thirteen-year-old son was a smoker and taken his lighter away.

He lit the propane in his lighter and touched it to the kindling. A small flame appeared and Dwain impatiently fanned the air above it with his hand, trying to make the flame grow. When the kindling ignited the wood, Dwain held his hands out to the heat that rose from the burning maple. A shadow passed over the window and Dwain turned to face the window and the door.

After several tense moments he turned back to the fire. The flames began to grow and most of the heat was being lost up the chimney. Dwain felt a draft of air coming down the chimney and saw smoke entering the room instead of the chimney. He remembered his grandfather adjusting something he called a damper. In the fireplace at the settlement there was a handle in the top of the hearth. Dwain ventured a quick look and bent in and looked up. There was a handle there and he grabbed it. The metal damper had been unused for who knew how long (possibly longer than Dwain had been alive) and refused to move. Dwain gripped it with both hands and tugged. It would not budge. In frustration he jumped up and kicked the stubborn handle. The damper let out a loud squealing noise as years of rust and corrosion broke away and it moved. Dwain grasped the handle and moved it until the gate closed enough to eliminate the downdraft, the fire was at a manageable level and most of the smoke was rising up the chimney.

The interior of the shack warmed quickly and Dwain realized that he was not out of the woods yet—now he realized he was hungry, but a quick search proved there was nothing edible in the shack. He stared at the window. He could find something to eat outside, but recalled the shadow he'd seen earlier.

Dwain stripped out of the heavy one-piece snowmobile suit and removed the exterior boots, keeping on the felt linings. He found a couple of old wooden chairs, placed one by the table, and sat down. He folded his arms on the edge of the table and rested his head on them. used one to hold up the corner with the broken leg, and sat down, resting his head on his hands. As the fire took hold and the interior of the house warmed, he felt drowsy and soon dozed off.

The Wendigo stared in through the dirty, film-coated window at the boy. The traces of heat that escaped the cabin seared his flesh and he stepped back a step. For over an hour he watched like a silent sentinel and then turned and walked into the woods. He fought against his urge to kill the boy and feed. When the need grew so strong that it was about to take control of him, he began to run.

26

State Route 161 along the Maine–New Brunswick Border

John Bear had just driven through Saint John and entered into Fort Kent when his cell phone rang. He glanced at the display and saw that it was the Regional Communications Center in Houlton. Maine had set up four 1-800 numbers through the public safety dispatch system so that anyone in need of a warden's services could reach one locally. Houlton was the one for the northern part of the state. John Bear pulled over to the shoulder and answered the call. "John Bear."

"John, Jane Lewis in Houlton."

"Hey, Jane what's up?"

"Got a call from a woman named Amy Dowd. She needs to speak with you as soon as possible."

John was surprised. The Dowds always avoided contact with law enforcement, in fact not once during his tenure in northern Maine had he ever been called by anyone at Dowd Settlement. To the best of his knowledge they didn't even own a phone. When Jane read the number he immediately recognized it as Del McBrietty's. "I'll call her right now."

He disconnected and entered the number for Del's. The phone was answered on two rings. "Del's"

"Del, John Bear. Is Amy Dowd there?"

"Yup, she's been pacing like a wolf in a small cage waitin' for you to call."

"Well, put her on."

He listened as the phone changed hands and then Amy Dowd said, "Warden Bear?"

"Yes, how can I help you, Amy?"

"My nephew Dwain has gone missing."

"When?"

"Sometime yesterday. He went to spend the day with his friend, Murdock Cochran. I went to get him and found his Ski-Doo on Camp 106 Road. Looks like the motor blew."

"Any sign of which way he went?"

"Ten inches of snow fell last night so any tracks have been covered up. I thought that he may have walked to Dickey checkpoint—"

"Which is unmanned."

"I called Little Black from the radio call box, but they said no one had called them. Then I headed over here to call you."

"Stay where you are. I'm in Fort Kent, but I'll be there within an hour." He called Norman Levesque, the RCMP officer in Claire, New Brunswick, and explained the situation.

"Okay, I understand," Levesque said. "We do need to talk though. Benny got some information for you—there's been more than twenty missing persons in and around the Quebec–New Brunswick border. Obviously, there may be as many or more over in Maine."

———

John Bear arrived at Del's shortly before ten a.m. Amy Dowd met him at the door and they walked into the dining area and sat below the moose head. Del brought them coffee and slid into the booth beside Amy. "Tell me everything you know," John said.

"Yesterday morning, Dwain was mad at his father. He wanted to go spend the day at the Cochran place. Buster said no. These killin's have got everyone's nerves on edge. Dwain got mad and I tried to intervene, but the boy must have heard his father and me arguing. That was the last time we saw him."

"When did you realize that he was gone?"

"Yesterday afternoon. Buster went looking for him and we found his sled was gone. We figured that he'd gone ahead and gone to the Cochran's." She sipped some coffee. "If we find that boy alive, Buster is gonna kick his ass big time. . . . It'll be quite a while before that boy will be able to sit without rememberin' the beating."

"Okay. Tell me about the sled," John said.

"When the boy didn't come home last night, I decided to go and fetch him—that was this morning. I knew the route he'd most likely taken so I took the same one. I found the old Ski-Doo on Camp 106 Road. Looks like the motor finally blew up. On account of yesterday's snow I seen no tracks so I figured that he most likely tried walkin' to one of the checkpoints. Dickey was the closest. I got no idea when he lit out, but if he got to Dickey before nine last night he could call Little Black and they'd send someone to fetch him."

"But they haven't heard from him."

"Not a word."

John drank the remainder of his coffee and turned to Del. "Okay if I leave my truck here?"

"Sure."

John turned to Dowd. "I'll offload my sled and follow you to where he left the Ski-Doo."

Camp 106 Road

Amy Dowd and John Bear stopped beside the incapacitated Ski-Doo. It only took a cursory inspection for John to determine that the sled would need a new motor before it would run again. If it wasn't used as a source of spare parts, it would end up on one of the many piles of scrap and junk scattered around Dowd Settlement. John studied the area looking for any sign of which way the boy may have gone. In short time he knew it was fruitless. The previous day's storm had completely filled in anything that would help him determine where he should start his search.

"You called the Cochrans?"

"Yes, they haven't seen him."

"Okay. Let's assume that he was walking to Dickey checkpoint. You know this area better than anyone, is there any place where he might have holed up—tried to get out of the weather?"

"Not that I know of. Of course the woods are full of deadfall and he could have made some sort of shelter."

"We came up that way and saw nothing. He would have heard us when we passed. What about the other direction. You think he might have decided to walk home?"

"Nope, Dwain may only be thirteen but he's been raised in these woods, he'd know Dickey was closer. Besides, I would imagine he's in no rush to face Buster."

As if on cue, they heard the sounds of several approaching snowmobiles. Amy looked up the road and said, "Speaking of the devil. . . ."

Four sleds rounded the curve in the road and John recognized Linwood Dowd immediately. "Looks as if the entire clan is here."

"That boy is going to be in a lot of trouble. . . ."

John looked at her. "Going to be?"

"Yup. Right now they're all worried about him, but once he's found, his hide's gonna be hanging on the shed next to them coyote skins."

The convoy of sleds stopped beside them and the riders dismounted. None of the Dowds wore helmets, preferring to don ball or watch caps. Buster wore a Boston Bruins cap with the visor pointed to the rear so that the wind wouldn't catch it. He reversed the cap, walked over to the inoperative Ski-Doo and stared at it for a few seconds before announcing, "Yuh, it's fucked. Only fit for the junk pile." Ignoring John Bear he asked Amy, "Any sign of the boy?"

Amy shook her head.

"He get to Cochran's place?" Lin asked.

"I called them and they said they ain't heard nor seen hide or hair of him."

"Looks a bit worrisome," Lin Dowd said. He turned, ignoring the warden as his grandson had. "Buster you run down to Little Black, see if anyone seen anything." He turned to Louis. "You run up the Hafford Pond, see what that nutty fuckin' Askook's been up to." He then turned to John Bear. "You, Earl, and me are going to search these woods."

"What am I supposed to do?" Amy asked.

"Get your ass home an' help the women take care of the rest of the brood."

"I want to go with you," Amy protested.

"If you'd a discouraged that boy rather than lead him on. . . ."

"Grandpa, that ain't fair!" she protested.

"You don't do as you're told, I'll show you what ain't fair. Now get on home!"

"Linwood," John Bear said, "this is an official missing persons search now. I got to call it in to the state police and the warden service—"

"You go ahead an' call anyone you fuckin' want—call the goddamned U.S. Army for all I care. But I believe one of them crazy fuckin' Indians got that boy and if I find out that's so, I'll kill whichever one's got him."

"Lin, you go takin' things into your own hands and you'll stir up more trouble than you either want or need."

"Warden, if someone's fucked with mine, I'm gonna fuck with his. Now you go call anyone you want, but me 'n Earl are going to find that boy."

John Bear said, "I'll go with you, but first I'm gonna call Ashland and set a search in motion."

"You got ten minutes," Dowd motioned to the rest of his family. "I told you all what to do, now git to it!"

27

Camp 106 Road

The search party stopped for a break and John Bear noticed that he had a text message from Murphy on his cell phone. He noted the time and realized that he was roaming on a Canadian tower. Regardless of the cost, he called Murphy; in order for the warden to call it must be important. The phone rang once and was answered.

"John?"

"Yeah."

"We got another body."

"You're shitting me. . . ."

"Wish I was—like the others, it looks like a berserk animal attacked the guy."

John said. "Where did you find it?"

"Not far from Frontière Lake."

"Approximate age and size of the vic?"

John saw the looks of concern the Dowds were giving him and knew that they too were holding their breath, hoping this victim was not Dwain.

"I'd say midthirties." Murphy must have realized what John's concern was and added, "Not the Dowd kid. Thank God."

"No one has reported a missing person?"

"No, but I got an ID. He has a fishing license from Quebec. I'll check with the authorities over there."

"Let me know as soon as you learn anything."

"You heading this way?" Murphy asked.

John looked at the Dowds and replied, "Not unless you need me."

"Shit, we've had so goddamned many of these I can do it in my sleep."

"I could be there in an hour if you want."

"It'll be night by then and I already spent one night babysitting a vic. The forensics guys are here and I want my bed tonight."

"Okay," John said, "Do what you got to and get the hell out of there."

"We still should meet and get one another up to speed and talk about something else."

"What's that, Murph?"

"You think maybe we ought to put a stop to this weekend's derby?"

"I do, but the organizers will raise holy hell. They been advertising this all year."

"Let them fish the other nine lakes and rivers. We get twenty, thirty, or more ice fishermen up here, many staying overnight in their shacks, this thing could hold an all-you-can-eat buffet."

"I'll see what I can do. Don't get your hopes up."

"I suppose you're right. There's one thing that we probably should be thankful for."

"Oh?"

"This thing leaves so little of its vics there isn't any fear of the morgue running out of space."

"This isn't funny, Murph."

"I wasn't trying to be funny."

"Yeah, I know. Keep me informed."

"How about we meet at the Little Black checkpoint. . . . Maybe they'll still have some hot coffee."

"You got it. I'll see you there."

John placed his cell phone back in his pocket and zipped it closed. He turned to face Linwood Dowd. "You heard. There's another body, but it ain't Dwain." He looked at the darkening sky. "Be dark soon and it'd make me feel better if you and your family went home. Let us handle the search, I will personally direct it and keep you informed."

"Who's this *us* you're talkin' about?"

"The Maine Warden Service, the Aroostook County Sheriff's Department, the Maine State Police, and the Aroostook County Emergency Management Agency. If needed we can also get assistance from U.S. Customs, Starling Woodlands, and volunteers."

"Bullshit. Other than the warden service how many of them know where in fuck they're goin' up here?"

"If nothing else the Starling people know the area."

"All Starling is interested in is rapin' our land and stealin' our timber. No thanks, Warden, we'll continue lookin' for Dwain, without you if we got to."

"Lin, you boys be careful that you don't break any laws."

"I already told you, we'll do whatever we got to do to get that boy back."

Dowd spun away and motioned for his son, Earl, to mount his sled. Before he drove away, Linwood Dowd said, "Mark my words, Warden. If we find that anyone has hurt our boy, he'll pay for it."

"Just so you're aware that the same holds true for you if you go vigilante."

Little Black Checkpoint

John Bear rounded a curve in the unplowed road and saw Murphy's snow-covered sled parked under the outside spotlights on the hut. John slowed and stopped beside the building. The door opened and Larry

Murphy walked out of a cloud of steam. "Hey, Murph. I got here as fast as I could."

Murphy had left his heavy parka inside the gatehouse. He stomped his feet and wrapped his arms around his torso. "This makes two of these I've found in the past week. Why in hell doesn't this shit ever happen in the summer?"

John stepped off his sled and glanced up at the white globe of the moon. Through the thin layer of clouds between them and Earth's only satellite it was reminiscent of a 1930s horror film, complete with a ring around it. "Let's go inside and you can tell me what you got over coffee. They do have hot coffee, I hope?"

Murphy led the way into the checkpoint as soon as John reached the threshold of the door and closed it behind him shutting out the below-freezing air.

"A couple guys going to Lake Frontière were unloading their stuff and saw it down a small ravine."

"Any identification?"

"The fishing license is made out to Guy Boniface. Says he lives in Rivière-Bleue, Quebec."

"I know where it is, on route 289, about halfway between Lake Frontière and Estcourt Station."

"Well, he looked like there may be parts of him in both places. How we going to notify his next of kin?"

"We'll notify the Canadian authorities. They'll probably let the RCMP handle it."

John poured a cup of coffee and sat on a cushioned bench that ran along the room's north wall. "You find any forensic stuff?"

"You're shitting me, right? This guy looked as if he'd been there for a few days and we've had a couple of good snows since he got hung up . . ."

"Hung up?"

"Yeah, I forgot to tell you, whoever killed him hung him by hooking his head in a fork on a big beech tree. Looks like the killer wanted to cache the body to keep it safe from predators."

"Now it's my turn to say, *you're shitting me.*"

"Afraid not. As my old drill instructor would say, *I shit you not—why you're my best turd.*" Murphy downed his coffee and sat beside John. He hung his head and his exhausted expression left no doubt the toll that the lack of sleep and the murders were taking on him.

John stood. "C'mon Murph, let's get out of here. You okay to ride your sled home?"

"Yeah." Murphy stood, seemed to sway on his feet. He reached out and placed a hand on the wall. "Maybe you should follow me?"

Big Twenty Township, T20, R11

Dwain added more wood to the stove and stared into the blackness outside. The gigantic thing hadn't come near him all day and he was getting hungry. He'd searched every corner and crack in the shack but found nothing to eat and he wondered how it was that the big creature survived. During his search for food, he found a box mounted to the outside window in the rear of the cabin. It looked like something you might store meat in during the winter, but it was empty. He walked to the table and sat. He wondered about the mysterious thing with which he'd found refuge. It had a human form, but the incredible height and serpentine looks indicated something else. The boy got up and grabbed a piece of tree branch from the kindling pile, and stirred the ashes in the firebox; which brought another weird thing about whatever it was. Never had Dwain met anyone so averse to heat of any sort. He had not set foot inside the shack since the fire had been lit.

He heard a noise outside and opened the door. It stood in the moonlight, holding something. The snow, which came to Dwain's waist, barely reached midway up its calves. It took a single step forward and thrust a hunk of what seemed to be fresh meat into Dwain's hands. As soon as the boy got a grip on the morsel, he backed away from the door as if the heat was searing his flesh.

Dwain's benefactor disappeared into the night and Dwain closed the door to keep the heat inside. He looked at the piece of, *what? What sort of meat is this*, he wondered. *Had the giant gone into Lyndon Station? If so, why hadn't he taken me?* Dwain's stomach cramped with hunger and he realized he hadn't eaten since yesterday. He looked around for a pan to cook it in and anything he could use as a utensil and settled for a pointed stick he saw in the pile of firewood. He stared at the meat. It didn't look like any meat he'd ever seen before. Rather than a healthy red tint, it was a dull gray, and he didn't know how old it was and was hesitant to try and cook it. He raised the meat to his nose and smelled it—no odor of rot or putrefaction. Finally hunger won out and he dropped the meat on the woodstove's hot metal surface.

A loud sizzling and popping filled the room, immediately followed by a strange smell. Dwain allowed the meat to sear for a minute before gingerly gripping the one-inch-thick steak with his right forefinger and thumb and flipping it. While the meat cooked he searched the cabin for something he could use as a cooking utensil. Hunger won out and he speared the food, and the smell of sizzling meat permeated the air around the stove. He began salivating. Unable to hold back, he pulled it off the hot surface, ignoring the heat, and bit into it, tearing off a piece with his teeth and swallowing it. He took another bite; the outside was charred black, but the inside barely warm. *Doesn't taste any different than a rare steak*, he decided, and ripped off another piece.

Dwain finished his supper and the door banged open. He stood outside, barely discernible in the moonlight. The man stood back, away from the warmth inside the shack. When he spoke, all Dwain heard were thunderous roars. It was like being in the middle of a thunderstorm.

Dwain clamped his hands over his ears and shouted, "What?"

It motioned for him to come outside and retreated into the night.

Dwain gathered his snowmobile suit and hesitated before putting it on. For some reason or another, the fire attracted his attention. Suddenly, it seemed to be somehow repugnant; so much so that he was reluctant to get close to it, even if only to pick up his boots. In spite of the room's multitude of cracks and openings from which heat could escape, the fire still felt stifling. He snatched up his boots, walked as far from the fire as possible, finished dressing, and walked out the door.

He was waiting, standing beside a Polaris snow sled with the motor idling. It motioned for Dwain to get on and once the boy was settled, it pointed north. Dwain opened the throttle and the sled raced across the moonlit snow. Dwain turned his head and almost crashed when he saw him jogging alongside the speeding machine. They traveled a mile and Dwain was sure he would be falling behind and ventured another look, but rather than lagging back, he kept pace and showed no signs of fatigue.

28

Dowd Settlement

L inwood Dowd flopped in the heavy reclining chair and looked at the old pendulum clock that sat on the mantle. He thought: *Seems like it should be later than ten past eight.* He pulled off his heavy boots and snowmobile suit, and then leaned back and closed his eyes. Exhaustion had worn the old man down, but pride and vanity would not let him show it to his children and grandchildren. He was still, and always would be, patriarch of the family, regardless of age and physical prowess. He heard a noise and when he tried to open his eyes, the lids felt as if they had two-pound weights attached.

Earl stood in the door, holding a mug of steaming coffee, which he offered to the old man.

"Any sign of the boys yet?" Linwood asked as he took the coffee.

"No. I 'spect they'll be back before sunrise though."

Linwood placed the hot mug on the table beside the recliner and leaned back. He closed his eyes and his head turned to one side.

"Dad, whyn't you head up to bed and get some sleep. I'll wake you when the boys get home."

Linwood forced his eyes open and looked at Earl. "I'm fine right here." He hoped that his son hadn't picked up on the fact that as much as the old man wanted to go to bed, he doubted that he would be able to climb the stairs to his bedroom. "Just leave me be."

Earl threw a few pieces of firewood into the fireplace, turned down the lights, and walked to the door. He stood in the threshold and studied his father's immobile body. For the first time he thought about how frail the old man had become. He still thought of his father as a tall, lean, and taciturn man with a strong dislike of government and politicians in general. However, Earl knew his father's closest secret. Not only had Linwood Dowd served in the U.S. Army, he was a war hero who'd saved the lives of a squad of soldiers in Gia Lai Province in Vietnam's central highlands. As an inquisitive kid, Earl had ventured into the uppermost reaches of the barn and come across an old wooden trunk with U.S. ARMY stenciled on its cover, and inside he had found unexpected treasures. A medal that he would later learn was the Silver Star along with a citation that told of Corporal Linwood Dowd's heroic stand that held a North Vietnamese army battalion at bay until his regiment could arrive and drive the enemy back into Cambodia.

Earl was also aware that as much as the old man tried to hide it, he was too old for running around the North Maine Woods in February. He closed the door that separated the living room from the kitchen and determined that if his father was still asleep when Buster and Louis arrived, he'd leave the old-timer to rest and he and his boys would continue the hunt alone. Earl dropped into a chair and finished his coffee. He yawned and thought: *Christ, my ass is dragging too—how in hell does the old man do it?*

Hafford Pond

Askook heard the whine of approaching snowmobiles and peered out the window in time to see two Arctic Cats stop outside his cabin. Even before the riders removed their dark glasses he recognized Buster and

Louis Dowd. He reached up and took his .357 revolver off the peg where he kept it. A visit from the Dowds was never a good thing. Before they dismounted their sleds, he opened the door and stepped outside. "What you boys want?"

"That ain't no way to greet company, Askook," Buster said.

"Ain't no way I'll ever consider you Dowds to be company. So, state your business and be gone."

"My boy's gone missing," Buster said.

"You think I got him? Well, I don't."

"We was wondering if you *found* him. His sled broke down sometime yesterday afternoon. We ain't been able to find no sign of him and any tracks he may have left were buried under the snow."

Askook relaxed and asked, "You notify the wardens? Lost people is their job."

"That Indian warden, Bear, is helpin' us. He ain't said as much, but I believe he thinks that whoever has Dwain may be the killer that's been killin' folks all over the area."

The Wendigo. Askook kept his thoughts to himself. *Wouldn't be the first time a Wendigo kept a victim to feed on later.*

"Well, all I can tell you is I ain't seen neither the boy or the killer. If I do I'll shoot the killer and send the boy home."

Buster and Louis stared at Askook for several moments. "You do that," Buster said. He put his glasses on and said, "Don't suppose you'd let us take a look around?"

"You can look inside."

When the Dowds dismounted, Askook pointed at Buster. "*You.* Not both."

Louis retook his seat on his sled, unzipped his suit, reached inside, and took out a pack of cigarettes. He placed one in his mouth and turned into the wind. He cupped his hands and bent over as he lit the smoke.

Buster gave Askook a wide berth as he entered the cabin. In no time he reappeared. He returned to his machine and straddled the seat. "He ain't in there," he told his brother without taking his eyes off Askook.

Louis took a deep draught of smoke then threw his cigarette into the snow. He looked as if he might decide to try something stupid.

Askook looked at the sky. "Won't be long till it's dark. You boys should be headin' back, don't yuh think?"

Buster started his motor and revved the motor. Louis did the same. Buster put his transmission into gear, spun around, and rode off with his brother behind.

T20, R12

The Wendigo felt the onslaught of hunger. He walked away from the boy who slept in the abandoned lean-to they had found. The Wendigo became aware of the hum of a plane flying overhead and looked toward the southeast. In summer it wouldn't cause him any concern, but it was February and the deciduous trees had long since shed their leaves, making it easy for an airborne observer to see through the trees. The drone of the motor became louder and he knew that he had little if any time left.

The plane appeared in the early morning sky. It dipped its wings and flew directly over his head. If the pilot notified the authorities of the location, the Wendigo's exit route to Quebec would be cut off. It had to get to the border between Kelly Rapids where there was a shallow place where the St. Francis River could be forded, once in Canada it would be easy to disappear.

The more he thought of Quebec, the more the Wendigo believed that to reach it was to reach safety. He returned to the sleeping boy and woke him up. The youngster was intelligent. He immediately mounted the sled and tried to start it. The motor refused to start. The boy unscrewed the gas cap and peered into the gas tank. "Out of gas," he said.

The Wendigo grabbed him and swung him onto his back and then ran into the woods.

Sébastien Lavallée banked the Cessna and stared down through the trees. Against the white backdrop of the forest floor he easily spotted the gargantuan figure standing beside a snowmobile. There was no doubt that he had found the man he and John had seen at Viverette Settlement.

Lavallée circled around and dropped down to get a closer look. Another figure appeared from some type of shelter and mounted the sled. He banked the plane into an even tighter turn and reduced throttle as much as he dared. He saw the giant grab the second figure, which by now he was certain was the Dowd kid, and run off into the woods.

He straightened the aircraft and keyed his microphone. He contacted the warden service's seaport base on Eagle Lake and requested they connect him with John Bear. Once the connection was made, he said, "John, I found the boy. He's about ten miles north of Hafford Pond."

T19, R12

John Bear raced along Estcourt Road. He was traveling at speeds he would not have been able to attain if the road had not been plowed; the hardpan snow filled in most of the potholes. His primary concern was that he'd meet a log truck on one of the turns. He saw a long straightaway before the sled and opened the throttle until the speedometer on the sled indicated sixty miles per hour. He'd placed the coordinates Sébastien had given him into his GPS and knew he was ten miles away. A feeling of incredible urgency came over him and he opened the throttle further.

T20, R12

John stopped beside the abandoned machine. He followed the smaller set of tracks into a copse of bushes and found a crude and obviously old lean-to. Fresh pine boughs covered the floor and he knew that Dwain Dowd had slept there. He saw no sign of the Wendigo having slept and he marveled at its stamina. John had slept for five hours the previous night and after his ride at breakneck speed was exhausted. He thought that an hour on those boughs would be bliss. He quickly removed his helmet and scooped a handful of snow. He washed his face with the frozen water and shook his head to rid himself of the excess.

Feeling temporarily alert, John returned to the abandoned sled and noted its Quebec registration. *Was this Guy Boniface's missing sled?* He walked to the Polaris and saw that the gas cap dangled from the tank by a chain. A quick inspection proved what he expected; Dwain had been riding it and it was out of gas.

He turned and trudged through the shin-deep snow to his sled. He donned his helmet, started the motor, and saw the Wendigo's tracks heading north, toward the Canadian border. John followed.

Hafford Pond

Megedagik Askook watched the Dowds depart and began gathering the gear he'd need to spend a prolonged period in the woods. He took his lever-action .308 rifle out of the corner where he stored it, even though he knew it would have little, if any, effect on the creature he would be hunting. He'd long suspected the area was the hunting ground of a Wendigo, but never before had he possessed enough proof to take action. When Buster and Louis Dowd arrived at his cabin doing everything but accusing him outright of the abduction of Buster's son, Askook knew he had to do what he could to stop the Wendigo. The Dowds were under the misguided impression that they sought a man, not the most evil of manitous.

Askook knew that the Wendigo would try to find sanctuary in the vast wilderness of Quebec. If he was still alive, the Dowd boy would slow it down and force the Wendigo to stick to trails over which the boy could travel. He also knew that due to recent weather conditions and snow accumulation there was only a single trail that would allow them to easily cross the St. Francis River into Canada. All he had to do was beat them there and wait. They would be coming sooner or later.

He carried his provisions to his snowmobile and straddled the machine. He sat on the seat and his legs almost obscured the machine. He looked like a teenager riding his six-year-old sister's bike. He started the motor and headed north.

29

Dowd Settlement

The sound of snowmobiles woke Earl Dowd and he leapt up from the chair in which he'd been dozing. He walked onto the porch and watched as his sons, Buster and Louis, turned into the yard. Rather than drive into the large barn where they normally stored the sleds, they drove up to the porch and shut off their motors.

Earl said: "You find the boy?"

Buster was the first off his sled. "No, Dad. Askook may be nuttier than a loon but he ain't had nothin' to do with Dwain."

"So, where does that leave us?"

Earl said, "C'mon in and have something hot. When'd you boys last eat?"

"Ain't had nothin' since before we left here yesterday," Louis said.

Earl nodded. "There's hot stew in the kitchen." He walked inside the main house and saw Amy standing on the stairway that led to the bedrooms on the second floor.

Her hair was disheveled and her eyes puffy from sleep. "They find Dwain?" she asked.

"No. I need you to cook up something. We're gonna eat and then me and the boys are goin' back out."

"What about Grampa?"

"He ain't up to it. . . ."

"The hell I ain't," Linwood Dowd protested. "I'll be goin' long after you and your boys have quit."

"Dad, I ain't sayin' you aren't in good shape for your *age*, but yesterday damned near killed you. You ain't nineteen anymore and that ain't no tropical jungle out there. You're damn near seventy and we're goin' to be pushing hard in below-zero temperatures."

The old man stood still, his fists clenched. However, the expression on his face told Earl that the old man was secretly thankful to have someone else make the decision. Still he protested. "Earl, I'm still the head of this family—"

"Yes," Earl said, "you are, and that's all the more reason why you should stay here and keep things together."

Earl looked at his sister. "Let's feed the boys and then let them get a couple hours' rest. I want us to be back out on the trail by seven."

T20, R12

The boy was awake and alert; the meal had revived him as the Wendigo knew it would. With each passing meal he was becoming stronger. Wendigo concentrated on the trail ahead as he ran through the soft snow. If he had not had to stop to feed the boy, they would be safely in Canada. He paused at the top of a ridge and looked into the valley below; on the precipice of the horizon he saw the glow of headlights and shrugged. The Wendigo knew the pursuit was the Indian warden and that he was following the trail. The Wendigo concentrated on the business at hand. There was no recourse but to leave a trail for the warden to follow. He dismissed the warden who was rushing to his death. He turned and in the distance could see the St. Francis River and Quebec beyond.

Suddenly, a tall man stepped from the woods beside the trail. He held a rifle and had covered himself with Anishinaubae symbols to ward off evil manitous, such as the Wendigo.

The Wendigo lifted Dwain from his back and placed him to one side. He motioned for him to step aside and turned to face the fool in the trail.

Askook was tall, but his height did not compare to that of his opponent. "Give me the boy and you may pass," he said.

The Wendigo responded with booming claps of thunder that sent waves of fear through Askook. Askook swallowed his fear and said, "Give me the boy, before it is too late for him."

The Wendigo took a menacing step forward, the talons on the end of his fingers shined in the dwindling sunlight, and displayed a malformed mouthful of jagged teeth and bellowed again.

Askook removed the rifle from the crook of his arm and aimed it at the Wendigo's chest. "I know what you are and I also know what is required to kill you."

The Wendigo ignored the warning and suddenly his torso became obscured by black storm clouds and the temperature dropped so fast that Askook saw two massive trees split with deafening cracks.

Askook felt an icy terror that threatened to consume his soul. With more bravado than he felt, he said, "I will kill your physical form, cut out your heart of ice, and will throw it in a great fire."

The Wendigo closed with Askook, who raised the rifle and fired without aiming. The silver bullet passed through Wendigo's side rather than hitting a vital place.

Surprised by the pain the bullet caused, the Wendigo stumbled. He quickly regained his feet and turned his attention to Askook. A whirling storm cloud enveloped the monster from its waist up and the temperature around him plummeted further. The wind increased from a gentle breeze into a driving blizzard. Driving putrid odor and chill before it, death charged out of the killing blizzard.

Askook levered the spent cartridge out of the chamber and loaded a second. He pulled the trigger and the weapon failed to fire. He turned the rifle, grabbing it by the barrel and, when the Wendigo was within reach, swung it with all his might. He stepped into the swing like a major league power-hitter swinging for a home run and drove the butt upward into its ribs.

Askook swung again and slammed the rifle into the Wendigo again. There was a loud crack and the rifle butt separated from the barrel and spun away, disappearing in the deep snow. He threw the useless rifle barrel into the snow and held his left hand in front of his body, hoping to ward off his attacker while he reached for his knife with his right.

The cold enveloped Askook and before he knew it he was in the grasp of the Wendigo. His talons raked along Askook's ribs and finally freed his knife from its sheath. The horrible serpentine face of the beast lowered, seeking Askook's neck. The fangs pulled back when the weakening man drove his knife upward through the bottom of the beast's chin. The Wendigo threw the Indian and was rewarded when Askook slammed into a large beech tree and yelled out in pain.

The Wendigo stepped forward preparing to finish the man.

Askook scrambled to his feet, holding his damaged side with one hand and his bowie knife poised to strike in the other.

The Wendigo was momentarily perplexed. *How was it that this man's weapons were capable of inflicting so much pain?* The knife blade flashed and the answer came: *Silver. . . . This one knew how to kill him!*

Askook went on the offensive and slashed its forearm. Blood flew through the air and stained the snow.

The Wendigo bellowed and then counterattacked with renewed vigor, driving Askook backward.

He grabbed Askook's throat with his left hand and drove the talons on the right hand deep into Askook's belly.

Askook grunted, bent forward, and backed up a step, freeing himself from the horrible claws.

The Wendigo stepped forward and retracted his hand from the Indian's stomach and then drove his talons into the Indian's chest. He shoved the hand deeper in the cavity, probing for the hammering heart with icy fingers.

The Wendigo dropped his vanquished foe onto his knees, stepped back, and glared at him.

Askook's knife dropped from his bloody hand as he stared up at his killer.

The Wendigo's triumphant roar echoed through the forest. He reached out and grabbed a handful of the dying man's hair and prepared to butcher him. But before he could strike, a snowmobile raced up behind him. He spun around and saw the warden racing up the ridge and motioned for the boy to come to him.

Rather than obey, the boy stood still, staring at the Indian who lay face down in the snow. The Indian's body was covered by a cloud of steam caused by the heat flowing out of his body. Suddenly Dwain spun and ran toward the approaching sled.

The Wendigo ignored the boy and stepped over the vanquished man's body. Askook rolled aside before the Wendigo could step on him and lay in the snow, staring at the darkening sky.

John Bear saw the Wendigo run away. Its speed astonished him; in three strides it was moving so fast that it was difficult to see. John gave up thoughts of pursuit and ran to Askook's aid. The amount of blood in the snow told him that there was no hope of saving the trapper. He raised the dying man's head and smiled when Askook said, "I held him as long as I could—what kept you? It was a Wendigo."

"I know," John said.

"I was wrong."

"About what?"

"Obviously these stupid Anishinaubae talismans and dream catchers ain't worth shit."

John couldn't help but smile again. "I don't know about that. I think you hurt him."

"Take my knife—rifle's broke."

John reached into the snow and picked up the bowie knife. "It's a nice blade," he said.

"Blade's coated in silver. Like werewolves, Wendigo don't like silver. . . . Don't try to arrest him. You know what you have to do." Askook's eyes glazed over and he was dead.

"He fought hard. . . ."

John turned to find Dwain Dowd standing behind him.

"You going after him?" Dwain asked.

"No, I have to get you home. Did he hurt you?"

"Naw. He took good care of me. You goin' after him?"

"I'd like nothing better, but I have to take care of Askook and I have to get you home." John looked around the area and added, "Did you see how Askook got here? He must have a sled someplace nearby."

"Didn't see nothin'—he stepped out of the trees over there—" he pointed to a spot in front of their position, "and stood in the middle of the trail when we got here."

"Well, what you say we check the area out a bit."

30

John Bear heard the sleds before he saw them, but once they rounded the curve in the trail he knew it was a posse consisting entirely of Dowds. Earl Dowd raised an arm and the following riders halted. Earl peered at John. "That my grandson behind you?"

"Yeah."

"Whose sled is he riding?"

"Askook's."

"So it was that asshole who had the boy."

John stepped off his sled and removed his helmet. "No. Something else had the boy, Askook stopped it."

Earl nodded. "I didn't think Askook was involved." He looked around the area. "How come Dwain is riding alone? Where's Askook? We owe him."

John placed his helmet on the seat of his sled. "You boys wouldn't happen to have a thermos of hot coffee would you?"

Earl lifted the seat of his sled and reached inside the storage compartment. He extracted a thermos and offered it to John. He stood silently as the warden twisted the cap off, removed the stopper, and poured coffee into the cap.

A small cloud of steam formed above the hot black beverage and John took a drink. The strong drink warmed him as it moved down his throat. He swallowed, handed the thermos to Earl, and said, "You're too late." He pointed to the eight-foot-long trapper sled attached to the rear of his sled. "That's Askook's sleigh—he's inside. The kidnapper killed him."

"Where's the kidnapper now?"

John swallowed the rest of the coffee and handed the cap/cup back to Earl, who screwed it onto the thermos. "Don't know. I came on them just as the fight was ending and it took off. I would imagine that by now it's either in Quebec or Estcourt Station—either way it's trying to get to Canada."

"You keep saying *it*, like this *thing* ain't human. What's that all about?"

John wasn't sure that the Dowds were ready to hear the truth so he tried to evade answering. "That's a subject for later."

Earl gave him a quizzical look, but obviously decided to let it lie.

Buster and Louis Dowd dismounted from their sleds and walked to their father's side. "You didn't go after him?" Buster asked.

"Nope. Askook was still alive when I arrived. Once he was dead I figured gettin' Dwain back was more important."

Earl nodded. "We appreciate that. We'll take him home."

"May want to have him checked out by a doctor," John said. "He's been out in the cold for most of two days."

Buster looked at his son. "You okay?"

"Yes, just a little hungry," Dwain answered.

"Okay, we'll take him from here, Warden." Earl turned to his sons "Guess our job here is done. Mount up and we'll get him home and feed him."

John said, "Take the sled with you. We'll want to talk with Dwain in detail later."

"You goin' after *it*?" Earl asked.

"Not much sense in it today." John replied. "I got to get Askook back to Lyndon and notify the RCMP and U.S. Customs to be on the watch—and to be careful, it's dangerous, crazy, and running scared. That's a potentially lethal combination no matter what you're dealin' with."

Earl nodded and then turned away. In seconds the posse had turned around and was headed back toward Dowd Settlement. John stepped aside as Dwain passed him on Askook's sled. The boy didn't acknowledge him as he passed. John Bear stood in the knee-deep snow and listened to the dying sounds of their motors.

Little Black Checkpoint

Once John Bear was within range of a cellular tower, he called for assistance and Larry Murphy, Bob Pelky, and an ambulance were waiting for him when he reached the small cabin that served as gateway to the northwestern section of Maine's north woods. Once Askook's body was transferred from the trapper sleigh to the ambulance, the three law enforcement agents entered the small shack. The warm interior made John aware of how fatigued he was. He'd had at most five hours of sleep in the last forty-eight hours and knew he had to get some sleep soon or he'd be useless.

Murphy poured three cups of coffee from the urn and handed one to John and another to Pelky. "The authorities on both sides of the border have been notified to be on the lookout for this thing."

"You emphasize how dangerous he is?"

"Definitely," Murphy said. "It was a bit uncomfortable when they asked for a description and when I gave it to them, the silence on the line was deafening."

"The state police are also on the lookout," Pelky said. "We've contacted the FBI because of the international implications. This is turning into one hell of a manhunt."

John drank the coffee and with his free hand rubbed his eyes, which were beginning to feel like two hot coals. "If it reached the Slash and crossed the border into Quebec, it could be anywhere. The only thing stopping it from getting access to the entire continent is the Saint Lawrence River."

"Something tells me," Pelky added, "that we haven't seen the last of this thing."

"In a way part of me hopes we have," John said. "Too many people have been its victims already—and who knows how many vics there are that we've never heard about."

"If nothing else," Murphy said, "his unusual culinary requirements should expose him sooner or later."

"Like I said," John intoned, "I hope we don't hear about it—in the meantime, I'm headed to my brother's place. I need sleep."

Big Twenty Township

The Wendigo followed the snowmobile until he heard the motor shut down. Another motor was running nearby and he followed his prey's tracks until he came to a lake. The prey was using a power auger to cut ice fishing holes in the ice. An hour later the Wendigo was feeding.

The Wendigo's arm ached where the Indian had cut it, but the bleeding had stopped and the gash was already healing. He walked along the top of the ridge, surveying the terrain for any landmark that would help determine his position. All he knew was that the St. Francis River, Maine's northern border with Quebec, was to his north. There were three towns in the vicinity: Rivière-Bleue, Estcourt Station, and Pohénégamook in Quebec. He was certain that he was west of Rivière-Bleue, but not certain if Kelly Rapids was close by, or if he was west of that too, which made Pohénégamook in Quebec and Estcourt Station in Maine the best options.

The more he pondered, the more confused he became. He started following the trail. He listened to the sounds around him as he walked.

Hungry again, he hoped to hear the drone of another solitary snowmobile rider but heard nothing but the sound of trees swaying in the freezing wind and the raucous cawing of crows and ravens. He walked on.

St. Francis River, Border of Maine and Quebec, Canada

The Wendigo came upon the river and checked the area before crossing. He saw a car with a light bar race by on the highway in Canada. A sound above made him look up and he saw a small aircraft flying along the river on the American side. He had no doubt that they were looking for something—and that that something was him. Obviously, alerts and warnings had been sent to law enforcement agencies in both countries. Escape was not going to be as easy as he thought.

The Wendigo moved away from the river, back into the safety and concealment of the trees. He needed transportation. There were hundreds of miles of border south of Pohénégamook and most of it was uninhabited.

Fort Kent, Maine

John Bear felt lousy. He'd returned to his brother's house and slept for three hours, but that was nowhere near enough. Tom had woken him up at one o'clock holding a cordless house phone. That was when John learned that a task force consisting of the RCMP, Maine State Police and Warden Service, and ICE had been formed. Law enforcement was pulling out all the stops in the manhunt for the Wendigo, which they were now calling the North Woods Killer. John entered the customs building and introduced himself to one of the customs agents. The agent directed him to follow a short corridor to a conference room where everyone was gathering.

When he entered the room he saw Larry Murphy and Bob Pelky already seated at a long rectangular conference table. He took a seat beside them. Pelky looked at him and said, "Jesus, John, you look like warmed-over shit."

"You think things look bad where you're sitting," John wisecracked back. "You should be sitting here looking out."

"You get any rest?" Murphy asked.

"A couple hours . . . what's up?"

"I think," Pelky said, "that this investigation is about to be taken out of our hands."

John leaned forward, rested his left elbow on the table and massaged his burning eyes with his left thumb and index finger. "That's all I need right now."

Over the course of the next fifteen minutes the room began filling up with various law enforcement people—many of whom John knew and greeted. Finally, Lieutenant Aurel Michaud, senior warden in charge of the Ashland Regional Headquarters, walked in and all conversation in the room ceased. Michaud walked to the front of the room and stood behind the podium at the head of the conference table. "Good afternoon," he said. Michaud turned his attention to John. "How you feeling, John? I hear you've had a tough few days."

John smiled and said, "I'll be fine Lieutenant—nothing a few days rest won't fix—once we bring this killer in."

"That," Michaud said, "is why we're here. To put our heads together and figure out how we're gonna catch this fucker."

John sat to Michaud's left and wondered if the senior warden had any clue what they were dealing with.

"ICE will be monitoring the border along with our aircraft out of Eagle Lake. Customs agents in both Maine and the Canadian provinces of New Brunswick and Quebec have been notified to be on alert for him." He turned toward Pelky and continued, "The Maine State Police will be watching all the roads between here and Patton, in the event he tries to escape to the south."

"We've been able to track this perp back to when he was a kid, down in the Swedish Colony. His father was brutally murdered and the kid disappeared. From what we can piece together, the old man was an abusive drunk. Beat the hell out of the kid for the slightest thing. Kid grew up and must have gone into one hell of a rage. He ripped the old man, one Wally Condor, to pieces. The body wasn't discovered for five days and no one has seen the kid since the day of the murder—until now."

John sat back lost in thought. If Paul Condor had become the Wendigo, he had been one for so long that not a single vestige of Condor remained. Rather than open himself up to verbal ridicule he opted to keep the true identity of the killer to himself. "What I don't understand," John Bear said, "is how these disappearances have gone unreported all this time. At the rate this is going we should have been swamped with missing persons reports and constant search missions."

"We're looking into that."

The meeting was interrupted by a knock at the door. A young woman in a customs uniform walked to the front of the room and handed Michaud a pink message slip. He thanked her and read the slip. He addressed the meeting, John and Murphy in particular.

"They found a body they think may be another of Condor's vics about ten miles east of Estcourt Station. John, you and Murph should head up there after the meeting. I'll have a CSI team meet you there."

Michaud concluded the meeting by asking if anyone had any questions. He then singled out John Bear and Murphy. "You guys done yeoman's work on this. If you hadn't, this guy would still be unknown to everyone."

This guy and what he's become, John thought, *is still unknown to most of you. . . .*

31

Big Twenty Township

John Bear and Murphy studied the gigantic footprints in the snow. "At least we haven't had a snowfall since it took off on foot," Murphy commented.

"Don't sell it short, Murph. We ain't dealin' with a normal perp here."

"John you ain't believing that this is one of them . . . what did you call it?"

"A Wendigo. Doesn't matter what I believe—it is what it is and that's what should concern us."

Murphy nodded. "Either way, what we got here is one big sumbitch who just happens to be a psycho."

"Believe what you will, Murph, but I'm not gonna sell it short." John returned to his snowmobile. "Let's see where the bastard went. Shall we?"

They followed the tracks as they skirted the St. Francis River, all the while headed toward Estcourt Station. The going was slow as they had to weave through trees and break their own trail, all the while keeping the mammoth footprints in sight. When the tracks left the trees and entered Airport Road they knew they'd lost him. "Tell you what," Murphy said. "You head west and I'll go east, maybe we'll pick up his trail again."

John Bear was looking at the sky over the road to the west. A murder of crows was swarming around the woods. "I don't think there's any need of that. Follow me."

They walked down the road a hundred yards and stopped. John stepped into the woods and the trees exploded with crows taking flight.

When Murphy reached John's side, he said, "Jesus, John, look at all the blood. You suppose it's . . . ?"

"It's arterial." John pointed to a long stream of blood that looked as if someone had shot it from a hose. He followed the blood trail deeper into the trees and found a copse of leafless red willow bushes. John called out to Murphy, "We got another victim."

Murphy followed, taking care to step in the tracks John had made. He found John squatting in the thicket, staring at a body. John looked up when his companion stopped beside him. Murphy's face contorted when he looked at the body. "Sonuvabitch," he said.

John picked up the dead man's hands. "He ain't been here long, rigor ain't full."

Murphy looked at the body. It had been eviscerated and there were various organs lying in the three-foot-deep snow. "Was he . . . ?"

"Eaten? Yes. His neck's been bitten open, that was the arterial blood we saw."

Murphy squatted beside John and said, "It's as if he was killed kosher."

John stared at Murphy for a second trying to determine if he was trying to be funny or if he was merely stating an observation. He decided that it was the latter.

"You think animals got to him?"

"He hasn't been here that long, but if he lies here much longer . . ."

"I know, I got to wait for crime scene. I'm starting to feel like the cadaver recovery unit of the warden service."

It took an hour for the crime scene technicians to process the scene. As limited as they were by the snow, cold, and terrain they gathered as much forensic evidence as possible. The only evidence they had on the killer was the gigantic tracks they photographed, hoping to match the tread to pictures they'd taken at the other crime scenes and around the shack in Viverette Settlement.

When the sound of the departing helicopter diminished, John announced, "I might as well go back with you. This trail has been beaten down so much I'll never determine which way it went."

32

Junction of Little Black River and Johnson Brook, Allagash, Maine

The Wendigo threw the bone into the trees. The femur was the last of his larder and already the never-ending hunger was driving him mad. No matter how much or how often he fed, the hunger was always there; the more he ate, the more he wanted to eat. To be a Wendigo was to be continuously on the hunt.

He stared at the open area where the summer hunt was always good. The site of a trailerable boat launch, there were always fishermen and campers here, but not in winter. In winter the lakes with their supply of solitary ice fishermen were a much better hunting ground. He stood and turned toward Dowd Settlement. Due to recent events he'd never be safe to hunt the area—they'd always be looking for him. He also knew that no matter what he'd never be able to hunt anonymously again. The Wendigo knew that his only chance of survival was to run; hide in the deep woods southwest of Allagash.

Dowd Settlement

Amy Dowd met John Bear in front of Linwood's house. "Mornin', Warden." Her body language and smile surprised him. Prior to his finding her nephew, he'd thought that the Dowds would never trust anyone in law enforcement, let alone a warden.

"Good morning, Amy. Any of the men around?"

"They ain't far."

"Well, I thought I'd stop by and see how Dwain was doing."

"He's . . ."

"Amy, who you talkin' to?" said a third voice from inside the house. In a few seconds, Earl Dowd appeared in the threshold of the door. "John," he said.

John stepped onto the porch. "I came by to see how the boy is doing."

"You get the bastard?" Earl asked.

"No, he killed a snowmobiler and took off into the deep woods. We lost him not far from Estcourt."

"I'll bet you guys are surprised when you find your fuckin' shoes in the morning."

"There are times when I surprise myself," John said.

"Who's that in your truck?" Amy asked.

John motioned and Laura Wells got out of the truck. "This is Laura Wells. She's a newspaper reporter who's writing a story about the hunt for this killer."

Earl turned his attention to Wells. "You gonna write about Dwain?"

"I was hoping to get to interview him," she said.

Earl stepped aside allowing them access to the house. "You want some coffee?"

"Sure, I'd like that," Laura said.

"C'mon in."

John and Laura followed Earl inside, with Amy following. After the subzero temperature of the outside, the fires from two fireplaces and a woodstove made the interior of the log house seem like a blast furnace and they took off their heavy parkas. Earl and Amy pointed to a couch in front of the hearth. "Have a seat," Amy said. "How do you like your coffee?"

"Black," John and Laura said in unison.

Earl sat in a recliner chair to their right.

"How's your father?" John asked.

"Not good. He ain't no spring chicken and all the commotion with Dwain taxed him a mite. He's been taken abed for the past two days."

"How is Dwain doing?" Wells asked.

"Seems okay, although he's took up some queer habits."

"Queer habits?" John asked. "What sort of queer habits?"

"Hates coming inside the house, says it's too hot for him. Last night he snuck out of the house and slept in the barn."

Amy came in carrying a tray with four cups of coffee on it. "You talking about Dwain?" she asked.

"Yup," Earl said, "I was tellin' them that since he got home he's been acting sort of weird."

"Well Dad, keep in mind that he went through a lot. After all, he's still a boy," Amy replied, trying to defend her nephew. "He'll be all right with time."

"He ain't had no appetite either," Earl added. "He don't snap out of it soon his father will take him over his knee."

"He's not your grandson?" Laura asked.

"My son, Buster, is his father," Earl said.

Laura took a notebook from her bag and jotted notes as Dowd spoke. "How is his mother reacting to this?"

"She don't live with us. She and Buster divorced." He turned to Amy, "Five years ago I think it was."

Amy nodded her head in affirmation.

"She was from away—" he made the comment as if it explained every-thing, "and wasn't able to adjust to life here."

"Where was she from?" Wells asked.

"Over by St. Francis."

John had to suppress a laugh. St. Francis was less than thirty miles away. But to the Dowds it may as well have been in South America.

Laura drank some coffee and placed the mug on the coffee table in front of them. "Is it possible to talk with him?"

"I got some questions I need answered too," John added.

Earl became suspicious and said, "If we can stay."

"Of course," Laura said.

John gave her a stern look. He'd hoped to get the boy alone, away from family where he may open up more freely. He turned toward Earl and saw stubbornness in the set of Dowd's jaw. "I have no problem with that," he said.

Dowd turned toward his sister and said, "See if you can find the boy." When Amy left he turned to John and Laura. "Don't be surprised if we have to go outside to talk with him. Like I said, since we got him home he can't stand heat."

Amy returned five minutes after she'd left—alone.

"Where's Dwain?" Earl asked.

"He won't come in. He said he'll talk with them but only if they come out to the barn where it's cool."

"Cool?" Earl said, his face red with anger. "Cool! It's ten below zero out there."

I'm sorry, Dad, but that's what he said."

"That's fine," Laura said. "We'll go out there, won't we John?"

John Bear agreed, but he was beginning to be concerned about the boy and his obvious aversion to anything approaching warmth. They donned their coats and followed Amy outside. Snow and ice crunched beneath their feet as they crossed the open yard. With each breath steam hung in the air before their faces and the moisture in John's nose froze.

The interior of the barn was dark and almost as cold as outside. Dwain Dowd stood well back in the dark recesses of the first floor. The smell of hay, old oil, and diesel fuel permeated the atmosphere. This was not an unused building. When they approached Dwain, John could see a gleam in the boy's eyes that had not been there yesterday. What really struck him was that he was certain Dwain Dowd had grown at least an inch, maybe even two or three in twenty-four hours. He looked at Amy with a quizzical look. Her only answer was to shrug her shoulders.

Dwain circled around and sat on a frozen bale of hay. "Hi, Warden," the boy said.

John Bear wasn't certain what to expect, but after rescuing Dwain he expected more than an aloof *Hi*. "Dwain. I have some questions to ask you," he said.

"I'll try to answer them." He looked at Laura.

"This is Laura Wells," John said, "she's a friend of mine who writes for the newspapers downstate."

"Hello, Dwain," Laura said. She held her hand out.

Dwain stared at the proffered hand but did not reach for it.

After several moments, Laura dropped her hand.

"So," Dwain said, "who's asking the questions?"

"Since this an active investigation, I am," John Bear said.

Dwain nodded and John noticed that as cold as it was the boy's coat was open and all he wore underneath was a thin undershirt. "How did you come to be with him?"

"I was going to see my friend, Murdock . . ."

"That would be Murdock Cochran?" John interjected.

"Yeah."

"Go on," John said.

"The old man . . . my father . . . didn't want me to go so I snuck out and left quick, never thought to check the gas and oil in my sled. The motor seized when I was just over halfway there. I figured that I was closer to the Cochran's than home and started walkin'. I got really cold and built a shelter by a fallen tree. I fell asleep and when I woke up I was in a cabin."

"Did he . . . ," John paused while he thought about the right way to ask what he was about to ask, ". . . harm you in any way?"

"No, he treated me real good, fed me and everything."

"Really?" John asked, curious now. "What did he feed you?"

"Gave me some meat to eat."

"Did he," John asked, "give you any indication of where he was headed?"

"He didn't talk. When he tried all he could do was roar really loud."

"He didn't hurt you in any way?" Laura asked.

"No, he was fine, until that crazy Indian attacked him and you come along. He took off—I think he run because he thought you'd arrest him, even though that fella he killed attacked him first. I hope he comes back—he's a really nice guy."

Big Twenty Township

Having eaten the last of his most recent kills, the Wendigo debated its options: one was to follow the Estcourt Road south and try to cross the border somewhere along the Slash. There was no way the cops could put a barrier and watch the entirety of the border and he could disappear into the hundreds of square miles of Canadian wilderness. His other option was to return to Lyndon Station—the last thing they would expect. He could go to Dowd Settlement and get the boy. He was surprised to realize that he missed the boy. . . . Maybe the boy would come with him willingly. If he didn't, it would be easy to take him.

Condor quickly made up his mind. He turned and headed south toward Dowd Settlement.

33

Dowd Settlement

Dwain felt his presence before he saw the immense figure framed by the light of the open door and he immediately knew who it was. He stood and ran to the silhouette and wrapped his arms around his waist. "I knew you'd come for me," he said.

The Wendigo turned and motioned for Dwain to follow him out into the frigid night. They crossed the open yard and entered the woods behind the log house. The behemoth broke a trail through the snow making it easy for Dwain. The unlikely duo crossed the open ground and disappeared into the primordial night.

Amy Dowd picked up the plate and, before walking to the barn, checked the temperature on the thermometer that hung outside the kitchen window—minus twenty degrees Fahrenheit. She shook her head, wondering how Dwain had been able to spend the night in the unheated barn. She left the warmth of the house, wrapping her coat tightly around her as she walked to the barn. The distance was short, not more than fifty feet, but by the time she got to the door her toes were stinging from the cold and her nose felt frozen. She saw a huge footprint in the snow that had mounded up in the threshold and her heart skipped. She darted inside and called out, "Dwain! I've got your breakfast. . . ." When she received no answer, she placed the dish on a bale of hay and searched the barn. Dwain was nowhere to be found. She grabbed the plate of now frozen eggs and ran back to the house. She placed the plate on a table beside one of the recliners and climbed the stairs to Dwain's bedroom. She opened the door and saw that the room had not been slept in nor was there any sign of her nephew. She ran down the stairs and into the kitchen, where her family sat at the table drinking their morning coffee. "Dwain is gone!"

Linwood looked at her and said, "What you mean *gone*?"

"Gone, he's not in the barn, he's not in his room, he's not nowhere."

Earl looked up. "You searched everywhere?"

"Only the barn and his room."

Linwood addressed the rest of the family. "I want every inch of this place searched." He directly spoke to Buster: "If that kid run off again, you better wear his ass out when we get him back. Now get to it."

"There's one other thing," Amy said, "I saw a giant footprint headed into the barn."

Earl, Buster, and Louis leapt to their feet, and Buster's chair fell over backward with a resounding *bang*. He stopped by the hearth and took a lever-action Savage .30–30 from the gun rack on the wall and grabbed a box of 170 grain cartridges. He fed ammunition into the rifle as he walked to the barn. Louis had also armed himself with a .44 Magnum revolver and was behind him. As they rushed inside the barn Buster said to his brother, "You check the loft, I'll look around here."

Louis walked to the threshold and studied the massive track in the snow. "That motherfucker come and took him."

Buster stood beside his brother, "Better get some food inside us, we're in for a long day. . . ."

Lyndon Station

John was having breakfast at Del's when Murphy walked in and sat across from him. "You heard?" he asked John.

"Yup, Amy called me a half hour ago."

"What's our game plan?"

"The first thing we got to do," John said, "is keep the Dowds from chasing after him—we don't need no vigilantes running around the woods, messing up any trail there might be."

"Unless I miss my guess," Murphy said, "we're already too late for that. Earl and his boys are most likely already on the hunt."

"You're right." John drank the last of his coffee and stood up. "We'd better get our asses out there."

Dowd Settlement

When John and Murphy arrived at the Dowd compound, Amy met them in the yard. "They left after him over an hour ago."

"Who went?"

"Everyone, including my grandfather."

John said nothing but was hopeful that the old man would slow them down a bit. He looked toward the back of the house and saw where several sleds had gone off into the woods. "That where they went?" John asked.

Amy nodded.

"Let's off-load our sleds, Murph."

The wardens took their snowmobiles out of the beds of their state-issued pickup trucks and then moved the trucks off to the side of the barn. They donned their cold-weather gear and started the snowmobile motors. After a few moments they took off after the Dowd posse.

They followed the trail about two hundred yards into the woods where they found the tracks. John and Murphy turned onto the path beaten into the snow by the Dowds and accelerated.

34

Little Black River, T19, R12

John Bear saw the Dowds ahead and gave his throttle a twist, sending him speeding forward. He passed the last sled in the line and recognized Louis Dowd. He believed that Earl and Linwood rode the two lead sleds. As he came abreast of the first sled, he motioned the driver to stop. As soon as the convoy halted and Murphy joined them, John removed his helmet and the lead Dowd rider did the same.

"Earl, what in hell do you think you're doing?" John inquired.

"I'm going after my grandson—*again*."

"This ain't the way to do it, man. It's a police matter and we'll take care of it."

Linwood Dowd sat on the second sled and he said, "*Police matter* my ass. This is a Dowd matter."

Fatigue was evident on the old man's face and John said, "Lin, you ain't up to this. You have heart attack or stroke out here and you'll be dead before they can get anyone to you—then where will your great-grandson be?"

"Fuck you, Bear. I'll be going long after you and these young pups have give out."

John leaned back on his seat. He realized that the Dowds were not about to forego the quest and opted to make the best of a bad thing. "Looks like he's running for Big Black River, and from there he can easily get to the border. How you boys fixed for gas? There ain't no place for fuel between here and St. Pamphile. Most likely, he'll head for St. Pamphile and try and cross over in the wilderness south of there. We've alerted the RCMP, the Border Patrol, and every other agency we could think of. They're patrolling the Slash from the air as well as from the ground, still there're hundreds of places where he can cross and we'd never know it. All that bein' said, why don't you boys head on home and leave this to us. Whether you believe it or not, we know what we're doing."

Murphy sat in awe. Never before had he heard John Bear talk so long. He also saw the Dowds thinking over what they'd been told. *Maybe*, he thought, *they'll listen.* His hopes were dashed when Buster said, "I don't give a shit about what anyone else does, but I'm going after my boy—and when I catch that crazy bastard . . . ," he slid his rifle out of the special scabbard that was mounted to the front of his sled, "I'm gonna kill the sonuvabitch."

"Buster, you do that and I'll have to come after you and place you under arrest."

"Ask me if I give a shit."

John turned to Linwood. "Lin, be rational about this. Go home, before this kills you. If your boy and his sons want to go on I won't stop them, but I don't want to see you die out here."

Linwood Dowd looked at John for a few seconds and then at his sons.

"He's right, Dad," Earl said. "We got to go faster, we don't know how far ahead he is. You'll only slow us down."

John saw a look of resignation cross Linwood's face. He knew the old man was here only because to turn back would be a tremendous loss of face and one thing Old Maine men had plenty of was pride. Linwood had fought valiantly in a faraway war, then returned home to forge Dowd Settlement from primeval forest and then fathered and raised a family on that land. Nevertheless, he was forced to accept the wisdom of Earl's words. He nodded in surrender.

"Okay, you boys go on, I'll head back." He pointed a warning finger at his son. "Earl, you bring that boy back no matter what it takes—or you'll all answer to me." As he made that last statement he looked John Bear squarely in the eye. "That goes for every damned man jack of you."

The senior Dowd turned his Arctic Cat around and headed down the trail they'd cut.

Murphy watched the old man depart and when he was out of sight said, "What do you think, John?"

"I think you should follow him. Once you see that he's safe get in touch with Michaud and tell him what's happened and get an air search going . . . have them place emphasis on the Slash between Lac-de-l'Est and St. Pamphile."

Murphy nodded and set off behind Linwood Dowd.

John turned his attention to Earl and his brothers. "If I can't talk you out of this, we might as well work together. Let's figure out what we're goin' to do."

T18, R13

The Wendigo stood in the trees studying the rudimentary cabin before him. Smoke furled from the chimney and hung low in the air, smelling of the not-unpleasant scent of burning hardwood. He motioned for the boy to join him and together they watched until an elderly man walked out of the cabin and followed a path of packed snow around the side of the cabin. Moments later he returned with his arms full of firewood.

When the man was back inside the cabin, the Wendigo led Dwain to a copse of alders.

"I know," Dwain said, "stay here."

The Wendigo returned to the spot where he'd stood vigil and waited for a few moments before approaching the cabin. Upon reaching the door he saw that it was secured by the simplest of door latches, a metal handle with a flat piece for the thumb to press down, releasing the catch inside. He yelled and kicked it open. The door broke into pieces and he was inside.

In minutes the Wendigo returned to the boy and handed him a piece of raw meat.

Dwain looked ravenous as his teeth ripped into the meat.

John stopped and spied footprints leading out of the trees. The scent of wood smoke was in the air and he removed a Maglite from his storage compartment. He trailed the light along the prints in the snow and followed them. He walked about fifty yards and saw the small cabin. A thin stream of smoke rose from the chimney and the door was either open or missing. As he approached he heard noise inside and he removed his service pistol from its holster. When he was within twenty-five feet of the door, he shined the light inside and called out, "Hello in the cabin . . ."

The only reply he got was a low guttural growl. In the harsh beam of the Maglite, he saw that the door had been smashed into several pieces. He took another step and heard movement inside. Suddenly four shiny dots appeared inside. Whatever the cabin held, predators—coyotes most likely—had found food and they were not about to give up their bounty easily. John stood still, raising the pistol up and aiming it at the door. Two coyotes appeared in the door, their snouts red with whatever they'd been feasting on. John fired a shot into the air and the two canines burst out of the cabin and bounded off into the woods.

John heard noise behind him and then Earl Dowd say, "What you got?"

Without turning, John replied, "Unless I missed my guess, I'd say they stopped here for supper."

They entered the cabin and John shined the Maglite around the interior. When the light beam hit the eviscerated corpse, he heard Earl spin and rush outside. Moments later he heard the unmistakable sound of someone vomiting. He ignored the activity behind him and studied the mess on the table. He'd seen worse carcasses before, but none of them were human. He took out his GPS and made note of the coordinates so that he could either return or send someone to recover the body—or what remained of it.

John turned and walked outside into the night. "Well," he commented, "I guess we aren't spending the night in there."

"No shit," Earl Dowd said.

John walked to his sled, threw one leg over the seat and said, "We need to find some place to settle down for the night—then I need to tell you guys what it is we're chasing."

John Bear and the Dowds found a thick stand of evergreen trees and used the snow-laden lower branches to create cover for themselves. The Dowds had come prepared for a prolonged stay in the woods and in no time had spread tarps on the ground and made crude shelters. Buster had a good-sized fire going, beside which they sat drinking hot coffee while they waited for Earl to finish cooking fish on a camp stove.

Earl turned away from the Coleman stove and used a pair of tongs to pick the hot fish out of the cast-iron skillet he'd cooked them in. When he tossed a portion onto John's plate he asked, "What's gonna happen to this sumbitch when we catch up with him?"

"I won't be able to arrest him," John commented.

"Why not?" Buster queried.

Earl scoffed. "Because some asshole judge will let him out, either on a technicality or he'll let him post bond—then he'll light out for the woods again—probably never again to be found."

John swallowed a mouthful of fish and washed it down with a drink of coffee. "Earl, this thing ain't human—it was once but no more."

"You lace that coffee?" Earl asked.

"Tell me something, you boys have grown up and made your living in these woods, right?"

"So?" Louis said.

"You ever before seen a track like this thing leaves?"

His audience was quiet.

John finished his coffee and reached for the pot. "This thing is old . . . real old. My people have known of its existence since the beginning of time—it's an evil spirit that we call the Wendigo. . . ."

35

T17, R14

The Wendigo looked east, where a distinct dark red slash ran horizontal across a section of the sky. The phenomenon, called the *crack of dawn* by the locals, was a harbinger of the approach of daybreak. He cast a look toward his backtrail, where he knew his pursuers were—and he knew they were coming, his senses told him so. The Indian warden and the boy's people were on his trail. He turned his head and looked at the sleeping boy.

The boy was still weak but there were signs that he was toughening up. Each and every day he was growing. He stared at the boy and wondered what was keeping him from feeding on him. He recalled the way the boy stood when they had first faced each other. The kid was not intimidated at all by the Wendigo's giant stature. He looked at him and showed not so much as the slightest nervousness—the boy had a strong spirit and if there was anything the Wendigo understood it was a strong spirit.

The Wendigo turned back to the east and saw that the light had become a wide swath and had changed from dark red to a lighter hue of pink. It was time to get moving, the boy had slept long enough. If all went as he planned they'd reach Little East Lake by noon. From there it was a short run to the easternmost shore of Lac-de-l'Est and the Quebec border. Once they were out of the soft snow and onto the hard pack and ice of the lake they'd be able to run faster. Once into eastern Quebec with its thousands of square kilometers—he had already started thinking in Canadian measurements—of virgin forest no one would ever find him, ever. The biggest challenge would be getting to the other side of the Saint Lawrence River, but once that had been accomplished there was an open gateway to the Saguenay River and the uninhabited millions of acres of Quebec's interior.

He shook the boy awake.

While the boy stepped off into the deep snow and trees to empty his bladder, the Wendigo took a piece of meat out of the pouch that served as his larder while traveling. When the boy returned, the Wendigo handed him his breakfast and waited as his friend gnawed at the sinewy meat.

Dwain swallowed the last morsel, looked at his mentor and said, "I'm ready. Let's go."

The Wendigo took the boy's hand and effortlessly lifted him onto his back and then loped off into the forest.

T18, R13

John Bear was already up and foraging for fuel for a morning fire when the Dowds shook themselves awake. It was the coldest morning yet and the day showed little promise of warming up. The air seemed crystalline, as if ice floated in it. There was a ground-hugging cold that seemed to penetrate John's bones and he had to force his body to move. He carried the deadwood he found back to the campsite and squatted down to start a fire. His cold, stiff legs ached and seemed to cry out for a return to the comforting warmth of the heavy goose down–filled sleeping bag.

The Dowds each returned from a short trip into the woods and set about breaking the camp down, rolling sleeping bags, and storing all their equipment in the sleigh behind Louis's sled.

"Colder than a well-digger's ass," Earl said, squatting beside John.

John grinned at Earl and stifled the urge to grunt and moan as his muscles, sore and stiff from sleeping on the snowy ground, cried out as he stood. He rotated his arms, forcing them to work and increase circulation. "We'd best get some food in us and get goin' if we want to catch them before they get across the line."

"Where in Christ's name is he headed? There's any number of places where this Wendigo, or whatever in hell it is, could have crossed."

"Can't tell," John replied. "But if I was to guess, I'd venture it's headed for the Slash."

"How much of a lead you reckon he has?" Buster asked.

"Hard to say, but I doubt it's much more than a couple of hours." John nodded at the single track that led off to the south. "Ain't no one cuttin' in here, so none of the roads are plowed. He's havin' to break trail the whole way. Slows him down some."

Buster Dowd crawled out of his sleeping bag and walked over to where John Bear was starting a fire. "Shouldn't we get our asses in gear? Once he gets to the Slash, they's nothin' to stop him from crossing over."

John reached into his pocket and removed a gray wad.

"What you got there?" Earl asked.

"Dryer lint," John replied, "makes it easier to light the kindling." To emphasize his point John slid the lint under some broken dried twigs, took a prescription-medicine container filled with stick matches from his pocket. He took out a match, struck it, and when it flared up, touched it to the lint. The linen fibers ignited and started the kindling burning. He remained in his squat and said, "Buster's right. There's no barrier to him crossing over to Canada once he reaches the Slash. However, due to its never-ending hunger, he'll want to stay where it can get food."

"Where you think that is?" Earl asked.

"Only places I can think of are St. Pamphile and Lac-de-l'Est. Lots of people for it to prey on in St. Pamphile—but, he'll probably steer wide of it. Anything as tall as he is would stand out. The lake is twenty or more miles north of St. Pamphile and there may be ice fishermen there, an easier hunt."

Earl once again took charge of the kitchen duties and made a large pot of coffee, which he served to the others. John sipped the steaming brew and felt the heat move into his core, warming as it went.

"Won't the Canadians fine him if they catch him?" Louis Dowd asked.

John gave Louis a brief glance and chose to ignore his comment. He fanned the flames and the fire.

"He's a fuckin' Indian," Buster said. "All he needs to do is show a Tribal ID and they won't bother him."

John grinned. "What makes you think he will go through Canadian customs? For one thing, every crossing along the Maine–Canada border has been notified that he's wanted in a string of brutal murders. But more than that . . . well, when you see this guy, you'll understand better."

"What about Dwain?" Buster asked. "Won't he present a problem?"

John Bear kept silent. It would do no good to tell him that the Wendigo would not allow the boy to be a problem.

36

T18, R13

The Wendigo, with Dwain still perched behind him, walked through the seven-foot-high snow drift, breaking a trail as he went. He felt the boy's presence and resisted the urge to kill the boy and devour him.

His senses were at their peak: he knew the posse behind him was closing the gap, thanks in no small part to the trail he was leaving for them. If he was going to make it to the Slash safely, he'd have to slow them down. He pulled Dwain from his back and searched the woods, looking for anything with which he could construct a crude booby trap.

The morning was clear and cold. John Bear urged his sled forward and found his mind wandering back to his childhood. It was something that he tried to keep from doing as it always left him in a foul mood.

―――――

Maliseet First Nation, Edmundston, New Brunswick, Canada, Twenty-Five Years Earlier

"John, Tom! Where in hell are you boys?"

John Bear crouched down behind the evergreen shrub that grew in front of the house. There was just enough space between the clapboards on the side of the rundown house and the small spruce to hide the diminutive boys. John placed a finger across his lips warning his younger brother to keep quiet and not give away their location.

"I know you two sons-a-bitches kin hear me."

Tom clasped his hand over his mouth, worry and fear in his eyes. Both boys knew from experience what would happen if their mother caught them—especially when she was as drunk as she sounded.

Aquene Bear stepped out onto the porch and John could see her ankle socks, one of which had fallen down and lay wrapped around the top of her dirty lace-up shoes. She hollered again and John heard Tom moan in fear. Although Aquene was mean and abusive when she drank, she could be a loving and caring mother when sober—the problem was that she was seldom sober after nine in the morning. She had her rituals, one of which was that after rising from bed she drank two cups of strong black tea, fortifying them with whiskey when she had it. There was always a pot of tea sitting on the heated top of the old wood cookstove. Aquene's other ritual was to dump loose tea into a saucepan of boiling water and through the week she'd add water, always keeping the tea hot strong enough to burn the finish off the black iron stove. Once she'd consumed the second cup of tea, it was time for Aquene to start serious drinking.

"I get my hands on you two, I'm gonna wear you out!" she shouted.

A few seconds later, John heard the screen door slam and the heavy thuds of his mother's feet as she trudged through the minuscule living room on her way to the kitchen. Once back in her favorite room, she would sit at the old kitchen table in front of the window, drinking straight whiskey. She'd stare through the dirty windows and imagine that all of the neighbors were talking about her. The more she drank, the more she envisioned the neighbors were looking down on her, and she became angrier and meaner.

John motioned for Tom to turn about and crawl around the side of the house. He followed his brother and when they were safely out of their mother's line of sight, the brothers jumped to their feet and dashed into the woods behind the house. Once they were safely inside the crude shelter they'd spent the summer building, Tom sat with his back against the circular wall, folded his arms around his knees, and said, "Why's Mère such a bitch?"

"I don't know. All we can do is stay out of her way."

Tom looked like a lost waif. "Can we stay here until Père comes home?"

John nodded at his younger brother. "Yeah, we can do that. . . ." What he didn't tell Tom was that there was no guarantee their father would come home. More and more of late Charley Bear would stay away for several days in a row. *At least*, he thought, *we'll stay here until after she passes out.*

The boys had built the wigwam that summer at John's behest, Tom being too young to plan more than whatever held his interest at any given moment. John wanted a shelter where they could flee when their mother was in her drunken rages. He had been the victim of his mother's wrath on many occasions and his back bore the scars to prove it. Charley and Aquene Bear had three children: John, ten years old, Tom, six, and an older sister, Danya, sixteen, who ran away six months ago and her whereabouts were unknown. John missed her a lot; she had done what she could to spare him from taking the brunt of their mother's rage. However, the beatings had become so savage and brutal that Danya disappeared one night and had not been seen nor heard from since. There were times when John wondered if Aquene had finally lost any semblance of control and beat Danya to death. Unbeknownst to anyone, John spent many hours searching the woods for an unmarked grave or human remains in the woods.

———————

Present Day

Thinking of his sister brought John back to the present. He still felt an emptiness inside whenever he thought of her. *Danya would be in her early forties now—if she's alive.*

All his life, John had heard tales of Wendigos and he had always been unable to understand what could be bad enough to push someone to the point where they'd eat the flesh of another human being. As traumatic as his childhood was he'd coped and had little if any empathy for those who couldn't or wouldn't.

A sudden commotion ahead snapped John out of his head and he throttled back the sled. The Dowds were all off their snowmobiles and had rushed forward. Buster had volunteered to give John a break and take the lead and there seemed to be a problem at the head of their convoy. John leaped into the thigh-deep snow. He pushed his way through the powdery snow until he was on the hard pack that their tracks had created and ran forward. He leaped over Earl's and Louis's sleds and saw Buster lying on the ground. "I'm okay, goddamn it!" Buster shouted. "Asshole set up a booby trap and I sprung it, that's all."

John saw the white birch that had been tied back and then the rope by which it had been tied and triggered.

Buster struggled into a sitting position, groaned, and laid back. His face was pale, a line of blood trickled from the corner of his mouth, and he grimaced. John Bear crouched over him and reached for the front of his snowmobile suit.

"What the fuck you doin'?" Louis asked.

"Opening his suit to see how badly he's hurt."

Buster looked at him. "I ain't sure what, but I think somethin' inside me is busted up bad."

"Where'd it hit you?"

Buster held his hands over his torso, just below his rib cage. "Here."

John removed his heavy gloves and unzipped the injured Dowd's heavy black coat. He reached inside, trying to be as gentle as he could, and unhooked one of the suspenders that supported Buster's snow pants. When he took his hand out it was red with blood. He looked at Earl, who was fixated on his son's blood as it dripped from John's hand into the pristine white snow. He turned back to Buster and said, "I ain't about to bullshit you, okay?"

Buster nodded.

"You're hurt bad. You need a doctor and soon." John looked at Earl. "You and Louis need to take him back. I'll go on alone."

John braced himself for an argument from one of the Dowds but none came forth.

"Which of you got a cell phone?"

Louis said, "I do."

"It's a sure bet that there ain't any towers out here. If you head north, as you get close to Estcourt Station you should pick up a Canadian tower. You'll be roamin'—"

"Don't worry 'bout that," Earl said.

John read off a number. "Enter that into your address book and as soon as you get a signal call them for a medical evacuation." He looked up at the sky and saw the deep-blue color of high pressure. "Weather's good and wind not too strong. They should be able to fly. If they can't get to you soon, take him across the line to Pohénégamook."

"Po-what?" Earl asked.

"Pohénégamook. A small town on the lake of the same name. Has a population around two thousand—which, when compared to Estcourt with its twenty-five people, constitutes a big city around here." John looked at Earl and knew what was on the man's mind. "Yeah, I think they have a small hospital there. If not they'll have phone service and can get help. Either of you speak French?"

"They both do, their mother was Acadian, she used to talk to them in French all the time." A wry smile covered his face. "I used to get pissed and tell her that I was American and for her to speak American to me." He looked up at the sky. "Now it looks like what she done may just save Buster's life. She's been gone for nineteen years now. But I'll bet she's lookin' down with that smug smile she always got whenever she proved me wrong."

John wasn't sure how to respond so he said, "Never hurt anyone to be bilingual."

"Bi-what?"

John resisted the impulse to say, *we just had this conversation.* Instead he said, "Bilingual, able to speak more than one language."

"Louis," Earl said. "Empty out a sleigh and make a bed for your brother." He turned to John. "We'll take care of Buster. You git on and bring back my grandson."

John nodded. There was nothing else to say, so he trudged back to his sled and mounted it. He started the motor and revved it a few times. He slowly drove around the line of sleds and saluted the Dowds as he forged ahead. As soon as he was clear of them, John opened up the throttle.

"Dad," Louis said. "You go with the warden. I'll get Buster back. Dwain is gonna need to see a familiar face."

Earl seemed divided between taking care of his oldest son and the need to save his grandson. "You sure, Louis?"

"As sure as I ever been 'bout anythin'. Go."

Earl jogged back to his sled, started it, and sped after John Bear.

The Slash, T18, R13

John Bear broke out of the trees and the instant he saw the Slash, his stomach turned. The entire length of the treeless corridor delineating the border between the United States and Canada was beaten down with the tracks of a multitude of snowmobiles. He released the throttle and the sled's motor dropped to an idle. He saw Earl Dowd's reaction and knew he was experiencing the same sense of frustration as John. Yet neither of them was prepared to accept defeat.

"We need to split up," John said. You head north toward Estcourt and I'll head south toward Lac-de-l'Est and St. Pamphile."

"How we gonna contact each other if we find something?"

John Bear pondered what he knew was the quintessential question. "I haven't a damned clue, Earl. In fact, I've about exhausted my supply of ideas."

Earl looked to the north. "What's that way?"

"Nothing until you reach Estcourt and Pohénégamook, Quebec."

"Let's head south together," Earl said. "If Condor wanted to go to Estcourt I don't think he'd have come all the way down here. I agree with what you said earlier, he's probably headed for someplace where he can get food."

"Tell you what," John said. "It's got your grandson; we'll go until you say we've gone far enough."

Earl nodded his approval. "Thanks, John."

John Bear and Earl Dowd traveled south along the United States side of the Slash. The snow was hardpacked and snowmobile tracks crisscrossed the terrain and wove their way around the myriad shacks that lined the Canadian side, facing the U.S. The first time they paused for a break, Earl asked, "What in hell are all of these elevated shelters? They look like ice fishing shacks on stilts."

"They're shooting stands," John replied. "The Canadians use them to shoot moose on our side of the border."

"You're shitting me?"

"No, I wish I was. They'll shoot a moose on this side and then haul it across to their side."

"And we can't do nothin' about it?"

"If we walk twenty feet to the west, the warden service has no jurisdiction. If we did, those shooting stands would have been torn down a long time ago."

Dowd unzipped his snowmobile suit coat, reached inside, and retrieved a pack of cigarettes. He held it up. "You a smoker?"

"Not regular, but I'll have one from time to time. I gave 'em up full-time a few years back."

Earl offered John the pack. "Would this be one of those times?"

"You know," John said, "it might be."

Dowd nodded and used his thumb to flip open the box. He took out a cigarette, cupped his hands around a lighter, faced into the wind, and lit it. Once his cigarette was lit he stepped off his sled, handed the pack of

Marlboros and the lighter to John, looked at the sky, and then his watch. "We only got about three hours until sunset."

John Bear lit a cigarette, handed the box and lighter to Earl, and sat silent, smelling the alluring scent of burning tobacco and feeling a slight buzz as the nicotine soaked into his system. He said, "Bitch of a habit ain't it? You can quit for years and still crave them. . . . What you want to do?"

"How far you figure we are from Lac-de-l'Est?"

"Couple miles. From there it's maybe twenty, twenty-five miles to St. Pamphile."

"How big is it?"

"St. Pamphile? Couple thousand people on the Canadian side."

"Canadian side? Is there a St. Pamphile in Maine?"

"Yeah, ain't much of a place. If it wasn't for the Quebec side of town the place would dry up and blow away."

Dowd took a final drag on his cigarette and threw the butt into the snow. "So if we was to go across and try and get a place to stay, how much trouble would we get in?"

"Depends. You got a passport on you?"

"Passport card. We do some business over in the provinces so we all got them. I always carry mine in my wallet."

"Then there won't be no problem. Customs down there is open until nine at night."

"Then I guess we oughtta get goin'." Dowd put his sled in gear and started driving south along the Slash.

Lac-de-l'Est, T17, R14

John was about twenty yards behind Dowd when they came upon the lake. Earl suddenly jumped from his machine and ran toward the icy surface. John Bear stopped behind the abandoned sled and saw Dowd on his knees, hugging Dwain. He leaped off his sled and ran to join them. Earl was on one knee, holding the boy at arm's length, and John heard him ask, "Dwain, are you okay? Did he hurt you?"

The boy said nothing. He merely stared at his grandfather as if he were a stranger.

Dowd raised his voice and John saw the man's relief turning to anger when his nephew wouldn't speak. "Goddamn it, Dwain. Talk to me!"

John placed his hand on Dowd's shoulder. "Take it easy, Earl. He's been through an ordeal."

Dowd stood up and walked a couple of steps away from the boy. "I s'pose you're right," he said to John. He turned and looked back at Dwain. "Where'd it go?" he asked.

Without saying a word, Dwain raised his hand and pointed at the frozen surface of the lake. The ice looked gray and foreboding. Ice fishing shacks were scattered along the shore. John knew there was no way they'd ever find the Wendigo. "I guess we head home," he said.

"We're not going after him?"

"We're standing on the edge of roughly ten and a half square miles of glare ice. It could have gone straight across to the south or gone over to Quebec Route 287. Most likely it left the ice someplace in between, no way in hell will we catch up to it. Besides, we could be standing in Canada and I got no authority here."

"I thought Indians could travel back and forth all they want."

"We can—as private citizens—as a game warden I can't. Take your grandson home, Earl. Find out how the boy's father is doing . . . if you can."

Dowd looked longingly at the nine square miles of the lake that was Canadian. After several seconds his shoulders slumped. "I suppose you're right, John. But I swear on everything that's precious to me—if that motherfucker comes after this boy again, I'll be shooting first and asking questions later."

Lac-de-l'Est, Quebec, Canada

The Wendigo stood back in the trees, watching the activity on the U.S. shore of the lake. He'd hated deserting the boy, but the warden and his partner had shown that they would not give up the chase as long as they thought he had the kid.

He remained in place until they mounted their sleds and raced away to the south—no doubt headed for St. Pamphile. He believed that as long as the Indian game warden was alive, the man would not give up the quest. He had to go back—not immediately, but soon.

A sudden hunger cramp bent him over and he wrapped his long arms around his middle. Still bent over he studied the ice fishing shacks, looking for a sign of inhabitants. Farther up the lake he saw a shack with two Bombardier sleds parked outside and a thin stream of smoke streaming out of a shiny metal pipe in the side. He ran out of the shelter of the trees and onto the ice—dinner was almost ready.

37

Dowd Settlement

Laura Wells stopped her rented four-by-four in front of the porch to the Dowd house and got out. She glanced around the yard, admiring the rustic beauty of the place. She smelled the enticing odors of freshly chopped wood and wood smoke. She heard the door open and close. She turned to see a young woman standing on the porch.

"Kin I help you?"

"I'd like to see Amy Dowd." The woman's *in-your-face* attitude startled Laura. But, rather than back down she became more dedicated than ever to getting the story she'd come here for. "And, you are?"

"I'm Francine, her sister-in-law. Amy's inside, but she's busy right now."

"My name is Laura Wells—"

"That s'posed to mean somethin' to me?"

"I don't suppose I could inconvenience you to tell Amy that I'd like to talk with her about her nephew, Dwain."

Francine paused before giving a curt "Wait here."

In a matter of seconds Amy came to the door. "Come on in, Laura." She turned, walked inside, and waited for Laura to scale the stairs and join her. When the reporter entered the large family room, Amy walked past her and headed for the kitchen, beckoning Laura to follow her.

When Laura entered the kitchen she immediately felt at home. The warmth of the room made it feel smaller and cozier than it was and the combination of coffee, cigarette smoke, and baked goods created a smell that was reminiscent of her grandmother's kitchen. "This is lovely," she said.

Amy indicated for her to sit. "Can I take your coat for you?"

"No, thank you," Laura said, "I'll just drape it over the back of this chair." She removed the heavy parka and hung it on the back of the chair as if it were on a hanger. She sat down and let her chilled body soak up the dry heat from the woodstove.

"I have coffee or tea. Would you like some?" Amy offered.

"Coffee, please."

Amy turned to a large cupboard, opened the door, and took out a mug. "Is a mug okay? Or, would you prefer a cup and saucer?"

For some strange reason, Laura felt as if the Dowd woman was mocking her. She let the slight bounce off her. "Mug will be great."

Amy removed a second mug from the cabinet, took an old metal percolator from the top of the stove, and poured coffee into the mugs. "Cream?" she asked.

"No, I prefer mine black, no sugar."

"Of course. Now I remember, you'll have to forgive my absentmind-edness. . . . There's been so much going on around here it's all I can do to remember my name."

"Amy, that's perfectly understandable. Don't worry yourself."

Dowd nodded, carried the mugs to the table, and placed one in front of her guest. She sat across from Laura and before she could say anything, her sister-in-law appeared in the door holding a large basket of folded clothing. "Thanks for the use of the laundry, Amy."

"It's no problem, Francine. Have a good rest of the day."

Once Francine had departed Laura said, "She's a good sentry."

Amy smiled. "As you've probably already learned, we Dowds take care of our own. Francine is a little blunter about it than most of us." She sipped from her mug and said, "Now what brings you out here?"

"The murders."

Amy nodded. "I suppose that'd do it—what do you want to know from me?"

"First, how's your brother doing? John told me that he'd been severely injured."

"Buster? He's still in the hospital. The doctor in the clinic in Pohénégamook—wherever that is—said that it was a good thing that they took him there and didn't try to go all the way to Fort Kent. The stub of a broken branch speared him in the side, just missing his stomach; if they'd tried to remove it Buster could have hemorrhaged and might have died." She got up, walked to a shelf over the sink and picked up a pack of cigarettes. "Do you mind?"

"No, my mother and grandmother were smokers. To be truthful, even though I've never smoked, I do like the smell."

Amy returned to the table, sat down, and lit a cigarette. "The doctor said that the piece of branch that was in Buster kept pressure on the ruptured blood vessels, keeping him from hemorrhaging."

Laura took a drink of coffee. "This is very good," she said.

"Thanks, I drink too much of it though."

"And your nephew and your father? How are they doing?"

"Hard to say. Dad hasn't done much other than sleep, since he got back. Dwain, he's worse than he was the first time he was with that psycho. Still stays out in the barn and won't say anything to anyone."

"You might want to get him into Fort Kent and have him undergo some counseling."

Amy snorted derisively. "It's not that I disagree with you. But you try and get my brothers and father to listen. They think that Dwain will come around, he just needs some time to get over things."

"But your grandfather, isn't he a Vietnam veteran? He should know about PTSD and its effects. If they don't deal with it now, it will only get worse and will have to be dealt with later on."

"Linwood Dowd, and all his descendants for that matter, are not about to admit that any of their kin are crazy."

"Crazy? I didn't say anything about him being crazy."

"Tell them that."

"Can I see him?"

"Who, Dwain or Dad?"

"Either . . . both."

"Not up to me. You're welcome to go out and see if Dwain will talk to you." She sat back, took a final drag from the cigarette, and ground the butt in an ashtray. "Beats me how that boy hasn't froze to death."

Laura finished her coffee and put her coat on. "Would you like to come with me while I talk to him?"

"Don't think it'll matter either way. He ain't talked to no one since he got home—just sits there with his arms wrapped around his gut, rockin' back an' forth. I ain't ever seen that boy with so little life in him. He won't talk, he won't respond to anythin', and he won't eat."

"That does sound strange."

"That isn't all," Amy said. "None of the animals will go anywhere near him—not even Shep—and that dog loves that boy to death."

Amy Dowd led Laura Wells out of the house. The wind blew across the yard at thirteen miles per hour, gusting to twenty-five, making the minus-thirty-degree weather feel like it was somewhere between minus fifty and minus sixty-eight. The cold hit Laura like a frigid wall. As the two women walked across the yard to the barn, ice crackled and crunched beneath their boots. "No one has been able to talk Dwain into going inside the house?" Laura asked.

"He can't stand heat."

"Be that as it may," Laura responded, "this is too cold for anyone to survive. Does he have any type of heat out here?"

"No. We tried and tried to get him to come inside, but he won't. Finally, Grandpa said, 'Leave him be. He'll come in when he's ready.' So that's what we done."

Entering the barn, Laura detected a subtle rise in temperature, which she credited to being out of the wind. Nevertheless, the temperature inside the huge barn still had to be minus thirty. She wondered how anyone could leave a boy in such a place—if Dwain had been her nephew, she'd have physically taken him inside. Her nose began to feel numb and, in spite of wearing heavy wool socks and winter boots, her toes began to sting from the cold.

Amy guided her to the far back corner of the barn, where the weak sun could not reach, therefore keeping the interior from warming up by even a degree or two. Laura shoved her glove-clad hands into the pockets of her parka. Amy stopped in front of a small stall and said, "Dwain, there's someone here to see you."

Far back in the darkest corner of the stall Dwain sat on a bale of hay, staring at them. "Hello, Dwain. Do you remember me? My name is Laura Wells."

Dwain remained sitting silent.

"Would it be all right if I came in?" Wells asked, hoping to get some type of response from him.

"Dwain," Amy said, "answer the lady—you been raised better than what you're acting."

Laura touched Amy's arm and said, "It's okay, Amy. I understand what he's dealing with. Why don't you go back inside? I'll stay here with Dwain for a few minutes."

"You're wasting your time."

"I don't think it'll be a waste of time," Laura said. "Will it, Dwain?"

His shrug was barely discernible in the dim light.

Laura said, "Really, Amy. We'll be fine."

Amy looked inside the stall and then at Laura. "Okay, it's your time." She turned her head back to her nephew. "You be civil Dwain, 'cause if you ain't your grandfather will be out here and you don't want that—he's really put out with your attitude."

Laura stood in place, watching Amy until she was outside. She turned back to Dwain. "I'm really tired of standing. Is it all right if I come in and sit down?" She took her left hand out of her coat pocket and pointed to a bale inside the stall and perpendicular to the one upon which the boy sat. She stepped inside the stall and he leaped to his feet. Laura immediately froze in place and looked at him. *My God*, she thought, *he's grown at least six inches in the five days since I saw him last!* Another thought came to her: *If what John says about the Wendigo is true, how tall must it be now?* She sidled over to the hay bale and sat on it, ignoring the freezing cold that penetrated her jeans and butt. "This is a close as I'll get, Dwain. I just want to talk to you."

He sidled away and sat on a bale across from her.

Laura sat silently, studying the dusty barn and pretended to be fascinated by the cobwebs that hung from the rafters. After a few moments she detected him relaxing ever so slightly. "I know what you're going through, Dwain."

She watched his face, which looked sullen. He shrugged again as if he didn't believe her.

"When I was about your age I was in a store that was robbed. The men that did it took me hostage when the police showed up." She studied his face, hoping for some indication that she was getting through to him—he gave her none. "It was the most helpless I've ever felt. Did you feel that way when . . . ?"

She paused to give him opportunity to respond. Again she waited for several long moments before deciding that he was not going to answer.

"I was scared every minute that they were going to hurt me. Did that happen to you?"

"No."

Laura felt as if she'd won a major victory and waited to see if he would go into more detail. When he didn't she said, "But there must have been a time when you thought he might hurt you."

Dwain gave her a look that bordered on being scornful. "No. He's a nice guy."

"But, he's killed people."

"I didn't see him kill anyone."

"What about the man named Askook?"

"That," Dwain said, "was self-defense. That man attacked him first."

Laura sat back and leaned against the wall. Her feet and face were numb with cold and she became concerned about frostbite. "But, he held you against your will—didn't he?"

"NO!" Dwain was on his feet, glaring at her with his fists clenched. "He did not. . . . I went with him because I wanted to." He exhaled and she realized that there was no cloud of chilled vapor coming from his mouth. She blew and saw her breath immediately cool and turn into a cloud before her face. *What is going on here?* She wondered.

He dropped back onto his seat and said, "No one understands him. You're just like *them*—always sayin' bad things about him . . . tryin' to turn me against him. Well, you ain't gonna do it, no more than they did. In fact, I want you to leave now. I want to be alone."

"But—"

"GET OUT!"

His shout startled her and she jumped to her feet. Her first impulse was to get angry, but then she realized that although he was only thirteen years old, she would be no match for him if he became violent. She walked out of the stall and stopped in the center of the barn. "If you want to talk, Dwain. Remember I know what you're going through."

His eyes seemed to flash and she heard him mutter, "Screw you."

38

Lyndon Station

John Bear was sitting in the dining room at Del's, waiting for Laura to join him for dinner. When he saw the look on her face as she entered the room, John knew something serious was weighing on her. She took her heavy parka off and threw it into the booth across from him.

"Bad day?"

"I went out to see Dwain Dowd today."

"Oh, how'd it go?"

"There are some strange things happening with that boy."

"Such as?"

"He stays out in a freezing barn and won't eat anything they bring him. Then there's the physical change."

"What sort of physical change?"

"I swear he's grown six inches since the last time I saw him."

"Really?"

Del walked over and placed a menu and glass of water in front of her. She looked at him without picking up the menu. "You still have salmon, Del?"

"Yes, ma'am."

"I'll have that . . . and a Manhattan—strong."

Del looked at her companion. "John?"

"The usual."

Del nodded and disappeared into the kitchen.

As soon as they were alone, Laura turned to John. "The thing that concerned me the most was . . ." She seemed reluctant to speak.

"What?"

"When he spoke there was no steam coming from his mouth."

Laura bent forward. "John . . . the only way that could happen is if his breath is as cold as the air outside—and it was thirty below in that barn." Her point being made, she sat back.

"I'll take a run up there tomorrow. I hear that Buster got out of the hospital today."

Dowd Settlement

Louis held the battery-operated lantern high as he guided his brother Buster into the barn. "This is friggin' nuts, Buster. The doctor only released you when you promised to stay in bed for three to five days. You should be in bed, not tramping around in the cold."

"Screw him. I want to see my boy. If that goddamned Indian did somethin' to him, I'll kill the bastard."

"Stop talkin' stupid," Louis said. "He's gone. You heard Earl. He left Dwain and run off into Quebec. We've probably seen the last of him— he's Canada's problem now."

"That may be so, but Dwain is my problem." Buster leaned on his brother's shoulder as they slowly walked to the rear of the barn. When they reached the stall where Dwain had sequestered himself, Louis said, "He's in here."

Buster pushed away from Louis and stumbled his way into the enclosure. He saw his son sitting on a bale of hay and moved toward him. When Buster turned and fell backward to sit beside his son, Dwain leaped up and moved to another part of the compartment. He sat so that he could watch both his father and his uncle without having to turn his head.

Buster gasped in pain and watched the boy. "How you doin' son?"

Dwain stared at his father.

It seemed to Buster that his son didn't know who he was. "Do you know who I am, Dwain?"

"Yeah." Dwain's look was as surly as his tone.

"And who is that?"

"You're Buster. . . ."

"I'm your father damn it! Be respectful when you speak to me."

Dwain's eyes seemed to flash when he answered, "Yes, *sir*."

Buster became enraged at his son's insolence and tensed to go after him. Pain ripped through him and he paled, slumping back onto the cube of hay. In spite of the subzero temperatures he broke out in a sweat.

Louis darted to his brother's side. "Damn it, Buster. I warned you not to overdo it."

Buster held his right hand up, halting Louis. He looked at his son, "You can't stay out here Dwain. It's freezin'. I want you to come in the house with me."

Dwain sat still and showed no indication of moving.

"Damn it boy, if you defy me I'll beat you within an inch of your life."

Dwain stood up. "I'll go in."

Louis helped Buster to his feet and said to Dwain, "Go in, Dwain, we'll be right behind you."

The boy walked out of the stall and Louis and Buster saw him in the transient illumination of the spotlights that lit the yard. "Jesus," Buster said. "He's grown almost a foot!" He hissed in pain.

Louis half-carried Buster out of the barn, keeping his eyes on his nephew. "Brother, I think the day is past when you can take that boy across your knee—"

Dwain lay on his bed in front of the open window. The curtains flapped with each freezing gust of wind. He stared at the ceiling through eyes that were dull, as if he were devoid of intelligence. The reality was that he was so hungry he couldn't sleep. He sat up in the bed and looked out at the moon reflecting off the pristine snow that covered the field between the house and the woods beyond.

Dwain sensed *him* and slipped out of the window onto the roof. He took three long strides and jumped to the yard below, landing soundlessly. He looked over his shoulder to see if he'd been observed—not that it mattered. He was going to *him* and he'd kill anyone who tried to stop him.

The Wendigo stood twenty feet back in the trees, watching the house. His hunger was driving him mad. All he had to do was go there. The house was full of nourishment. He fought against the pangs of his empty stomach. He watched the boy slip out of the upstairs window and leap to the ground. As he watched him racing across the snow, the Wendigo emitted a piercing whistle, calling him.

Amy Dowd woke up. She thought that she'd heard something. She lay quiet, listening to see if the sound would be repeated. An ear-piercing whistle, followed immediately by a sound that she thought was a clap of thunder, made her snap up in the bed. The whistle was repeated, a different voice this time, younger, as if the person doing it was an adolescent. *Person?* Amy whispered "Why did you think that?"

She heard another thunder clap and it made her think of a creature suffering from some soul-wrenching agony. Then a word entered her mind . . . *Hungry!*

39

John Bear and Amy Dowd drank the last of the coffee she'd made for them and walked out into the icy, snow-covered yard. "You say that he was in his room when you went to bed last night, but back in the barn when you woke up?"

"Yes. There were other weird things last night too."

"What sort of things?"

"As cold as it was I heard thunder, not once but several times. Don't ask me why, but I thought someone or something was in terrible . . . I don't how to describe it—the only thing that comes to mind is someone was suffering from a terrible hunger. Then there were these loud, shrill whistles. It creeped me out so much that I wanted to hide under the covers."

"Where did the noises come from?" John asked.

Amy pointed toward the woods beyond the barn. "It was late and I was half-asleep, so I can't be positive, but I think they came from over there."

John Bear looked up at the cloudless azure sky. "Did you see anything?"

Amy flushed. "To be truthful, Warden, I was too friggin' scared to get out of bed and check. It took all my courage to bring Dwain in from the barn this morning."

"Unfortunately, I understand you," John said. He pulled the zipper of his parka up as far as it would go and added, "You go check on Dwain. I want to look around a bit."

Amy disappeared up the stairs and before John was out of the living room door she reappeared. "He's not in his room."

"I'll look around outside," John said. He stopped in front of the barn, staring into the dark interior. Amy ran across the yard, putting on a parka as she jogged inside the barn. From the back stall John heard her say, "He's here."

John circled around the building following a path worn of packed snow. He saw where a set of footprints had scaled a five-foot-high snow-bank and entered the field beyond. A trail had been broken through the thigh-high snow and John followed it. He was forced to raise his legs high while trying to place his feet in the tracks left by his predecessor. Before he was a quarter of the way across the open expanse, his thighs and calves were throbbing with exertion.

John persevered, ignoring his various aches and pains and following the tracks into the woods and saw where they met an even larger set of tracks. If the tracks he'd followed belonged to Dwain, then there was little doubt in his mind what this new set belonged to. The Wendigo had not stayed long in Canada. John wondered what the link was between it and Dwain Dowd. He studied the area, following the two sets of foot-prints with his eyes. He saw where they had sat side by side on a large downed pine tree, its needles, brown and withered. There was no way of telling how long this midnight rendezvous had lasted, but instinct told him it was no chance meeting—it had come looking for the boy. The one unanswered question was *why*? This was the third time the two had paired up and John was baffled as to what was the hold that they held over one another.

He followed the tracks he believed to be Dwain's. They led him out of the trees and back across the field to the barn. When he slid down the snowbank, John stomped his feet to remove the snow that stuck to his boots and inside the cuffs of his green trousers. He circled the barn and entered it.

As soon as he stepped out of the cold breeze into the calm of the farm building he noted the difference in the temperature that resulted from the loss of windchill. Without the sound of the blowing wind everything seemed deathly quiet. He was surprised to hear Amy Dowd talking to her nephew in a subdued voice. Whether or not the boy had answered he wasn't sure as a gust of wind created a sudden cacophony of noise inside the barn. Air sought out cracks and openings in the wall and the building seemed to sway and moan. He was confused; minutes ago Amy had said that the boy was not in the stall, yet here he was—he must have been somewhere else in the barn. Still John couldn't stop wondering how they'd missed him.

"Dwain," Amy said, "you're scaring me."

When John walked up and stood beside her he heard Dwain say, ". . . trying to scare you, Aunt Amy."

John filled in the earlier part of the conversation and realized that Dwain was trying to ease her mind.

"I just can't stay in that house. It's too hot."

The boy seemed to tense when he saw John step into view.

"Hello, Dwain," John said. "Do you remember me?"

The boy's eyes narrowed. "I know who you are. You want to kill him."

John stood his ground. "No, I want to help him—to make him stop killing people."

"He knows what you are. You're an Indian and he doesn't like you."

"That," John countered, "is because he's afraid."

Dwain looked defiant when he said, "He isn't afraid of anyone or anything."

"Oh, yes he is," John said. "He's especially afraid of me because he knows that I know *what* he is—and he knows that I'm probably one of a handful of people who know how to stop him."

"That's a lie! He's a great being—a god!"

John refused to react to the boy's elevated voice. Rather than return aggression with aggression he kept his voice calm and under control as he said, "I agree with you: he is a god—an evil god."

Dwain seemed to disappear as he backed deeper into the shadow.

John and Amy stood on the porch in front of the main house. "What's happening to him?" Amy asked.

John had strong suspicions as to what was going on with Dwain but opted to keep them to himself until such time as he had definitive proof. "He's just confused," he said. "It helped him when his sled broke and he was afraid he'd freeze to death. He saw it fight Askook, who he is convinced was the real criminal—and now Dwain is dealing with a strong case of hero worship."

"You're sure that's all there is to it?"

"I'm sure." John stepped off the porch into a whirlwind of snow that raced across the yard, coating everything in its path, including him, with a fine dusting. "Try to get him to eat something and if you can't coax him out of that barn take him a sleeping bag or some heavy blankets."

The door to the house banged open and Buster Dowd stood in the threshold. John immediately saw the pain in his features and heard the anger in his voice. "That goddamned boy out in the barn again?" His words were directed to Amy, but his eyes remained on John Bear.

John was certain that Amy did not want to risk upsetting her brother any more than he already was and it didn't surprise him when she turned, lowered her eyes, and nodded yes. She then darted past Buster and disappeared inside the house.

Buster let her pass without any comment. He kept his gaze on John and said, "That stupid kid met *him* last night—didn't he?"

"It looks that way, Buster. How are you doing?"

"I been fuckin' better. The doctor says I'll be all right. Friggin' piece of branch stuck me like a stake. It'll probably take the rest of the winter and most of the spring, but I should heal up okay." He pointed toward the barn. "What's goin' on with him?"

"I'm not sure. You might want to get him some counseling."

"Counseling? What for? That son of a bitch do something weird to him?"

"No, nothing like that. But there are times when a kidnapping victim starts to identify with and bond to his or her kidnapper—shrinks call it Stockholm syndrome, look it up."

"That's the craziest fuckin' shit I ever heard!" Dowd's voice rose and he began coughing. He doubled over and appeared to lose his balance.

John bounded up the steps and reached him at the same time that a pair of massive arms encompassed him. John saw Earl Dowd's face over his son's shoulder. "I got him, John," Earl said.

"Let me help you." John grabbed hold of Buster and helped Earl move him inside. They laid him on a couch in front of a blazing fireplace, the flames so high that their tops were not visible within the hearth. Once Buster was down, John turned and shut the door.

"Ain't good for him to get riled up," Earl said.

Amy rushed into the room, saw that Buster had lapsed into a state of unconsciousness and said, "Oh my God, what happened." She cast an accusatory look at John. "You should know better than to upset him."

"Amy," Earl said, "shut up and go get a blanket and cover him up."

Her face reddened and she spun around and ran up the stairs to the second floor.

Earl motioned for John to follow him into the kitchen. Once they were there, he closed the door, turned, and said, "You want coffee?"

"Sure—black."

"Good, that's the only way I know how to serve it." Earl grabbed two ceramic mugs from the cupboard and poured them full of coffee from the pot that sat on the woodstove.

John carefully sipped the near-boiling beverage and said, "Strong, but damned good."

Earl Dowd gave him a piercing look and said, "John, what the fuck is happening to my family?"

"Earl, I told you what we're dealing with. This thing has powers that are beyond belief—do you know that it doesn't actually kill its victims? Most of them die of fright before it devours them. All I can say is that I'm trying as hard as I can to bring it down."

"I heard Buster when he said that Dwain went off to meet with him last night. I'll tell you this, I'm lockin' that kid in his room at night. If I see that crazy bastard anywhere close to here, I'm gonna kill him."

If he doesn't kill all of you first, John thought.

40

Lyndon Station

John Bear sat at the bar in Del's Place. He and Murphy were in civilian clothes, with half-consumed beers on the bar in front of them. "Do you realize that we've been working this case for over three weeks now?" Murphy commented.

"I've worked longer ones," John replied. "But never one that frustrated me like this one. We know what the perp is, but we don't know where it is."

"Do you think someone out there is helping it?" Murphy asked.

John raised his glass to his lips, took a drink of beer, and said, "I don't think it needs help. Like a male bear lived up there in Viverette Settlement alone and survived. It's like the coyote in Indian folklore, it's a trickster. We know it's out there but it always seems to be one or two steps ahead of us."

"Maybe," Murphy said, "we should go after it like we would a coyote?"

John's brow furled and he grew pensive. *Maybe Murphy was on to something? How did one hunt the elusive coyote? You bait them, and I know just what to use.*

When John finished off his beer and stood, Murphy said, "What I do—say something stupid?"

"No, Murph. The opposite, you just told me how we may be able to get him."

"Really?"

"Yup. See you around, I got some things to do."

John walked out into the night air. The ice on the parking lot surface crunched beneath his feet as he approached his truck. Suddenly the hair on the nape of his neck stood up and he felt as if he were being watched. He stood beside his truck, key poised before the lock, and slowly searched the area as much as he could without moving his head enough to be seen doing so. He paid particular interest to the trees across the road from the parking lot and thought he detected a form standing there. He unlocked the door, opened it, and reached across the seat for his service pistol. He felt an immediate feeling of relief as his hand tightened on the handle of the familiar weapon. He straightened up and turned to face the dark shape he'd seen. It was gone.

He heard a door open and spun toward it. Murphy stood in front of the door to Del's Place, his hands raised to his shoulders. "Whoa, John! It's me . . . Murphy."

John lowered the handgun and said, "Someone or something was in the trees over there. I'm going to check it out."

"Hold on, I'll grab my piece and join you."

John waited for several moments and when Murphy joined him holding his nine-millimeter service pistol in his right hand and a Maglite in the left, they crossed the road and headed toward the place where John believed he had seen the stalker.

They scaled the snowbank and slid into the four-foot-deep snow on the backside. Murphy took the lead and shined his flashlight into the trees as he broke trail. "Where did you see it?" he asked John.

"That fir to your right. It was under the branches."

As they pushed their way beyond the deeper snow that had been piling up over the past three months, John felt his legs straining. "You know," he said, "this is the second time today I've done this."

"Really, where else did you do it?"

"Dowd Settlement."

"Dwain acting up again? Hell, you just chased that kid halfway to Mount Katahdin."

The snow depth decreased and was only eighteen to twenty-four inches deep and Murphy shined the light into the tree line. "Got something," he said.

When John reached Murphy's side, the senior warden was breathing hard from the effort required to wade across the twenty or so feet between the roadside snowbank and the woods. He looked at the area that Murphy was illuminating and saw the gigantic footprints. There was a smell of putrid meat in the air.

"Do you smell it?" Murphy asked.

"That seals it," John said. "There's not a doubt in my mind—the fucker's back."

Murphy used the flashlight's beam to follow the tracks as they disappeared deeper into the trees and snow-laden bushes. "We going to follow him?"

John's breath sent steam spiraling into the freezing night air when he said, "Be a waste of time and energy. It can travel one helluvalot faster than we can. It could be in Piscataquis County in a few hours."

Murphy turned his head, studied John's face for a second, and then said, "Why do I get this feeling that you aren't joking?"

"I've tracked it through the woods. It ain't human the way it can move through the snow."

Larry Murphy switched off the television as soon as the late-night news finished. He didn't like the weather forecast, which was snow for the next two days and then more snow for the days after that. February usually had the third-highest average snowfall in Lyndon, however there was only a three-inch difference between it and January, which was the snowiest month with an average 25.2 inches. Normally the local news from Presque Isle was of little interest to him, but the station's meteorologist was more accurate than many Murphy had seen, especially when it came to forecasting winter storms. Of late, however, he'd developed a great deal of interest in the Aroostook County news.

Murphy adjusted the auger feed on the pellet stove that provided all the heat he needed in the two-room cabin and walked into his bedroom. He rolled into bed, read a book for a half hour, and then turned off the light. In minutes, he was asleep.

The smell of a decaying body was so strong that it woke Larry Murphy up. He glanced at the digital clock on his nightstand and then laid quiet, listening for whatever had aroused him. He heard the wind gust and he looked out the window. Murphy always slept with his blinds open, allowing ambient light to illuminate the room. He watched a gust of wind push snow across the hard crust layer that had formed after the brief warming period known as the January thaw. The building creaked as it stood firm against the wind. Snow was falling and it was evident that it was going to accumulate—he recalled the late-night weather forecast, which had called for eighteen to twenty inches of new powder.

He laid back and closed his eyes. Just as he was about to fall asleep there was a soft rattle at his front door, as if someone was trying the knob to see if it was locked. Murphy's holster, containing his service pistol, was draped across the wooden chair that sat in the corner at the foot of his bed, and he got up and took out the pistol. He checked the load as he softly crept out of the bedroom. He stopped beside the door, holding the pistol in both hands and pointed toward the ceiling. Slowly, so he wouldn't alarm whoever was on the other side, Murphy unlocked the door and waited for the intruder to try it again. The smell of rot was so strong that he thought his stomach would void.

The wind gusted, rattling the door, but there was no attempt to open it from the outside. Cautiously, Murphy turned the knob and another gust of wind blew the door inward. Murphy spun around, stepping into the threshold and aimed his nine-millimeter pistol outward. There was no one in sight. Murphy stepped to one side and visually searched the right side of the entrance—seeing no one, he stepped across the doorway so he could see the opposite side and repeated his search. He turned his attention to the ground and saw the giant footprints filling with wind-blown snow. He inhaled and realized that the rotted corpse smell had diminished to a mere trace, which the wind carried away.

Murphy closed the door and locked it again. He kept his pistol in hand as he walked around the interior of his home, looking out each of the windows for any sign of someone moving about. Other than the footprints he'd seen in the snow, there was no sign of the intruder. He looked at the wall clock over his sink and decided there was not much use in going back to bed as he would be getting up in an hour and a half—and, as hyped as he was, he doubted that he'd get back to sleep. He turned to the small gas stove in the kitchen and ignited the burner beneath the percolator of coffee he'd prepared before going to bed.

Murphy turned on the television and sat at the table oblivious to the all-news channel as he thought about the implication of the killer's tracks being at his door. He heard the coffee begin to percolate and turned off the burner. As he poured a cup he looked at the clock again and wondered whether he should wake John up or wait until five. If this thing, whatever it was, was going on the offensive, John would want to know.

41

Del's Place, Lyndon Station

Murphy met Bob Pelky and John Bear for their ritual of morning coffee at Del's Place. He sat down and Nellie placed a mug of coffee in front of him.

"Rough night, Murph?" John asked.

"You could say that. I had a visitor in the middle of the night. . . ." Murphy related the events of the previous night to them.

"You're sure it was Condor?" John asked.

"If you're askin' did I see him—no. But there were tracks the size of snowshoes around the house. I'm positive they were his. I can't think of another person in the area with a hoof that big."

John sat back and looked pensive. "Sounds like it's taking the fight to us. . . ."

"I'll report this to the barracks in Houlton," Pelky said. "They'll send a couple extra troopers up here."

John remained quiet for several moments.

"What's on your mind, John?" Pelky asked.

"We better keep a close watch on anyone close to us," John replied.

"Do you think he'll make a play for our families?"

"At this stage I don't have so much as a single goddamned clue what it'll do. However, its tracking Murph to his home is of concern."

Pelky stood up. "I think I may send Elaine to see her mother down in Presque Isle for a few days." He turned to John. "You should warn your brother and his wife . . . and Laura. He could go after any of them.

All three gulped down their coffee and stood up.

"I'll do that," John said. "Then I'm going out to your place, Murph. Maybe we can pick up the trail."

Murphy looked through the steamy windows at the steady falling snow. "We already had six inches since last night. Doubt that there'll be much to see at my place."

"Be that as it may," John answered. "I know one thing—I ain't waitin' for it to come after me. I want whatever advantage I can get."

Home of Tom and Clarisse Bear

His brother and sister-in-law were having breakfast when John walked into their kitchen.

"Well," Tom said, "the prodigal returns."

John felt his face flush and swallowed the retort he would have made had Clarisse not been in the room. He retrieved a mug from the cupboard near the sink and filled it with coffee from the coffee maker on the counter. He sat at the table across from his brother, Clarisse to his left.

"You want something to eat, John?" Clarisse asked.

"No, thanks, I had breakfast at Del's with Murph and Bob." He looked at his brother. "How long since you been over home, Tom?"

"A while."

"You might want to consider spending a few days over there. . . . Spend some time with the old man and Clarisse's family."

Tom studied his brother for several seconds. "What's goin' on, John? Why you tellin' us to get out of town?"

John took a sip of coffee and leaned back. "You know this case I been working on?"

"Yuh, the murders. You got any idea who done them?"

"Yes, a Wendigo . . ."

Tom looked concerned. "Maybe you should tell us what in hell you're talkin' about, big brother?"

John spent twenty minutes relating the events of the past few days, including his pursuit of the Wendigo, Dwain Dowd's abduction, and Murphy's belief that it was roaming around his place the night before.

When John finished, Tom said, "Do you honestly believe this thing will try and get at you through us?"

"I don't know, Tom. The only thing I know for certain is that it's a Wendigo."

"You say it kidnapped the Dowd boy?" Clarisse said.

"That I ain't so sure of. I do know that the kid's snow sled broke down and it picked him up and took him with him. The kid says that nothin' happened—which I believe. But, the second time it looks to me like the boy went willingly."

"If," Tom interjected, "this killer is a Wendigo, why didn't it—?"

"Devour the kid? That's the part that has me stumped."

"It abandoned the boy to get you and the boy's uncle off his trail?" Tom said.

"Yeah, we believe that's what it did. But, there's evidence that it didn't stay in Quebec—and I think it's been meeting with the boy in the woods late at night."

Clarisse got up, retrieved the coffee pot, and refilled John's mug. While she did that, Tom left the room and returned in a few minutes, carrying two pistols. John immediately recognized one of them as the .45-caliber Hi-Point he'd given Tom as a Christmas present a few years ago. Tom placed the smaller of the two handguns before his wife. "Since October fifteenth," he told her, "you no longer require a state-issued permit to carry a concealed weapon in Maine. I want you to take this with you wherever you go."

Clarisse picked up the .32-caliber pistol and expertly dropped the magazine from it. She pulled back on the slide and checked the chamber to insure there was no live round in it. She released the slide, inserted the magazine, and once again pulled it to the rear. She released the slide, loading a bullet into the chamber. She checked to see that the safety was on and placed the gun on the table. "I gather we're staying here and not going to Canada," she said.

McBrietty's Cabins

John knocked on the door of Laura's cabin and heard her moving inside. She called out, "Who is it?"

"John, can I come in?"

He heard the security bolt slide and then the door opened. Laura stepped back from the door and John entered the small rental cabin. Her hair was disheveled and her eyes appeared puffy. When she spoke her voice was congested and she generally looked terrible.

"Are you all right?" he asked.

"I got a cold," she said. "Possibly the flu, too."

"Have you taken anything?"

"No, I just need to rest, by tomorrow I should be okay." She waved for him to follow her deeper into the room, away from the door. "The weather isn't helping me either. How much snow are we supposed to get?"

"The weatherman is hedging his bets, he won't narrow it down more than to say we'll get between eighteen and twenty-four inches."

"A foot and a half to two feet! Oh my God. How do you people live in this climate?" She walked to her bed and fell into it.

"Laura, we have to talk. . . ."

She held up her hand, bolted from the bed, and darted into the bathroom, slamming the door behind her. He heard the toilet flush and the sound of her retching and then another flush. After a few minutes she reappeared, quickly shutting the door behind her. "John, I'm not up to talking now. Every orifice in my body is secreting fluid. Could you come back later? Maybe by tonight I'll be able to talk."

John nodded. "I'll try and come by this evening. Can I get you anything?"

"Does Del sell over-the-counter meds?"

"I'm sure he has some cold stuff."

"Would you be a dear and get me some nighttime cold medicine, aspirin, and any type of decongestant he might have." She reached for her purse. "I'll give you some money."

John held his hand out in the universal signal to stop. "I got it. You just rest."

"I'm going back to bed. I'll leave the door unlocked. . . ."

"I'd rather you didn't do that. Just give me your room key."

She raised her head and said, "What's wrong? You seem nervous."

"That's what we need to talk about when you're up to it."

"Okay." She reached over to the dresser and handed him her room key. The effort seemed to take every bit of strength she had. She walked to the bed and fell backward onto it. In minutes she was asleep and snoring as she breathed through her mouth.

John returned from the general store with as much over-the-counter cold medicine as he could find. Fortunately, Del knew that cold and flu season was an annual event in Lyndon Station and he kept a wide variety on hand.

His entrance must have awakened Laura. She lay on her bed watching as he unloaded enough medication to treat a marine division. "How many people do you expect to come down with this?" Laura asked. She laughed and immediately broke out in a fit of coughing.

John got her a glass of water and carried a couple of the medicine bottles to her. He shook out two tablets of cold medicine and handed them to her along with the water. "Take these."

Laura's cheeks and nose were a hot-pink hue and her eyes puffy and tearing. She gave him a half-hearted smile and opened her mouth and tossed the pills inside, immediately washing them down with a long drink. She placed the glass on the nightstand and dropped back, her head settled on the pillow. "You're a darling, John." Speaking must have aggravated her sore throat because she rose up on one elbow and retrieved the water and finished it off.

John refilled the glass and placed it beside her.

"What is important enough that you'd brave catching this bug to talk to me?"

"The Wendigo."

"So you're sure that the killer is one . . . have you caught it?"

"No, but we think it's back in the area."

She frowned and John clarified his statement. "Last night, Murph heard someone or something prowling around outside his house. When he investigated, all he found were tracks like the ones we've found at all the crime sites."

"Okay, so it's back. Why should this be important enough for you to come running over here?"

"Laura, we can't eliminate anything with a Wendigo. It wouldn't surprise me if it may know about . . ."

"Us." She finished the statement for him.

John hated the way he stammered when he said, "Yeah. It could know about us—or at least I'm going to take steps based upon that assumption. I'm telling everyone close to me to get out of the area until we catch him."

She laid still, staring at him for several long moments. "I'm not leaving."

"Laura this guy is extremely dangerous, more than anyone I've ever encountered."

She held up a hand, silencing him. "Hon." Her use of the term of endearment took him by surprise. "I'm in no condition to travel and—even if I was—I have a job to do, too. If I let this thing run me off I'll be back to reporting on the local garden club's meetings. I've been on this story since the Kelly boy went missing and I am going to see it through to the end." She gave him a smug smile. "Here's what I'll do. You promised to take me with you and as of yet have only done it once. I'll be your shadow, that way you can protect me from him."

When she flopped back on the bed and said, "Now go away and let me get some rest," he knew that the discussion was over.

42

Larry Murphy's House, Lyndon Station, Maine

John and Murphy stood on the front porch, studying the indentations in the snow. John glanced up to the sky and said, "You followed the tracks?"

Murphy nodded his head. "They go back into the woods about fifty feet or so. I couldn't tell which way he came from nor which direction he went."

"At the rate it's snowin' we'll never find out."

Murphy turned to the entrance to his small house. "Coffee's ready. You want some?"

"Yeah, not much else to do."

They entered the small house and John sat at the small table in the center of the common room. Murphy had sectioned the room by arranging the kitchen furniture in one corner and the living room in another. The bedroom and bath were the only other rooms in the house. John felt at home in Murphy's house and wished that he had a similar place. *Maybe*, he thought, *I'll build a small place like this for myself and get out of the apartment in Ashland.*

Murphy walked to the kitchen area and filled two mugs with coffee and returned to the table. "You got any type of plan in mind?" he asked John.

John looked past Murphy at the falling snow, which had increased in intensity. "Nope, the way the snow is comin' down his tracks will be gone in an hour, if not less."

"So we wait for him to show himself again?"

"That's basically the plan. Although, it may be wise to keep an eye on the Dowd place. Condor seems to have developed some sort of bond with Dwain."

"You think we should head on out there?" Murphy asked.

"I have to report to Lieutenant Michaud," John said. "Tell you what, let's drive into Fort Kent and fill the lieutenant in. First thing in the morning we'll go to Dowd Settlement."

The North Maine Woods, Near Dowd Settlement

The Wendigo walked through the deep snow and leafless bushes. He was aware that everyone north of Bangor was probably looking for him and as a result he was hypervigilant. A gust of wind swept through the trees creating a white whirlwind of snow that cascaded down, coating his head and shoulders until he resembled a white statue. He shrugged and set a course for Dowd Settlement. He glanced up through the pines and leafless deciduous trees while trying to determine the sun's position above the low-hanging overcast that covered the area. Experience told him there was more snow in the offing—all the better to hide any sign of his passing.

Upon arriving at Dowd Settlement he stood back from the edge of the woods and studied the barn through the falling snow. He looked over his shoulder at the steep incline behind him. If he was caught, his best avenue of escape would be that way, to the top of the beech tree–covered ridge. He squatted behind some evergreen trees and waited for darkness.

Darkness chased the light away and the Wendigo left the trees that concealed him from the sight of anyone who would casually scan the woods. Two steps brought him to the edge of the trees. The world was a monochrome tapestry, white snow and black buildings and terrain. It was a world in which he was at ease. He scanned the open field and then stepped out into it.

He was halfway to the barn when he heard the whine of approaching snowmobiles. He turned toward the sound and saw one machine round the left corner of the barn and head directly at him. He looked toward the right and saw another sled appear from that direction. There was a sharp crack as a bullet passed through his side. He'd walked into a trap! He spun and fled toward the safety of the woods.

The Wendigo's long legs served him well. He glided through the snow, but the increasing cacophony from the sleds told him that they were closing fast. There was a loud *snap* of a bullet breaking the sound barrier. He broke left, ran two strides, and then went right, hoping to throw the shooter off.

He was almost to the trees when he heard one of the sleds immediately behind him. He turned, emitted a thunderous roar and backhanded the rider, throwing him from his seat. His first instinct was to carry the still figure with him, but reconsidered when another bullet snapped past his head. He spun around and bolted into the safety of the woods.

Earl Dowd stopped his sled and ran to see how badly Louis was hurt. When he reached his son, Louis was sitting up and holding his head, the remnants of his helmet in his hand. Earl squatted beside him and asked. "You okay?"

"I ain't dead or crippled if that's what you're askin'."

Earl turned his head and looked at the track in the snow where the giant had fled.

"We goin' after him?" Louis asked.

"Not by ourselves." Earl stood up and offered his hand to his son. "Let's get back to the house. I want to check you out, then we're gonna form a posse. I want every male Dowd armed and on a sled within the hour."

He helped his son onto his sled and they turned and raced back to the house. An hour later a convoy consisting of eight men—all armed with high-powered rifles, formed up in the Dowd dooryard, and set out in pursuit.

43

Del's Place

John Bear and Laura Wells had just sat down when John's cell phone rang. He glanced at the display, muttered "shit," and answered. "Yes, Amy."

"How'd you know it was me?"

"Caller ID. What can I do for you?"

"That thing was here tonight."

"When?"

"I'm not sure, but not more than two or three hours ago."

"And you're just calling me?"

"This was the first chance I got. Dad and Louis spotted him and took off after him. Somehow it knocked Louis off his sled and got away. Now, Dad, Louis, and six relatives are out looking for it."

"How long ago did they leave?"

"Fifteen minutes, no more."

"Thanks for calling, Amy."

"Warden, they're all carrying guns and I don't think that they intend on bringing it back alive."

"Okay, Amy. I'll get out there as soon as I can."

John broke the connection and Laura said, "Trouble?"

"The Dowds are at it again. They spotted the Wendigo and went after him. Some way or another, it got away—now the entire clan is chasing him."

"What are you going to do?"

John leaned back. "By the time I get out there they'll have at least a couple hour's head start. I might as well eat, then grab Murph and head up there."

Dowd Settlement

John and Murphy parked off to one side of the plowed open area that the Dowds used as a front yard. Amy met them before they were halfway across. "Thank God you're here. Dwain has gone missing!"

"You're sure?" John asked. "Maybe he's hiding someplace."

"I've looked everywhere. He's nowhere to be found."

"I'll see if there is any sign of which way he went," Murphy said. He walked toward the barn.

"He went by himself," Amy called after him.

Murphy turned toward her. "You sure of that?"

"He didn't get within fifty yards of here." She pointed toward the trees over a hundred yards away. "Louis and Dad saw him when he was coming across the field. That's when they went after him and he knocked Louis off his Ski-Doo and took off. Dad came back here, got every man in the settlement, and they took off after him."

Murphy remained where he was. "John? How you want to handle this?"

"Amy already searched the property, so doing it again is a waste of effort. Let's get our sleds off the trucks and see if we can catch up with them." He looked at the cascading snow. "Before we lose their trail." He looked across the open field and saw the wind pick up the loose surface snow and spin it into a whirlwind which darted along the ground.

The wardens pulled their snow machines out of the beds of their pickups. John reached into the back of the extended cab and removed his cold-weather suit. Once he had the suit on, he sat and removed his boots, slid the felt booties out of the rubber-soled snowmobile boots, put them on, and then slid the bulky outer boots over them. Ready for prolonged exposure to the winter weather, he saw that Murphy was likewise ready. They straddled their sleds and started the motors.

John turned to Amy. "If any of them return, tell them to stay here or I'll arrest them."

T17, R12, North Maine Woods

Back in the woods and secure in his element, the Wendigo decided to go on the attack. He hid beneath a tall evergreen tree beside the trail. In short time he heard the Dowd convoy and prepared to strike. Headlights illuminated the trees around his hiding place and for a brief second he worried that the rider of the lead snowmobile would see him. He let the file of men pass and when the last sled was abreast of him, he struck.

He leaped from his hiding place and hit the unknown rider, driving him off his sled and into the deep snow. He straddled the man and raised his hand, prepared to smash it into the rider's face. Suddenly he was in the center of a beam of light and he heard a shout. He'd miscalculated; there had been another member of the group who'd lagged behind. He turned toward the light and saw a flash immediately followed by the impact of a bullet. He rolled off the downed Dowd and heard another shot. The man on the ground grabbed a knife from his belt and drove it into his thigh.

The Wendigo roared his rage and smashed his huge right fist into the knife-bearer's face. He felt bone and cartilage break and the man went limp. The trailing man raised his rifle and fired a third shot. Again the Wendigo felt a bullet's impact. He coiled, preparing to leap at this new threat. Suddenly the road was bathed in light; the rest of the party had turned around and were racing toward him.

The Wendigo leaped over deadfall and burst through a copse of frozen ice-covered alder bushes, loud voices behind him. He paused long enough to see his footprints and knew that stealth was out of the question. His only hope lay in flight.

T17, R12, North Maine Woods

Earl Dowd waded through the knee-deep snow and saw Louis and two family members squatting over a body. As he got closer, Earl saw the dark spot in the snow that he knew would turn red as he got closer to it. "Who is it?"

Louis looked at his father and said, "Cully. I ain't never seen nothing as strong as that thing. The bastard killed him with one punch."

"I shot him—twice," another voice said.

Earl turned to see his nephew, Kane, standing to one side, still holding his Remington 700 .30-06 semiautomatic rifle. "You sure of that, Kane?"

"You know me, Uncle, I hit what I shoot at."

Earl nodded. Of all the Dowds, Kane was the best shot. "Someone needs to take him home," Earl said. "As for the rest of us, there ain't nothin' to be done for Cully. So go after the sonuvawhore. This time we ain't goin' back until we've killed the fucker."

Earl looked at the circle of family members and pointed at the two youngest. "You boys been ridin' double?"

"Yes, Uncle Earl."

"Then you're the funeral detail." Earl stared into the black forest and in a low voice said, "Too goddamned young to be involved in this." He turned to the boys. "Take him home—and stay there. We'll end this tonight."

44

John and Murphy followed the trail into the forest, and when they saw headlights coming toward them, they stopped and waited for the sleds to approach. The two boys stopped and John recognized them as being Dowds. "You boys headin' home?"

The first rider said, "Yes, sir."

John looked past him and saw the dark shape of a sleigh. "What you haulin'?"

The boy looked as if he'd been caught chewing gum in class and looked at his companion.

"I asked you a question, son," John said, keeping his voice and tone at a reasonable level.

"My cousin, Cully. Fuckin' asshole killed him—"

John nodded, "Who killed him?"

"That thing we was chasin'. Crushed his head with a single punch. None of us ever seen anything like it."

"Tell me what happened. Don't leave anything out."

The boys related the events of the evening and concluded with: "Uncle Earl sent us back with the body and said we was to stay at home."

"Sounds like good advice to me," Murphy said.

"How long ago did all this happen?" John asked.

"'Bout three hours ago."

"Okay, you boys go about your business, and when you get home call the state police and tell them what happened. They'll send someone for him."

John and Murphy watched the Dowd boys ride away and sat quiet for a few moments. "What you thinking about, John?"

"I'm thinkin' that this could turn into one hellacious blood bath in a hurry."

"If it hasn't already," Murphy said.

The Wendigo looked down the ridge and watched them setting up a camp in the valley below. There were fewer of them now, only five—and they were about to become fewer still. His attention was drawn to the east where two additional sleds approached. He remained back in the trees watching. The snowfall had abated and the wind picked up, driving the windchill into the minus-thirty range. He relaxed; things were working out perfectly. Even the weather was helping him—what was freezing cold to his pursuers was comfortable to him.

The new arrivals stopped at the camp and dismounted. The first of them removed his helmet, and the Wendigo immediately recognized the Indian warden. He walked away from the precipice and strode deeper into the woods. He stared at the posse one last time and wondered how they'd react if they knew how close to them he was. A gust of wind sent a cloud of snow into the air and he let it settle on his head, face, and shoulders. As he descended the steep slope of the ridge, trees creaked and swayed in the wind, frozen dead branches broke off some of them and fell into the four-foot-deep snow with muffled thumps. He turned toward Rocky Mountain, where he knew of a cave where he had a cache and could hide.

John Bear and Murphy were exhausted when they drove into the small valley and found the impromptu camp the Dowds had established. John dismounted and pulled his helmet off. He immediately felt the sweat that the insulated protective headgear had caused begin to freeze in the frigid wind. He reached inside a pocket of his snowsuit and retrieved his warden service hat and put it on. He saw Earl Dowd standing beside a small fire holding a steaming cup of coffee.

"Earl," John said with a nod of his head. "Got any more of that coffee?"

Dowd pointed at the pot sitting on a bed of smoldering coals. "Help yourself."

John saw a row of metal coffee mugs lined up on a snowmobile seat and retrieved two. He returned to the fire, tossed a mug to Murphy, and then used one of his heavy insulated mittens as a potholder to hold the hot percolator

Steam hovered over the rim of the metal camp cup as John gulped down a burning mouthful of the hot liquid. The hot beverage seemed to scorch his throat as he felt it make its way down his esophagus before disappearing deep into his body. "I guess you know why we're here."

"To stop us from getting it. . . ."

"To help you get it—and stop you from killing him."

Dowd sat on a dead tree that lay near the fire. "We got you outnumbered."

"How many more of your relatives are you willing sacrifice to get him?"

Earl seemed to pout as he sat forlorn on the snowy tree. "I gather you met up with Billy and Mikey, and Cully—Cullen."

"Yes," John saw movement to his left and turned that way. Louis Dowd appeared at the edge of the trees. He must have been taking care of personal matters and was slipping his snowsuit trouser suspenders over his shoulders. His face was swollen and one side a spreading bruise. Something had hit him hard and John didn't think it was a branch. He nodded at Louis and asked, "You all right? Looks like you kissed a runaway truck."

"I'll live." Louis helped himself to a cup of coffee. "What brings you out here?"

"Amy called and said you guys had had a run-in with it yesterday and that you were chasin' him." He paused to let his words sink in and then added, "She also said that she didn't believe you'd be bringing him in alive."

Louis looked at his father. "She's out of control, Dad."

"Yeah," Earl replied.

"She's got a good head on her that's for sure," John added. "You kill him without him attackin' you and I'd be forced to bring you in too. Right now, he's a person of interest, not a fugitive for anything except maybe kidnapping—and I ain't so sure that Dwain didn't go with him on his own."

Earl stiffened. "You sayin' my grandson wanted to run off with that freak?"

"Yup, and from your reaction, I'd say you think so too."

"So," Earl said, "now that's all been said. What are you going to do?"

John squatted in front of the fire and warmed up his coffee from the remnants of what was in the blue metal pot. "Take charge. It's now an official manhunt. We bring him in alive if we can, otherwise, we do what we have to to end this thing."

Earl stared across the fire. After several tense moments of silence he said, "You gonna deputize us or something?"

"No need for all that; besides I don't have that authority. But you take your orders from me or, in my absence, Murphy."

45

Rocky Mountain, T18, R12, North Maine Woods

The Wendigo squatted in the mouth of the cavern he'd used for hibernation since before the whites came into the world and studied the slope below. He saw no sign of activity and after twenty-five minutes turned and scrambled deeper inside. Halfway down the narrow chasm he stopped beside a bear den and looked in. He saw movement and heard the sow grunt in her sleep, it was then he realized that she'd given birth, which made him leery. It was not unknown for she-bears to come out of hibernation when they gave birth. For several minutes he stood bent over so he wouldn't bang his head on the roof of the cave, and studied the miniature bear cubs, which he estimated to be less than a week old, as they scrambled for a warm spot near their mother's teat. The sow was about three-quarters deep into her hibernation state and there was a GPS collar around her neck—which didn't concern him. If biologists from the Department of Inland Fisheries and Wildlife should appear to do a check on the cubs, he'd deal with them.

Satisfied that the new mother posed no threat, he crept past the den and moved deeper into the cavern. Within fifty feet of the den, the cavern opened up into a wide area with several tunnels branching off it. The Wendigo scrambled to the first tunnel on the left and darted into it. He lay down and closed his eyes, fighting against the overpowering hunger that threatened to consume him. He stayed that way for over an hour and then got up in frustration. He went back to the entrance, and once again taking care not to crush one of the tiny cubs beneath his huge feet, he circumvented the comatose she-bear.

The sun was already well into its afternoon descent when he low-crawled out of the pile of deadfall that obscured the entrance to the lair and he breathed in fresh cold air, which was manna after the stuffy, moldy smell of the bear den. He stared off in the direction where he'd last encountered the posse and fought back his desire to give in to impulse and set off in that direction to obtain food. He turned in the opposite direction and climbed further up the slope. There were logging roads in that direction; thoroughfares where food might be found. He stopped, turned, and stared wistfully downslope, where he *knew* food existed.

T17, R12, North Maine Woods

The search party had spread out, hoping to cut the killer's trail. They had spent the morning hunting in vain. If the fugitive had left any tracks, the wind and drifting snow had filled them in. As the afternoon wore on toward sunset, the search had turned from a manhunt into one of finding a suitable campsite for the night.

John and Earl Dowd were drinking hot coffee at the campfire that was maintained at a central location from which the area had been searched in quadrants. "Ain't natural that he can disappear like this," Earl said.

John knew that if there was one thing Wendigos were not, they were not natural—if anything, they were a perversion of nature. They thrived on cold, eating mankind, and had supernatural abilities. He'd heard tales of them having the ability to shape-shift their appearance. They also were capable of self-healing and resurrection if their bodies were not burned in a raging bonfire. Still he knew that if he was to tell Earl his thoughts and beliefs, he would think John was just another crazy damned Indian. John sat on the seat of his Ski-Doo and finished his coffee. He looked off at the silhouette of Rocky Mountain, barely visible through the fine sheet of falling and drifting snow, and knew that they need not look for the Wendigo. It's all-consuming hunger would lead it to them. John refilled his coffee mug and said, "I think that drinking this much coffee is a mixed blessing."

Dowd understood what he meant and smiled. "Yeah coffee and beer have one thing in common. You never own them, only rent them." He indicated to the bulky one-piece snowmobile suits they wore. "These suits are a pain in the ass when it's time to pay the rent."

They heard a sled approach, stood up, and waited until it stopped near theirs. Louis Dowd raised the visor of his helmet and said, "I hope you two ain't drunk all the hot coffee."

"Anything?" John asked.

"Nothing but snow, dead trees, more snow blowing from the trees, and cold. Other than that I ain't seen shit." He threw one leg over the sled and dismounted. He retrieved a mug and, when he held it out, John filled it. Louis took a drink and said, "Ain't no one seen nothing. It's like the ground swallowed him up."

"It probably did," John replied.

The Dowds said nothing and John added: "Wouldn't surprise me none if he ain't found a lair where he's layin' up—probably burrowed down, waiting for us to give up the search."

"Well," Louis said, "he's in for the shock of his life. I ain't goin' back until we got him—one way or the other. I don't care if I have to stay out here until spring."

"I don't think it'll come to that," John said. He turned to Earl. "We may want to send a couple of the boys back to get some supplies. This could run into a week or more. I'll send Murph. One of us has to update the brass on what's happening."

"I'll send two of the boys back in the morning. No sense in doing it today, it'll be dark in a couple of hours and it's five or six hours each way to the settlement. If they have to run into Lyndon it could be a couple days before they get back."

John nodded and looked toward the mountain again. "You ever been up there?" he asked.

Earl looked in the same direction as John and said, "Rocky Mountain? Long time ago the old man was gonna cut wood up there back in the late seventies, early eighties. We never did though."

"Why not?"

"Beats me, the old man never said why he changed his mind."

"Maybe," John said, "he couldn't get a permit to cut."

"Doubt that, Linwood Dowd could care less about permits. Back then it was Seven Islands that held the cuttin' rights, and they were tough but you could work with them guys. Today it's Irving from Canada. They're a whole different type of animal. If they had their way wouldn't be nothing left of these woods but clear-cut and mud. Northern Maine would look like Southern California—a mud slide waitin' for a rain storm . . . or the spring thaw. And if they get their way, they'd own every tree that was cut."

"Anything up there?"

"Nothin' worth goin' out of your way for. The forest service has a lookout tower, but that's unmanned this time of year." He gave John a quizzical look.

"What?" John asked.

"I'm surprised you don't know the place."

"Why should I?"

"Well, there's a warden cabin about a mile below the lookout tower on the summit."

"No shit? I've never been a patrol warden up here. The state did most of that down in Oxford and Hancock Counties. Murph'll know."

"Murph'll know what?" said a new voice.

John turned to see Murphy enter the camp.

"About the warden cabin on Rocky Mountain."

"Not a bad idea. We could set up there and coordinate the search. Not to mention we can get out of the weather there."

"Is it heated?" John asked.

"Last I knew there was a woodstove there. Ain't much, just a place for us to crash while checkin' out the area."

"Might be worth checking out," John said. "What's access like?"

"No road, but the trail is wide enough for a sled or an ATV to get up there—at least it was last time I was there."

"In the morning," John said, "we'll go up there and make it a base-camp until we've determined if this thing is in the area or not."

Rocky Mountain

From his perch on the mountain's summit, the Wendigo observed the activity around the small cabin below. He had no idea how they had found him, but knew that if he was to survive he had to go on the offensive. To remain hidden, in hope of outlasting them, was not going to work. He needed to eat, it had been two days since he'd eaten and the need was driving him toward taking hasty action—if he didn't get something soon, he'd return to the cave and have a bear feed, although wild game was not his first choice of food.

The snow had stopped and high pressure had settled over the area, driving the overcast that held the heat near the ground. The night was clear, causing radiational cooling, and so many stars were visible that they seemed to smear themselves across the galaxy. He felt his strength returning, but then he always felt stronger and more vital after the sun set. A wave of hunger pangs constricted his stomach and he made up his mind that he would give the posse one more hour to settle in—then he'd strike.

About one hundred feet back in the trees, the Wendigo circled the camp, paying attention for any lookouts they may have posted. He made two complete revolutions around the perimeter before he was certain where the sentries were located. He knew that his presence so close to their camp was risky; if one of the humans should find his tracks, they would lead them to him. If that should happen, he'd be forced to move to another of his lairs. He should leave now, get away while he still had time—but there was the *hunger* . . .

He saw a pile of firewood and knew that they would assign someone to keep the fire going through the night. All he need do was wait. He positioned himself close to the wood where he could see the seven snowmobiles that were parked around the camp. Seven sleds meant at least that many drivers.

The Wendigo settled back to watch and to wait.

Sleeping bags surrounded the fire and their lumpy appearance intimated that they were occupied. A lone man patrolled the campsite. He walked to the woodpile. He gathered an armful of hardwood and turned toward the fire. Before the man could sound the alarm, Wendigo's powerful hand gripped his throat, crushing his larynx and stifling any sound. With his free hand, he thrust his talons into his chest. Blood pulsed with each beat of the skewered man's heart.

The Wendigo threw the still-warm body over his shoulder and ran into the protection of the trees.

———————

The cold woke John Bear up and he slipped out of his sleeping bag. He looked at the fire, saw that it had burnt down until all that remained was smoldering embers. He knew that Galen Dowd had taken the first fire watch and must have gone to get more wood. He shoved his feet into his boots and, without lacing them, walked to the woodpile. He found pieces of firewood spread around, but no sign of Dowd. He called, "Galen, you out there?"

No answer.

"Galen—you out there?"

As soon as John stepped outside the camp's perimeter he smelled the sickening odor that had become too familiar. He followed a set of footprints into the trees and saw a dark spot in the snow. He walked to it and squatted down. He heard a noise behind him and looked up. Earl Dowd stood behind him. "That smell is him, ain't it?"

"Grab a flashlight, will you, Earl?"

The senior Dowd disappeared and in short time returned, shining a beam of light ahead of him. "Where the fuck is Galen?" he asked.

The beam flashed across the dark spot at John's feet, which turned dark red. "Gone," John said.

"What the hell you mean, gone?" Earl focused the light beam on the spot. "Is that blood?"

"Yup." John stood up and said, "You armed?"

Earl stared at the red oval in the white snow. "No—but I will be in a minute." He jogged to his snowmobile.

John heard voices, followed by Earl's curt voice. When Earl returned he gripped a .30-30 lever-action rifle. "You think . . . ?"

John pointed to a large track in the snow. "Yeah, I think it got him."

Murphy stood beside the fire and called, "John?"

"Over here, Murph. Bring my pistol and coat will you?" He squatted down and zipped his boots.

Once he was armed and dressed, John led Earl and Murphy away from the camp, following the tracks. "He must have taken Galen," he said. "Notice that blood trail headed upslope?"

Earl passed John and began plowing his way through the thigh-deep snow, following the grisly trail.

John and Murphy followed, content to let Dowd break a trail for them. They heard Earl curse and saw him try to run through the snow.

"He's here!" Earl shouted.

Galen Dowd's body lay beneath the wide bottom limbs of a towering pine tree. As his body had cooled, the snow beneath him had melted and he'd sunk down below the surface of the snow—John thought he looked as if he'd been laid out in a white coffin. If they had any doubt about who'd killed him it disappeared when they saw that like all of the Wendigo's victims his body had been ruined. His blood had frozen in the minus-twenty-degree temperature and sparkled like crystal.

"What the fuck?" Earl said.

"This," John said, "is what I've been trying to tell you. This is not a human being. It's a cannibal on steroids."

"Why didn't he mutilate Askook?"

"We came up on it too soon."

Earl shined the light and the tracks were easily visible as they disappeared into the night. Earl started to follow, but stopped when John Bear placed a hand on his shoulder.

"We'll wait for daylight," John said. "These things are formidable in the day, but they're unconquerable at night. All we'll do is screw up the trail and leave ourselves open to attack."

Earl's shoulders dropped in resignation. "At this rate I'll have no family left. . . ."

"We take after this in the dark and you'll be right." John saw him shiver and realized that Earl wasn't wearing a coat nor insulated pants. All he had to ward off the frigid night was a flannel shirt and jeans.

"Let's go back," John said, "before we freeze to death."

"What about Galen?" Murphy asked.

"We'll take what we can of him back to the camp so that coyotes and other natural predators can't get at him."

46

Warden Cabin, Rocky Mountain, T18, R12

The posse arrived at the cabin at the base of Rocky Mountain shortly after noon. It was the consensus that they would spend the afternoon setting up a base camp from which they would operate. They unloaded their sleds and moved sleeping bags, food, and firewood inside.

John started a fire in the woodstove and as the inside of the building warmed he felt the fatigue brought on by days of running through the woods in pursuit of the Wendigo. He rested his head in his hands and was tempted to take a short nap.

His eyes closed and he was on the edge of sleep when the door opened and Earl Dowd walked in, allowing a blast of cold air to follow. John raised his head and blinked his eyes against the bright light from the outside.

"Sorry," Earl said. "I didn't mean to startle you."

"That's okay, the heat was getting to me and I dozed."

Earl opened his winter suit. "Heat sure feels good. It's been a long couple of days."

John stood up and stretched.

"You got any idea how we're gonna do this?"

"Yes, I do. However, there isn't much we can do until Murphy gets back from Lyndon Station with supplies."

"Well," Earl said. "We got to tell the boys something."

"Yeah, I suppose we do." He put on his winter parka and walked outside.

John saw the Dowds gathered around a fire in the fire pit that sat in the middle of the open area around the cabin. They turned toward him and Earl patiently waited for them.

Earl walked over and joined his kinfolk. "John has something to say," he told them.

John studied the faces of the men who stood before him. The Dowds—Earl, Louis, Carlton, and Alton—looked skeptical of anything John might say.

Galen Dowd's remains were wrapped in a blue tarp and lay on the packed snow in front of the cabin. The four survivors of the manhunt may not have been saying anything, but John had no doubt about their resolve to find Galen's killer. That resolve was driven by a desire for revenge and John sensed it.

"I know you're pissed," he said to the assembly. "But we still got to do this the right way."

"The right way?" Earl's fists were clenched. "This bastard has killed two of my kin, kidnapped my grandson, and almost killed my son—I'm gonna kill the fucker *the right way*."

"Earl, use your head for something other than a hat rack." John kept his voice as calm and nonconfrontational as possible. "If you kill him without cause—"

"Without cause? Ain't you heard nothin' I said?"

"Yes, I did. If this isn't done right my higher-ups and the state police are going to look into our actions and a couple of things could result. First, whoever kills him could end up facing a murder charge. Second, if we don't do this correctly and don't kill it, it'll disappear into the wilderness and continue stalking and killing."

Earl exhaled and kicked a clump of ice and snow. "Where in hell is the rights of Cully and Galen? Don't the law care about them?"

"Earl, I ask myself that when I go to work every day," John said. "The philosophy is that it's better for a hundred guilty men to walk free than one innocent man be convicted."

Earl pointed in the direction that the tracks had gone. "Well, this sonuvawhore ain't innocent. Besides," he turned toward John. "You say this thing ain't human. If that's so it's a rogue animal and we got every right to kill it."

"That's one way to look at it," John said. "The problem is as big and ugly as it is, it still stands on two legs and looks kind of human."

"Well, we ain't gonna do anything if all we do is stand around ratchet-jawin'," Earl countered. He turned to the remaining Dowds. "Carl, you take your brother home and stay there. Your mother has already lost one son, and I ain't about to put her sole remaining one in jeopardy."

"I want to stay, Uncle—"

"I know you do. But there are times in life when we got to do what we need to do, not what we want to do. Do as I say and take your brother home."

"What about his sled?"

"The only way to tow it would be to take the belt off the clutch. Unless you got tools, we'll leave it here and come back for it once this thing is done. Shit, before this is over we may have them spread from Allagash to Estcourt." Earl turned and addressed Louis and Alton. "I won't hold it against you boys if you was to head home—your decision."

Alton Dowd looked indecisive for several moments and then said, "I got tools, Uncle Earl. If it's all the same with you, I'd like to head back. My mother will freak out when she hears about Galen."

"Well," Carl said. "I guess I'm stayin' then."

"No," Earl said. "You ain't. Even the military won't send a sole-surviving son into combat. You're goin' home."

"Dad," Louis said, "if you stay, I stay."

"Okay, it's settled then. Now all we got to do is figure out how we'll get Galen secured for the ride back."

"As little of him as is left will fit in my trapper sleigh," Alton said. "If you're goin' after that thing, then you better get movin'."

John Bear walked out of the warden cabin and took a pair of snowshoes from the storage component of his Ski-Doo and fastened them to his feet. He heard the sound of a sled approaching and saw Murphy break out of the trees.

He waited until Murphy turned off his motor and then walked to him. "Were you able to get everything?"

"Yeah, but you're going to owe your sister-in-law big time."

"Owe her for what?" Earl asked.

John turned and said, "Her silverware."

"What the hell for?" Earl inquired.

"Wendigos are like werewolves; silver can kill them."

"Ain't no such thing as a werewolf," Earl said.

"Two weeks ago you didn't think there was such a thing as a Wendigo," John countered.

"Don't see how silverware will help. What you gonna do—invite it to supper?" Earl replied.

John laughed. "Nope." He asked Murphy, "You get the other stuff?"

The table was transformed into a workbench. John cut two pieces of the silverware and placed it along with a silver ring into a small foundry crucible. He lit and positioned a portable propane torch so that it heated the container, and then used a second to directly heat the silver inside.

Murphy, Earl, and Louis stood to one side observing the process. "Why two torches?" Louis asked.

"Silver melts at 1763 degrees Fahrenheit or 961.8 degrees Celsius," John answered. "It would take hours to do it with a single torch. The first torch will heat the crucible and the second the silver itself. Murph, did you get the molds?"

"Yeah, Wilmer Johansonn lent us his set. It's got every conceivable caliber mold we'd ever need."

John nodded. Johansonn was a local gunsmith who reloaded ammunition for most of the hunters and target shooters in Lyndon Station and the surrounding communities.

As the silver heated, John asked, "What caliber is your rifle, Earl?"

".30-30 Winchester."

"I'll need some of your cartridges."

Earl walked to the corner of the room where his sleeping bag and gear were stored. He opened a small canvas pack and took out a box of ammunition. He returned to the table and placed it beside John. "That enough?"

"More than enough, I'll be making five rounds for each of our weapons . . . odds are we'll be lucky to get off more than two shots apiece. Before we could shoot a third time it'll be on us and we'll be dead—if we're lucky."

"Louis—caliber?"

"Rifle's a Remington semi-auto, shoots a .30-06 Springfield," Louis answered.

"I'll need five cartridges. What about sidearms?"

"Me and Louis are carrying Hi-Points, uses nine-millimeter Luger." Earl looked at John's pistol which lay on the table. "What do you guys carry?"

"Sig Sauer Model 226, fires a .357 Sig cartridge. Murph you want to get the molds out?"

"Earl, in the bag is a bullet puller, looks like a plastic hammer. Pull the bullets and pour the powder in a container."

In less than an hour, John had made forty silver bullets and was melting more silver."

"What's this silver for?" Louis asked.

"We're going to coat our knife blades with it. A Wendigo can strike faster than anything you've ever seen. Once it has its hands on you, your knife may be your only usable weapon."

"I feel like I'm starring in a horror movie," Louis said.

"We are," was John's taciturn reply.

John was standing outside the cabin, snowshoes strapped to his feet."

Murphy walked out of the building, saw John, and said, "You going after him on foot?"

John looked up and saw Earl Dowd standing on the top step of the small porch that led into the cabin. "You're taking a big chance, John."

"Yup, it's on foot, so one of us should track it the same way. You boys can scout around the bottom of the mountain, it'll probably try to avoid you and if you make enough noise you could drive him to me. If I need you I'll get Murph on the DIF&W radio."

John tightened the last fastener and straightened up. "We can't make any assumptions with this thing. Wouldn't surprise me if it isn't someplace where sleds can't go."

"This killer is a sly one, that's for certain," Dowd said. "Don't go nowhere for a minute." He disappeared inside the cabin.

John took a last-minute inventory, to ensure he had everything he thought he might need. He heard the cabin's door slam and turned.

Earl Dowd walked to him carrying a bolt action rifle. He held the weapon out and said, "Take this. It's Galen's Remington Model 700. The civilian version of the rifle marine snipers used in Vietnam."

John took the rifle and inspected it. "This is a nice piece," he said.

Earl handed him the silver .30-06 cartridges. "I think that Galen'd be pleased to know that his rifle was the one that got his killer."

"Earl—"

"I know you want to be like that old-time animal guy, Frank Buck. . . ."

"I don't know him."

"Doesn't surprise me. He was big stuff back in the twenties and thirties. Wrote a book, *Bring 'em Back Alive*."

"You can rest assured that I won't go out of my way to avoid killing it . . . if I can," John said.

Earl looked up the mountainside and said, "One thing is for certain: it thinks the same. You want to put an end to this, you got to be as ruthless and vicious as it is. Okay?"

"Don't worry about that, I've seen enough of its handiwork to know how dangerous it is."

Murphy held up his two-way radio. "I'll be monitoring the frequency all day," he said.

John nodded and with a wave of his hand turned into the woods. He immediately retraced their tracks to where they'd found Galen Dowd's body and followed the Wendigo's tracks.

––––––––––––

The Wendigo heard the sound of the sleds even though he couldn't see them. He turned away and scaled the steep tree-covered slope. The feat of hiking the wintry terrain with its hidden barriers of downed trees and buried bushes took superhuman effort, and it felt safe; a human being would have to be in the best of physical shape to travel through the midwinter woods. As he vaulted over a downed maple, he fought against the hunger and decided to take the fight to his pursuers.

The sun filtered through the trees and the air was frigid—however, he was a manitou, a Wendigo. He scoffed at the stupidity of the posse. Their precious machines made so much noise he'd have to be deaf not to hear them.

He paused, taking a moment to study his backtrail, and froze. He detected movement on the lower slope. Someone was tracking him. He stepped behind a snow-laden pine tree and peered down toward the forested valley below. The figure looked familiar. The Indian. A mixture of rage and fear filled his entire being. He looked back toward the summit. If the warden wanted to track him, he'd give him something to track. He nodded to himself. Once he crested the peak, he'd find a suitable place to ambush the warden and, after that, take better care to conceal his tracks and movement.

He heard the sound of an airplane and looked upward. A small plane was slowly circling overhead. The warden must have requested an aerial search of the area. The Wendigo knew that from the sky he would stand out and if he was to lie in wait for the Indian, he'd need shelter from above as well as from the ground.

He turned and walked upward.

Sébastien Lavallée maintained a tight circle above Rocky Mountain. He saw a lone person in the woods and banked so he could get a closer look at him. When the solitary man waved and took his hat off, Lavallée recognized him.

He returned the wave with a wiggle of his wings and turned his attention upslope. He maintained his airspeed to just above stall-speed and peered down through the foliage-barren trees. Their trunks looked like black pins sticking in a white pincushion and all that broke the grayscale world below was the dark green of various types of evergreen trees. He saw something large standing behind huge pine tree and dropped down to get a closer look. Lavallée saw someone standing behind the tree in such a way that he would be undetected by anyone downslope—and the only person downslope was John Bear.

Lavallée snatched his microphone from its hanger and made contact.

John had turned off the speaker of his radio, electing to use an earbud instead. He was studying the terrain ahead when Lavallée's voice came through advising him that the warden-pilot had spotted someone higher up the incline. The figure was hiding behind a large pine tree, no doubt hoping to ambush any pursuit. John knew immediately that he was close to the Wendigo. His belief was confirmed when a draught came down the slope, carrying the smell of rot and decay. He checked his rifle, ensuring that it was loaded and free of any ice and snow.

Climbing the mountainside was exhausting work. Even with snowshoes, navigating through the snow was like wading through thigh-deep water and in a short time John developed a sense of admiration for soldiers and marines who assaulted enemy beaches while wading ashore. He slipped off the surface of hidden rocks and on several occasions almost tripped over buried deadfall and other pieces of debris and plant life. His chest began to ache and breathing was an all-consuming activity. The snowshoes proved to be more of a hindrance than an aid on the steep terrain, so he removed them. Uncertain where the trail would lead him, John did not want to discard them and strapped them to his back in the event that he would require them on more suitable terrain. The sound of his progress was hidden or at least muffled by the snow. During any other time of year, dead foliage and trees that had been accumulating for years would make his movement loud enough to be heard for a long distance.

Knowing that the Wendigo knew his location made John even more cautious. Rather than keeping his attention on the tracks in the snow, he now divided it, watching up the slope as well as his backtrail and the woods to his right and left. After Lavallée's warning, he paid particular attention to the pine trees, especially the large ones whose boughs were laden with snow and drooping downward, perfect cover for a lurking enemy.

Lavallée's voice came through his earphone again: ". . . Suspect is on the move, headed toward the summit . . . over."

"Roger," John replied.

Lavallée said, "Suspect has just entered a pine grove. It's too dense for me to see anything, over." Then he said: "I can't stay on station any longer, fuel is getting to the point where I'll have to return to Eagle Lake to refuel, over."

John keyed his mic and said, "Roger, thanks for the assist. Out."

The airplane dipped its wings again and veered away in a southeasterly direction.

"John, I'll try and get back if I can. Out."

John acknowledged the transmission, but doubted that he'd see Lavallée again that day. By the time he flew to the DIF&W float-plane base on Eagle Lake, refueled, and returned, it would be close to dark. In minutes the sound of the plane faded and all John heard was the wind gusting, trees creaking, and the occasional call of crows.

He stared toward the top of the peak and began following the tracks up with his eyes. As he struggled against gravity and the deep snow, he vowed to end this hunt that day.

47

Rocky Mountain

John lost the Wendigo's trail on the summit. The rocky ground was barren of snow and it had obviously taken to avoiding stepping anyplace where its tracks would show. He looked at his watch and then at the heavy overcast that blocked his view of the sun. It would be dark shortly and he would need to find shelter if he was going to spend another night in the woods.

John cautiously slid sideways down the icy surface, trying to control his descent with his leading foot. There were just enough patches of bare rock and dirt to allow him to reach the trees below the summit while staying on his feet. Once he entered the shelter of the forest the temperature seemed much warmer, almost comfortable in comparison to the windswept peak. He looked skyward and shook his head. The clouds hung low in the sky and presaged yet more snow. Any accumulation of more than a couple of inches could obscure any tracks he might find. John was also cognizant of the fact that for safety, he'd have to make a cold camp, as even the smallest fire would shine like a beacon and lead the Wendigo to him. He turned to his right, planning on circling the summit until he came across his trail.

The Wendigo easily eluded the Indian warden and moved swiftly down the mountain. He heard the sound of snowmobiles and turned in that direction. He descended the mountain as if it were a gentle, rolling hill and hid beside the snowmobile/ATV trail near the bottom. He squatted behind a massive pine tree, letting the snow-laden lower boughs conceal him. He studied the surface of the trail and saw that the fresh snow was undisturbed. He settled in. If these men were serious about finding him, they'd check out every trail and road in the area. All he had to do was wait.

Murphy slowly followed the logging road, breaking trail as he progressed. He scanned the trees on either side of him and, other than a small doe, saw little. The recent snows had driven most of the smaller denizens of the forest deep into their burrows. He saw a set of tracks where a moose had crossed the trail, and coyote tracks not far from them. All of the signs were what one would expect in the forest after a couple days of snow.

Even through the smoky dark face shield the winter world made him feel as if he were watching a black-and-white movie. The entire world appeared in grayscale; white snow, black and gray trees, and dark overcast clouds. The only thing that broke up the monochromatic scene was the green of the evergreen trees and the occasional colored plastic ribbons the logging companies used to indicate various things, such as property lines and trees slated for harvesting. To add to his discomfort, the wind was whipping the fresh powder into mini-hurricanes that covered him with a fine coating of snow. The snow penetrated the opening between his insulated suit and the helmet and melted, causing cold water to soak his undershirt.

The miserable conditions distracted Murphy and he stopped beside a huge pine. He removed a glove and fished around in his coat pocket, removing a white handkerchief with which he wiped his neck. He turned and looked back, wondering where the Dowds were.

The attack was sudden and lethal.

Murphy detected movement from the corner of his eye, but before he could react, the Wendigo was upon him. The last thing the astonished warden saw was the large claw-laden hand as it penetrated his chest— ripping into him again . . . and again . . . and again.

Earl and Louis Dowd were about one hundred yards away when they saw the huge figure bending over a prone figure. It heard their approach and when it looked up, Earl recognized it. He quickly stopped his sled and grabbed for his rifle. He used his teeth to pull his right hand glove off and quickly centered the crosshairs on it. The boom of the .30-30 rifle broke the silence of the forest and echoed across the mountain.

The Wendigo jumped up, which convinced Earl that his bullet had found its mark, and fled into the woods.

Louis raced past his father. Earl slid his rifle back in its sheath and sped after his son. They reached the body on the ground and saw the blood that stained the snow red.

"Jesus Christ," Earl swore. He grabbed his rifle, leapt off his sled, and scanned the trees in the immediate area.

While his father kept watch, Louis squatted beside Murphy. A horrific gash had laid his chest open. "He's dead, Dad."

Earl continued searching the trees and replied, "I knew that without lookin'."

"What we gonna do?"

"He got his radio on him?"

Louis quickly studied the corpse, taking care to avoid touching the lacerated organs and blood. He found a small black device attached to the suit near Murphy's right shoulder. He took it and handed it to his father. "Ever use one of those, Dad?"

"No," Earl said. "But it can't be all that difficult." He studied the device for a minute and saw that it was powered on. He spoke into it, "John? You there, John?" and then listened for a reply.

"There must be a button you have to push," Louis said.

Earl looked at the radio, turning it over in his hand. "Looks kind of like a cell phone," Earl commented. "Here, you take it."

Louis took the radio and pressed the talk button. "Warden, you there?"

Immediately he was answered. "Murphy?"

"No, sir, this is Louis Dowd."

"Where's Murph?"

"He's dead. The monster ambushed him and killed him."

"Where are you guys?"

Earl took the device from Louis, who showed him which button to push. "John, this is Earl. We're at the base of the mountain, on the tote road directly below the watch tower."

"Stay there, I'm on my way. It'll be at least a half hour."

"I got a shot at it, think I hit him—he run off into the woods. Maybe I should follow while the trail is fresh."

"No. Stay where you are. It's gonna be dark in a couple hours," John said. "You get caught in the woods after sunset and he'll have the upper hand."

It was dark when John Bear came off the steep mountain slope, wading through knee-deep snow. He was hypervigilant, not sure whether or not the Wendigo was in the area. He came out of a copse of leafless willow bushes and stepped onto the tote road. Even though the snow was as deep as it had been in the woods, walking was easier on the unplowed road. He used his radio to contact Earl and Louis. They confirmed their location, and John turned south.

John saw the Dowds before they saw him. He trudged onward, ignoring the throbbing ache in his legs, which were fatigued from hours walking in the snow. As he closed with them he saw the tarp-covered lump in the snow. Even though he'd been told that Murph was dead, it didn't really register with him until he saw the silent shape.

He was within fifty feet of the Dowds when Louis spotted him. He spoke and Earl spun around, his rifle ready if needed. He recognized John and lowered the rifle. "Am I glad to see you," Earl said.

John stopped beside the two tired men and asked, "How'd it happen?"

"Don't really know," Earl said. "He got ahead of us somehow and when we come around that bend it was bent over him—I got a shot at the sonuvabitch, might even have hit him." Earl point toward a white birch tree. "These silver bullets must work, though. He took off and headed up the mountain like a homesick angel—through there." Earl sounded wistful when he added, "Still think one of us should have gone after him."

"You'd have ended up like Murph." John raised the tarp and looked at the body of his colleague and friend. He saw the gash in the chest and said, "Was he mutilated?"

"I think his heart's gone, I ain't no doctor, so I cain't say if anything else was took," Louis said.

John dropped the tarpaulin and then dropped, exhausted, onto the seat of Murphy's sled. He looked skyward and said, "Be dark soon, let's get him out of here and up to the warden cabin. This is gettin' out of hand. It's time I call in reinforcements."

48

Warden's Cabin, Rocky Mountain

John Bear placed his radio on the table and reached for the mug of coffee that Louis placed before him. The hot beverage burned his mouth and he felt the burn continue as the liquid traveled down his esophagus to his stomach. In spite of that, after hours in the arctic-type cold, it felt good.

Earl sat back and said, "You change your mind yet?"

"About?" John said.

"Bringing this sonuvawhore in alive. If there was ever anything needed killin' it's this."

"Maybe he has no control over what's possessed him."

"What the hell are you talking about?" Earl asked.

"Sounds like Indian mumbo-jumbo to me," Louis said.

John took another drink of coffee. "Okay, it's about time you guys learned everything about what we're fucking with here."

"I would think so," Earl said.

Rocky Mountain

The Wendigo stood in the woods, looking down upon the cabin. He knew that the rules were about to change—killing the warden was certain to escalate things. He was dealing with a dilemma. The Indian warden would bring in reinforcements. By midday every available member of the warden service, state police, and possibly even the border patrol would be involved—and they'd be looking for any excuse to kill him. His dilemma was that on one hand he desired to attack, assault the three men in the cabin. He reached down, felt the gaping wound in his side, and a small flame of fear sparked. The men were armed with weapons strong enough to kill him. He thought about the eons he'd spent drifting in the void, waiting for someone to summon him and did not want to be relegated to that existence again.

His other choice was to flee, run into the thousands of square miles of wilderness in Canada, but food was scarce in the tundra and frigid country to the north; if he went there he'd be forced to find a lair where he could go into hibernation. Years of sleeping was not something he looked forward to.

He turned and started up the mountain. As he scaled the steep slope he stopped on several occasions to look down on the cabin, fighting against the impulse to turn back and attack—before he did that he needed to find out what sort of weapon they were using. Whatever they'd shot him with hurt him badly.

He would have to do something soon though—the *hunger* was becoming all-consuming.

John stared into the fire, letting its heat penetrate his body. As he warmed, the soreness and aches of prolonged exposure to the elements became more evident. He heard the Dowds as they moved around the cabin, but was so engrossed in his thoughts and anger that they may as well have been on the moon. Murphy's death had rattled him more than he would have thought. They were friends and had worked together for more than ten years. John realized that the longer he pursued the Wendigo, the more personal the hunt was becoming. He smelled frying potatoes and heard the scrape of someone turning them in a black castiron frying pan. Earl appeared beside him.

"Supper's ready," Dowd announced. "It ain't much, just some coffee, fried potatoes, ham, and biscuits that Amy packed for us."

John stood up and turned toward the table that was centered in the room. "Smells as good as any feast I've ever eaten."

Louis carried the heavy twelve-inch frying pan to the table and placed it in the center. He used a spatula to serve the ham and fried potato hash onto three plates. He returned to the stove and retrieved a pan of biscuits that had been warming and the coffee pot. Once he was seated and they began eating he broke the silence. "What's our game plan?"

Earl looked at John. "You got anything planned?"

"First, we should have reinforcements here in the morning. I contacted Lieutenant Michaud. He'll have a task force here in the morning."

"Task force? You sound like we're at war, not after one asshole," Earl said.

"This *asshole* has killed how many people?" John replied.

"Don't have a clue," Louis said.

"Exactly," John retorted. "We know of seven—and he almost killed Buster. That, along with the fact that he knows these woods like the back of his hand, tells me that the three of us ain't got a snowball's chance in hell. He'll pick us off one at a time. So in the morning we'll have every warden north of Bangor, along with the state police, border patrol, and county sheriff's department up here." John ate a mouthful of food. "If I was Michaud, I'd be bringing the National Guard along too."

The Wendigo passed the hibernating bear and entered the bowels of the cave. His side still pained him and he needed to find out why. He came to the rear of the cavern and sat against the wall. He probed the wound with the long claw of his right index finger. He felt something hard and it made his finger burn. Ignoring the pain he worked the small projectile out and studied it—a bullet. His fingers burned where it touched the round and he knew why it had hurt him so much. It was a silver bullet. If he had any doubts that the Indian warden knew how to kill him, they were gone. This called for a change in strategy. He leaned back and let his body rejuvenate now that the silver was removed.

49

Warden's Cabin

John heard the sound of snowmobiles and walked to the door of the warden cabin. He opened the portal and stood in the threshold watching representatives from every law enforcement agency, state and Aroostook County. The lead vehicle was a John Deere trail groomer. When it stopped, the door opened and two men scrambled out of the enclosed cab. John immediately recognized them as Lieutenant Michaud of the warden service and a state police sergeant who he knew was the leader of the SWAT team. The groomer was followed by a convoy of snowmobiles of various manufacture.

John nodded to Michaud. "Where'd you boys steal that?" he quipped.

Michaud looked over his shoulder at the groomer. "Belongs to one of the local snowmobile clubs. When I told them what we needed, they lent it to us. Their club members want this over as much as we do so they can start riding again. Of late they been too damned scared to venture out into the woods."

John looked at the armada of snowmobiles and said, "I hope you brought supplies and some sort of shelter. There's nowhere close to being enough of either for the army you brought."

"Don't worry about that. We brought everything we need to set up a base camp here," Michaud said. He climbed the three steps and entered the cabin, followed by the SWAT leader. "Now suppose you fill me in on what the fuck has been goin' on up here. I particularly want to know how in hell Murphy got killed." He pulled off his gloves and opened his coat. "I hope you got some coffee. . . ."

"It's on the stove. Mugs are over there on the counter," John said, bracing himself for the ass-chewing he knew was sure to follow.

When Michaud had his coffee he sat at the table and, for the first time, noticed that he and John were not alone. Louis and Earl Dowd walked through the door and Earl said, "If you want to know what happened to Murphy, it's us you want to talk to. John wasn't there. He was up on the mountain following its tracks."

"So you saw his murder?" Michaud said.

"Not exactly. We were behind him and he'd gotten quite a ways ahead of us. When we caught up with him, his killer was bent over him . . ." Earl hesitated and then said, "We think that's when it opened him up and—"

"So," Michaud said looking at each of them in turn, "he'd been—"

"As far as we could tell his heart was ripped out," John said.

Michaud shook his head. "What the fuck is with this guy?"

"He's a Wendigo," John said.

"A what?"

"A Wendigo—the physical form of an evil spirit that roams the woods preying on solitary hunters, fishermen, whoever it can find."

Michaud stared at John. "An *evil spirit.*" His tone and attitude indicated his disbelief in what he'd been told.

"It's a cannibal. It eats its victim."

"Is this some of that Indian bullshit? Like that *Jeremiah Johnson* story where Indians believe that if they eat the heart of a brave enemy they'll somehow get braver?"

"No," John said. "This is a manitou, a god, if you will."

Michaud stood up. "John, I think you been chasing this guy too long. . . . You're making him sound like a super-villain in a movie."

"Lieutenant, no movie character could be anywhere near as dangerous as this thing. We believe that it was once a kid named Paul Condor."

Michaud stood up and looked through the window at the activity in the yard. "How in hell has he stayed below the radar this long?"

"All I can figure," John said, "is it finds its victims in the middle of the woods. Unless it's hunting, it avoids any contact with humans, especially those traveling in groups. It's obvious it's been at this for a long time, so we shouldn't underestimate it."

"So," Michaud asked, "how do you want to do this?"

"Encircle the mountain, keep it from getting off and running for Canada."

"He won't be able to go there," Michaud commented, "we've alerted the RCMP about what's going on here. They're watching the border."

John grunted.

"What? You don't think they can stop him?"

"Lieutenant, they can't even stop hunters from shooting Maine moose and lugging them across the Slash. There's no barrier between our countries and neither we nor the Canadians have enough manpower to watch the entire border."

"Well, it is what it is, we'll do what we can." Michaud switched the subject. "Once we have the mountain cordoned, then what?"

"Then the SWAT people and I go up the mountain and drive it down."

"What about Louis and me?" Earl Dowd asked.

"You can join the guys surrounding the base or you can come with me." John looked at Michaud, who nodded his agreement.

Michaud started for the door. "I'll get things going. We'll have a command post with radio comm set up by sundown." He watched two of his wardens loading Murphy's body into the trail groomer. "And John . . ."

"Yes, sir?"

"Shoot the bastard first. Then, if he's still alive, we'll worry about reading him his rights."

———————

Rocky Mountain

The Wendigo circled around the mountain, amazed at the sudden increase in activity below. The humans were surrounding the base and setting up outposts; it was obvious they were prepared to be there for a while. Immediately, he knew that to attack would mean death, especially if they were armed with silver. The now-healed wound had cost him the opportunity to take the fight to his enemy— with the arrival of this new group, they were too numerous. His objective changed from that of observing what all the activity was about to that of finding a way through the cordon of armed men that hemmed him in.

He took his time circling the ridge. There was four hours until sundown and he wouldn't be able to do anything until then. One thing about the situation did make him feel secure—finding food for his trek was no longer a problem.

———————

Lieutenant Michaud listened to the reports from the various outposts on the two-way radio that had been set up in the warden cabin. He looked up when John Bear entered, bringing in a blast of freezing air with him. "Everyone is in place," Michaud said.

"How many men per outpost?" John asked.

"Three, I gave them orders that two were to be on watch at all times."

"I hope this doesn't backfire on us. This thing is anything but an everyday perp."

"John," Michaud didn't try to hide his irritation, "I hope you aren't gonna go on about some crazy damned Indian myth."

"No, I'm not. I'm thinking about seven bodies, all killed and similarly mutilated. What or whoever this killer is, it knows these woods and how to move around in them better than anyone I've ever encountered."

Michaud listened to the warden service's most experienced criminal investigator, acquiescing to his knowledge and experience. "Well, at least you haven't tried to convince me that he's some sort of supernatural demon. . . ."

"Oh, I believe it's not entirely human, that's not an issue. Nevertheless we have to take into consideration what it's capable of. He's avoided us and outsmarted us at every turn. I firmly believe it's a Wendigo and I will take whatever action I can to kill it."

"Okay. I'll accept that he's off his nut and thinks he's some sort of evil god. How does that help us?"

"Lieutenant, maybe I should explain to you what it takes to kill this."

Michaud walked to the stove and filled a ceramic mug with coffee. "Maybe you should."

"The Wendigo has preyed on the Anishinaubae people since the dawn of time. The Native American peoples' struggle against starvation during the long, cold winters has always given it opportunity. As the food supply dwindled, hunting parties had to travel farther and farther from their territory. A lot of them got turned around and lost. These were the Wendigo's prey—lost and solitary people in the woods were an ideal source of food. When a Wendigo feeds, it grows and so does its hunger and its need for more food. Hence, the more it eats, the more it needs."

"Okay, so the more this guy kills, the more he has to kill. Am I interpreting what you're saying correctly?"

"Yes. Now the rest of the myth. A Wendigo is incredibly strong. It can run so fast that a human can't see it. Silver can hurt or kill it." John reached into his pocket and took out a silver bullet. "I made these and Earl shot it with one, otherwise he and Louis would, in all probability, be dead. Even if you render it unable to fight, you can't assume that you won. It also has the ability to resurrect. The only way to make sure you killed it is to cut the body into pieces and throw its heart—which is made of ice—into a bonfire."

"That's absurd."

"You're probably right, but it's what the Anishinaubae peoples, as well as other nations, and I believe."

"I'm struggling to see your point, John."

"My point is that his powers are most strong at night, that he can attain gigantic height, and cannot be killed by any mortal human. Think about most wartime heroes. They seem to be possessed of some powerful source of energy while they are performing their heroic deeds—many of which seem insane to rational people. However, we aren't dealing with a rational being."

"Let's hope that what you describe isn't the case, that all we're dealing with is just another nutcase. What's your suggestion?"

"By now he's aware that he's surrounded. The Dowds, the SWAT team, and I will head up the mountain tonight."

"John, climbing a mountain in the dark during winter will be tough going. It's supposed to clear off tonight and thermal cooling will drop the overnight temperature well below zero."

"Our best chance of finding him will be when he's moving around and that'll be at night."

"Okay. Have you notified the others?"

"I did that before I came in here." John turned toward the small room where their sleeping bags were spread. "I figure we'll head up around eight tonight, so I'm gonna get a few hours of sleep. In the meantime, we got to make some silver bullets—at least one or two per man."

50

Del's Place

Laura Wells was surprised to see the bar at Del's Place was full of local men, all listening intently to Del, who stood behind the bar and looked like a judge holding court. She walked to the door between the dining room and the bar, leaned against the door jamb, and listened.

"What in hell is goin' on up at Rocky Mountain?" Bill Kelly shouted to be heard over the chatter.

"You guys shut your pie holes and I'll tell you what I know," Del raised his voice and the din ceased. He placed his hands on the edge of the bar and leaned forward. "A couple of the Dowd boys were in the store early yesterday afternoon. They told me that Earl and a bunch of his kin had cornered the killer, up at Rocky Mountain."

"They get him?" asked Phil O'Connor.

"I'm gettin' to that." Del was obviously enjoying his role as being *the man in the know*. "To get to the point, no. As a matter of fact Cullen Dowd got killed."

A rumble rolled through the room as everyone began talking at once.

Del raised his hands and shouted for quiet. "I ain't done yet." When the room quieted down he continued, "John Bear and Murph caught up with the Dowds and took charge. They camped up at the warden cabin on the mountain—that night Galen Dowd got killed."

Again a fervor of protest filled the crowd. "What the hell are they doin''bout this?" O'Connor shouted, taking on the role of spokesman for the group.

Del ignored him. "You boys . . ." He noticed Laura standing in the threshold of the door to the dining room and nodded. "You folks may have noticed all the cops and wardens that were here this mornin'— well, I heard on the scanner that one of the wardens was killed yesterday afternoon."

Again everyone began talking at once. Laura felt her knees go weak. *A warden dead!* She felt a stab of fear. She raised her voice and, in a tone she hoped sounded like a dispassionate reporter and not a scared significant other, asked, "Did you hear which warden?"

"Nope, but there's cops of every sort up there." Del waited a second for his words to sink in and then added, "no matter which warden it was I don't think the killer will be coming down from that mountain alive . . ."

Laura didn't hear the rest of the conversation. She darted out of the building, jumped into her SUV, and headed for Dowd Settlement.

Dowd Settlement

The lights were on when Laura turned into the yard at Dowd Settlement. She pulled up in front of the main house and shut off her motor. Amy walked onto the porch as Laura exited her vehicle and stood with her arms wrapped around her torso, looking haggard and worn in the harsh illumination of the spotlights that lit the area. She stared at Laura for a second, looking like she was at a loss for words, and then said, "You heard?"

"Yes. I'm so sorry—"

Amy turned as if to brush off Laura's words. "Come on in. I can't stay out long, Granddad's taking this hard. Whatever this goddamned thing is, it will be the ruin of our family."

The sudden transition from twenty below zero to the super-heated atmosphere of the house was like walking into a wall, and Laura immediately took off her heavy parka and placed it over the back of one of the recliner chairs that faced the raging fire in the large stone hearth. She sat and turned to Amy. "How are you handling this?"

"I'll be all right. You want some coffee?"

"That'll be great."

Amy turned toward the kitchen.

While Amy got the coffee, Laura sat, bent forward with her arms resting on her knees, staring at the wood fire. The flames mesmerized her and she thought about the dead warden and tried to imagine how she'd handle it if it was John. The sap in one of the logs boiled to steam and snapped when the log burst open. She jumped and broke away from her reverie.

Amy placed a serving tray on the small coffee table that sat between the couch and the hearth and then sat on the opposite end of the couch. "You all right?"

Laura realized that Amy must have seen her jump when the log burst open and said, "Yes. I just got lost inside my head for a moment."

"You take it black, right?" Amy asked.

"Yes." Laura looked Amy in the eye. "I should be serving *you*."

"No, I need to have something to do or I'll completely lose it."

"Have you heard which warden was—?"

"Killed? No, I haven't. In fact all I know is what Alton told me he heard on his scanner. The wardens and the cops know that many of us have them, so they're very careful what they say over their radios."

Laura nodded that she understood. "Which of your relatives—"

"My nephews, Cullen and Galen."

"How many of your people are left out there?"

Amy paused for a second appearing to hold a roll call in her head." My father, Earl, my brother, Louis, and my cousin Kane are there. Buster wants to join up with them, but he's still laid up from the last time they chased it."

"Do you know that the hunt has grown? They've called in people from every level of law enforcement."

Amy grew pensive. "I heard that on the scanner. But I don't know if that's a good thing or not."

"Oh?"

"That bastard will know about them and be on his toes. A single man who knows his way around the woods will have a better chance of finding him—especially if it doesn't know it's being hunted." She stared at her hands for a few moments. "At least that's what I think."

Laura gave thought to what Amy had said and she had to agree with her. However she didn't like the idea. The only man capable of tracking it was John—if he was alive.

The front door opened and a young woman entered. "Amy, any word about Dwain?"

"No,"

"He's been gone for two days now and not a sign of him."

"What's that, you say?"

The three women turned to see Linwood Dowd helping his grandson Buster down the stairs that led up to the second floor. The bandages wrapping Buster's chest were visible through the open buttons of his heavy wool shirt. Linwood's face was red with anger and once he had his grandson off the stairs he released Buster's arm and his voice rose as he asked, "Why in hell hasn't anyone told us?"

Amy's face reddened, but stood her ground and absorbed her father's anger. "Granddad, don't be getting yourself all worked up, it ain't good for you."

"Nothin's good for me . . . at my age a man's livin' on borrowed time anyways. Now what's this about Dwain?"

"He took off again—we didn't want you and Buster to get all upset, so me'n Dad decided to keep it quiet."

"You checked everywhere?"

"Me'n Alton looked ever'wheres and he ain't nowhere to be found."

Linwood assisted Buster to a chair and then walked across the room and flopped into one of the easy chairs that fronted the hearth. "Gone off with that goddamned killer agin, ain't he?"

"We don't know that for certain," Amy countered.

"Girl, you know as well as Buster and me do that Dwain ain't been actin' normal since we got him back from that crazy bastard—he's gone off to find him and there ain't no doubt about that."

North Maine Woods, T17, R12

Dwain Dowd broke a trail through the deep snow. The walking would have been easier if he stayed on the woods roads but he wanted to avoid being seen by any people who might be hunting for *him*. There were snowmobile tracks everywhere and on several occasions a low-flying airplane passed overhead. He sensed *his* location and was determined to reach it before the men surrounding the mountains killed him.

The night sky was clear of clouds and the temperature plummeted to thirty below zero, but the boy was ambivalent to it. For all that the frozen environment affected him it may as well have been mid-July.

Rocky Mountain

The Wendigo remained near the top of the mountain, making sure that he stayed beneath the cover of the large evergreen trees that covered the lower slope. A short time ago he had heard something—a sound not of the forest—and had come to this side of the incline to investigate.

His eyesight was superior to that of a human and he was able to see in the darkness better than a man wearing a night-vision device. He found a place that allowed him to observe a game trail while remaining hidden. Men, he knew, were like water; they always took the path of least resistance. If they were coming to the summit, they'd most likely pass his hide.

He'd been squatting motionless for thirty minutes when he saw them coming from below. The lead gunman wore night-vision goggles and moved through the deep snow with an ease that told the Wendigo he was familiar with the woods.

The Wendigo waited for the searchers. He hadn't seen the Indian warden, but was certain that if he wasn't with them he was close by. All it took was patience and they would come to him.

John stayed back and watched the sniper in the point position creep slowly up the incline. The point's attention was more on keeping on his feet than on observing the area around him. John's head was turned, checking the positions of the rest of the team when he heard a brief shout. He turned in time to see the point man's feet disappear into the snow-laden boughs of a large evergreen. A dark cloud surrounded the tree and a sound that resembled a thunder clap brought snow cascading around him. John quickly aimed his rifle up the slope, expecting an attack from the tree.

"What the fuck happened?" called a voice to John's rear.

John turned to tell the trooper to shut up. Before he could speak there was another rumble of thunder and the Wendigo charged. Behind him, the terrified policeman dropped to the ground. John took his rifle off safe and pointed it at the dark cloud that raced down the slope. He aimed at the center of the cloud and fired. He knew he'd scored a hit when he was knocked off his feet by a primordial shriek that he was sure had punctured his ear drums. He ejected the spent cartridge and loaded a second silver bullet. In the dark it was almost impossible for him to discern anything. He wished he had a pair of night-vision goggles. He'd requested a pair when they'd set out, but was told they had only enough for the SWAT team members. He looked for the SWAT officer and couldn't find him. John hoped that he was only lost in the dark and not taken by the Wendigo.

John slowly raised himself up into a crouch and began to slide back-ward, all the while keeping his profile below that of a fallen tree.

A shot rang out and John saw the remaining three SWAT snipers hiding behind trees. One of them pointed to a position directly in front of John. "I got a location on him," the sniper called. He peered through his scope and stepped away from the tree for a clear shot. He didn't get it off. As soon as he was in the open, the dark cloud enveloped him and he screamed. As fast as it had descended, the cloud receded up the slope. The SWAT officer was on his feet and staring at John. A large section of his neck had been ripped away, sending a stream of pulsing blood shooting from a severed carotid artery. His eyes were wide in disbelief and he toppled forward into the snow.

"Stay under cover!" John ordered the remaining two snipers.

John began to dig a small tunnel beneath the dead tree, hoping to create enough clearance for him to slide under and possibly get off a shot or two. "Keep me covered," he called to the men behind him.

"Gotcha," came the reply.

John burrowed under the tree and when he hit frozen ground, scooped out a fighting hole in the snow until he was under the fallen beech and had an opening on the far side. He took a moment to brush off his rifle and checking that all of its operational parts were free and clear of anything that may cause it to malfunction. He peered upward, ignoring his telescopic sight, which he believed was useless under the circum-stances. The telescope attached to his rifle with a mount that allowed him to aim using the rifle's sights. He waited, watching for any move-ment up the grade.

Suddenly the wind picked up, sending a gust of air so frigid that the trees on the slope cracked and split. The dark cloud disappeared into the night, driving a wall of drifting snow before it. Thunder rolled again and John raised his head. The Wendigo stood in front of a rock outcrop. John immediately shifted his aim and fired. The sound of his rifle fire was barely discernible against the crash of thunder and then the Wendigo was gone.

Afraid of being trapped in his impromptu hide, John scurried back out of the burrow. He crouched behind the tree and cursed when the air warmed and freezing rain engulfed the mountain, coating everything, man, beast, and flora, in a heavy layer of ice.

After several minutes, during which he became thoroughly soaked, John took a chance and stood up. The remaining members of the search party gathered around him. Everyone had their coats open and their rifles inside against their bodies, protecting them from the elements.

The sergeant in charge of the team blinked against the lashing rain. "What the fuck was that?"

"Our quarry."

"Jesus, I've never seen anything like that in my life."

"Let's hope that you never see it again."

"So I guess we carry our dead down to the camp."

John looked around and shook his head. "You can look if you want." John pointed upslope at the tree from which the Wendigo attacked. "but you won't find him." John stared into the black sky, the freezing rain hitting his face like frozen bee-bees. *This is gonna make things tough. There's gonna be a crust over everything and we'll never get close to him.*

51

Warden's Cabin

John Bear led the survivors of the search for the Wendigo into the open area around the warden cabin and saw Michaud standing on the steps. He walked to the foot of the stairs and without saying a word, nodded at his superior officer. Michaud turned and walked inside and John followed.

Once inside, Michaud inquired, "What happened?"

"Don't know what to tell you other than we got ambushed."

"Ambushed?"

"Somehow or another it knew we were coming."

"It's darker than the inside of a reefer out there—you think he's got night vision equipment?"

John walked to the counter, picked up a coffee mug, and looked inside to see how clean it was. "Don't have a clue, Lieutenant. I doubt it'd need it though—"

Michaud interrupted, "John, don't give me that supernatural power crap, okay? We need to understand what we're up against."

"What we're up against, sir, is something that most likely possesses that *supernatural crap* and is very proficient in using it."

Michaud stood and watched John as he walked to the stove, picked up the coffee pot, and filled his mug. "Okay, don't get touchy. I'm going to have to explain the deaths of three officers to Augusta. That's the only reason they'll approve the manpower and money this is costing and if I tell them about some Algonquin shaman—"

"Manitou," John corrected him.

"Manitou. . . . They're gonna think we've all been out in the cold so long that we're delusional."

John sat at the table and, for several seconds, hung his head over the mug of coffee, inhaling the aroma of the hot beverage. As his body warmed he felt a debilitating exhaustion. When Michaud sat across from him, he raised his head and looked at his superior officer.

"John, you been burning the candle at both ends since you got this case; I want you to take some downtime. Spend today at base camp. We've got the mountain surrounded and I'll send out a couple of patrols at day break."

"Lieutenant, all sending men out there will do is get more of them killed. In fact, it'll just look at it as a replacement of supplies—remember, it's a cannibal. Regardless of how tough the terrain, we can't leave a wounded or dead man intending to come back for them, it'll—well, you get my drift."

"So, what do we do?"

"You keep the cordon around the base of the mountain. I'm gonna get a couple of hours sleep and then I'm going after him."

"I'll tell the state police to have a team ready to go with you."

"No, I'll go alone—it'll be easier for me to follow him and hopefully get close enough to apprehend or kill him."

"What about the Dowds? You could take them with you."

"The same thing I said about police holds true for them. Keep them on guard duty."

Michaud sat silently, as if he were processing John's plan. After several moments he locked eyes with John and said, "Don't worry about apprehension—kill the sonuvabitch."

They sat quietly, listening to the sound of heavy freezing raindrops hitting the cabin's metal roof. John finished his coffee and stood up. "I'm gonna get a few hours."

Michaud looked toward the ceiling. "It's goin' to be a miserable night."

"It's already been a miserable night," John answered.

"I promise you one thing, John."

"What's that?"

"We aren't leaving here until that goddamned thing is dead. . . ."

"Thanks, Aurel."

Michaud ignored John's informality and smiled at him, "Go on, get some sleep."

Rocky Mountain

Dwain Dowd reached the foot of the mountain prior to sunup. He circled the base, looking for a trail that he could follow to the summit. He was fatigued after his all-night trek from Dowd Settlement, but wanted to meet up with *him*. Dwain felt linked to the Wendigo in some metaphysical way and was certain that he was preparing to leave the area.

Dwain's state of lethargic exhaustion allowed his attention to drift and when he rounded a turn in the unplowed, snow-laden road he stopped abruptly. There were three men sitting around a small fire and one of them was staring at him.

"Who're you?" the man asked.

Dwain stopped walking and stared at the men. Two of the men sat with their backs to him, one turned, and then stood up. "Boy," Louis Dowd said, "what the fuck you doin' here?"

The sun was visible through the barren trees when John left the warden cabin and entered the woods. The freak rain storm of the previous night had created a crust of thin ice and frozen snow. Everything, tree limbs, bushes, rocks, and deadfall was coated with ice. Brushing against anything caused it to explode in a shower of icy spray and particles.

Each step he took resulted in his feet breaking through the hard surface with a loud crunch and John knew there was no way in hell he was going to take the Wendigo by surprise. The sound of his passage through the woods would be audible to a deaf man. Walking was treacherous and every step carried the risk of spraining or breaking an ankle. Each time he placed a foot down the crust broke and his foot drove into the softer snow beneath the hard surface layer. When he raised a foot to take the next step, the sharp edges of the top layer barked his shins. In short time his legs pained him and he was certain his lower legs were scraped raw and bleeding. Still he pushed forward.

John felt the sun's warmth on his back. He glanced at his watch and saw that it was almost eight in the morning and he decided to take a few minutes to catch his breath. He found an old stump and cleaned the ice from its top and sat. He inhaled deeply and pulled up his left pant leg and saw bloodstains on the long underwear. He felt the insulated undergarment pull away from something to which it was stuck, raised it and saw the bloody scrape. He dreaded starting out again. It was then that he noticed the faint impression that indicated a trail. He stood up and made his way to the barely visible path. While still snow and crust coated, the covering on the trail was below the tops of his boots. *At least it ain't barkin' my shins*, John thought.

The path, however, presented him with a different problem. The surface was packed hard and the resulting layer of ice made walking treacherous. Several times he slid backward, and he cartwheeled his arms to stay on his feet. Because he needed his hands free to grab bushes and tree limbs, his rifle was a hindrance, so he suspended it from his shoulder with the leather sling and continued climbing the treacherous path.

John propelled himself upward for the better part of an hour and his heart pounded and his arms ached from pulling his way up the icy trail. He came to a short span where the trail appeared level and stopped. His breath was labored and he bent over, resting his hands on his thighs. He studied his surroundings and realized that he had in all probability only traveled a half mile. *At this rate,* he thought, *I'll be all day getting to the top—if I make it that far.*

After a brief break to allow his heart rate to drop and his breathing to return to normal, John once again started up the treacherous trail. As he slowly ascended the slope he wondered where the path led. It was obviously a game trail and ended at some water source below, but where on the mountain did it end? Curiosity spurred him on and he struggled upward.

By noon, John was starting to think that he was at best on a fool's errand and began entertaining thoughts of heading back to the cabin. The trail suddenly changed direction and rather than ascend the mountain, turned to the right cutting across the side of the ridge. He decided to continue on for another half hour and if he hadn't found any sign of the Wendigo by then, he'd head back. Less than a hundred yards from the turn, the trail abruptly ended at what looked like the entrance to a small cave. John stopped immediately and studied the opening. It looked to be an ideal den for a hibernating bear and, knowing that it was the time of winter when hibernating sows gave birth, he did not want to enter a den to come face to face with a half-awake, surly she-bear. A sow protecting her young was problem enough, let alone being confronted by her in a confined place. John slowly approached the opening.

He stopped beside the portal and ventured a look inside. He realized that, rather than a small enclosure, the opening led into a large cavern. He removed his rifle from his shoulder, operated the bolt, and loaded a round into the empty chamber. He dropped down and slid inside.

Once he was clear of the low overhang above the entrance, John found himself in a cave big enough for him to stand upright. He slowly stood, studying the dark interior. His gaze moved from the black depths to the ground around his feet. The temperature inside the grotto was low enough for him to see his breath spiraling in front of his face, but within ten feet it was warm enough that the ground remained unfrozen—then he saw the footprints. They were the Wendigo's.

Warden's Cabin

The heat from the cabin's woodstove was oppressive and Dwain tried to stay as far away from it as possible. The old game warden sat at the table in the center of the main room, listening to what Dwain thought was indecipherable chatter from the radio that sat on a small table by the window against the front wall.

The warden looked up and stared at him. "You sure you don't want something to eat, boy?"

Dwain shook his head and remained sitting on the floor in the far corner of the room.

"I got to say," the warden said, "you're the quietest goddamned kid I ever met."

Three heavy thumps sounded as someone stomped their feet to remove snow from them. Dwain turned his attention to the door as his uncle entered.

"I heard you got my grandson in here," Earl Dowd said.

Michaud pointed to the corner. "He's been like that since your brother brought him in a couple of hours ago. He ain't said a word, just sits there staring. He acts as if it's too hot in here for him."

Earl unzipped his parka and said, "Probably is. Since he was abducted by the Wendigo he hates the heat. Over home he's been staying out in one of the barns."

Earl walked around the table and stood before his grandson. He said nothing and just stared at Dwain.

After a couple of seconds, Dwain crossed his arms and enclosed his knees in them. He dropped his head, hiding his face from his uncle.

"You want I should leave you two alone?" Michaud asked.

"If you don't mind," Earl answered.

"No problem." Michaud stood up, grabbed his parka from the back of the chair he'd been sitting in, and put it on as he opened the door and stepped outside.

Earl remained silent until the sound of the warden's steps faded. Then he turned to Dwain. "What the fuck you think you're doing?"

When several moments passed with no response from the boy he said, "Answer me! What are you doing here?" He took a step forward and then stopped. "At least give me a reason not to beat the shit out of you."

Dwain raised his head and stared at Earl. "You touch me," he said, "and I'll kill you."

"What?"

"You heard me. If you touch me, I'll kill you." Dwain stood up and confronted Earl.

Earl realized that the boy he'd towered over two weeks ago was looking at him eye to eye. He felt a brief instance of fear. Dwain had grown a full foot or more since he had been taken by the Wendigo. His anger got the best of him and he reached for Dwain.

The boy grabbed his uncle's arm and tightened his grip.

It took all of Earl's willpower to keep from crying out at the boy's vice-like grip.

"Grandpa, you got no idea who I am. I don't think you ever did. Don't make me hurt you." Dwain released Earl, pushed him back, and started walking toward the door.

Earl rubbed his throbbing arm and stared open-mouthed at his grandson. He realized that Dwain was right. He didn't know who—or what—the boy had become. "Dwain, what has happened to you?"

Dwain looked over his shoulder at Earl. "I got free."

"Free? We always let you do whatever you wanted, within reason anyways."

"Well, ain't none of you got any say no more."

"Where you going?"

"To *him*."

Before Earl could say anything more, Dwain left the cabin. Earl ran to the door and flung it open. Dwain was nowhere to be seen.

52

As John Bear slowly followed the tracks he was amazed at the vastness of the cave's interior. He hadn't known such a place existed in Maine. He passed by a small chamber on his left and heard a grunt in the darkness. His nose told him more than his eyes—*bear.* The last thing he wanted to do was to disturb a hibernating bear. He moved beyond the small grotto where the sow was, taking great care to do so quietly.

Past the bear cave, the light diminished to a treacherous gloom. John retrieved his Maglite from his pack and shined it around the subterrane. The narrow entrance had opened up and exposed an open cavern from which a warren of smaller caves disappeared into the darkness. John's first thought was that he'd stumbled upon an abandoned mine. But he'd never heard of anything this big—but then it wouldn't be the first time that a mine had been abandoned and then all knowledge of it erased. He panned his light around the ground and saw no evidence of the Wendigo in the rocky, packed soil. He shined the light beam in all directions as he slowly advanced deeper into the labyrinth. Suddenly, the futility of his actions registered; the very same light that made it possible for him to see where he was going broadcast his location to the Wendigo—if it was in fact in the cave.

Once again he stared into the cavern. John realized that he was not equipped to explore the deep recesses of the cavern; he needed more men and equipment. He turned to backtrack his way out when he caught movement between him and one of the grotto's tunnels and the pervasive smell of grave rot filled the cavern. He concentrated the light in that direction and raised the rifle with his free hand. He detected movement again and then the Wendigo stepped into the light beam.

Dwain scrambled over a slope of snow-covered loose shale. Several times he'd slid backward as the loose rocks shifted under his feet and he'd had to crawl forward on hands and knees. Once he'd entertained thoughts of quitting the quest and returning to the camp below. Then he sensed that *he* was close, which gave him incentive to continue on.

He saw the dark opening and knew it was the entrance to the cavern where *he* was waiting. He quickly approached the opening, dropped to his knees, and crawled inside.

John dropped his Maglite and fired a shot at it. The rifle's sharp *crack* echoed through the cavern and the flash from the barrel lit the interior like a flashbulb. Realizing that the rifle put him at the disadvantage of not having a light source, he placed it on the ground, took out his service pistol, and retrieved the Maglite.

He shined the light in the direction where he'd fired, hoping to see its body lying there, but it was not. John scanned the cavern again, trying to locate his quarry. He was sweating heavily and not sure whether it was due to heat or fear. He shook his head, trying to shake off the sweat that threatened to get in his eyes and ruin his vision. He began to slowly circle the cavern, staying close to the wall. He heard a grunt behind him and spun the light in that direction. The bear stood, outside of the hibernation den, and when John's light hit its eyes they shined like red lasers in the black face. Suddenly the animal spun around and bellowed a pulsing roar at something or someone behind it that had it spooked.

John suddenly felt like a kernel of corn in a grinding mill. He had the Wendigo in front of him and the irritated bear behind him. He turned his light back and saw someone move on the other side of the bear. He dropped to one knee, to steady his aim, and sighted at the bear.

Dwain saw the bear and stood still. Under any other set of circumstances he'd shout and wave his hands and feel confident that the animal would run in the opposite direction. However in this situation he knew there was no such option. He knew that the smart thing to do would be to retreat and hope that it would return to its den and hibernation. But *he* was here, Dwain knew it; he sensed his presence.

A light shined in his direction. Dwain knew it had to be a human. *He* wouldn't have need of a flashlight to see in the darkness.

Dwain looked around for something to use as a weapon and saw a stone twice the size of his fist. Without taking his eyes from the bear, he squatted down and picked up the rock.

John Bear moved to his right, hoping to get a better angle, one which minimized the risk of hitting the person behind it should he have to shoot the bear. He stumbled over a rock and fell, losing his grip on the flashlight. Before he could regain the light and his feet, the bear emitted another pulsing roar and then a dark shape appeared before it. John immediately knew from its size that it was the Wendigo.

The Wendigo met the bear with such force as to drive the bear back a step. The startled animal retaliated with a mighty swing of his right paw. In the beam of the flashlight, John saw the Wendigo stagger back a step, regain his balance, and rush the bear again. This time the bear was fully awake and in defensive mode. It crashed with the Wendigo, wrapped its forelegs around its torso, and raked its back with its long, curved claws.

The Wendigo strained and forced its way out of the bear hug, its back ripped open and blood flowing down it. It drove its talons into the bear's chest and the beast bellowed in pain. It swiped again, this time sweeping its sharp claws across the Wendigo's face. It pushed forward and the Wendigo fell onto its back with the wounded, angry black bear on top.

The bear jumped up and down on the Wendigo's chest, smashing into its flesh so hard that blood flew into the darkness. The Wendigo drove its long claws deep into the bear's soft underbelly. The bear drove its hind feet into the Wendigo's stomach and kicked backward, eviscerating him.

All fight went out of the Wendigo, but it shoved its hand deeper into the bear's gut before releasing its grip and settling back onto the ground. The eviscerated beast pounced and reached forward trying to bite its enemy's head, but before it could do so it collapsed in a bloody heap. John was certain the bear was dead and hoped the same was true of the Wendigo.

As if it read his thoughts, the Wendigo rose to a crouch. In the dim light, John could see its eyes; they seemed to be floating around in bowls of blood. John raised his Sig Sauer P226 and aimed it between the eyes.

The Wendigo opened its mouth to roar, but before it could emit its debilitating thunder, John fired twice. The two silver .357-caliber bullets flew true and entered the front of the Wendigo's head, blowing the back off as they exited.

He turned his attention to the bear, which lay on her side. In the narrow beam of light John could see the damage she had absorbed during the fight. A spark of life remained in the sow and she snarled at John.

John stayed back and watched her crawl into the den. Even though mortally wounded, she growled, defending her cubs to her death. Keeping an eye on her, John cautiously moved along the wall opposite the den. All the while, he watched the hibernation den; one never knew what a badly wounded animal would do—especially one whose only exit was through you.

Reaching the Wendigo, John took a cursory glance at it. The enraged sow had opened its thorax and abdomen and the internal organs were torn and ruptured. The area was rank with the smell of blood, half-digested intestinal matter, and feces.

John moved the light to see its head. The back of the huge skull was open and looked like it had fallen ten stories onto a concrete slab. Nothing, not even a Wendigo, could survive that much damage.

John shined the light inside the den and saw the bear lying on her side. Her eyes shined in the light and her side heaved up and down with each of her labored breaths. Her three cubs, so young their eyes were not open, scrambled toward her to suckle. He heard a noise and turned to see Dwain staring at the Wendigo's body.

The boy looked at John and in the dim light, John thought that he looked like a normal, if tall for his age, teenage boy. Shock was written on Dwain's face. He had a bewildered look as he scanned his immediate location. The boy didn't have to say anything for John to understand that he was wondering how he'd gotten here. Whatever spell the Wendigo had over him was gone—or so John hoped it was.

"Dwain," John said.

The boy was staring at the eviscerated body and didn't reply.

"Dwain," John said louder and with a more forceful tone.

The boy's head snapped up and he looked at the warden.

"Go outside, there's nothing for you in here." He waited for a few seconds and when Dwain remained in place, he said, "Go on now, get outta here. I've got something to do, then I'll meet you, and we can go down the mountain together."

The boy turned and, after a couple of faltering steps, ran toward the grotto's entrance.

John turned to the Wendigo.

Base Camp

It was dark when John and Dwain reached the base camp at the warden's cabin. They stepped out of the woods and saw that several fires were burning around the open area where a number of arctic-capable tents were erected. Earl and Louis Dowd stood in front of one, drinking coffee from metal cups. Dwain looked at his grandfather and uncle and seemed hesitant. John placed a hand on the back of his shoulder and said, "Go to your people. Everything will work out—when it comes to family, there is nothing that can't be resolved with a simple heartfelt *I'm sorry* and a *thank you.*"

Dwain looked at him, his eyes beseeching him to help. "You don't need me boy. It's your folks you need—now go."

John stood still, hoping he'd been correct in what he'd said, until Dwain reached his uncles. When Earl grabbed him and hugged him, John knew it was going to be all right and turned toward the cabin. Michaud stood on the porch, his hands on his hips. "Well?" the lieutenant said. "Did you get it?"

"It's no longer a problem."

Michaud nodded and beckoned for John to enter the cabin. Once inside John dropped his pack beside the door and before saying anything, poured a cup of coffee. When he returned to the table, Michaud asked, "I take it he's dead."

John nodded.

"You kill him?"

"Not yet."

"What do you mean *not yet?*"

John walked to his backpack, opened it, and took something out. He placed the wrapped bundle on the table and unveiled what appeared to be a human heart—only it was made of ice.

"What the fuck is that?"

"Wendigos have a heart of ice. If you don't destroy it they will resurrect. . . ."

John picked up the ice heart, walked to the woodstove and opened it. He opened the damper until the fire was as close to a raging inferno as the old metal stove could handle. He tossed the heart into the fire. The stove began to pulse and vibrate and there was a howl loud enough to shake the windows and be heard for miles. Flames belched out of the stove and then there was a loud noise as if something had passed by at an incredible speed. Within seconds there was an urgent banging at the door. John opened it and Earl Dowd stood on the steps. "What was that?" he asked. "The whole cabin shook and the inside lit up like it was on fire—then there was a loud fuckin' noise and then this jet of steam shot out of the chimney—reminded me of a steam train climbing a grade—and then . . ." Earl snapped his fingers ". . . just like that, everything returned to normal."

"I stoked the fire," John said.

"What you stoke it with, jet fuel?" Earl said. His face turned serious and he said, "Dwain told me that the Wendigo's dead. . . ."

John looked at the stove and replied, "He is now."

"Where's the body?"

"In a cave near the summit; I'll collect it in the morning. You can come along if you like."

"I just might do that," Earl said.

53

Dowd Settlement: Four Months Later

John Bear and Laura Wells sat in front of the huge hearth, drinking a hot beverage, and talking in low voices. "I want to do an article on the family, how they're dealing with the deaths, Dwain's kidnapping—everything."

John smiled at her. "Sounds as if you're going to ride this horse to the finish line."

She stared at the fire for a few moments. "My paper has bought the *Aroostook County Tribune.* . . ."

"Really."

"I've grown to like it up here and I'm considering requesting a transfer to Caribou."

He turned to face her. "Isn't that a step down, career-wise?"

"Living in a city isn't all that great. . . ."

"Do you think you will be able to survive in a town where the most upscale store is a dollar store?"

She smiled. "It's only a two-and-a-half-hour drive to the mall in Bangor."

"And," he said with a smile, "only a twenty minute drive to my place in Ashland."

"Is that so? The thought never crossed my mind."

Their discussion was cut short by the entrance of Amy and Earl Dowd. They sat in easy chairs so that the foursome created a half circle. Once he was settled, Earl said, "John, Laura, thank you for coming."

"I should have come sooner," Laura said.

"Well, it is a long drive up," Amy commented.

A gust of wind rattled the front door and Earl looked out the window at the wind-driven rain that pounded the area. "Seems like my whole life it's rained at every funeral."

"I was sorry to hear about Linwood's passing," John said.

"He was never the same after what happened last winter," Amy said.

Earl turned to John. "There's one thing about that whole deal that you still ain't explained to me. What in hell did you throw in that stove that almost blew that cabin to hell?"

"The Wendigo's heart."

All three of his companions turned to John. "It's heart?" Amy said. "Why on earth would you do that?"

John knew that what he was about to tell them would be difficult for them to accept but he decided to take the risk. "It was a Wendigo."

"You've said that any number of times," Earl commented.

"Wendigos," John explained, "are not human. They will inhabit and possess a human body, but they themselves are not human—they're the most evil of all Algonquin manitous. Gods, if you will. They have many powers, among them the power of resurrection."

"Surely, you don't believe such a thing exists?" Amy said.

John replied, "Years ago, I asked that same question of my grandfather. He replied: *No, but I saw his tracks once.* . . ."

"Okay, let's accept that such a thing exists, why did you burn its heart?" Earl inquired.

"There's only one way to kill one. You cut out its icy heart and burn it in a fire."

"Help me understand this," Earl said. "You burned it's heart in the fire?"

"Yes. The next day when you and I returned to the cave and you saw its body, I had you take the bear cubs down the mountain."

"I wondered about that bear," Earl said. "Why didn't you bring the cubs down after the sow killed the Wendigo?"

"She was still alive."

"Why didn't you put it out of its misery?" Laura asked.

"It had recently given birth to three cubs and at the time I was not able to bring them down, so I left them there where they could curl up beside their mother until I could get back. That night, Aurel Michaud contacted a biologist and a wildlife rescue shelter in Saint John. After I finished what I had to do, I brought the cubs down and sent them to the shelter."

Laura gazed at him. "John Bear, you are a man of many faces. On one hand you can cut up a human being with a chainsaw and then carry three newborn bear cubs to safety."

John chuckled. "Keep in mind that the bear is my totem . . . sort of like your guardian angels. It would be wrong for me to abandon them to starve. As for the Wendigo, we've already determined that even though it looked human, it was not."

"I been trying to figure out why you carried a chainsaw up to the cave."

John didn't answer, he sat quiet with a knowing smile on his face.

Laura, Amy, and Earl sat silent, obviously processing what he'd said and, John thought, wondering how much to believe.

After several moments John said, "How's Dwain doing?"

"Fine," Earl said, "he's growin' like a damn weed. Must be well over six and a half feet tall and strong as any three of us."

"Surprisingly," Amy added, "he eats less than what it would take to keep a bird alive. . . ."

"Really?" John replied. "Is he around? I'd like to see him."

"You'll get your chance. He should be at the funeral." Earl looked at his watch. "Speakin' of which, we better be goin."

They departed the house and were immediately drenched by the driving rain. John hunched over and took Laura by the arm as they walked into the gusting wind.

Earl said, "The cemetery plot is over by the woods in the far corner of the clearing."

"We'll follow in my truck," John said.

There was little conversation as they drove around the barn and followed Earl onto a muddy lane that meandered toward the tree line. The windshield wipers made a thumping noise as they tried to get ahead of the deluge. John and Laura stared straight ahead. The combination of the cold spring rain and their amassed body heat fogged the side windows of the truck and the defroster could barely keep the windshield clear enough for John to drive.

As they approached the burial plot, John saw a yellow backhoe and a cluster of trucks, all indistinguishable from one another due to the coating of mud that each wore. June is a rainy month in far northern Maine and the ground was swampy from the accumulation of new water and the snowmelt of the past winter.

Laura broke the silence. "When does it warm up around here?"

"Next month," John said, "set your alarm for four in the morning and get up as soon as it goes off. One day it'll hit seventy-five and if you oversleep you could miss the entire summer."

"Really?"

John chuckled. "It ain't that bad. But I will say it seems like the winter is ten months long. It usually warms up in late June, but by late August you can start seeing some foliage turning."

Laura looked at him. "You *are* pulling my leg, aren't you?"

"Stick around and see," John answered.

The four-by-four stopped and when they disembarked, Earl stood beside his truck and said, "Welcome to the Dowd family plot."

John saw a burial ground that encompassed almost an acre of cleared ground. "How'd you ever get approval for this?" he asked.

"What the friggin' guvmint don't know won't hurt them."

John held the door for Laura and when she stood beside him they studied the assembled Dowd clan. The vast majority of the assembled mourners were unknown to him, although he did recognize Buster and Louis.

Laura tightened her grip on his arm and when he inclined his head toward her, she whispered, "Are these all Dowds?"

He shook his head and said, "Most are local people."

He guided her around the periphery of the assembly, stopping when they were beside the Dowds. John immediately saw Dwain and did a double take. The thirteen-year-old was well over seven feet tall and towered over everyone there. He and Laura took their place between Dwain and Earl. A short, slightly obese man in an expensive suit stepped forward and stopped beside the grave. John looked at the gathering and saw that beneath their rain gear the men wore a lot of flannel shirts and the women wore dresses and huddled beneath umbrellas trying to keep their hair from being destroyed by the gale force wind and pounding rain. Laura wore a fashionable suit with pants rather than a skirt, which John was sure she was thankful for each time a gust of wind swirled around her legs.

The new grave was open, a casket covered with an American flag draped over it. Beyond it John saw other new graves. *Galen and Cully*, he thought.

The short man held a Bible, a dead giveaway that he was the minister. John hoped that he would keep his eulogy short, the day was windy enough. The preacher must have read his mind. He spoke for ten minutes, led the congregation in several prayers, and then turned things over to the family to say their final goodbyes to Linwood Dowd.

In all, the service lasted just under an hour and John led Laura to the truck. When they passed Dwain he nodded and said, "It's a shame ain't it?"

"Your great-grandfather was a well-liked man," John said. "He lived a long life."

"Oh, I know that," Dwain answered. "What's a shame is burying him in the ground to rot . . . such a waste."